HELL ON HORSEBACK

Taking his time, Morgan passed out of range of the big rifle, but he kept on riding easy. It galled him to have a rifle and pistol and still be riding back to be put in handcuffs. Yet the only other way was to come in like a storm and hope to kill Stretch and the Indian before they killed him. Stretch would have a rifle on him by now. So might the Indian.

He kept coming, still thinking of the guns he had and wasn't going to use, ready to halt when Stretch yelled her warning. It came, loud and threatening. Then he saw Stretch come up from behind a clump of brush. The rifle was rock steady at her shoulder and aimed at his chest.

"Let the guns slide," she yelled. "Don't even think what you're thinkin', Big Boy. Watch him, Pretty." Morgan didn't turn his head, but he knew the Indian was rising up from somewhere with the shotgun.

GIANT SPECIAL EDITION

BUCKSKIN

MUZZLE
BLAST

— Kit Dalton —

LEISURE BOOKS **L** **NEW YORK CITY**

A LEISURE BOOK®

January 1994

Published by

Dorchester Publishing Co., Inc.
276 Fifth Avenue
New York, NY 10001

Printed in the United States of America.

Chapter One

Niles City, the signboard said. The sign was neatly painted—black letters on a white background—and the pole that supported it stood up straight. Morgan rubbed his mouth with the back of his hand and thought about beer. Even in the remote northern Arizona Territory a place that claimed to be a city would surely have a long-neck bottle of Pearl beer, the best beer in the Southwest or anywhere else. Maybe even a cool bottle of Pearl, provided they kept the bottles in some kind of cellar. A cold bottle of Pearl was too much to hope for. This bump on the backside of creation wasn't likely to have Oregon pond ice shipped south and layered in sawdust and straw, then wagoned across country, dripping every lurch of the way.

He touched his horse's flanks and went over the hill to the start of the main street. Just before he got there, out of the high country wind, he heard the woman yelling. He got closer, and when he was past the straggle of Saturday afternoon farm wagons, he saw the woman, already mounted up, and the three rowdies who were giving her a hard time in front of the saloon. A bunch of loungers stood on the boardwalk, whistling and catcalling, egging on the three rowdies, drunk by the look of them. The woman wasn't calling for help, just swearing a blue streak at the three drunks who were slapping their thighs with their hats, whooping and hollering like the fools they were.

Across the street from the saloon was a town marshal's office and lockup, but not a badge in sight. By now the woman's horse was wild-eyed and ready to throw her. Morgan just wanted a few beers before he continued on his way, but there was no way out of it. Oh Lord, he thought, ain't there any Galahads in this tidy-looking town besides me? The three turned to gape at him as he rode in close—three red-neck cowhands, full of beer or whiskey, all wearing guns. Suddenly it got quiet except for the skitterish movement of the woman's horse.

"Let her be, fellas," Morgan said. "You don't stop that she's going to get hurt." He said it as hard and as easy as he could, like a sensible man pointing out the error of their ways. But his face told them he was ready to see this through if that's what they wanted.

Maybe they weren't as drunk as they were letting on. On cowhand wages they'd probably been drinking beer. It was hard for a grown man to get too drunk on beer if you were used to drinking it. He glanced at the woman, and she stared back at him. She had short blond hair and was a real looker. No time to get a better look at her. At least she had the horse under control.

"You can ride out now, ma'am," he told her.

They didn't try to stop her when she turned the horse, but she hadn't gone more than 40 feet before she turned the horse again so she could see what was happening. Morgan damned her silently for not doing what she was told. The three clowns looked unsure of themselves. Some of the boardwalk gawkers laughed, and that didn't go down too well. It could still come to killing, Morgan knew, but he also knew he could kill the three men before their guns cleared their holsters. Even so, by the time he finished doing that, other guns could be firing at him from inside the saloon. And if he stayed alive no matter what, there would be the marshal to deal with. A stranger always got the blame. He got the feeling that the marshal wasn't that far away. Could be he was watching the show from behind the barred windows of the jail. Morgan wanted to turn his horse and ride out, but if he had to die he would rather do it facing them than be shot in the back. He sat on his horse, waiting.

At last, one of the sports said in a high, jeering voice, "What's your interest in this, drifter? Who asked you to stick your long nose into this? Case you can't count, there's only one of you, a whole lot of us." A skinny kid no more than 20, he looked a little smarter than the others. "You think you can handle all that?" He waved his left hand to include the loungers on the boardwalk.

Most of the onlookers didn't want to be included. Some went back into the saloon, while the others edged out of the line of fire. The blond woman continued to watch. She was wearing an ivory handled .38 belted high. That didn't say she knew how to use it or would side him if shooting started.

Morgan said, "I don't know how much I can handle, but I can handle you. You decide if I can or not. You boys been bothering this young woman, and I don't like it. Dumb horseplay, if you ask me." He thought of a lot worse things to say, but didn't say them. If he said them, they'd have to draw. If it started, it would start with the kid.

Making sure his two friends hadn't wandered off, the kid said, "Nobody is scared of you if that's what you're thinkin'. You talk like you think you're fast, and maybe you are. Fast men get buried every day. What're you doin' in Niles anyhow? Ain't no range wars around here. You look like you could be runnin' from the law."

It was a standoff of sorts. The kid seemed to know Morgan wouldn't draw first, so he could brazen it out a bit, maybe even make himself sound like a man not to be fucked with—as long as he didn't push Morgan too hard. Talk, talk, Morgan thought, ready to settle for talk.

"I'll be going now," he said. "Got to see a lady safe home." He knew the kid wanted to let it go, but something kept pushing him. This was the kid's small moment of glory, and he wanted to make the most of it. This little set-to would be good for a lot of stories until the kid grew out of it or some short-tempered man put an end to his life.

"Lady!" The kid spat to show his contempt for the blond woman waiting nearby. The gawkers laughed; the kid was a card all right. "You mean that back shootin' murderin' cunt over yonder? She may drop her drawers for you—you bein' her champeen an' all—but you best let your cock dangle or she'll murder you like she did poor ol' Crockett Mapes. Was there justice she'd a hung for it. 'Stead of that she's ridin' around like her ol' man still runs this fuckin' town."

This was dragging on too long. Morgan edged his horse away without making a full turn. There was danger if he listened to any more bullshit. The kid was working himself into a rage. No shots came at him, but the kid was still mouthing off about the blond woman. Well, she's not my wife or ladyfriend, not my sister, Morgan thought. He'd been gallant enough for one day.

"Let's go," he said to the woman.

"I'm not afraid of that trash," she said, but she set her horse to walking. "There was a time . . ." She didn't finish the sentence. No need to. Morgan figured there must have been a time, the way she spoke and carried herself and the kid's remark about her old man running the town at one time. And a fat-looking town it was, with a new town hall, a bank and newspaper building, two white churches, two streets branching off the main street. Must be a sorry comedown for her to be bullied in public by three drunken rowdies. Was a time when the marshal would have come running to break it up. Now he was hiding.

Still there were no words of thanks by the time they reached the end of the street. Maybe she thought what he'd done was no more than her due. Why not? Women were precious commodities. He'd have done the same for a crib girl. Difference was, a crib girl would have thanked him. If she planned to drop her drawers like the kid said, that was fine with him. Better than a peck on the cheek or a hearty handclasp. She hadn't said her name yet. There was something peculiar about her, but that was inside her head. The rest of her was good to look at. Fairly tall, about 23, she had whitish blond hair, pale blue eyes, and a body just made for a mattress. A formidable woman! How formidable was she in bed? He hoped to find out.

She didn't say anything until they had cleared the town. "I'm Molly Niles," she said. "I own a horse ranch about ten miles out. My father was Territorial Representative Alonzo Niles." She said the last part as if she expected him to have heard of her father and be impressed.

"Lee Morgan," he told her. "Used to have a horse ranch myself." The town was well behind, but he checked to see if they were being followed. With a few more drinks in him the kid might decide to take up where he left off.

Molly Niles didn't look back. "What happened to the ranch?" she asked.

"Horse thieves," he said. "Wiped me out." He said nothing about the Jack Mormon renegades that had slaughtered most of his stock, burned his house and murdered the few men left to watch the place. "Hit me when I was away with the boys on a buying trip." He didn't tell her that he had tracked the Jack fanatics, who hated all but themselves, to their mountain hideout and wiped them out.

It was getting to be late afternoon and he could do with a rest. A horse deal that went sour had left him smack-dab in the middle of the terri- tory with nothing to show for his trouble. The so-called horse rancher, a front man for a gang of horse thieves, was already on his way to jail, the horses seized by the law, by the time he got there. Other horse buyers were as burned as he was. The location of the so-called ranch should have been a dead giveaway as well as the low prices being touted around. Reason given was the owner wanted to sell out fast because he was in bad health. Fuck it! All he'd lost was time, of which he had plenty. Now he was heading north by the back trails and he'd ridden 30 miles since early morning.

"You want to get back into horse ranching?" Molly Niles asked.

"Been thinking about it," he said. "I like the work." He wasn't about to tell her his life story. Getting a big enough stake together was the hardest part of it. A few times he'd come close. Sure as hell he wasn't going to start over with nothing but a few horses and a shack. The hell with that shit! Start right or let it go.

"You want a temporary job while you're thinking about it?" she asked. "I'll pay you five hundred dollars to help me drive two hundred horses to Fort Buell as soon as possible. Major Van Horn needs the horses since half his mounts are dead of bloody flux or have to be shot, and I need the money. No one around here will work for me— white men, that is. That's what the trouble in town was about. I was trying to hire a few men."

"I could use the five hundred," Morgan said; then he waited. It was up to her to say more. He didn't give a damn who this Crockett Mapes was or why she'd killed him. Shot him in the back if the drunken cowhand was to be believed. It was likely she had. Usually back-shooting wasn't to his liking, but if that was the only way to kill Mapes, then it was the smartest if not the most sensible thing to do. Maybe not too sensible because she'd been seen doing it, or so it seemed.

Molly Niles said, "Perhaps you won't want to work for me after I tell you a few things about myself. I did shoot Crockett Mapes in the back, and I'm glad I did." She paused to think, as if she hadn't thought about it before. "I wouldn't do it again but I'd want to. I was released from Yuma Prison six weeks ago after serving one year of a fifteen-year sentence. The sentence would have been longer if my attorney hadn't convinced the court that I was in a disturbed state of mind. Like hell I was! Crockett Mapes crippled my father, destroyed our lives, and I killed him for it. I got a full pardon, not because the governor believed me any less guilty, but because my father all but beggared himself, bribe on top of bribe, to get me pardoned. My father died a few days after I was released."

They rode in silence for a while; then Morgan said, "What you just told me makes no difference. I'll work for you if you want. About me, I could tell you anything at all. No easy way to check it. You'll have to take me on trust."

She gave him her second tight smile of the day. "Hardly on trust. You may be good with horses, but there's no way you could steal two hundred horses by yourself. And I'll have very little money until I get the ten thousand dollars sale money from Major Van Horn."

Morgan gave her a tight smile of his own. "I could waylay you when you start back with the ten thousand."

Their eyes locked for an instant. "You could but you won't, unless I'm a bad judge of character. Anyway, I'm sure Major Van Horn will provide an escort for the journey back."

There was another lull in the conversation; then out of nowhere she told him what had led to the killing of Crockett Mapes. She started by saying, "I suppose you're wondering how it all came about."

"Only natural," Morgan said. It wouldn't be polite to say that all he'd been thinking about was how to get her clothes off and get her legs spread. Sometimes being tired could make you very horny. It had been three weeks since his last woman, far too long to his way of thinking.

"It began a long time ago," she said. "What I mean by that is there was bad feeling between my father and Alamo Mapes, Crockett's father, ever since he came here from Texas fourteen years ago. His real name is Lamar, but everybody calls him Alamo—it means so much to him. Every year he gives a big barbecue on the anniversary of the Battle of San Jacinto, when Sam Houston avenged all those massacred at the Alamo. Mapes named his five sons Crockett, Bowie, Travis, Austin and Houston. Heroes of Texas history, and fine, honorable names for a family of thieving white trash. Alamo Mapes is proud of Texas even if Texas isn't proud of him. Father looked into his background and found that Alamo Mapes left Texas because the law was getting too hot for him. Oh, he's done well for himself in Arizona—a big ranch, a sawmill, a freight company—but it wasn't always like that. For all his barbecues and backslapping, he remains what he always was—vicious, no-good, white trash. A family of barn burners is what my father called the Mapeses."

"Surprised they got away with that in Texas," Morgan said.

"A figure of speech," she said with something like irritation. "They didn't burn any barns in

Texas. But Alamo Mapes grew up changing brands, then running stolen horses and cattle into Mexico."

"What's he done here?" To Morgan, Mapes didn't sound very different from a lot of self-made men in their younger days—cutting corners, bending the rules, skirting the law. Every wealthy man got bad-mouthed even if he was completely honest, which was seldom.

Molly Niles said, "He did plenty of things that couldn't be proved. Never enough evidence. People have always been a little afraid of him—everyone except my father. My father always believed he murdered a rancher named Leydecker to get his land. It's true Leydecker had a number of enemies, men he owed money to and wouldn't pay, or insulted when he was drunk, which was most of the time. He fathered two children by two different women, then laughed at their families when they tried to persuade him to do the decent thing. No one was ever arrested for his murder— he was shot from ambush—but my father was certain Alamo Mapes was behind it. A nephew of Leydecker's, a store clerk in Bisbee, inherited the land but sold it cheap to Mapes. My father said he was afraid not to."

Morgan got a picture of Niles as a pompous old man who was all puffed up with his own importance—a big bullfrog in a small pond. His daughter had gotten her haughty manner from someone.

"How my father despised that man," she went on, "and he never hesitated to say so. The bad feeling grew worse when Mapes began to take an interest in politics. That was after he started to make money. Hambro, my father's main political rival, was—is—all for statehood. My father opposed it, said we weren't ready for it. Mapes put money into Hambro's campaign, supporting him all the way. My father lost the last two elections to Hambro, but that didn't silence him. He used his newspaper to attack Hambro and Mapes as crooks and opportunists, men who saw statehood as a way to line their pockets."

"He ever get sued?" Morgan asked.

"No. Nothing as civilized as that." Molly Niles's jaw had a bitter set to it, and she chopped off her words like wood chips. "My father had just printed another editorial exposing Hambro's partnership in Mapes's sawmill, which had supplied the lumber for the new town hall at inflated prices. The day that week's newspaper went on sale, Crockett Mapes confronted my father as he was crossing Main Street and said he was going to flog him until he admitted that his charges were lies. Crockett raised a horsewhip with his left hand. My father tried to draw a pocket pistol to defend himself. Crockett, a dead shot, drew his own pistol and shot my father six times— one bullet for each arm, two bullets for each leg. My father survived but was confined to a wheelchair, his right arm and right leg withered and useless. A hopeless cripple at the age of fifty-nine. Crockett Mapes stood trial but was acquitted. Witnesses, most of them Crockett's friends, testified that Crockett merely shook the whip, which he habitually carried. They swore my father drew first."

Morgan knew he was expected to say something. He didn't want to say anything, but she had paused so he could. It sounded like a straight enough story except she was leaving something out. Fucking Crockett Mapes hadn't been mentioned, not that he'd expected her to mention it.

Something made him think the drunk kid had been telling the truth about that. Hard to keep secrets in a small town. But why in hell had she back-shot Mapes on Main Street in front of witnesses when she could have ambushed him in some lonely place? The town might know she'd done it, but proving it was something else. That she'd done it in the heat of the moment didn't wash. Molly Niles was a cold one. Didn't take long to see that. Morgan knew she was still waiting for him to say something.

"Sounds as if Mapes planned it," he said.

"Alamo Mapes planned it," Molly Niles said. "Crockett did what his father told him to do. You're wondering why I didn't kill the father. I should have, but I didn't get the chance. I went looking for him at the freight company, but the men there didn't know where he was or weren't telling. I went to the saloon, thinking I might find him there. Crockett was coming out when I got there. He smiled at me, then walked on by. That's when I shot him in the back."

All that Morgan could think to say was, "Well, it's over and you're free."

"I'm more than that," she said, but didn't elaborate. When they topped a rise in the road, she pointed to a windbreak and ranch buildings in the far distance, way off to the east. "My father's ranch is mine now. We owned all the land along the county road, twenty miles of it. I intend to get it back. My father had to sell it, the newspaper, other good land and go deep into debt, just to get me out of prison. I don't know how many people he had to bribe to do that. It might have been easier if he'd still held office. We had an experienced foreman and good wranglers, but they're gone—no money to pay them. Now I have to make do with a small crew of Mexicans. They're lazy and unreliable, like all Mexicans. I pay them what I can, and they're glad to get it. They let the place run down after my father was crippled and I was in prison. That's all going to change."

There was a hardness about her that would have put him off if she hadn't been so good looking, so perfect for bed. The year in Yuma had hardened her, as it would harden anybody. All the same, there must have been a certain tough streak in her to begin with. Yuma hadn't broken her—that was plain to see. She was so goddamned sure of herself. Unless he had her age figured wrong, she couldn't have been more than 21 or 22 when they put her in a cage. Of all the women's prisons in the country, Yuma was the worst. The wild women there must have drooled over her firm breasts, rounded ass and long muscular thighs. Just thinking about it gave Morgan an iron hard-on.

They started down a side road that went to the ranch. Morgan hadn't asked her anything about the drive to Fort Buell. Best to let her talk herself out before he started on that. It seemed like she hadn't talked to anybody for a very long time. He decided he liked her well enough. Only one thing bothered him—why was she willing to pay him so much? The thought crossed his mind that she might try to knock him down on the money when the drive was over, or maybe not pay him at all. That, he decided, would be the biggest mistake of her young life.

Mexicans came out of the darkness to greet them. There were lights in the main house and the bunkhouse, along with the smell of wood smoke. Horses moved uneasily in a string of corrals. Molly swung down and gave her horse to one of the

Mexicans. Morgan said he would see to his own horse.

"My house is your house," Molly Niles said in stilted Spanish, the kind they taught in young ladies' academies. It was an attempt at humor, Morgan realized, but Molly Niles had no humor.

"Your ass is my ass," he said to himself.

Chapter Two

The house was old, built in the style of a Mexican rancho, and it had a low-peaked roof with red tiles and thick adobe walls, small windows with inside shutters and a massive oak door. An old Mexican with a long mustache and a threadbare black suit bowed and held the massive door open wide so they could go in. Five other Mexicans, four men and one woman, stood around in the dull yellow light of the doorway. The woman was young and good-looking in a sullen way, thin and very dark, with surprisingly big breasts and long black hair skinned back and fastened behind her head with a silver clasp. Her elaborate silver earrings tinkled softly in the night wind. She stared hard at Morgan.

Molly Niles spoke to one of the men—she called him Trinidad—and said they would talk about the drive to Fort Buell in the morning. Then she waved them away. She didn't speak to the woman, who was the last to leave. Something there, Morgan thought.

The main room was long and wide, with glass-fronted bookcases, framed maps and oil paintings. Navaho rugs were scattered here and there on the flagged floor. A piled-high log fire blazed in an enormous stone fireplace. Molly Niles went to the fire to warm her hands, saying, "It can get cold at night even in late April. Sit down, Morgan. Make yourself comfortable. Ignacio"— that was the old Mexican house servant—"set out the drinks and then you can go." She took a key from the pocket of her short riding skirt and gave it to him. The old man unlocked a massive, elaborately scrolled sideboard and put glasses and bottles on top of it.

Morgan was in a deep leather armchair to one side of the fire. Molly Niles went to the sideboard and talked over her shoulder as she fixed the drinks. "Jack Daniel's all right with you? It was my father's favorite whiskey. Mine, too. I keep it locked up, as you see. You can't trust Mexicans when it comes to alcohol."

Morgan was glad the old man had left the room. He had nothing for or against Mexicans, but why hurt somebody's feelings for no reason? Like as not, the old man didn't give a shit as long as he had food and a bed. Molly Niles gave Morgan his drink and sat down in the armchair facing him. Morgan's glass was half-full, as was hers. She might be niggardly with the hired hands, but she didn't stint on the whiskey.

"Here's to a successful drive," she said and downed half her drink.

Well, now, Morgan thought, here's a girl who knows how to drink—no ladylike sipping, no pretend gagging. Her eyes grew brighter, and she didn't mind the way her short skirt rode up on her smooth, muscular thighs. Neither did he. His hard-on, which had flagged a bit, came back full force. After three womanless weeks, he was ready to go anytime she was. The thing of it was, how soon would that be—if at all?

Now she was drawing his attention to the huge oil painting that hung above the fireplace. It showed a thick-bodied man in early middle age with a florid face and a mane of white hair. Morgan thought the man in the painting should have had porky jowls and a bigger belly. No doubt the artist knew which side his bread was buttered on. He had given the face in the painting a man-of-destiny look.

"My father," Molly Niles said, getting up to admire Alonzo Niles in all his glory. Morgan stood up too, though he wanted to stay where he was. Anything to get this gorgeous creature closer to bed. Molly Niles finished her whiskey standing up, then stretched out in her chair. She held out her empty glass, and Morgan poured a fresh drink in it. After she drank most of it— Morgan was still working on his first drink—she sat up straight and gave him a hard look.

Oh, Christ! Morgan thought.

"I've been noticing that you don't call me by any name. I call you Morgan because it suits you better than Lee for some reason. You don't call me Miss Niles or Molly. Why is that? I think it must be deliberate."

Morgan drank a little whiskey. "What would you like me to call you?"

"I'd like you to call me Molly. But you mustn't get ideas, if you know what I mean. We'll be together a great deal, and I wouldn't want you to . . ."

She finished her drink without finishing the sentence.

"Of course not," Morgan said, not entirely convinced that she meant what she said. Just the same, if that's what she wanted, he wasn't going to come at her like a randy mountain man. That wasn't his style, and there was always the 500 to think about.

"I'd like us to be friends," she said in that bright voice of hers. "I like you, Morgan, but a woman in my position has to be careful. I'm sure you understand that."

"Sure thing," Morgan said, thinking he might as well have another big drink. If she wasn't going to spread them for him, then he might as well drink. The hell of it was, he still had a hard-on. Small wonder! Her skirt was practically hiked up to her crotch, and unless the whiskey was playing tricks with his eyes, she wasn't wearing any underwear. Maybe he should show a little of that mountain man spirit, after all.

She got up suddenly, as if reading his mind. "You must be hungry," she said. "I certainly am. I'm no great cook, but I can make something you can eat. Ham and eggs, something like that? Nothing Mexican."

"I fixed a big meal just before I got to Niles City," Morgan said sourly. Fuck ham and eggs! She'd probably burn the fucking things. "If you don't mind, I'd like to get some sleep. I've been on the go since five this morning."

She drank her third drink at the sideboard. "Then you must be tired. How thoughtless of me not to see that." She seemed to be mocking him. "I'll show you where your room is, just down the hallway from mine, it so happens. Riggs, our foreman, slept in the house after my father became an invalid. No reason why you shouldn't. I'll sleep better knowing you're in the house."

She laughed, as if mocking the idea that she needed any man to protect her. Morgan drank the rest of his drink and followed her through an archway and down a hall with doors on both sides. With most of a pint of whiskey in him, he didn't want any more. What he wanted he wasn't going to get, it looked like. Still and all, it was a shame they couldn't have a friendly bed rassle before starting out for Fort Buell. He realized he was slightly drunk but not at all sleepy. He still had the hard-on, and she knew he had it. How could she not?

She opened a door and showed him into a room with a big double bed that stood high off the floor. There was a wardrobe, a long table and two squat chairs, all as solid as the oak trees they started as. An oval mirror with a gilt frame hung on the wall between two windows. Not much light came from the hall, and when they bumped together Molly Niles said, "Oh, my goodness!" Morgan reached out for her, but she ducked away and lit a candle that stood in an old iron candlestick. "Sleep well, Morgan." She patted the brightly colored quilt before she went out quickly and closed the door behind her.

Might as well try to get some sleep, Morgan decided, knowing he'd sleep all right after his hard-on subsided. He pulled a chair close to the bed and put his gunbelt and his father's old silver watch on it. It was five minutes to ten when he undressed, blew out the candle and got under the covers. He was drifting off to sleep when two women, screaming and yelling, jerked him awake. At first he thought he'd been dreaming, but as the yelling continued and got louder, he went to the door and opened it a crack. He recognized Molly Niles's voice. The other woman's voice was Mexican. There was a crashing sound as if a glass had been thrown. A chair or something like it went over with a louder crash. Both voices were shrill with anger, but he could understand Molly Niles better than the woman she was fighting with. The sullen Mexican with the earrings? Maybe. Maybe not. Whoever she was, Molly Niles was calling her a dirty filthy cunt and ordering her to get out of the house. The Mexican woman was yelling in Spanish and English, but all Morgan could make out was, "Go fuck your new man wit' hees big cock. Son ob a beech come in de house showin' off de beeg steef cock in hees pants. How jew you teenk I feel? You are the dirty feelthy cunt, Molly." There was a loud slapping sound that went on and on. The Mexican woman began to scream. More furniture was overturned, followed by the slamming and bolting of the front door. The door was pounded for a while; then it got quiet.

Morgan closed the door and got back into bed. Not for a moment had he considered trying to break up what sounded like a strictly private quarrel. Quarrel, hell! They'd gone at it hammer and tongs right in front of Alonzo Niles. But what in Christ's name was it all about? If Yuma had turned Molly queer, the fight made some sense. If not, why was the fight so savage, and what was the reason for it? All right. Suppose Molly was queer, had woman-fucked the Mexican and was now tired of her. Why was the Mexican still around? It was easier to think of the two women as lovers rather than friends, but Molly was so casually contemptuous of Mexicans that it was hard to think of the two of them naked together.

Was it possible that Molly and the Mexican were half sisters, the Mexican sired by Alonzo Niles more than 20 years ago? Bullshit! Next he'd be writing spicy stories for the lady trade.

But he was still thinking about it when Molly came in naked with a lighted candle in her hand. She set it down with the elaborate care of someone who'd been drinking too much and got under the covers with him. Morgan pretended to wake up, yawning and rubbing his eyes.

"You mean you slept through all that uproar?" Molly asked.

"What uproar?" Morgan replied, pulling her close. "I heard some frogs croaking before I dropped off, then nothing. Was there an uproar? What kind of uproar?"

Pressed tightly against him, she began to stroke his cock. "Well, not really an uproar. You saw that Mexican girl who was outside the house when we arrived? Well, I've been trying to get rid of her since I got out of prison, but she keeps hanging on, goddamn her to hell! Her mother used to cook for my father in the old days. He had a soft spot for Mexicans, loved Mexican food. I don't. After her mother died, my father allowed her to stay on in the little house where she'd lived with her mother. She was fifteen at the time. There was no question of sending her away after my father discovered that she was a better cook than her mother. And as I've told you, my father liked Mexicans. That was fine as long as my father was alive. Now he's dead and I certainly don't need her."

She talked steadily and too much. He didn't mind talkers as long as they were doers as well. This one was. Loosened up by liquor and ready for a big dick, she still sounded like the lady of the big house—but what a difference! If she stayed like this on the trail, it would be a drive to look back on. His hand went between her legs, his middle finger into her. With a heartfelt groan, she closed her thighs on his hand, pushing her tongue into his mouth. She opened her thighs, and his finger slid up and down on her knob. It was well-developed, and he knew she used her own finger a lot. Only natural for a strong-willed woman who'd spent a year behind bars and the last six weeks on a ranch with a bunch of Mexican men she didn't like.

She pulled him on top of her, spreading her legs and raising her knees. His balls were pulled up tight and his cock was like a pole, as he went deep inside her with one long thrust. Her heels drummed on the bed, and she cried out, "All the way in! All the way in!" She clutched him desperately as he pulled back for another thrust. Most women did that, but this one seemed to have some kind of frantic fear that he would pull his cock out and not put it back in. But that's how she wanted to do it, at first—long penetrations of her body, then a pause and the wild clutching of her hands, then another powerful thrust. Any way she wanted it was fine with him. A man is always a guest between a woman's legs, Morgan thought, and his cock is what gets him invited.

He knew she wanted him to fuck her faster when she started to push upward with her crotch. Quick little bumps seemed to vibrate in his cock, but she didn't want short quick thrusts. She wanted long, long thrusts, but she wanted them faster. She even said it. "Do it faster. In and out, out and in— faster, faster!" And as he quickened his thrusts they became like a machine, his ass-powered rigid cock driving in and out like a piston. He had a big cock and she was tight, but she was so thickly wet that it was like driving it into hot, heavy oil, so smooth was the thrust and withdrawal, the push and the pull.

She didn't come right away, though she trembled on the edge of it. She was like a man who holds back his come and tightens his muscles to delay his come, so he can build up his come into something like an explosion. But she was close to it and getting closer. Her face was contorted like someone in agony, and the pleading cries coming from deep in her throat threatened to turn into screams. His hands, cupping her ass, lifted her and pressed her up into him. Then, with a wild twisted shuddering that was almost a fit, she came as her hands slid between them, pinching her own nipples and milking herself of pleasure. Milking herself like that, she couldn't stop coming. Her other hand reached down, and she pushed her finger inside herself so she could stimulate her clit as Morgan drove in and out of her. Then she took her finger out and put it in Morgan's mouth, and it tasted salty as he sucked on it. Everything she did excited him. She was very young, but she used her body like a high-priced, much-in-demand prostitute—not a slick operator who went through the motions, but more like a happy amateur enjoying sex in every possible way. She built him up to his orgasm, working on him with every part of her body, and when he couldn't stand it anymore, when the tension became unbearable, he shoved it in to the hilt, held it there with the weight of his body behind it—and came like a gushing hose. It had been three weeks since his last woman, and all his stored-up jism shot into her. He lay on top of her, gasping and sweating, hardly able to move at first, drained and pleasantly exhausted, knowing this was just the start of the night.

As she moved under him, his cock began to swell and harden. As she felt it getting big again, she groaned, reached between them and circled the part of his cock she could get at with thumb and forefinger. Her fingers were greased with his juice and hers, and when he began to move again it was like he was fucking two different cunts at the same time. But then, when his cock grew thick and hard, she took her fingers away and put her middle finger in his ass and massaged him there, tickling and rubbing, and it drove him wild. He wanted to keep his cock in her cunt, and at the same time, as it bulged and throbbed, he wanted to put in her ass and her mouth and under her armpits and between her breasts. This time they came together, now fully aware of each other's needs and longings and wanting to share the intense pleasure coursing through their bodies.

In a few moments, while he rested, she pushed up and rolled him over on his back. Then she kissed him on the mouth and on both sides of his face, moving her head down to his chest, where she pulled on his chest hair with her teeth. Then her mouth moved down to his crotch, and she lifted his cock and took his balls and sucked on them. She sucked his balls into her mouth and made as if to swallow them. Morgan's cock stood up again, and she stroked it up and down with her hand. Her mouth closed over the head of his cock, and there was a hint of danger in her small, sharp teeth. Her teeth nibbled at his cock, and her tongue tickled it. Next she placed her head so she could move her mouth up and down on his cock. It felt like he was fucking her in the mouth, and his balls tightened in preparation to come, and he would have shot off in her mouth if she hadn't pressed the big vein of his cock with her fingers. Easing the hold on his cock, she continued to suck him, and the same thing happened. She kept cutting off his come, keeping him from what he longed for, and there was something close to anger in him. His hands, which had been caressing her face, suddenly gripped her head and pushed her mouth down on his cock. Feeling the fierce need in him, she sucked him with equal fierceness, and when the come shot out of him into her mouth, she swallowed it and swallowed it, and he kept coming and she kept sucking.

This time, at last, he had to rest, and they lay together, their arms crossed, her fingers fondling his limp cock, his fingers tickling her clit. The bed was wet with sweat and come, and the room had the sweet smell of sex. It was good to lie beside her in the dark room in the silent house and know there was nothing to disturb them. This Molly Niles was something of a puzzle—the way she changed from proper lady to voracious sex in a few hours—but he wasn't going to rack his brain trying to solve it. Most people were a bit of a puzzle. For him, right this minute, it was enough that he was in bed with a beautiful, willing women and had a job that would put money in his pocket. He wasn't going to spoil it by thinking too hard. Sometimes, to raise money or just to get by, he had worked for other people, some stingy, a few generous. But he'd never had a deal like this. Five hundred dollars for a walk in the country, so to speak, and a woman like this as a bonus. Damn it, he was going to be the best trail boss there ever was. She deserved nothing less than that.

At last, she stirred and spoke, fumes of stale

whiskey coming from her. "I'm going to get another drink to put me to sleep. Would you like one?"

Morgan didn't want any more booze, but it would have been unmannerly to say no, the nice way she asked. She slipped out of bed and came back with two big glasses of Jack Daniel's. She got back into bed and pulled the crumpled quilt over them. There was an early morning chill, and she snuggled close to him after belting down the whiskey. Morgan took a short drink, then reached down and put the glass on the floor.

"You must wonder at me," she murmured, but that thought was forgotten as the whiskey took effect. If there was any wondering to be done, he did it about her lovemaking and not about her character. Just then, he didn't give a damn about her character. A woman with hands like hers—body, breasts, mouth, everything—just had to have a fine character. That was the way he felt, and there was no reason to change his high opinion of her, as long as she stayed in bed. To think otherwise would be boorish and ungrateful. What a wife she was going to make for some lucky fellow if he lived beyond the wedding night. And if he did die, it couldn't be for a better reason. Men picked up the fallen standard and ran full tilt at Gatling guns. Others dived into icy rivers and drowned, trying to rescue a struggling child. But this was the way to check out.

The whiskey had worked its magic and she said, "I'm thinking of the nights out there. I have a tent that will keep the rain off. We can sleep on blankets, and it will be warm and cozy. We can listen to the wind and the rain and know they can't get at us."

Morgan nodded so she could feel him nodding.

A bit of a dreamer, this girl, and what she was saying was a relief from what too many woman said. Did you enjoy it, darling? You mustn't think because I did that I'm a wanton woman. I've never done that even with my husband. You bring out the wildness in me, you big devil. Worst of all were the ones who began to hint at matrimony. From these he ran like a greyhound.

But Molly Niles said none of that, for which he was thankful. It would have been better if she hadn't talked at all. Still, you had to take the good with the bad, and with her the bad wasn't so bad and the good was better than great.

She talked as she got him in shape for the next bout. Playing with his cock, she said, "You really stood up to those awful men in town. The way you were ready to kill all three of them. Well, I knew I had found the right man."

Morgan didn't say that it waren't nothin', ma'am. It was never nothing when you had to kill men and you stood a good chance of dying yourself. Anyway, the bashful shit-kicking act wouldn't work here. She was too smart for that, not like other women he'd used it on.

"I couldn't let them bother you like that," he told her. "You could have been hurt. I guess you could have taken care of yourself if I hadn't happened along."

That was a nice touch, he thought, and she liked it. She was one of this new breed of free women, and what he'd said was right up her alley. "I'm sure I could have handled them," she said, "but it was just as well it turned out the way it did. If I had been forced to shoot them, it would have been no more than they deserved."

From her tone, Morgan was sure she would have done it if she'd been able. It wasn't that, so much as the way she said it—so matter-of-factly, as if the three men were burrowing pests making a nuisance of themselves in the lady's flower garden. Morgan would have killed them too, if they had forced it on him, but he wouldn't have been pious about it.

"Who were they anyway?" he asked.

"I don't know their names," she answered. "They work for Mapes."

"Has Mapes bothered you since you got out of prison?"

"No, he hasn't bothered me. Mapes never bothers anyone himself. He gets others to do it for him. I don't want to talk about Alamo Mapes, if you don't mind."

Morgan didn't mind, far from it. For all he cared, Mapes could be down a well. He tickled her clit and felt her respond, while his cock responded to the quick strokes of her hand. No more talk for a while. You could talk anytime. Now there were more important things to do. One of them was to take her from behind, and she told him what she wanted by turning over and lying flat. Morgan carefully mounted her that way. Doing it from behind took a little more care, but she had moistened his cock with her spit, and it went in smoothly after a few tries. Anything she wanted she was going to get.

She liked it as much as the regular way. Morgan liked it any way he could get it. He had long since realized he was a horny man who could never get enough. Women in their way were more important than food and drink. If push came to shove, you could always find something to chew on and a mouthful of water to wash it down. Women were harder to find, especially in some of the places he found himself in—and not just a lovely woman like this, but any woman. When you did find one who looked and fucked like a lonely cowboy's dream, you made the most of it, as he was doing now.

Groans broke out of her, and she begged him to get it in all the way. It *was* in all the way and still she couldn't get enough of his cock. She had a tight ass and she made it tighter, hurting him as he must be hurting her. But the pain was pleasure for both of them, and she dug her fingernails into his hands until that hurt, too. Thinking to pleasure her more, he freed one hand, slid it under her, put his middle finger inside her and began to tickle her clit. She came with a scream that would have been heard in the bunkhouse if she hadn't muffled it by burying her face in the pillow. Morgan's orgasm was right on top of hers, and she kept coming after the last juice drained out of him. He kept her orgasms coming with his finger, and they were so frantic and violent that he thought she was going to shake the bed apart. Then she turned her head, blew out a long breath and relaxed.

"Major Van Horn really needs my horses," she said, sitting up. "He can't get them any closer, and my price is right, slightly under the market price. I've cut the price a little because I need the money as much as he needs the horses."

Morgan felt like saying, "Whoa there! How did the bluecoat major get into this bed?" The whiskey was dying in her, and it was time it did. There was most of a big drink on the floor on his side of the bed, but he didn't mention it.

"Well, I must get some sleep," she said, meaning in her own bed. She got up and went out without a farewell kiss. That was all right. She'd done enough with her mouth for one night.

Morgan was trying to straighten the bedclothes

when he heard a sound close to the open window. It could be some prowling night animal, but somehow he didn't think so.

He pulled back the curtains just in time to see the Mexican woman disappearing into the darkness.

Something there all right. Still none of his business. He wouldn't mention it to Molly.

Chapter Three

Molly said Fort Buell was more than 100 miles to the east, with no settlements or ranches in between. Beyond the fort, going toward the New Mexico line, there was nothing for 60 miles. Then you hit a trading post that doubled as a saloon and whorehouse. The place did a good business because it was all there was.

"I've never been there," Molly said, looking at the rough map that lay between them on the kitchen table. It was early next morning and Morgan was eating ham and eggs that he had fixed himself. Molly was drinking black coffee. Funny, Morgan thought, after last night I can think of her as just Molly. No last name. Nothing like bed to bring people together.

Earlier, before Molly was up, on his way to the kitchen, he'd found the old Mexican house servant cleaning up the mess in the main room. He looked startled when Morgan said good morning.

The only damage that Morgan could see had been done to the portrait of Alonzo Niles. Something, probably a glass, had hit him squarely in the face, ripping the canvas and ruining his looking-to-the-future expression.

Morgan turned the map so he could look at it. They would have to drive the horses through foothills, high plains and short stretches of desert. The route was direct enough, but here and there it wandered off because they had to drive the horses where the water was. Arizona was the driest country north of the Mexican border. Morgan didn't think it looked too bad, better in fact than some trails he'd been over. No Indian trouble this far north, Molly said. Except for a few scattered bands of diehard Apaches still raiding on both sides of the border, most Indians were on reservations. Horse thieves hadn't been a worry since the last of the rustler gangs was wiped out five years before.

Molly poured another cup of coffee. "You make the strongest, blackest coffee I've ever tasted."

"No half measures for me." There had been no half measures the night before, not a one. Morgan felt pretty good. He had fucked a brittle, edgy, beautiful woman into a state of dazed contentment. At least, that was how she'd looked when she finally went to her own room. Now she was all business, as if Morgan had never given her a dick or a lick.

Morgan pushed his plate away. "You ever been on a drive?"

"Unfortunately no," she said. "I was always away at school in St. Louis. My father bossed the drives when he was a young man. Later, after he went into politics, Riggs and the foreman before him did it. We did business all over the territory in those days. By the time I grew up the ranch wasn't doing as well as it had been, not for a good many years. My father lost two elections, one after the other, and it took some of the heart out of him. He devoted too much time to the newspaper, not enough to the ranch."

Morgan didn't have anything to say to that. Old Niles's newspaper had done him in. Fearless crusading wasn't such a great idea in this part of the world, unless you were fast with a gun.

Somebody knocked on the kitchen door, and Trinidad, the Mexican foreman, came in. Molly didn't offer him coffee or tell him to sit down. He was about Morgan's age, late thirties, tall for a Mexican, handsome and proud of it. There wasn't much Indian in him and he spoke good English.

"This is Mr. Morgan," Molly said. "You will take your orders from him. You were on the last drive before Mr. Riggs left, so you know the country. Can you think of any problems we might run into?"

"I can think of no problems, Miss Molly," the Mexican said. "No big problems. Small problems, yes. There is always snakebite and jimson weed to look out for. Sprung tendons, you know."

"You're sure the count is right?"

"Yes, Miss Molly." Morgan thought the Mexican was slightly uneasy. "Two hundred and seven horses is the count. It was two hundred and five, but yesterday we found two strays hiding in the deep brush in the canyon."

"Good work, Trinidad," Molly said. "That means another hundred dollars."

"How soon do we start the drive, Miss Molly? The horses are nervous from being in the corrals so long a time. Some are still half wild from running on the open range. If they break out of one corral, the others will break out, too. It would take a week or more to round them up again. The wildest ones will go where it is hard to find them."

"No!" Molly banged her mug down so hard coffee slopped on the table. She looked from Trinidad to Morgan. "We can't let that happen. I thought it would be all right to wait until tomorrow morning, but if there's a chance the horses will break out, we'll start today. The wagon is loaded. Tell Carlos to get the chuck wagon ready."

Trinidad nodded and started for the door.

Morgan stood up. "Everybody hold on a minute. I want to look at the horses. See if they can be driven on such short notice. You mean none of them have been gentled?"

"Not many, Mr. Morgan," Trinidad said, not happy about it. "I have only three men besides the cook. Manuel is a cook and no good with horses. I do the best I can."

Suddenly Molly was in a bad temper. "That's not good enough, Trinidad. You don't work hard enough, that's what's wrong with you."

Trinidad put his hat on and straightened it. "You are calling me lazy? I am not here to be insulted. Take your horses to Fort Buell any way you can. I am leaving unless you apologize. If I leave, the other men will follow. They stay only because they have my promise that they will be paid."

Morgan kept out of it. Molly's face was white, and she had to swallow several times before she got the words out. "I . . . I'm sorry I spoke like that. I know you're not lazy. Far from it. Will you stay?"

The Mexican nodded. "I will stay. But when will we start the drive?"

Molly started to say something, but Morgan cut in. "We start at first light tomorrow morning, if I think we're ready."

Molly's reaction was fierce. "We start today. This is my ranch, that's my herd, and you're working for me. We will move out as soon as the wagons are ready."

"No good. I want to take a look at the horses. Some may be too wild to take along this trip. You agree, Trinidad?"

The Mexican didn't want to side with Morgan against Molly. "Miss Molly wants to take the greatest number of horses."

"If they stampede on the trail it'll be worse than on your own range," Morgan said to Molly. "We're shorthanded as it is. If they run off you'll end up with maybe half of what you have now."

Molly said, "It's your job to see they don't run off. What do you think you're being paid for?"

Morgan didn't put on his hat and walk out. He wasn't Mexican and didn't go in for dramatic scenes. Besides, he needed that $500. With horses scattered all over the country, Molly wouldn't want to pay him a cent.

"I'll earn my pay," he told her. "After I look at the herd I'll tell you what I think. Then you can decide."

"Meaning *you* can decide."

"No," Morgan said. "You make the decision. I won't back out now, but I won't say yes to everything you say." Some rules had to be laid down right from the start. Otherwise she'd walk all over him, which was fine in bed if she did it with bare feet.

In the end, Morgan got his way. Molly joined him, with Trinidad trailing behind. The horses were in two corrals when there should have been a third. A bit late to be building another corral at this point. These were big four and five year olds out of western mares by Eastern hackney stallions.

"I guess we can take them all," he told Molly when he got through. "But we have to go easy even if it slows us down a bit. A few days maybe."

"No more than that," Molly said to show her authority.

"Won't be," Morgan said. Unless something goes wrong, he thought. Anything could go wrong anytime, anywhere.

Molly turned away from him and asked Trinidad if he'd seen Ana that morning. "You want her, Miss Molly?"

"I want her gone today," Molly snapped irritably. "She was supposed to leave yesterday."

The Mexican shrugged. "I told her she had to go. I gave her the money you gave me. It is hard for me to talk to her. When I told her yesterday she said she does not deal with hired hands. If you could tell her yourself. . ."

Molly didn't want to listen. "I did tell her. Get rid of her any way you can. I don't care how you do it."

Trinidad walked away, looking unhappy.

Molly said to Morgan, "I told you about Ana last night." Morgan nodded, though he hadn't been too interested in Ana just then. Molly had been stroking his cock at the time. "I don't want her getting into the main house while I'm away. God knows, she's emotional enough to do anything, like setting fire to the place. Ignacio has two grandsons, boys really, coming to help him guard against thieves. I doubt if they'd be any match for Ana. I think I'll . . ."

Molly changed the subject in mid-sentence. "I'd better see what I'm going to wear. Oh, I don't mean my trail clothes. I'm sure I'll be having dinner with Frederick—Major Van Horn—Captain Todd and his wife, other officers and ladies at the fort."

Morgan wanted to smile. Frederick was a bachelor or a widower, it seemed. Was he supposed to be jealous? He got the feeling that Molly would have been happier if Frederick was a colonel. Had a classier sound to it. But a remote post like Fort Buell wouldn't rate a colonel.

"What will you be doing?" she asked.

"Getting to know the other Mexicans."

"Whatever for? You've talked to Trinidad. Anyway, you'll get to know them on the drive. As much as you'll want to."

"Best do it now," Morgan said. "If there's anything to be set to rights, I'd like to do it before we start."

"Now is not the time to be firing anybody," Molly said.

"I know that. Just a little chat, is all."

"Suit yourself."

Molly walked away, and Morgan smiled after her. It was the first time he had worked for a woman, but he thought he'd get the hang of it. Sure as hell he wasn't going to work for her steady, even if the drive went as smooth as melted butter. He didn't want to turn gray before he was 40.

He found Carlos, the cook, cursing at the chuck wagon. He was drunk, but that wasn't surprising. All cooks drank, but most managed to do their job in spite of it. This one was no different from the others Morgan had come across. Old, skinny, bad-tempered. Cooks were the tyrants of the trail, the terrors of the bunkhouse—and they got away with it. He started laying down the law as soon as Morgan came close. His English wasn't too bad.

"Listen a me, boss. I cooks wat I cooks, hokay. Hew don' like wat I cooks hew gotta cooks youself."

Morgan grinned at him and went to look for the other hands. He found Hector and Manuel shoring up a loose corral post with rocks. From the way they moved he could tell they'd been drinking. He figured he couldn't get too tough about it. They were working for next to nothing. But he had to say something.

"Who told you you could drink?" he asked them in English. Since he knew only a few words of Spanish, he might have to call Trinidad to make himself understood.

Both men weren't much more than 20. Brothers, he figured, short and wiry and dark. Smiling, one of them said, "We drink today cause we feelin' good. Soon we gonna get all a our back pay. Trinidad say we get back pay at Fort Bew-well. So we steal bottle from de cook and we drink."

Morgan nodded. "Finish the bottle, but no drinking on the trail."

The other one smiled fit to unhinge his jaw. "Bottle is fineesh. We don' drink on trail cause we got nothin' to drink. No money, no bottle. Sonbitch, we got to stay sober."

"Good idea," Morgan said. "Where's the other man? Cesar."

The older brother smiled apologetically. "He is sleepin'. He drinks and he have to sleep. Good man, no drinkin' on de trail."

Cesar was sleeping peacefully in his bunk until Morgan shook him awake. Then he came up swinging. He landed a blow on Morgan's shoulder before a backhander brought him to his senses. He mumbled, "Hew don' have to hit me, boss. Was jus' restin' couple minutes."

"Do your resting at night," Morgan told him. "Find some work to do before I find it for you. Now get the hell out of here."

Cesar swung his legs off the bunk and stared at Morgan. "You are de boss of the drive, not the boss here. We don' start yet."

"I'm the boss everywhere," Morgan said.

Next Morgan checked the big wagon that was to carry everything they might need—Molly's tent, spare wheels, wagon tools, a bucket of axle grease, rope and stakes, carpenter tools, slickers, kerosene. Trinidad had done a good job. Nothing important had been left out. But what in hell was the box of dynamite for? He had pried open the box and was looking at the dynamite sticks when Trinidad showed up.

"The dynamite is for the fort," he said. "It is new, not sweated. It is safe. I checked it myself."

"Why can't the major get his own dynamite?"

The Mexican shrugged. "I think the major asked for it in the letter he sent about the horses. A trooper brought it. The fort is far from everything, you know. The dynamite is safe, Mr. Morgan."

"A bullet could set it off," Morgan said.

Trinidad looked puzzled. "What bullet?"

"Any bullet. Bullets come when you least expect them. Put sandbags around the box."

"Whatever you say, Mr. Morgan. We will all be safer like that."

There was a slight sneer in the Mexican's voice, but Morgan didn't respond to it. Vain, handsome Trinidad was jealous. Nothing he could do about that. Trinidad had his eye on Molly *and* the ranch.

Both were beyond his reach, the poor son of a bitch.

Morgan knew he would have to keep his eye on Trinidad.

There wasn't much to do after checking the wagon. He went back to the house and knocked on Molly's door—a little afternoon fucking wasn't a bad idea—but she wasn't in her room or she wasn't answering. Last night had worn him down a bit, so he stretched out and slept. It was getting dark when he woke up and went back to try Molly again. Same thing. No response to his knock. Simmer down, boy, he told himself. If you don't get your ashes hauled tonight, you have all those nights on the trail to make up for it.

There was plenty of food in the kitchen—Molly ate as well as she drank—but he didn't feel like cooking anything. The Mexicans were eating supper when he went over to the cook shack. They were surprised but courteous, making room for him when he came to the table with the food the cook gave him, a plate heaped with all the things Molly would turn her nose up at. The food was better than he would have expected Molly to provide, and there was plenty of it, which made him wonder if Trinidad hadn't cut out a mount or two. He wouldn't get $50 apiece for stolen horses, but he'd get something. No wonder he looked nervous when Molly asked about the count.

Naturally the cook wanted to know how he liked the food. Morgan said it was better than the big expensive dinner he once had in the fanciest restaurant in Mexico City. That was a joke and they laughed at it, all but Trinidad, who just smiled a thin smile. Morgan thanked the cook and said he'd see them in the morning.

On his way back to the house, he decided the hell with Molly. If she wanted it, let her come to his room the way she did the night before. He took his rifle and gun-cleaning kit to his room and worked on his guns until he got tired of it. Usually, working on his guns relaxed him, but not tonight. He wondered if Molly could be getting to him. Fuck that shit! He'd fucked more women than he could remember and was still his own man. By any yardstick Molly was a bitch, and yet he had to admit there was something about her that got under his skin.

Finally, he got into bed and tried to read a fat leatherbound book that lay on the table. It was Alonzo Niles's life story, written by himself and dealing with his first 40 years in the Arizona Territory. It was so dull and so pompous, he figured it would take 40 years to read. He was of no mind to spend the evening with Alonzo Niles, so he put the book back on the table and blew out the light. Some time later he awoke from a restless sleep and heard someone moving quietly in the hallway. Then he heard an old man's cough and knew it was Ignacio, the house servant, making his rounds.

Molly didn't come to his room.

Chapter Four

They moved out at first light. Far to the east, a good day's travel from where they were, the sun was coming up behind the bald top of Duckegg Mountain. Below it, the foothills were still in shadow. It had rained the night before and there was a thin fog that would remain until the sun burned it off.

Molly drove the freight wagon, Carlos the chuck wagon. The horses were skittish when the corral gates were opened, but now they were moving at a slow but steady pace. There had been no wild break for freedom, something Morgan had been afraid of. Horses weren't as stupid as sheep, but it didn't take much to make them panic. A snake, a loud noise, a fast-moving cloud shadow could set them off.

Molly was doing all right with the big wagon. It didn't take much skill to drive a loaded wagon pulled by steady work horses. Morgan smiled at

the way she sat ramrod straight on the box. She'd
have to loosen up a bit or she'd have an awful
backache by the end of the day. All he'd gotten out
of her so far was a brisk "Good morning" when
she strode from the house all ready to travel. She
had traded the short riding skirt for a pair of Levi's
that took nothing away from her long legs and
firm ass. The two brothers, Hector and Manuel,
rolled their eyes until Trinidad hissed at them.

The sun was full up, the fog gone, and cotton-
ball clouds hung motionless behind the top of
the bald mountain. A cold east wind blew, but
the clouds looked as if they were anchored to
the top of the mountain. After six hours on the
move they were in the foothills, skirting the lower
slopes of the mountain. Tall pines grew thickly on
the slopes, and there were patches of mountain
meadow with good grazing. Halfway around the
mountain the trail started on a downward slope,
but they still had a long way to go before they
got out of the high country. Up high there was
good grass and water, and the only danger was
prowling mountain lions. As a rule, mountain
lions did their hunting at a higher elevation, but
the smell of so much fresh meat on the move
might draw them down after it got dark and the
herd was penned in for the night.

They stopped at noon in a narrow valley with
a rapidly flowing creek and good grazing. The
horses cropped the grass along the side of the
creek but made no attempt to cross it. Cesar
and the two brothers watched them to make
sure they didn't try. Molly took a picnic basket
from the wagon and spread out a lunch of cold
beef sandwiches and a pot of coffee reheated on
Carlos's cook fire. Carlos watched her with a
sardonic smile that he didn't do much to hide.

Trinidad ate refried beans and looked at the horses.

It was the first time Morgan had seen a picnic basket on any kind of drive, not that there was anything wrong with a picnic basket. The sandwiches were good and the coffee was—well, it was hot. The only thing wrong with any of it was Molly's attitude. For one thing, she didn't offer Trinidad a sandwich. The man was her foreman and she could have offered him a sandwich. Things like that didn't make for loyalty.

"We're not moving very fast, are we?" she said as if Morgan hadn't explained the reason for that.

Morgan drank some of the reheated coffee. "We'll make better time tomorrow. The herd is settling down. Mind if I ask you something?"

"You mean, why am I so impatient? I'm impatient by nature, but this is different. I want to get the money for the horses so I can start rebuilding my ranch. Those horses are just about all I have left."

"All the more reason not to lose them. But like I say, we'll set a better pace tomorrow. We'll set it and stay with it."

"If I say so, Morgan."

Morgan looked up at a hawk wheeling and banking in the sky. Better than seeing buzzards. The buzzards would appear right after they lost the first horse. You always lost a few no matter how careful you were, but Molly would blame him for that.

"You're back to that, are you? I thought that was settled. I won't let you bollix up this drive." Morgan meant what he said.

She flared up at that. "It's not a matter of letting me do this or that. I'll decide what has to be done."

Morgan threw out the dregs of the bad coffee. "What's your decision right this minute?"

"This minute? This instant? We move on without any further delay."

Another brick wall. "The hands haven't eaten yet. The idea is to watch the horses while they eat. We stand our night watches so they can sleep, but now they've got to eat."

"Let them hurry it up then." She fastened the lid of the basket and put it back in the wagon. Morgan didn't know how much Trinidad had heard. He wasn't that close, and his face was deadpan. Maybe he was thinking about the sandwich he hadn't been offered.

They got the horses and wagons across the creek. It was deep and swift, still fed by snow melting from the mountains. One horse broke a leg and Morgan had to kill it, but he waited until the herd was across before doing so. Lunchtime for the buzzards, he thought. Fifty dollars less for Molly.

She didn't like that, and she didn't like it when Morgan told Cesar to drive the freight wagon across. The horses were moving on ahead, easy to handle after plenty of grass and water. "I can drive the damned wagon," Molly protested but gave the reins to Cesar when Morgan said they could lose half their supplies if the wagon overturned.

A late spring shower hit them in the afternoon but was gone in minutes. The herd was moving along fine. Manuel and Hector were good with horses. Whenever one of the horses started kicking up, they moved in fast on the troublemaker. Cesar wasn't as fast or as willing, but he did his work. Trinidad kept an eye on everything.

Now and then, Morgan felt Trinidad's eyes boring into him. He never caught him doing it, and he didn't try. Only natural, he thought. The man had stayed loyal to the Niles family after the old man had screwed up, Molly was in prison, and the money was starting to dribble away. Now, just as Molly was coming into some money, he had been pushed aside in favor of a gringo.

Morgan still hadn't figured out why she was paying him so much. What was she afraid of? There were no horse thieves out here. Was she afraid of the Mexicans? She didn't like or trust Mexicans. It was only human nature that young bloods like Hector and Manuel would want to shove a cock into her, but wanting and doing were very different things. Morgan just didn't see the two good-natured brothers as dangerous. Anyway, they'd have Trinidad to deal with if they even started to get out of line. Trinidad himself was another story. Unless he was dead wrong, Morgan thought Trinidad wanted to fuck Molly as a way to becoming a rich and respected man. Driven far enough by ambition, such a man could be dangerous. Was there something about Trinidad that Molly hadn't told him? For all her defiant manner and abrupt way of speaking, she was not a woman who told the complete truth.

Was she afraid of Alamo Mapes? It could be that. But why would Mapes wait so long to kill her? A man like that could arrange to have her killed in prison. Nothing too hard about that. Another thing to think on. She'd been out of prison for six weeks, riding around on her own. Why hadn't Mapes killed her or had her killed in all that time, that is, if he meant to kill her at all.

Morgan had no clear picture of Mapes. Molly's accusations were all he had to go on. That he was crooked and greedy might very well be true, but that didn't make him a killer. Very possibly he wanted to forget about Alonzo Niles and his dead son, Crockett. He was middle-aged and making money; respectability was smiling his way. It wasn't too farfetched to see a political career in his future—Senator Lamar "Alamo" Mapes of the new state of Arizona. Stranger things had happened.

Sunset wasn't far off. Morgan rounded his horse and rode back to see how Molly was doing. They were moving through a narrow gap in the hills, so she couldn't drive the wagon to one side of the herd. Her face was coated with the dust kicked up ahead of her. Morgan told her to wet her kerchief and pull it up over her mouth and nose. That got an angry stare, but she did it.

"How soon do we make camp?" she wanted to know. She reached behind her to massage the small of her back.

"Soon as we find a good place to pen the horses. You can stretch out on your cot, and I'll give you a back rub after the herd is set for the night. If you want one, that is."

Her pale eyes were angry in her dusty face. "There's nothing wrong with my back, Morgan. You're a lot older than I am. How old are you anyway? Perhaps you're the one who needs the back rub."

Morgan, who was 38, said in a quavery voice, "My poor old back sure could do with a rub. I sure appreciate your kind offer, Miss Molly."

That got her madder. "You're a blasted idiot, that's what you are. You think I'd dirty my hands rubbing your sweaty back? Stay away from my tent and stay away from me. Now go about your business. My business is your business, and don't you forget it."

"Yes, ma'am," Morgan said.

He was still grinning when he saw Trinidad staring at him. No mistaking the sullen anger in the other man's eyes. Then Trinidad looked away and shouted something to Cesar. Morgan couldn't see that Cesar was doing anything that called for shouting. It was Trinidad's way of breaking the tension of a moment before.

Something there, Morgan thought, and not just ordinary resentment. Maybe he should start sleeping with his gun in his hand.

They found the right place for the horses, a small, shallow valley with grass and a rocky pool that spilled over enough water for the herd. It branched off the trail and there was a narrow way out at the far end, but a man posted there could turn back the horses if they tried to get through. Trinidad said he remembered the place, but the pool had been dry when he'd taken part in the last drive to Fort Buell two summers before.

They set up two rope-and-stake fences, one long fence at the mouth of the valley and a shorter one at the narrow end. It was close to dark by the time Molly's tent was secured and the fires were going. Hector, Manuel and Cesar took the first watch. The cook would bring them their food when it was ready. Carlos had taken on a load of whiskey, and he cursed and sometimes sang as he prepared the food.

Morgan looked the horses over, then came back to the fire. Molly insisted on having her own cook fire. "I'll do the cooking," he called to her. She was in her tent and didn't answer, so he said it again, this time louder.

"As long as you don't ruin it," she called back.

Morgan smiled as he set two ham steaks in the fry pan. In her present mood, nothing sat right with her. He knew he was a better cook than she was, which wasn't saying much. When he could he preferred to eat his meals in restaurants. On the trail he made do with anything. Coffee was the only thing he took pains with. It had to be strong and black. That was the kind he made now, and it was ready before the fried ham and beans.

"Coffee's on!" he sang out. He didn't know if she expected him to bring it to her tent. He didn't give a damn one way or another, but he didn't want to do it in front of Trinidad and the cook. Anyhow, he hadn't hired out to be a waiter. If she wanted waiting on she should have brought along the old man.

He heard the creak of the folding cot as she got up off it and came out. It was dark now, not chilly yet, but the heat of the fire was welcome. Molly sat on the ground and sipped the scalding coffee while Morgan turned the ham steaks.

"How far have we come?" she asked, staring into the fire.

"Fifteen miles or so. Like I said, we'll do better tomorrow. We'll get there."

Like the horses, it didn't take much to set her off. His last remark did. "Of course we'll get there. The only trouble is, I'll be an old woman and you'll be on crutches by the time we get there."

"All I want is a decent funeral," Morgan said.

She stared at him. "How can you take life so lightly?"

Morgan said, "How else should I take it?"

"I don't care how you take it. I could never be like you, and I wouldn't want to be. I mean to make something of my life."

Suddenly he felt sorry for her. Spoiled bitch or not, there was something vulnerable about her. An old man's foolhardiness had shattered her life, and she didn't seem to know how to put it together again. He was sure she had lied to him about Crockett Mapes and Ana, the Mexican at the ranch, but it didn't matter. He still felt sorry for her.

He expected her to say more, but she didn't. Instead, she said she wasn't hungry and took the mug of coffee back to her tent and closed the flap. Morgan ate the two steaks and most of the beans, then stretched out under the freight wagon and slept until it was time to stand his watch. He went to Molly's tent and called her name—they would all stand watch, it had been agreed—but she didn't answer. Not that it made any difference. The horses were quiet and stayed that way for the rest of the night.

The grass was wet when they started out next morning. During the night, at the narrow end of the little valley, Morgan thought he'd heard the cough of a lion. Lions didn't hunt in the rain, but he walked around in his dripping slicker just in case. The rain beat down for hours, then stopped abruptly, as if a lever had been pulled to shut it off. The rain, which came mostly at night, would be gone before they were far into May.

It wasn't fully light yet. If Molly wanted early starts and long days, that's what she'd get. She drove the wagon with one hand and held a mug of coffee with the other. Morgan left her and rode ahead. It was good to be working, even for someone else.

They were still in the foothills. If nothing went wrong they'd be clear of the hills and moving out onto the plains sometime tomorrow. It would be hotter there and the horses not as manageable. It wasn't a big herd. A herd of that size would have no built-in dangers if there had been enough men and enough time to work on the horses before they were loosed from the corrals. As it was, the herd was moving just fine, and even though passage across the plains would make it harder to keep it together, there was nothing too bad ahead that he could think of. The stretch of desert would be the worst part of the drive.

The noon halt was just that—ten minutes so they could stretch their legs and get down some cold food. There was grass but no water, so they moved on before the herd spread out too much. In the high places they could see the plains spread out far below. Morgan scanned the flat country with his binoculars. Nothing moved as far as the eye could see. Earlier he'd climbed to a high rise and checked the country behind. Nothing there either. If anything was back there, it wasn't showing itself. He got some curious looks, but he didn't explain.

They made 20 miles by nightfall, five miles more than the day before. Fort Buell was still 100 miles away, maybe more than that, Morgan thought. This part of the territory hadn't been properly mapped because the only places in it of any consequence were Niles City and the fort. Most of Niles City's business came from west of it, where there were ranches, mines and a big Mormon colony.

They drove the horses into a grassy basin, wide but not very deep. Rope-and-stake corrals were built in the low places where the horses could break out. A place like that needed more men to make it secure, but Morgan decided it would do well enough. By midsummer the creek that ran through it would be dry. So far down from the mountains, the water in the creek didn't run fast or deep, but it was more than enough.

Darkness dropped down like a curtain, the way it does in that part of the country. Morgan got a fire going and started with the supper. No ham steaks tonight. The meat had a peculiar smell, which didn't mean that it wasn't fit to eat, but he didn't want to take the chance. The last thing he wanted was Molly puking up her guts or running to shit every five minutes. That, to say the least, was unladylike and would slow them up next day.

Molly was in her tent, and Morgan called her when the coffee was ready. No reply. Same thing happened with the bacon and beans. Well, sir, he wasn't her mother and if she didn't want to eat, the hell with it.

He didn't know she was drinking until later. That was after he'd washed his plate and scoured the fry pan with sand and water. Molly's plate was set aside on a flat rock with a bed of coals underneath to keep the food warm. There were no shadows on the wall of the tent because she'd turned the lamp down to a glimmer, but he heard her moving around. After a while, she came out and wanted to know where her supper was. Her eyes were bright in the firelight, and her manner was haughty as she took the plate he handed her.

She said, "I told you before we started that you mustn't get any ideas. Nothing has changed since then. I don't like to have to remind you."

Whiskey affected people differently, Morgan thought. Henpecked husbands talked back to their wives. Church elders shook their dicks at little girls. Sewing circle ladies did the cancan. Molly wasn't like that. The first drinks made her prim and proper, while the ones she took later turned her into a no-holds-barred cock lover. Right now she was at the prim and proper stage.

Standing there holding the plate, she said sharply, "Did you hear what I just said?"

"Yes, ma'am," Morgan said, holding back a smile. No point making her mad. "Why don't you sit down and eat your supper? Coffee's still hot."

That was the wrong thing to say. Anything was. "Are you suggesting that I am in need of black coffee? Of course you are. Well, I don't need coffee, and I don't need you. Do you know what your trouble is?"

"No, ma'am."

"You don't know any better, that's what. I am going to my tent now, and I do not wish to be disturbed."

Morgan looked over to where Trinidad and the cook were sitting by the fire. The cook's work was over, so he was drunker than he was during the day. He was half-drunk during the day and completely drunk during the night. When Morgan looked a second time, Trinidad was still by the fire and the cook was rolling into blankets underneath the chuck wagon.

Trinidad looked up when Cesar came to the fire. Morgan heard him say, "Why have you left your post?" in Spanish. Morgan could make out that much or most of it. Anyway, the reason for the question was obvious. Cesar, who was on the first watch with Hector and Manuel, should have been watching the herd.

Cesar clutched his stomach and said he was very sick and wanted to lie down. Trinidad rattled

off some Spanish, picked up his rifle and walked
away to take Cesar's place. Cesar rolled himself
in a blanket and lay down beside the fire. In a
while, Morgan heard him snoring.

Morgan had been sleeping under the freight
wagon, using his saddle for a pillow and an oil-
skin to keep from getting soaked when the wind
blew the rain. The wagon was a good distance
from the fires because a spark that turned into
a fire could blow them all to kingdom come. The
box of dynamite over his head didn't bother him.
If it blew, the force of the explosion would be felt
far beyond the camp.

He was lying on his side, thinking about Molly,
when he saw her coming toward him. Without
saying a word, he held back the covers and she
crawled in beside him. The whiskey smell coming
from her was strong. Except that the surround-
ings were different, it was the same as it had been
that first night at her house.

"I got to thinking about you," she murmured,
"and here I am. I thought you might be needing
me. Don't be bashful. The Mexicans are asleep.
Fuck the Mexicans!"

"Take it easy," Morgan said and started to take
her jeans off.

"I don't want to take it easy. I want a good fuck.
I want you to fuck me, Morgan."

Chapter Five

The tent would have been better, but Morgan thought you ought to take it where you could get it. Morgan liked women as much as he liked to fuck them. A lot of men had no use for women except to poke them. Sure, the tent would be better with the pallet from the cot on the floor and the door flap closed. The two Mexicans in camp didn't bother him. They were asleep and the wagon was a good distance from where they were. But even if they'd been awake, what business was it of theirs? If they knew about it and got horny, there was a remedy for that.

Trinidad was different. The handsome Mexican had a bone in his pants for Molly and plans for his future, and his feelings had to be respected. More or less they had, but not to the extent of kicking Molly out of bed. Let Trinidad take care of the owner's horses. He would take care of the owner.

It would have been hard to stop even if he wanted to. He had Molly's jeans off—no drawers for this girl—and her shirt and canvas coat open. She held onto his cock while he shucked his pants and pulled his shirt and undershirt over his head. They both smelled of sweat, but they hadn't been on the trail long enough for it to smell bad. It wouldn't have made any difference if it had. The night was cool, but Molly was sweating with excitement. She kept telling him to fuck her, and for a girl educated in a fancy school in St. Louis, she sure had a dirty mouth. Her legs were spread, and she was sopping wet down there. Hot woman juice ran down the inside of her thighs. "Hurry, Morgan! Hurry! Hurry!" she pleaded as he climbed on top of her and drove his cock in all the way. It went in as smoothly as a piston in an oil bath, and her legs came up and locked behind his back. Her hands were all over him, soothing him and hurting him at the same time. She came right away, and that was just the start of it.

There was no end to the number of times she could come. One orgasm convulsed her as much as the one before. Morgan found himself thinking how lucky women were to be able to come like that. She was tall, so he didn't have to bend too far to suck her firm, upthrusting breasts. The nipples were erect, hard with excitement, and while he sucked them his hands cupped her rounded ass, squeezing and letting go, squeezing and letting go. She gasped and shuddered when he pulled his cock out nearly all the way, then drove in again, giving her its full length.

She loved his cock, and she moaned and crooned over it, how big and long and hard it was. "Don't come, Morgan! Don't come yet!" she kept warning him. Her crotch bumped his, and her ass, slick with sweat, squirmed under his hands. "Don't stop! I'll kill you if you stop! I'm sorry I said that, Morgan! No, I'm not! Fuck me rough! Hurt me with your cock! Fuck me like a stallion fucks a mare! Make me whinny, Morgan!"

Morgan lifted her ass off the ground and drove his shaft into her at a different angle. He had to stifle a scream by clapping his hand over her mouth. She tried to move her head and bite his fingers, and it was all he could do to keep the scream bottled up. Jesus Christ! he thought crazily. I don't want to be the first man in history that started a stampede with his cock. Before he took his hand away, he whispered in her ear, "Scream and I'll knock you cold. I'll hit you so hard you won't wake up till tomorrow. Shake your head if you understand what I'm saying."

Molly nodded and gasped when he removed his hand. He hoped he'd be quick enough if she started to let loose again. Even if the scream didn't stampede the horses, Trinidad and the two brothers would come running with their rifles at the ready. Cesar, maybe even the cook, would turn out, and none of it would be very funny. Maybe he should fuck her gently for a while. That was his idea, but not hers. Quieter but still quivering with the need for more cock, she hissed at him angrily. No, he was wrong about the anger. It was more a wild, desperate need to be driven crazy with a hard-driving cock. More than anything, she was a woman with two very different sides to her nature, kept apart by a flimsy wall that disappeared when she drank too much whiskey. But if he wasn't her mother, making sure she ate properly, neither was he her father. In the end, like everyone else, she would have to find her own way.

The whiskey must have been dying in her because she whispered, "I want to feel you coming in me, Morgan. I want to feel your hot juice shooting into me. I want to feel your hot juice mixing with mine."

Just talking about it made her wild again, and it was like she'd been hit by a violent shock from an electric battery. A fierce surge of energy surged through her body, and he had to fight to hold her down. He gripped her ass, shafted in and out of her three or four times, then shoved it in hard all the way and sent his jism volleying into her. His come was so violent that he began to shake and was still shaking when she went into a frenzy of orgasms that looked like it would never stop. Her eyes rolled up in their sockets, and she bit hard into her lower lip until blood came. Then her body began to relax, not all at once but gradually, as if inch by inch, until she lay limp beneath him.

"Molly," he whispered before he realized she was asleep. At first, her breathing was quick and shallow; then that slowed down, too, and she didn't even stir when he buttoned her shirt and pulled the blanket up over her. A sound nearby made him hold his breath, not so much a sound as something moving without making a sound. It could be nothing more than some prowling animal, and yet he didn't think so.

He pulled on his pants and shirt, eased his boots on and stood up with his gun in his hand. Cesar and the cook were still asleep, and though he couldn't be sure, something told him that they hadn't moved from where they were. He circled the camp and saw nothing and heard nothing but the night wind. Rain clouds hid the moon, and he had to tread carefully as he made his way to the corralled horses in almost total darkness. Neither Manuel or Hector heard him as he passed them like a shadow. He reached the place where Trinidad ought to be, but he wasn't there. That didn't have to mean anything. Trinidad could be taking a look around, part of a night guard's job.

Just the same, Morgan waited, out of sight behind a clump of brush. Still waiting when the moon cleared, he saw Trinidad coming along the side of the rope-and-stake fence. Even in the moonlight, he could see the crazy look on the Mexican's face. Trinidad, usually so deadpan, was boiling over with barely controllable anger. As Morgan watched, he stopped and picked up his Winchester carbine from the grass where he had left it. Morgan hadn't seen it in the dark. The carbine was wet, the barrel glistening in the moonlight, and Trinidad dried it with his kerchief. It took several trys before he managed to roll a cigarette, and this was a man Morgan had seen rolling cigarettes with one hand on the back of a moving horse. A match flared as Morgan edged away.

Molly was gone from underneath the wagon when he got back, and when he went to her tent, the flap was unfastened and she was inside, sleeping on her back on the cot with the blankets pulled up to her chin. He fastened the flap and hunkered down from the fire in deep shadow, his Winchester cradled in the crook of his arm. From there he could watch Molly's tent and the way Trinidad would return to camp. In about 45 minutes he would see how it was with Trinidad and what he wanted to do about what had made him so angry.

Morgan had no proof that Trinidad had been sneaking around in the dark. He wasn't going to accuse him of anything or ask him why he'd left his Winchester behind, something no night guard would do. The way Trinidad carried himself, how he talked, how he looked would tell him what he wanted to know. A man in the grip of some violent emotion couldn't hide it so easily, no matter how practiced he was at maintaining a poker face. The Mexican was good at looking like nothing could get under his skin; he had been dignified rather than angry when he threatened to quit on Molly. That was probably an act, but this was altogether different.

Morgan knew the Mexican's murderous anger was because of Molly. What else could get him so worked up? An hour or so might cool his outward signs of anger, but the hate would be there in his eyes—dark, deadly, smoldering. Morgan didn't care how much Trinidad hated him as long as the hatred didn't come at him with a gun or a knife. The world was full of hate, not all of it expressed openly. Hate in some men festered for years, and sometimes it erupted into bloody violence and sometimes it didn't. He didn't want to kill Trinidad, but he would if he had to. It was as simple as that.

He stood up when he heard Hector whistling. Hector and Manuel came into camp, but Trinidad wasn't with them. They built up the fire until it was shooting sparks into the night air, all the while complaining about why it had been allowed to die down.

Trinidad didn't appear for a good five minutes, and when he came into the light his face wasn't just blank, it was rigid. Hector turned away from the fire to ask him something and got no reply. Asked the same question a second time, Trinidad snapped off a few words of Spanish. Hector shrugged at Manuel before he put the cold coffeepot on the edge of the fire. Manuel shrugged too, pursed his mouth in a silent kiss, then closed his fist and made a jerk-off gesture in Trinidad's direction. Trinidad was looking at Molly's tent and didn't notice any of this. But he spun around and brought up his rifle when Morgan came out of the shadows.

"What is happening?" he asked in a steady voice. "Did you hear something out there?"

"I was taking a piss," Morgan said. "Came to warm myself at the fire, then had to take a piss."

"Do you always carry a long gun when you take a piss?" Trinidad caught himself and tried to smile. "I mean I saw your long gun and thought there must be trouble."

Morgan smiled back at him. "No trouble. Carrying the old Winchester just gets to be a habit, I guess. Anything happening with the herd?"

"The herd is quiet," Trinidad said, turning to glance at Molly's tent. "Will Miss Molly be standing watch?"

Morgan saw the hate in the Mexican's eyes when he mentioned Molly's name. It was gone in an instant, but it had been there all right, dulled now by an effort of will. "Molly won't be standing watch," Morgan said. "I don't think she's feeling well."

"No doubt something has tired her out," the Mexican said in his careful English. "I will stand watch in her place. You can't do it by yourself."

That wasn't what Morgan wanted to hear. "Maybe Cesar isn't so sick now. Talk to him. See how he is."

"I have already done that. Cesar is sick. A sick man is no good for anything. I will guard the herd with you after I drink some coffee."

It was going to be a long night, Morgan thought. Cover wasn't so good where he was, and he looked around for something better. Clouds covered the moon, but light kept breaking through. He found a rock and put his back to it. A few minutes later it began to rain, a steady downpour that looked as if it might last for hours. Without a slicker he was going to get soaked, and if the rain lasted long enough it was going to turn everything to mud. The good side to that was, a man coming over muddy ground, his boots squelching with water, wouldn't find it easy to sneak up on him. It was hard to shoot right in heavy rain unless you were up close. Trinidad could try for a long shot, but he'd have to get lucky. Any other time, shooting so close to the herd would send the horses into a wild panic.

Trinidad could stampede the herd by shooting into it. Darkness, rain and confusion would hide his movements. He couldn't run the horses over Morgan because there was a hill behind him and the horses wouldn't make for high ground when there was an easier way to get loose.

He could have shot Trinidad when he walked into camp, but that would have been murder. The Mexican hadn't done anything. To try explaining that he didn't like the look on the Mexican's face and the other Mexicans would start shooting. Even if he managed to kill all of them, where would that leave him? Anyway, there was no guarantee that he'd be able to do it. The two brothers were clear targets, but Cesar and the cook were under the chuck wagon. Carlos, the cook, kept a sawed-off shotgun close to him

at night. He was an old man with watery
eyes, and he trusted his shotgun. Twin barrels
blasted together would reduce a man to stew
meat.

Nothing happened as the night dragged on. The
rain thinned just after first light, and now it blew
this way and that, driven by gusts of wind. As
the light grew stronger, he heard the cook's sad,
whiny songs coming from the camp. Morgan gave
it a little longer before he got up and stretched
his legs, stiff from holding the same position too
long. Along about now, Manuel and Hector would
be drinking coffee by the fire. Cesar? Cesar was
sick, or said he was. Molly? Hard to tell what she
was doing. A whiskey head wasn't enough to keep
her in bed when there were horses to be sold at
$50 a head.

Everybody was up and about when he went to
the fire. Molly stood by herself drinking some coffee. Rain slid down her slicker and dripped from
her hat. Trinidad, crouched by the fire, looked
at Morgan without saying anything. Carlos cursed
Hector for whistling and cursed the rain for
making a mess of his cook fire, and the tin shield
he rigged up over it blinded everyone with smoke.

Trinidad was in a black mood. No one else
seemed to notice it because they had their own
reasons for feeling low—rain, mud, soggy food.
Sure as shooting, Trinidad was working up to
something, and Morgan could only guess when it
would come out in the open. Too bad the Mexican
couldn't get hold of himself, accept the hard fact
that he didn't have a prayer with Molly and go
on from there. A bitter pill to swallow, but other
men had done it. Morgan had done it. A gawky
kid of 18 at the time, he wanted an older woman who was 25 so bad that he couldn't eat or

sleep. He wanted to kill the man she later married. Naturally he didn't. With all the years gone by, he no longer had a clear picture of what she looked like.

No such commonsense way out for Trinidad. Pride was a good part of it. These Mexicans were so goddamned proud, especially the ones with a high opinion of themselves. A handsome fellow like Trinidad would be unable to understand why Molly wasn't panting for his prick. That didn't just make him mad; it made him murderous.

They moved out with the rain still falling, and there was some trouble with the wagons in the deep mud. In a week this country would be without rain at all, and later it would be as dry as a sun-bleached bone. On toward nine o'clock, the rain stopped and the sun came out strong. The sun grew hotter, and Morgan took off his lined canvas coat and laid it across the saddle in front of him. Up on the wagon box, looking sour, Molly was shucking her coat. Morgan wanted to smile. Molly, with her sober self and her whiskey self, was a caution. Question was, which self was the real self? Maybe both.

They were starting out onto the plains when Trinidad started to act up. It began with little things, nothing that mattered a hell of a lot. He kept coming to Morgan with dumb questions, like asking if Morgan was sure they were heading in the right direction, wanting to know if they shouldn't stay closer to the hills. Morgan remained patient, knowing what the Mexican was up to.

"You were through here two years ago," Morgan said to him. "Don't you remember the route?"

"I am afraid I do not. You see, I was just a poor Mexican following orders. Riggs the gringo was in charge, just as you are in charge now. A poor Mexican is not paid to think, just to do what he is told."

"Keep the herd going the way it is," Morgan said.

Trinidad inclined his head in mock deference. "I will do what you say, Morgan. I hope you will not object if I stop calling you mister. It is so formal."

"Call me anything you like. If you want to follow orders, ride on ahead. The herd is moving out too wide on your side."

Another slow nod of the head. "Why did I not see that, Morgan? A gringo is always smarter than a Mexican."

Trinidad turned his horse as easily and gracefully as a circus performer. Morgan looked after him. The son of a bitch sure knew how to ride. Like all Mexicans of his stamp, he would be good with a pistol and a knife. From his belt hung a Bowie knife only slightly bigger than Morgan's, except it was fancier, with silver inlay decorating the haft and silver wire stitching in the sheath. His pistol was a long-barreled Colt .45 in an open-ended holster, and the butt was ivory, not pearl—a pistolero's gun. An odd thing to see on a ranch foreman's belt, but there it was.

Later, while they stopped in a grassy dip in the plain, Molly complained to Morgan about Trinidad's strange behavior. She was outraged. "Have you noticed it?"

"Tell me what he's done."

Molly said, "He pretends he's joking, but he's not. Trinidad never jokes. He hardly ever smiles. Now he smiles all the time. He smiles and calls me 'Molly Darlin'.' That's the name of an old Irish song, goddamn it! I warned him to stop, but he just smiled. 'But you are my Molly darlin',' he said. I won't be spoken to like that by a Mexican. Talk to him, Morgan. Tell him to apologize, or I'll send him packing."

It was hot, and there was no water where they were. Morgan thought the herd wasn't as settled as it had been. "Not right now," he said. "This isn't the place or the time. I'll talk to him tonight. That'll have to do."

"You think he'll stop?"

"No, he won't stop. I don't know what he figures to do, but he won't stop. You have to get ready for trouble."

"Why is he behaving the way he is?" Molly pushed up her brim and wiped sweat from her forehead. The booze coming out, Morgan thought, booze and a hot sun. Time to tell her the truth. Hard to believe she didn't know it already.

"He wants you, and it's making him crazy." Morgan hated to talk about this kind of shit. "You never saw him looking at you?"

Molly flushed angrily. "Of course I have. Men look at me. Old Mr. Fisher at the bank looks at me. You mean . . . ?"

"Trinidad wants to do more than look. He wants to marry you and become an Arizona gentleman."

Molly was horrified by the idea. "Marry me? He must be insane. Get rid of him, Morgan."

She had used much the same words when she ordered Trinidad to run the Mexican woman, Ana, off her property. "Not yet, I told you. I'd say keep him if you could. I don't think you can. He's not American, so I can't beat sense into him. Problem is, we're not just talking about Trinidad. That day he threatened to quit, he said the other Mexicans would quit, too."

"Carlos won't quit," Molly said. "He doesn't like Trinidad."

"A drunken cook is no use to us."

"I don't want Trinidad around. There's something sinister about him. I never noticed before, but I do now. What are we going to do, Morgan?"

Morgan saw Trinidad staring at them. He was too far away to hear what they were saying, but he kept on staring.

It was past time to move on. "I don't know what we're going to do," Morgan said. "Let me think about it. I'll do something before the day is over. One last thing: how much do you know about him?"

Molly looked over at the Mexican, then looked away. "Not a lot. About three years ago, he turned up at the ranch looking for work. Riggs, the foreman, didn't want him. My father took him on. After Riggs and the white wranglers left, Trinidad became foreman. Of the Mexicans here then, he was the best man for the job. Why do you want to know?"

Morgan was thinking of the pistolero's gun. "He's no kid. He could have done a lot of things before he came to you."

"You think he's wanted for crimes in Mexico?"

"I don't know. Either he's an honest man or a badly wanted killer lying low," Morgan said.

What he really wanted to know about Trinidad was how fast he was with that shiny .45.

Chapter Six

Morgan finished his supper as Molly ate hers. There was no one else in camp but Trinidad, who hadn't eaten anything. Cesar was still complaining about his stomach, and the two brothers were standing the first watch. It was dark, and they had been there for two hours. After putting his cooking utensils away, Carlos had wandered out of camp and hadn't come back. That wasn't his usual routine, Morgan thought. A man of fixed habits, the old cook always got under the chuck wagon and into his blankets when he finished work. If he'd just gone to drop his pants or take a piss, he was taking too long.

The herd was corralled in a saucer-shaped hollow with a shallow pond in the middle. Fed by a spring, it overflowed, making the ground around it soggy. The summer sun eventually would dry it up, but it now provided enough water for a small herd. Circled by alders, with tall rushes growing down to the water's edge, it couldn't be seen from the camp. To get out of the high plains wind, which was hot by day and cold by night, they had made camp in back of a low ridge with a wide gap in it.

It was time to have it out with the Mexican. Trinidad had been acting like a real bastard in the late afternoon. A couple of times Morgan had found him riding alongside Molly's wagon when he should have been seeing to the horses. Ordered to get back to work, he had done so but with a sneering humility that was worse than outright defiance. It was time to set him straight or to bury him.

"Go to your tent," Morgan said quietly. "Do it, Molly. I'll try to talk to him man to man with no woman around."

Molly went into the tent and ran out a few seconds later, stumbling and yelling. "There's a snake on my bed. A rattlesnake." She stopped, drew her .38 and turned back toward the tent. Morgan jumped up and told her to hold back.

"You hold back, gringo," Trinidad shouted, coming toward them with the long-barreled Colt .45 in his hand. "Drop the gun, Molly darlin', or I'll kill you. I can shoot your eyes out before you can pull the trigger." The Mexican came closer. "Unbuckle your belt, gringo, and let it drop. I am not boasting when I say I can shoot her eyes out."

Morgan let his gunbelt slide and told Molly to let go of the .38. Finally, looking daggers at the Mexican, she dropped it at her feet. Fierce anger glittered in her eyes.

"Walk away from the guns and stand together," the Mexican ordered, taking a coil of long rawhide thongs from his pocket with his left hand. "Ah, yes, the two gringos together, the lady and the drifter. I will now tell you what I am going to do."

"You're going to steal my horses," Molly said angrily, her voice heavy with contempt.

The Mexican smiled. "I am not going to steal your horses, gringa, but the others think I am. We will steal the horses, I told them, and we will get the money from this major at the fort. This major he knows me. He has been to the ranch, and he will give me the money. Then we will divide the money and go to Mexico. This is what they believe—the cook, the brothers, Cesar. I will handle the gringos, I told them. Just stay out of the way."

Molly stamped her foot, a childish thing Morgan had seen her do. Whatever she was, she had plenty of nerve, maybe too much. "Why don't you kill us and get it over with? You're going to do it anyway, you greasy mongrel!"

Trinidad's face twitched as if it had been slapped; then he smiled. "I will kill Morgan but not you. You, Molly darlin', I will rape. I will make you suck my greasy mongrel's cock before I do it. I will defile you. I will piss in your mouth, all over your gringa body before I am done."

"Fuck you, you bastard!" Molly shouted.

"Your sweetheart is so angry," Trinidad said to Morgan. He was enjoying this, making the most of it. "The others, my Mexican friends, will be angry when I stampede the horses, scatter them, and ride away leaving your naked sweetheart as their only consolation. They will beat you, Molly darlin', and rape you till your cunt is sore and bleeding. You will enjoy that, no? All that cock and all for you. I have heard you crying out for cock."

He threw the bunch of thongs at Molly's feet. "Tie your sweetheart's hands and feet. Down on your face, Morgan, so Molly darlin' can tie you. I will not kill you until I am finished with your woman. She can make her way home if my friends do not kill her, but without the money, she will lose her ranch, lose everything."

Molly picked up the rawhide and tried to slash at the Mexican's face. She was still coming at him when he hit her in the forehead with the gun barrel and she dropped like a stone. Trinidad looked at Morgan. "I did not hit her hard. I will wake her when I am ready. Turn around so I can tie you. You can lie or your side and watch, or turn the other way.

Suddenly, the Mexican stopped talking and hit Morgan where the shoulder muscle joins the neck. Bright lights flashed in his head, but he didn't black out. He let his body sag forward and hit the ground when Trinidad kicked him in the back of the knee. Trinidad had to stick his pistol in his waistband before he could use the rawhide thongs. He kicked Morgan in the upper arm to deaden it; then he grabbed the numb arm and jerked it behind Morgan's back. He was reaching for the other arm when Morgan turned and grabbed him by both arms to keep him from getting at the pistol. Morgan was hurting bad from the blow and the kick, but the pain gave him strength. He pulled the Mexican down on top of him, and they rolled over twice until Molly's body got in the way.

Molly groaned, and Morgan felt a fierce surge of anger. By slashing at the Mexican's face she had given him a chance to save his life. One of the Mexican's arms tore loose, and he fumbled for the pistol in the waistband of his pants. His fingers closed over the butt and the pistol started to come out, but the long barrel made it difficult. The pistol came out at last, and the Mexican pulled back in an effort to jam the muzzle into Morgan's chest. Again the long barrel made that hard to do so he tried to bring the muzzle up under Morgan's chin. Before he could do that, Morgan let go; then his hands clamped down on the Mexican's forearm. He jerked his head forward and sank his teeth into the other man's wrist. Trinidad screamed, and the pistol flew out of his hand. He reached for his knife, but Morgan grabbed his wrist before he got a grip on the handle. A sharp downward twist failed to break the wrist. Morgan punched him hard in the mouth and felt teeth break. The Mexican spat blood and broken teeth in his face without getting at his eyes. With Morgan still gripping his wrist, the Mexican twisted to one side, then tried to break Morgan's nose with his forehead. Instead, their two foreheads cracked together, and Morgan was stunned for an instant. The Mexican jerked the knife loose, but Morgan turned it and tried to shove it through the Mexican's belly. Twisting again, he evaded the blade by inches, and it stabbed into the ground. Steel rasped against rock, the blade stuck, and Morgan tried to dig it in deeper by throwing his weight on the handle. Their faces were close together, and Trinidad's jagged, broken teeth snapped at Morgan's nose.

Trinidad was shorter but wider in the shoulders and as strong as a bull. His free hand came up, grabbed Morgan's hair and jerked his head forward. Bone cracked on bone. The Mexican had a forehead like rock. Morgan felt himself being thrown off. Trinidad jerked the knife free and sprang after him. The knife flashed down, but Morgan rolled away from it and staggered to his feet. He staggered again until he righted himself and turned to face the Mexican with nothing but his bare hands. He spotted the Mexican's pistol in the grass, too far away to get to before the big Bowie was buried in his back.

Smiling, knees bent, the Mexican came at him in a crouch. He held the knife with the blade down, beckoning with his free hand, talking in his careful English. There was a shake in his voice that he wasn't able to control. "No good, gringo. No matter what you do, you are going to die. I will cut off your balls and shove them in your mouth. The cock as well as the balls. The big cock Miss Molly loves so much. But she will have the cocks of my friends to enjoy. She will find other cocks if they do not kill her."

The Mexican was trying to make him mad enough to be careless. But his anger had ebbed, and there was nothing but cold hate in his head as the Mexican talked and came forward an inch at a time. Morgan backed away and did some talking of his own.

Trinidad didn't expect that. "Why are you smiling, gringo?"

Morgan said, inching back as Trinidad inched forward, "I'm smiling at you, you Mexican pig. Where is your pistolero's shiny gun? How did you get it? Did you steal it from a real pistolero when he was dead drunk? Do you practice in front of a mirror and say bang-bang like the little boys do? Molly is just a girl, but she sees what you are—a thief and a sneak, a liar and a coward. You could not face me like a man so you put the snake in her tent. Is it a dead snake? Is it as dead as your cock?"

Trinidad jumped forward and slashed at Morgan's throat with the knife. The knife missed, but the force of the swing threw him off balance. Morgan kicked him in the knee as he turned. He grunted with pain, and his leg wobbled. After that he was more cautious, holding Morgan off with the knife until he was ready for the next attack. Morgan kept on with the badmouthing, calling him a pervert, a peeper into women's tents, a stealer of ladies' underwear, a masturbator who'd never gone to sleep without his cock in his hand.

They circled warily. Molly groaned again, but neither of them looked at her. Morgan knew he had to get the knife or make the Mexican drop it. Unless he did, the Mexican would kill him. It couldn't go on the way it was. Sooner or later the Mexican would stick him like a pig, chop off an arm or sever a leg. The Mexican's back was to Molly. Morgan yelled, "Shoot the son of a bitch! Kill him, Molly!" Trinidad spun around, and Morgan jumped on his back and clamped his hands around his throat. A bone cracked in the Mexican's throat and he started to black out. The knife fell from his hand, but he managed to throw Morgan over his head. Morgan landed on all fours without breaking anything. The Mexican was bending, grabbing for the knife. A kick in the face knocked him on his back and he lay there, choking and gasping. Though his face was mottled and his breath rattled in his throat, he tried to struggle back to his feet. Morgan let him get up all the way before he drove the blade through his heart.

A woman's voice came from the dark. "Throw

the knife away, Big Boy. There's nine guns pointing right at you."

Morgan dropped the knife beside the dead man,
and six women and three men, all armed, came
into the firelight from all directions. The long,
lanky woman who he took to be the leader of
this outfit was shaking with laughter. Kind of
good-looking in a horsy way, she had a Winchester .44-40 resting on her hip, and she poked him
hard in the belly with the muzzle when she got
close up.

"What the hell?" Morgan said.

That got another laugh. "You mean who the
hell are we, and where did we come from? Guess
you didn't catch on we been watchin' you an' this
dead greaser waltzin' around the last ten minutes
or so. We was sneakin' in when you an' the señor
was just startin' to mix it up. Let the best man
win, I decided. We'll kill the loser if he ain't dead
at the finish. Ain't no room in my plans for two
dangerous men. Don't look so surprised, big boy.
We bring you greetin's from Yuma." Another hard
poke with the rifle. "Molly ain't dead, is she, Big
Boy?"

"Molly? You know Molly?" Molly was groaning,
and Morgan turned to look at her. A violent shove
sent him reeling, and the lanky woman walked
past him and stooped down beside Molly. The
lanky woman slapped her face and jerked her
to a sitting position. Molly mumbled and raised
her hand to her forehead. It was swollen but not
discolored yet.

The lanky woman's shadow cut off most of the
light. "Morgan?" Molly said.

The lanky woman took her by the shoulders
and shook her. "It's me, your old jailmate Stretch.
Wake up, sweet pussy. Lord, how I been thinkin'

'bout you these last long six weeks. We broke out, honeycunt, an' we didn't need no Joshua to help us with the walls. Come on now, ain't you goin' to gimme a welcome kiss?"

"Get away from me!" Molly yelled. "I don't want your hands on me!" She tried to break loose but was jerked to her feet like a light, skinny child. The lanky woman slapped her, then pulled her close and kissed her on the mouth. Molly jerked her head back and spat in the woman's face. The slap she got nearly knocked her down.

Stretch took her by the arm and led her over to where Morgan was. There was nothing he could have done with eight guns aiming at him. "Was you and the Mex fightin' over this sweet little gal? 'Course you was, an' I don' blame you one bit. But you have to know, Big Boy, men ain't the only ones to fight over this blue-eyed creature. Wasn't hardly a day behind the walls somebody wasn't after this one's sugarbox, tits an' ass. Gals got their way of lovin' other gals an' to my way of thinkin' it's heaps sweeter'n some smelly man pawin' at your crotch."

"Oh, for Christ's sake!" one of the other women said.

Stretch pointed at her and laughed. "Molly an' Big Boy, I want you to meet my second-in-command, Dallas Eberhart. Couldn't of made it this far without her, she thinks, but a good ol' gal just the same."

"Kiss my ass!" Dallas said, scuffing up dirt with the toe of her boot. She was tall and good-looking.

"Now you're talkin' my language, gal," Stretch said. "Might as well interduce you folks to the rest of the bunch. These here Yuma College graduates are Cat Shawnessy, Sister Nunn, Luz

Carrasco, and last but surely not least, Pretty Woman. Pretty Woman slit the throats of the three greasers guardin' the herd. Slick as a hot pussy she did it."

"The cook?" Molly said.

"Not the cook," Stretch said. "First rule of any drive—don't kill the cook. He's old an' a drunk. What harm can he do? Couple of you boys untie him an' get him in here. I'm so hungry I could eat a . . ." What she didn't say made her laugh like mad. "I nearly said eat a woman, but I'll settle for somethin' hot an' tasty an' a lot of it."

The two men sent to get Carlos came back dragging him by both arms. As soon as they let go of him, he collapsed. "Start cookin', cookie," Stretch told him. The two men who got the cook had the look of tramp cowhands. The other man, though he wore denim pants and a cord coat, looked like a store clerk or a schoolteacher. Stretch used the Winchester to point at them. "The one with the cockeye is Jimmy Tuttle. Next to him, beer belly an' all, is Lester Murfree. Warmin' his ass and lookin' nervous is Ned Geer who once upon a time was the prissiest assistant bank teller you ever saw. Jimmy an' Lester was cowhands till they took to stealin' what they shoulda been herdin'. Sit down, Molly. You too, Big Boy. Get comfortable. Everybody get comfortable."

The men didn't look like much. Morgan looked at the women. The young Apache who killed the Mexicans was well-named—Pretty Woman, and so she was. A long, thin-bladed skinning knife in a sheath with copper rivets hung from her belt. About 25, she was short, wiry and had the color of a penny. Cat Shawnessy was perky looking, black-haired, with fair skin reddened by the sun. Sister Nunn, thin as a rail with mousy hair and poor sight, seemed completely out of place. Luz Carrasco was a fat young Mexican with staring eyes.

After yelling at the cook to get a move on, Stretch said to Molly, "Been watchin' you good people since noontime." She tapped a pair of binoculars slung from her neck. "Hung back real far, miles back, raised no dust, country soaking wet. Got this far north, then cut in on your trail. Was thinkin' of headin' for New Mexico. Lost the so-called Arizona Rangers days back."

Molly gave her a mean look. "They'll catch up to you."

Stretch laughed. "They'll be sorry if they do. Only four of them now. Big posse after us when we broke out. A lot of local men no doubt figurin' big reward money. Got discouraged and dropped out after the first few days. Territory only pays fifty dollars a head for escaped prisoners. You'd think they'd pay more for escaped killers."

Stretch didn't go to the chuck wagon when the food was ready. "You go get it, Big Boy," she told Morgan. "Molly can call you Morgan. I'll call you Big Boy. Bring the plate, Big Boy." A finger snapped. "Say, nobody's watchin' my horse herd. Lester, Jimmy, you too, Ned, go keep an eye on the horses."

They settled down to eat the food. By the look of them, they hadn't eaten for days. Morgan and Molly didn't eat. Stretch, shoveling it in, said to Morgan, "Just because you downed that Mex don't mean you're tough enough to take me on. I'll kill you quick if you make a tricky move. Any one of us'll kill you. See, Big Boy, we're all killers here. Anyway the ladies are. All servin' long to life sentences for murder. They'll hang us if they catch us. That's Territory law. No appeal from it. Killers that break out get the rope. They got a double reason to hang us. We killed two guards on the way out. Jimmy, Lester and Ned'll hang, too, so we got absolutely nothin' to lose."

As Stretch talked Morgan was trying to figure out the setup here. Stretch was the boss, an iron-clad dyke, either born one or turned into one by the Yuma women's prison. Yuma, far south, was a prison for men, a hellhole in the desert. Part of it, much smaller, was set aside for hardened women. Everybody knew how bad Yuma was. It had cages instead of regular cells, and diehard troublemakers were housed in barred caves dug into the cliffs that surrounded the prison. Reformers were always writing long letters to the newspapers. Suicides in Yuma happened all the time.

Dallas, Stretch's so-called lieutenant, was no dyke, no matter what she'd been through. No love was lost between the two women. More likely it was hate. Not being a dyke didn't make Dallas any less bad than Stretch, who was, according to herself, "the toughest, baddest woman that ever lived." More than once she spoke of herself as "Stretch Harrelson, the famous bank robber." Morgan had never heard of her.

Dallas didn't say much of anything, and he wondered what she had done to get herself caged up in Yuma. A killing, sure, but there were all kinds of killings. Not knowing anything else, he could only guess. Same for the others.

Stretch tossed her plate away and said to Molly, "Where are you takin' my horses, sweet crotch? They was yours, but now they're mine—ours. Speak the truth now, or I'll make you cry."

"Fort Buell," Molly told her. "I have a deal to sell them to the army."

"How much?"

"Ten thousand dollars, fifty dollars a head."

Stretch whistled. "Ain't that somethin' now! This mornin' we was penniless gals. Now it's only the night of the same day and we're rich. Nothin' like what I took from the banks, but enough, more'n a thousand apiece."

Dallas said drily, "Share and share alike."

"Nothin' but," Stretch said. "Now, Molly m'love, how is this deal to be handled?"

Molly said, "I have a letter from Major Van Horn stating the number of horses and the sale price."

"Better an' better. Go fetch it, honeymuff."

Molly got the letter from her tent and handed it to Stretch. It took her a while to read it; then she gave it to Dallas. "Here's what we're going to do," Stretch said to Molly. "You're going to write a letter on the back of the major's letter authorizin' nice, respectable Ned who used to work in a bank to pick up the money after the herd is delivered. Lester and Jimmy will be Ned's drovers. I wouldn't want the boys to get tempted, so I'll go along as cook. By the way, they got a telegraph line to the fort?"

Molly shook her head.

"Who says God ain't good to poor women? With no telegraph this major can't check on the sprained knee that's keepin' you home. Write that part in. After you get through and if it looks right, you can get some sleep. We all got to get some sleep. Sorry you an' Big Boy got to be handcuffed to the wagon spokes. Took some of them new Yuma handcuffs along. You never know. Pretty Woman'll watch you meantime. Remember what she did to them Mexes.

The freight wagon had been moved closer to

camp on Stretch's order. No one looked under the tarpaulin that covered the supplies, and Morgan said nothing about the dynamite. Compared to this bunch, a fire and an explosion didn't seem so bad. Anyway, it wasn't likely to happen.

A rock and a hard place, Morgan thought.

Chapter Seven

Molly fell into a deep sleep as soon as Pretty Woman handcuffed her right wrist to a wagon spoke and covered her with a blanket. Before the Indian went to sit and watch them, she tested the wagon spokes to make sure they wouldn't come loose. Once Molly sat up yelling but settled back before she was fully awake.

Lying awake with his eyes closed, Morgan tried to hear what Stretch and Dallas were talking about on the other side of the fire, but their voices were too low.

In spite of all the snappishness between them, it looked like they could cooperate when they had to, but it might be different when they got closer to the money. Gangs often split apart over money.

Done with talking, they stretched out and slept. Except for Pretty Woman, the others had been asleep for an hour. Even if Pretty Woman had dozed off, not a likely thing, Morgan knew the wagon spoke he was handcuffed to couldn't be loosened by pulling on it. The wheels were sound. He had checked them every night when they made camp.

Morgan slept because there was nothing else to do. Someone coming close woke him a good bit before first light. Stretch tossed him the key to the handcuffs, and he caught it with his free hand. "Put the cuffs on both wrists—do it right, Big Boy—and throw the key at my feet. Don't be throwin' it at me or . . . That's the ticket. Time we had a talk."

At the fire she told him to sit cross-legged while she poured the coffee. She set the mug down where he could get it, but he had to lean forward and put his elbows on the ground to lift it. "A cautious gal is what I am," she said. "Times that don't always work. Right now I'm cautious. Didn't break out of Yuma just to be dragged back there to hang."

Morgan sipped the scalding coffee. "You wanted to talk?"

"What we got to talk about is how you want to do this." Stretch tried to keep her rasping country voice as low as she could. "You can make it easy or hard for Molly. That gal's got a temper like a tiger. You look like you got a level head on your shoulders. You been fuckin' her, ain't you? Was that what the fracas with the Mex was about? I can tell you this. Molly wasn't fucking no Mex. She don't like greasers. Was it the Mex wanted to fuck her, and you didn't like it? Answer up, Big Boy."

"Something like that," Morgan said.

"Didn't I tell you? Well, sir, I mean to fuck her myself. Don't mind sayin' I been wantin' to do that a long time. You'd think fuckin' her would be easy inside the walls, me bein' what I'm like and all. Wasn't for want of tryin', I can tell you. Problem was, Molly always had a little smuggled-in money an' could buy protection. So nary a time did I get a tongue into her. This here's different—no protection here. It's always been my belief Molly is a woman-lover at heart. Just needs to be broke in, that's all. Now's my chance to find out. Makes no mind whether she likes it or not. I'm going to do her till she don't know the day or month or year. That kind of talk shock you, Big Boy?"

Morgan ignored the question. "Why would you want to do something like that? You can't hate her that much."

Stretch had the coffeepot in her hand. For an instant Morgan thought he was going to get it in the face, but she managed to control herself. "You ain't got the sense I thought, sayin' a thing like that. Hate her? Why I think the world of Molly. That gal's been on my mind since the first day I laid eyes on her. It ain't just the fuckin' part. I got feelin's for Molly."

She stared into the fire and told Morgan to shut the fuck up when he tried to say something. Finally she said, "We was talkin' about drivin' horses. Here's my deal. Molly hired you, but now I'm your boss. Get the herd to the fort same as you would for her, and I'll let you live. Molly, I think, will be comin' with me when we head out with the money. She don't want to do that it's okay with me. Fairer'n that I can't say."

Fair, my ass, Morgan thought. She'd kill him because she felt like it. The rest of the gang would be killed or double-crossed. Molly? No way to tell what Stretch had planned for her. Chances were she didn't know herself.

"Well, what do you say?" Stretch prompted him.
"I'll do like you say," Morgan said. "I wouldn't
want anything to happen to Molly. She saved my
life with the Mexican, and I owe her."

When Stretch stood up her eyes were mean.
"Don't get teary-eyed on me, Big Boy. That ain't
your style. It's not just Molly's life we're talkin'
about. You try fancy-dancin' with me and I'll give
you to Pretty Woman. You won't be singin' any
songs when she gets through with you."

Stretch wanted to move the horses faster when
they started out. "You figure the Rangers will
catch up to us if you move them slow?" she said.
"You're draggin' your feet, Big Boy."

Morgan said, "They're moving just right. Your
boys are nowhere as good as the Mexicans, and
the horses sense it. You'll never catch them if they
break loose. We're not long down from the hills.
That's where they'll head. Time lost now may be
time saved in the long run."

"I don't want to hear none of your country
sayin's. Time lost is time the Rangers can use
to be sniffin' at our ass. Step it up a bit."

No use arguing with her. He rubbed his wrists
as he rode ahead. It was good to get the goddamned handcuffs off. They'd taken the handcuffs off Molly, but Luz, the fat Mexican, rode
beside her on the wagon box. Sister Nunn, the
frail one, rode in back, wedged between the tarpaulin and the sideboard.

Jimmy and Lester, Cockeye and Beer Belly, as
Morgan thought of them, weren't doing too badly
with the horses, but they didn't have the easy
swing of Hector and Manuel. They weren't even
as good as Cesar. Stretch was good, riding with
the ease of the ranch kid Morgan figured she

must have been not so far back in the past. Dallas, no experienced rider, was doing her best to pick up the routine. Silent and swift on a cow pony, Pretty Woman was the best of the lot. Like a good shepherd dog, she went after the stragglers and the breakaways.

When he could do it without Stretch catching on, Morgan checked the trail in back. Nothing there that he could see. If the Rangers were there, they were taking their own sweet time. They could be anywhere. They could be headed for Niles City, hoping to put together a new posse. If Stretch could be believed, there were only four of them. Popular opinion said they couldn't hold a candle to the Texas Rangers. Morgan wasn't sure he wanted them to catch up. There would be shooting even if Stretch tried to play the hostage game, and there was the dynamite to think about. He couldn't tell her about the dynamite because she might take it into her head to blow them all to smithereens if it looked like she was going to be captured and hanged.

No rain now. Soon they would be raising dust as the country dried out. Overhead the sky was more white than blue, and the sun felt good after the rain and the cold nights. Down from the high plains, crossing the long stretch of desert, the sun would become their enemy. So far the horses were well watered, moving along all right, but they'd be put to the test in the desert. Three places with water were marked on the map. The bad part about desert water was that it had a way of drying up. A spring that had bubbled for hundreds of years suddenly would turn into a dry hole in the sand.

There was no noon halt because Stretch wanted to push on. No one dared complain, not even

Dallas. Morgan thought it was just as well. There
was no water for the horses and there wouldn't be
for at least another ten miles. It would take them
the rest of the day, maybe some of the evening, to
reach what was marked on the map as Red Rocks
Pool. Morgan didn't look forward to another night
handcuffed to the wagon.

Now and then Stretch would round her horse
and ride back to the freight wagon to talk to
Molly. Morgan didn't know what was said, but
whatever Stretch was saying was bound to get
Molly's back up. It was one hell of a situation, one
that could only get worse. Here was the braggart
killer Stretch, full of "feelin's" for Molly, trying
to woo her like a kid with a candy cane. The
look on Stretch's face when she returned to the
herd from these side trips told him the courtship
wasn't going well. If the others found it funny,
they didn't so much as crack a smile. To do that
would be like teasing a rattler.

The afternoon dragged on. Nothing much happened except that Stretch yelled at Jimmy and
Lester for not keeping their mind on the job.
She lost interest before they had a chance to say
anything. Morgan got yelled at, too. Even Ned,
the former bank teller, came in for some abuse
though he was doing his best to keep out of the
way. Dallas, Pretty Woman and Cat Shawnessy
didn't get any of her bad mouth.

Morgan still hadn't figured what the setup was.
Unless he was way off, Dallas was no dyke, but
what about the others? In his time, Morgan had
fucked a few dykes under what could only be
called unusual circumstances, yet his knowledge
of these women was limited. And if she was as
crotch-crazy as she said, it seemed likely that
she'd been doing one or more of these women in

the weeks after they broke out of prison. Fat Luz
and shaky Sister didn't fill the bill, so it had to be
Cat or Pretty Woman, maybe both. Indian wom-
en weren't often pretty by white standards, but
Pretty Woman really was pretty. Cat just missed
being pretty but was good to look at with her
dark hair, fair skin, greenish eyes and firm young
body.

Some women, he knew, turned queer in prison
as a way of getting along. These could be divided
into the women who discovered they liked it and
remained that way after they got out and those
others who went back to lying down for men.
No matter what people said, there was no way
to tell a dyke unless she was so brazen about it
you couldn't help knowing.

Thinking about women could always give Morgan a bulge in his pants. In days he might be
dead, but since that hadn't happened yet, he was
going to do his damnedest to see it didn't. No plan
presented itself, but any move he made would
have to include Molly. On his own he could cut
loose, make a run for it and hope they wouldn't
bring him down with bullets. But with Molly to
think of, goddamn it, he had to stay with this, no
matter how it ended.

The sun told him it was six o'clock or there-
abouts. No sign of the red rocks where the water
was. Still a good ways to go. Real trouble could
flare up there anytime during the night. No telling
what Stretch would do. Best as he could figure,
the way they were moving, it would take another
seven or eight days to get close to the fort. Crossing the desert might add a few days.

The sun was throwing shadows before the clus-
ter of tall red rocks could be seen jutting up from
the flatness that surrounded it. It would be dark

when they reached them. The rocks looked like a small castle in the middle of nowhere. "Go on ahead and take a look," Stretch told Pretty Woman.

The Indian woman raced away, light and swift on the cow pony. "Don't want to walk into nothin'," Stretch said to Morgan. "Somebody could be layin' for us in there. Would be bad if they kept us from the water. Look to the horses, Big Boy. They smell water and want to get at it."

Pretty Woman came back, reining in hard on the lathered pony. "One old man camped in there with two burros." Her voice was almost a whisper.

"Did you kill him?"

"I killed him." Pretty Woman let her hand slide down to the haft of the skinning knife.

"Good gal." Stretch was like a teacher praising a kid for giving the right answer. "Hear that, Big Boy? You'll be ridin' backward on a burro if you don't behave."

Pretty Woman was distressed. "I killed the burros."

"You done right. Just funnin', Big Boy. All right, folks, let's check into the Red Rocks Hotel."

It was a good-sized pool, but the passage between the rocks was narrow and the horses had to be driven in ten at a time. That took some time, and it was dark when the horses were watered and penned in a half circle of rocks with a rope-and-stake fence covering the open side. The horses didn't get as much water as they wanted, but that couldn't be helped. They'd have to be watered again after the empty pool filled up during the night.

Morgan looked at the dead old man before Pretty Woman threw a rope on his head and dragged him far out from camp. Close to 70, bearded and bald, he had nothing in his pockets but a clasp knife and three silver dollars. Had to be a prospector heading for the hills and the lower slopes of the mountains. Old men like that spent their lives looking for gold one place or another. A battered tin alarm clock went off while Stretch was kicking at his belongings, and she thought that was funny. Morgan thought it would be a pure pleasure to kill this woman.

Stretch had taken over Molly's tent and folding cot. She had set up the cot by the fire and was stretched out on it. Except for Jimmy and Lester, who were guarding the herd, they all sat around the fire. Her mood was better than it had been earlier. Morgan thought she might be thinking of some new way to break Molly down. "This is the life," she said, "as the bull said to the heifer. Think on it now, if it wasn't for ol' Stretch all you gals'd still be rottin' away in Yuma, breakin' your backs twelve hours a day every day, eatin' hog slop with the shit bucket only a few feet away, runnin' sweat in summer, freezin' your asses off in winter, gettin' punished for nothin' a-tall. And the fuckin' turnkeys down on you round the clock."

"We can't thank you enough," Dallas said.

Somehow Stretch didn't mind that. "You can stick your snotty remarks up your ass. You know I'm speakin' the truth. You think you're better than me, but who got you out of Yuma?"

"You did," Dallas said. "You planned it, but you only took us along because you needed us. Those two guards would've shot you if I hadn't shot them. You think about *that*."

Stretch told Pretty Woman to pull her boots off. "I do think about it," she said to Dallas. "You're a good shot all right. You sure as hell shot your rich husband when you caught him fuckin' your kid sister. You shot the sister while you were at it. Now I ask you, was that nice?"

"Go to hell!" Dallas said.

"Ah, that feels good." Pretty Woman was rubbing Stretch's feet. "Say what you like, Dallas ol' gal, I got you out of Yuma. It was me made the plan. You remember Crazy Ellie?" Stretch said to Molly. "The little loony that was married to Big Meg, big strappin' gal with the real high voice. How can you not remember Crazy Ellie, looniest loony in the place?"

"I remember her," Molly said.

"Well, now," Stretch said, warming to her subject, "things was goin' along fine till Big Meg took a fancy to some new gal they brung in. After that it was nothin' but yellin' an' fightin' tween Ellie and Meg. Meg said they wasn't married no more and Ellie could go diddle herself. The long an' the short of it is, one night when Big Meg was sleepin', Ellie put a sharp sliver of wood to Meg's ear and drove it through her brain with a rock."

"Jesus Christ!" Dallas got up and walked out of camp.

"Anyhow," Stretch said to Molly, "poor old Ellie was sentenced to hang; only it dragged on and on, with the prison doctor sayin' she was crazy and oughtn't to hang and the Territory doctor arguin' the law had to be upheld. Well, I figured they'd hang her when all the smoke cleared, and that's when I got word to good ol' Ned. Ned was holdin' money for me from the time we robbed the bank he was workin' at. Ned told us when the bank would be fat so my word to him was come see me or I'll spill the beans. The upshot was, the day before Ellie was hung, ol' Ned delivered a real nice coffin full of guns to the prison. The coffin was for Ellie, and Ned was her grievin' Uncle John. Wasn't too hard to get at the guns while Ellie was puttin' on a real wild howlin' show on the gallows. Jimmy and Lester was waitin' with the horses. Boys rode with me on a few bank jobs and wasn't caught like I was, but I could nail them anytime I liked."

Dallas came back and sat by the fire. "You all through with your story?"

"I think Molly found it interestin'," Stretch said. "Specially with her such a big part of it."

Molly had been staring into the fire. "What the hell are you talking about?"

Stretch put on a roguish face. "You helped plan it, gal, and don't you deny it. You got a pardon but couldn't stand the thought of us gals, your close friends, rottin' away in there. You was more than ready to help when Ned come to you with my plan. It was you provided the money for the guns, the coffin, the horses—everything."

Molly's voice was choked with anger. "Nobody would ever believe such a story. Everybody in Niles City knows I'm close to broke. Why would I risk my freedom?"

Stretch said slyly, "Nearly broke ain't broke. Besides, what you think is broke wouldn't look like broke to other people. Wasn't that much money anyhow. You could get it. As for riskin' your neck, you was mad, see, hated what they'd done to you an' wanted to get back at them."

Molly would have jumped up if Morgan hadn't held her back. Molly said furiously, "You can't drag me into this, you bitch!"

Suddenly Stretch's eyes were narrow and mean. "You're already in it, gal. That's why you'll be comin' along with us after we get the money. The thing of it is, gal, a lot of people will be ready to believe the worst about you. You got off too easy is what people will be thinkin', and who's to blame them? Your old man bribed you out of Yuma and everybody knows it. The law gets after you, you'll hang."

"Why?" Molly managed to control her voice. "You have my horses and soon you'll have my money. Isn't that enough for you?"

For a moment Stretch was flustered; then she smiled. "I—we like your company. Fiery gal like you don't want to settle down like some frump. There's the whole wild world waitin' for you out there. Excitement, gal, that's what you need. Fat banks just waitin' to be robbed with payrolls bulgin' at the seams. Think of the great times we can have—our pockets stuffed with the green, the fine hotels and restaurants, men waitin' hand an' foot on us."

Dallas's smile was twisted and skeptical. "Where will we be having these fine times of yours? Some hideout in the mountains? Some rathole in a town with a crooked marshal who'll turn us in when the money runs out?"

"Not a-tall." Stretch turned over so Pretty Woman could rub her back. "We'll light out after a few big jobs and go to the city. Not Denver or some western city where they might be lookin' for us. New Orleans I'm thinkin about, maybe Chicago or New York. Lose ourselves in the crowds till they ain't lookin' so hard to catch us an' the banks ain't so nervous. Then out we come an' hit them again. An all-woman gang is what I have in mind. Men are not reliable."

"Like your husband," Dallas said.

"Listen, you, we don't talk about that."

"If you can talk about my husband I can talk about yours. Left you lying wounded in the street outside the bank. At least my husband wasn't that kind of man."

Stretch heaved herself up on her elbow. "No, he just fucked your little sister. What the hell! Talk about it all you like. I mean to catch up with the bastard some day if the good Lord lets me live that long. I hate fuckin' men. That goes for you, too, Big Boy."

Morgan shrugged but said nothing.

"You don't have to come with us," Stretch said to Dallas. "There's the door, so to speak, only you won't find it so easy on your lonesome. A woman alone is a mark for every horny fucker she runs into."

"I can take care of myself."

"In a pig's prick you can. One man maybe you can handle, but suppose you're out there alone on the prairie or in some cowtown, any fuckin' place, an' you run into two, three, four bastards that decide this one looks good, let's fuck the ass off her, keep her a few days, then maybe kill her. What're you goin' to do? Run cryin' to the law? Bullshit! You can't go home. You can't go nowhere you'll be safe."

Listening to all this, Morgan knew Dallas was going to give way. Intelligent and well-brought up, she didn't have the other woman's nerve or cunning. "I never said I wouldn't be coming with you," she said at last.

Stretch said, "Don't agree with me too fast or I'll get suspicious."

"I have to be realistic."

"'Course you do, gal. What you need is a good fuck. Pity you're that way. In the end, though, you'll come around to my way of thinkin'. Until that great day in the mornin', what you need right now is a good fuck. I seen you lookin' at Lester an'

Jimmy an' givin' them thumbs down. Can't say I blame you, one with the cockeye, the other with the bloat belly. What would you say to fuckin' Big Boy here? Got to keep you happy, gal. Morgan's a man, but if you need a stiff one that bad, he ain't the ugliest thing I ever seen."

Dallas didn't blush, but she wasn't too embarrassed to cast a sideways glance at Morgan.

Stretch whooped. "Looka here now! We got ourself a couple of bashful lovebirds. What's the matter with you two? Granny's asleep an' granpappy's drunk in the cellar. What do you say, Big Boy? You don't mind, do you, Molly? It ain't like you was engaged or somethin'."

No one answered her, but she pushed on with it. "You got my blessin', children. Anythin' to keep my favorite gal happy. I seen you lookin' at Dallas, Big Boy, and don't tell me you wasn't. Tell you what. I'll turn you loose of the cuffs and you can bed down under the wagon. Molly'll have to be cuffed to the chuck, but she can sleep just as good over there. Can't have the two of you free to run off."

Later, with some of them asleep and some guarding the herd, Morgan lay under the wagon with his hands behind his head. Stretch said she was going to sleep, and Pretty Woman followed her into the tent. No sounds came from the tent. Free of the cuffs, Morgan felt bad about Molly, who lay beside the chuck wagon on the far side of the fire.

Just one more of Stretch's bad jokes, he thought. Nothing that Stretch said to Dallas was to be taken seriously—or was it? In spite of everything, he found himself waiting.

Chapter Eight

The wind picked up, blowing sand and muffling other sounds. Dallas rolled out of her blanket, stood up and walked over to Morgan. Morgan held up the blanket and she crawled in beside him. She smelled of horses and sweat, a woman who wanted a man. It was the only way she could have done it, and she did it right. The fact that she had killed four people—husband, sister and two prison guards—didn't weigh on his mind. She was here, and he wanted her.

She talked softly but didn't whisper. "Are you surprised?" she asked.

"I don't know. Maybe I am," Morgan said, pulling her close.

There was some awkwardness between two people in a strange situation. They took off their clothes, quickly and easily. "No gun," she told him, "so don't look for one. I don't take weapons to bed." She didn't say all she needed was his weapon. There was nothing coy about Dallas.

Soon they were naked under the blanket. She fondled his cock and shuddered. Suddenly the lust in her was like a savage animal breaking out of its cage. She was strong and pulled him on top of her, already bumping her crotch into his. Her legs opened so wide that her toes nearly touched the inside of the wagon wheels. Her legs kicked and locked behind his back as he drove into her, and her cunt tightened at the same time. At first, the grip of her cunt muscles was so tight he could hardly pull back for another stroke. It was like she didn't want to let his cock go, now that it was deep inside her. But he broke her grip with the force of his cock, and soon he was thrusting in and out of her, steady and remorseless. She didn't have the weight, but her body was toughened by hard work, and she fought him while she showed the need to be dominated. It was a fight between a man and a woman, but there was no real roughness in it. While he fucked her with long thrusts, her hands wandered all over him, and she murmured in a sort of wonder that she had a man on top of her who was fucking her.

"So long. It's been so long," she murmured, and he guessed she was thinking of the lonely prison nights with caged women calling out in their sleep or lying awake as she was, wanting the hardness of a man inside her and thinking maybe she'd never feel it again. Now she had it, and there was wonder in her voice.

Morgan figured Stretch was trying to listen, but he didn't give a damn. Sudden death in the form of a crazy woman was right out there, and he still didn't give a damn. He didn't know what Dallas was thinking, only what she was saying. "I thought I'd never . . . I wanted it so bad . . . it was . . . thinking about it and knowing . . ."

What she said was desperate and fragmented, a woman thinking with her body instead of her mind. His hands kneaded the firm muscles of her ass. She hadn't come yet, but he felt her tensing up to it. Then she came, so suddenly and violently that he had to fight to keep her pinned to the blanket underneath. Instead of gasping or panting, she sucked in a long, deep breath and let it out slowly as she came. But even when her orgasm had ebbed, her body continued to quiver. She wasn't a woman who had quick, frantic orgasms, one right after the other. She came as if in the grip of some deep emotion.

Now she lay quietly under him, holding his face with both hands, and said, "Thank you, Morgan. Thank you for that." Morgan didn't know what to say. Women usually thanked him with their cries or moans or the way their bodies jerked and spasmed. Odd to hear it put into words. As he quickened his thrusts, her quiet mood passed and new sweat broke out all over her body. Both their bodies were slick with sweat, and sand blown by the wind stuck to their skin. Morgan sucked her breasts and felt damp sand grinding between his teeth.

He came hard as she held him close, her hands squeezing his ass, her mouth sucking in his tongue. Then her hands pushed at his shoulders, indicating without words that she wanted to get on top of him. His sweaty body moved off her, and she threw her leg over him and moved into the new position. His cock, still in her, began to get hard again. A downward movement of her crotch made it feel like his stiff cock was standing up straight in her, and she rode up and down on his cock, moaning softly. She put her hands, palms down, on either side of his neck and raised her crotch so it felt like she was fucking him, as if she had a cock. Her moaning stopped, and she rode him with silent energy, driving his cock deep inside her. When she came, hard and fierce, she pushed down so far on his cock that it hurt. Again there was the long intake of breath, then the complete relaxing of all her muscles. Morgan came again, volleying upward into her. His juice dripped out of her, as did hers, and she reached down, wet her fingers and tasted it.

It went on like that for a long time. At last, tired and satisfied, she lay with her head on his chest. Except for the wind, it was quiet. He could tell by her breathing that she wasn't asleep.

"You're thinking how you can use me to get out of this," she said.

"Yes," he said.

"All the time you were . . . ?"

"Not all the time."

There was a tiny bit of truth in that. Using her was always in his mind, but there were moments when he hadn't been able to think about it. Now there was nothing else in his mind.

"We could get away from here together," she said. "Make a break for it and ride away fast. Stretch wouldn't follow us. The herd and the money . . ."

"Can you ride a horse without a saddle? That's how it would have to be."

"I think I could. I did it as a child."

Morgan smiled, thinking maybe she'd done it on a fat, tame pony. "I couldn't leave Molly behind. I don't know if she'd do the same for me, but I won't run and leave her to Stretch."

Dallas kissed his chest. "Molly would run the first chance she got. I knew her in Yuma, and she hasn't changed. You're making a mistake. There's no good in her."

"Is there in you?" Morgan asked. He wasn't thinking of the four people she'd killed. The husband and sister had it coming, and the two guards stood between her and freedom. He knew he'd kill two guards to get out of a place like Yuma.

"Some good." She raised her head and looked at him. It was dark under the wagon, but he could see her well enough. "I know that's hard to believe."

"Not so hard." He paused to think over what he was going to say. It hardly mattered how he said it if it got him killed, not after Stretch got the money but right now or very shortly thereafter. Very possibly this whole thing with Dallas was a setup. "Not so hard," he repeated.

"What were you going to say, Morgan?"

"I was going to say the only way to end this is to kill Stretch and the Indian. The others are nothing without Stretch."

"You want me to kill her?"

"Get me a gun and I'll kill her, as well as the Indian. I'll kill the others if they get in the way."

Dallas was laughing soundlessly. "All of them, even poor Sister? My Lord, but you're a hard man, Morgan. I don't know I could bring myself to kill poor little Sister. You know, before I killed my husband and sister I never thought I could kill anybody."

"What about it?" This was wandering too far. "Give me a gun, or leave it where I can find it. She's been letting me move around a bit. I know she's watching me, but she can't watch me every minute. Make up your mind. You know she has no intention of sharing the money. She knows she can handle the others. You're different."

"Yes, I know she means to kill me," Dallas said. "All of us, even Pretty Woman. Pretty Woman is her killer, but she'll kill her too when she no longer needs her."

Morgan didn't think he was making much progress. "Why are you so afraid of her? If you know she's going to kill you, what is there to lose?"

Dallas shivered, and it wasn't from cold. "I don't know. Everything I ever had is gone. If I'm caught they won't put me back in prison. They'll hang me. I'd rather hang than spend my life in Yuma, but I don't want to do either. Even if I killed Stretch, where would I go? I have no friends, nowhere to hide. And if I could hide, for how long? They'd always be looking for me. Four murders—they wouldn't give up."

Morgan felt hope slipping away. "I'd help you," he said, trying to keep the desperation out of his voice. "They can't look for you forever. I'd find a place you'd be safe. Canada. South America. If I give my word, I'll keep it."

"That would make you as wanted as I am. God, I never thought I'd end up like this. Sometimes at night I wake up and think this can't be happening to me. My family was well off, the man I married was rich, I was the envy of my friends. . . ."

Morgan cut in with, "Kill her or let me do it."

The brutal interruption didn't work. "I'm tired and confused, Morgan. If I fail to kill her, she'll hand me over to the Indian. On the way here, a very old man, a storekeeper, refused to tell where his money was hidden. Pretty Woman used her knife on him. It still makes me sick to think about it. She'd do the same to me before I died, but that's not all of it. I hate Stretch and want to kill her, but at the same time I don't. She got us out of Yuma, and she's held us together. At times it looked hopeless if not for her. Can you understand what I feel?"

Morgan didn't get a chance to reply. Stretch came out of the tent with the Indian behind her and went to the fire. Yawning and limbering up her arms, she raked a bed of coals together and put the coffeepot on to boil. "Lovely night, ain't it, Pretty? We ain't got lovebirdies, but we got coyotes singin' their music out there." Pretty Woman, whose face never changed, said nothing, and Stretch continued. "Don't see ol' Dallas nowheres. Wonder what mischief that gal has gotten herself into?"

Dressed by now, Dallas got out from under the wagon. "Ah, there you are, girly," Stretch said. "Had a good time, did you? Enjoyed yourself, did you? Course you did, or so I hope. But you know what they say? All good things must come to an end. Time you let your crotch cool off and got some sleep."

Dallas walked past Stretch without a word, but that wasn't the end of it. "That you in there, Big Boy?" Stretch said, bending down to look under the wagon. "Take a look, Pretty. The answer to a maiden's prayer. How'd you make out, Big Boy? Whispered sweet nothin's in the lady's ear, did you?" Stretch's voice turned mean. "A lot of fuckin' good that's goin' to do you. Stick your hand out, Big Boy. It's handcuff time."

Morgan dropped off to sleep after Stretch and Pretty Woman went back into the tent. He didn't know how much he'd accomplished by talking to Dallas. Maybe nothing. Yet there were moments when he thought he felt her teetering on the edge, wanting to come in with him, knowing it was her only chance. Stretch was a force to be reckoned with, all right. The big killer bitch had a hold on these women that would be hard to break, and it wasn't just the gun she carried or the Indian who did her bidding. A sort of strange bond between them was the best he could make out of it.

In the morning, eating beside the fire, Molly had nothing to say. She didn't even say good morning, and Morgan wondered if she thought he was making a deal with Dallas that didn't include her. Dallas, for her part, gave no sign of what had happened under the wagon not so many hours before.

Time was wasted getting the horses in and out of the narrow passage to the pool. To do it before first light would cause confusion. Stretch was impatient but saw the sense of it. Finally, in Stretch's words, they got the show on the road.

The sun came up strong, and the plain shimmered with heat waves. There wouldn't be any water for the horses until they came to the end of it. After that, they would be moving down to semi-arid country that went on for miles before they hit the desert. Water would get scarcer as they moved along, but the map said there would be enough.

Everybody but Stretch was beginning to look down in the mouth. Morgan could only wonder what Pretty Woman was thinking because her impassive face never changed. Dallas kept away from him, and Stretch yipped at the horses. As the miles passed, Stretch looked like she thought she had everything under control. Fact was, she had.

They pushed on without the noonday halt, chewing biscuits and sipping water. Looking like a man on his way to the gallows, the cook drove his wagon and tilted a bottle when he thought no

one was looking. Most cooks drank openly, but
Carlos knew better than to do it with this outfit.
Morgan hoped he would run out of whiskey before
long. It would be hell if Stretch started with the
bottle. Bad enough as she was, she would be a
lot worse with liquor in her. For reasons of her
own, though, she showed no inclination to drink,
and Morgan was glad of it. If Stretch didn't drink,
none of the others would dare to. Like her or hate
her, they did what they thought she wanted them
to do—all but Molly and Dallas, who defied her
in their different ways. How long their defiance
would last Morgan could only guess. If the lanky
killer decided to break them, really put her mind
to it, she could probably do so.

That night in camp was much the same until
Stretch started needling them. Molly and Morgan
were let alone. Morgan couldn't figure what her
purpose was. To make them more edgy than they
were? Or just out of plain meanness? Meanness
bubbled out of the woman like a poisoned spring.
It started with jittery, frightened Sister Nunn, who
never had anything to say.

"How're you this fine night, Celia?" Stretch
asked, using the scared little woman's given
name.

Sister was as startled as if Stretch had asked
her to break a wild horse. She had been pushing
her food around on the tin plate. "Fine," she said,
"I'm just fine, Stretch."

"Think you'll ever fall in love again, Celia?"

"Please, Stretch . . ." Sister leaned forward over
her plate, trying to hide from everyone.

Stretch said, "No need to be bashful, gal. It's
every woman's right to fall in love, even if the
man is a rotten, stinkin', two-faced deceiver." To
Morgan she added, "Poor little Celia stole from

the emporium where she kept the books. Owner was too cheap to hire a man. Doin' good at the job till this sly bastard come around and started makin' sheep's eyes at our little gal here. Never havin' a man even look at her before, poor ol' Celia went weak in the legs and wet in the crotch. Wasn't nothin' she wouldn't do for this weasel, includin' dippin' into the bank deposits and other crookedness. It was over the hills and away we go and weddin' bells when there's enough money, this weasel says. Only he takes the whole bundle and skedaddles, leavin' poor Celia droppin' bitter tears on her weddin' dress."

Sister tried to get up. "Stay," Stretch ordered. "Sit the fuck down. I'm tellin' your story so these gals can take a lesson from it. You gals've heard it before, but you can't hear it too often, specially you, Dallas."

Dallas remained silent.

"And the lesson to be learned," Stretch went on, "is never trust a man. They'll soft-soap you till you're full of suds, then run out on you. Anyhow, to get back to the story, Celia was spunky enough to go after this snake. Found him, faced him, and he laughed at her. For this he got six bullets up close, and Sister got forty years. Thirty for the killing, ten for stealin' from the store. Makes you think, don't it?"

"I wish I'd stayed where I was," Sister said with a meek defiance that seemed to surprise her. "I wouldn't have lived long in Yuma. Why did you take me along?"

"Cause I like you, gal. You was my cagemate. Besides you always said this New Mexico merchant was rich. That's when you was complainin' about how he pressed the stealin' charge so hard. I thought let's us pay this rich guy a call and see what he's got hid, like they all do."

Dallas spoke up. "You mean that's the only reason we headed for New Mexico?"

"You think we should've crossed the river into California?" Stretch shook her head at the other woman's question. "First place they'd look, for fuck's sake. Besides, there ain't nothin' that part of California but desert. So we headed the other way. Didn't fool them for long, but it gave us a start. New Mexico looked as good a place as any."

"I never said I knew where Mr. Stainer's money was hidden. I don't know if he has any money hidden. He always put his money in the bank." Sister was frightened enough to want to set this straight.

"Except when you was stealin' it," Stretch said, laughing at her own joke. "Don't fret, gal. Forget about his money. We got ten thousand warmin' in the oven. Course I wouldn't mind if we just stumbled across him. Pretty Woman would make him talk in two minutes flat."

Ned Geer, of all people, tried to change the subject. Morgan knew he was deathly afraid of the Indian woman. Small wonder; she was enough to scare anybody. The former bank teller said, "It won't be long before we're out of Arizona. That ought to make us all feel better."

It was a harmless remark, but Stretch didn't like it. "What's so good about New Mexico?" she asked him. "What're you figurin' to do? Get another job in a bank? Change your name and think they won't check back on you?"

Ned said nervously, "I don't intend to stay in New Mexico. I came from the East. I'd like to go back there. Get a job in some city and stay out of trouble for the rest of my life."

Stretch stared at him with contempt. "You'll get into trouble as long as there are young boys around. As long as you get shit on your dick you're goin' to get into trouble. A bugger an' a sucker is what you are."

"You promised to stop that kind of talk."

"So I did," Stretch said. "It just keeps slippin' out. What're you shamed for anyhow? You like to gobble the goose, don't you?"

"See, you're still going on about it." Ned looked as if he wanted to bury his head in the sand. "I can't help the way I am. I've tried to resist temptation. But I'm no saint and neither are you."

Stretch pretended to be shocked. "That's a hell of a thing to say, Ned Geer. Mighty hurtful, too. I can't speak for these gals, but deep in my heart I know I'm a saint, the holiest fuckin' saint that ever was. Jesus sees my heart, and so does the Virgin Mary. Soon as I get to heaven I'm goin' to find out how true that virgin shit is. 'Course I won't be seein' you up there, Neddy. Jesus don't like your kind."

Dallas spoke up again, as if getting back her nerve. "Why don't you let the man alone? You're always picking on someone. Does that make you feel better?"

Stretch turned to Ned. "My joshing don't make you feel that bad, does it?"

Ned mumbled something.

"You call it pickin'. I call it havin' a little fun," Stretch said to Dallas. "What would you do if I started pickin' on you?"

"Try it and find out," Dallas said.

"I never try to do anything," Stretch said. "I just do it."

Just another cozy evening round the old campfire, Morgan thought, and he felt something like

relief when Pretty Woman handcuffed him and
Molly to the wagon and left them there for the
night. They lay without talking, the length of the
wagon between them. Morgan thought it was up
to her to say something, and finally she did. "Are
you proud of yourself, Morgan? Morgan the stallion, Morgan the stud. It's any hole you can stick
it into, isn't it? You thought I was asleep. How
could I sleep?"

Morgan felt like a straying husband getting
cracked on the skull with a frying pan. A good
thing she didn't have a shotgun.

"I thought she might help us," he said. What
the hell was she so mad about? It wasn't like they
were in a honeymoon cottage with roses round
the door.

"You're lying," she said. "You're thinking of no
one but yourself. What did you promise her, Big
Boy? That you'd take her back to Idaho, just the
two of you, and hide her in the woods? You don't
fool me for a minute."

Morgan told her to keep her voice down.
"Nobody's trying to fool you. What should I have
done? Turn her out? Would you rather have her
as a friend or an enemy?"

Molly rattled the handcuffs chain. "Goddamn
these things and goddamn you. She may be your
friend, but she's not mine. Did you make any
extra effort to please her, you slimy bastard?"

"I tried to get her to kill Stretch or give me
a gun and let me do it. I think I made some
headway."

"Then why are we handcuffed to this wagon?"

"She hasn't made up her mind."

"More lies," Molly hissed. "I never thought you'd
do this to me, Morgan. You'd be dead now if I
hadn't attacked Trinidad. A lot you care about

that. No wonder she wouldn't give you a straight answer. She sees through you, and so do I."

"See what, Molly?" Morgan was sick of this.

"I don't care what she sees," Molly said, "but she'd have to be dumber than she looks not to see it. You'd double-cross her and you'd double-cross me to save your dirty skin. Come on, Morgan, what did you promise her?"

"I promised to find her a safe place to hide."

"She didn't believe you, did she? I don't want to talk to you anymore, is that clear?"

"It would be a mercy," Morgan said.

Chapter Nine

Early next afternoon, moving ahead of their dust, a single shot sounded far off in the distance. If the wind had been blowing the other way, they wouldn't have heard it at all. Stretch rode forward to where Morgan was.

"I heard it," he said.

"What do you think it is?"

Morgan started to answer, but she cut him off. "Shut up and listen." No other shots were carried on the wind. "It's no gun battle," she said. "They could be lyin' for us in a roll in the ground."

"Who is they?"

"Rangers, bounty hunters."

"So they fired a shot to let us know they're there," Morgan said. Dyke or not, she was just like any other woman in some ways. Didn't always make sense, added two and two and got three. "We can follow along or ride ahead and see what's doing."

114

"Let's do it then. No tricks, Big Boy." Stretch whistled, and Pretty Woman left the herd and came up fast on the cow pony. Morgan was told to ride ahead of the two women. They had put about two miles behind them when Stretch yelled, "I see them! Three men straight ahead!"

Stretch let her binoculars drop down on the leather thong and caught up with Morgan. Pretty Woman rode behind so she could watch Morgan's back. They rode past a dead horse with a US brand on it. The three men ahead, one staggering under a cavalry saddle, didn't hear them until they got close. Stretch yipped at them the way she did at the herd. The one who turned first was a red-faced cavalry sergeant of 40 or so, a thick bodied man with a couple of weeks' beard growing high on his cheekbones. Weighted down as he was, the man with the saddle was the last to turn. Both men wore manacles, wrist irons joined by a chain.

"What you got there, Sarge?" Stretch asked.

"The name's McCluskey, and you're lookin' at a couple of deserters. Major's orders was to find them and bring 'em back. Took a while. They was headin' for California. Fetchin' back deserters is my job, lady. What in blazes are you folks doin' out here?"

"Pickin' daisies, Sarge. So you're in the way of bein' some kind of army lawman."

"Pickin' daisies, huh?" The sergeant didn't know what to make of Stretch or Pretty Woman. "That's an Injun, ain't it?"

"She's my sister," Stretch told him. "Geronimo's only daughter, if you have to know."

The sergeant laughed uneasily. "Geronimo's only daughter. That's a good one. Guess we'd better be movin' along. Fort's a good ways off."

"Hold your horses, Sarge." Stretch's voice cracked like a whip. "I'd like to hear more about these deserters. You make them walk all the way back?"

"Well, you see, lady, there ain't no trains this part of the territory. These men sold the army horses they stole, so they're walkin' home to the guardhouse. You notice I'm walkin' myself. Horse broke a leg, had to shoot it."

"But you rode a good part of the way back. You enjoy makin' them walk, don't you?"

Morgan didn't have to wonder why she was taking so long to kill the three men. McCluskey represented some form of the law and had to be killed like a snake. First she wanted to make him suffer, beg for his life.

"Enjoy ain't zackly the right word, lady. Hard on them, I admit. They ought of thought of that before they deserted."

"You an' your fuckin' army law!" Stretch's gun came out fast. "I'm goin' to kill you, Sarge. You think you can get to that gun before I do?"

The sergeant's heavy Colt .45 single-action was stuck in his stiff, hard-leather holster with the flap buttoned. "Why would you want to kill me? I'm just doin' my duty. Who are you, lady?"

He held out his hand, and Stretch shot his thumb off. "Jesus, lady! You don't want to kill me! You got no reason! Mother of God, please don't kill me!"

Stretch shot him in the head; then she turned the gun on the prisoners and shot them too. It was the first time Morgan had seen her shoot, and she was as good as she said she was.

Covered by two guns, Morgan searched the sergeant's body—gold watch, a pocket knife, a cracked leather wallet with five ten dollar bills in it. Money to pay off informers, if need be.

Stretch took the money and the watch and gave the knife to Pretty Woman. The bodies lay in the hot sun, waiting for the buzzards to come flapping down. Pretty Woman drew her gun and held it on Morgan as Stretch pushed out the spent shells and reloaded. They worked well together, these two killer women. The Indian was Stretch's pet killer and bedmate. What did she think of Stretch's twisted courtship of Molly? She understood English, though she seldom spoke it, so she had to know. Stretch made no secret of her fierce longing for Molly by all those side trips back to the wagon during the day and the things she said at the campfire at night. Pretty Woman showed no resentment, showed nothing at all.

They rejoined the herd and made a wide sweep around the bodies and the buzzards tearing at them. Even at a distance, the smell made the horses skittish, but there was no panic. Unlike everyone else, Stretch was in a jubilant mood, bragging about how she had made the "bullshittin' sergeant" beg for his life. It didn't bother her that sooner or later she'd have army investigators hunting for her. You couldn't just kill soldiers and get away with it. Morgan didn't think it mattered a whole lot. He wasn't going to leave the killing of Stretch to the military. But how was he to do it? Maybe he deserved his nickname—Big Boy. Stretch laughed at him and defied him to make a dangerous move, and maybe she wasn't far wrong.

It was close to dark and still no sign of water. On the map, it was marked by a signboard, but that could have been blown down by the wind. There was nothing else to do but keep the herd moving. The horses weren't smelling water or they would have known it, which meant the water had dried up or was still far ahead. Here was the first real danger of a stampede.

Stretch had the map and was trying to look at it by striking wooden matches. Since the wind kept blowing the matches out, she had to get down off her horse and try again. Morgan knew she wasn't going to find anything different on the map. He had checked it, and so had she. But in spite of the wind and the dark, Stretch kept looking. With the mind of a mad child in a grown-up body, she kept trying to will the water to be there.

"You changed the map!" she screamed at Morgan. She crumpled the map and made as if to toss it away. The wind would have taken it far beyond finding. Morgan spoke sharply to her, and she smoothed out the map, folded it and put it in her shirt pocket. No more was said about changing the map, but she stayed mad at Morgan, as if he was to blame for the water not being where she wanted it to be. For a while it looked as if she might shoot him, and to hell with the consequences.

But the killing mood passed, and she was ready to ask for his advice. The high plain was a mesa, one end higher than the other. It sloped down to the east, but over the great distance they had to travel, the long slope was hardly felt. But there was a point, marked on the map, where the mesa ended and there was a drop, gradual in places, abrupt in others, to the rocky, dry country below. It would be crazy to try to move the herd down in the dark. It would be dangerous even with a full moon. But the light was very bad, the spring sky thick with rolling black clouds. A good time to start a stampede, Morgan thought. He decided against it.

"We'll have to hold the horses here as best we can," he told Stretch. "A rope corral and everybody turning out to stand guard. Has to be. Too dark to go on. You want to lose them down a drop?"

Stretch had to agree. "This is goin' to be a bitchin' bastard of a job. There's streaks of rock runnin' through here. How're we goin' to get the stakes set?"

She knew the answer to that. They had to do it the hard way, by looking for soft places to drive the stakes in. Everybody was hungry and tired, wanting to get the work done so they could eat and stretch out by the fire. Morgan had to tell them to work as quietly as they could, and then he had to tell them again. They weren't as afraid of him as they were of Stretch.

Even Ned and Sister and Luz were pressed into service, not that it did much good. Stretch told them they had to earn their keep. Morgan said they would cause less confusion sitting by the fire. Stretch cursed them—"good for nothing freeloaders"—and told them to get the fuck out of the way.

It was hard working in the dark, but finally the corral started to take shape. Morgan walked along, pulling on the stakes, driving them in deeper or moving them when they weren't secure. The hammer he carried would have been fine for crushing Stretch's skull, but he didn't get the chance. Pretty Woman stayed behind him all the time he was working. Every time he turned, thinking to kill her first, she moved back with the gun in her hand.

Finally the corral was as strong as it would ever be. At best, though, it was just rope and wooden stakes, and Morgan knew the horses could tear loose anytime. The horses moved restlessly, but so far there was none of the biting and kicking that comes before a breakout. It could go two ways, Morgan knew all too well. The restlessness could turn into something worse, or the herd could gradually settle down. If the quieter horses settled down, so would the others. Either way they would have to be closely watched all through the night.

They took turns eating. Morgan went to the fire, followed by Stretch and Pretty Woman. Luz, the fat Mexican, was shoveling in a plate of rice and beans. "Sister actin' crazy over dere," Luz said without turning her head. "Cryin' an' moanin' wit the blanket over her head. Look for youself."

Stretch looked. "I don't see her doin' nothin'. What the hell you talkin' about? Quit stuffin' your fat face an' go stand watch."

Luz stood her ground. "She been actin' crazy. She stop now, but she been crazy before."

Stretch told Luz to get out of there. "You better not be lyin', taco eater. Nobody messes with Sister long as I'm around," Stretch said. She went over to where Sister lay rolled in her blanket with her head covered. Sister tried to hide her face with her hands when Stretch pulled back the blanket. She started to cry.

Pretty Woman didn't watch Stretch. She watched Morgan.

"What's the matter, gal?" Stretch said, bending down to put her hand on Sister's head. "What you pullin' away for? This is Stretch talkin' to you."

Sister continued to cry. A new side to Stretch, Morgan thought. This crazy woman had so many sides to her.

"You got to stop that, hear?" Stretch said, not angry yet but on the edge. "You ain't cut out for this life. Nothin' to be done about that. Not right now. So dry up and shut up. If you're through eatin', make yourself useful. I ain't got time to coddle you along."

Eating rice and beans, Stretch said to nobody, "That poor gal ain't right in the head. What to do with her I don't rightly know. You think she's crazy, Big Boy?"

Morgan said, "Just peculiar. Nerves all shot, but not crazy."

"That fuckin' Luz, she should talk. A whore that killed one of her customers for pissin' on her favorite statue. She ain't even a real Mexican. From Panama, some place like that. Fuckin' foreigner. I'd have to be real hard-up to climb into bed with a pig like that."

Ned came into camp to get his supper. "You think Sister is crazy?" Stretch asked him before he could get the food. Ned looked startled, as he always was when Stretch spoke to him.

"I . . . don't know," he stammered.

"Spit it out. Say what's on your mind. You're an educated man. You ought to have some opinion."

Ned wanted to say the right thing, but he didn't know what it was. So he hedged. "Maybe slightly crazy. That's not quite right. More like very nervous. Being nervous can make you appear a little crazy."

Stretch thought about it while Ned filled his plate with beans and rice. "I think you said it right. Sister's betwixt crazy an' nervous. Long as she don't go full crazy, that's not so bad. We'll let her go on like she is and see what happens. A mad person could be a burden."

"I agree with you," Ned said. "We'll keep an eye on her."

Stretch said, "You mean *you'll* keep an eye on her."

Ned nearly dropped his plate. "Good Lord, Stretch, I'm not qualified to look after a crazy woman."

"Why not? You're an old woman yourself. You said she wasn't crazy. Let's stick to that. She's in your care from here on in. No argument about it. You know I don't like arguments."

"I know you don't," Ned mumbled into his plate. Morgan didn't think he'd ever seen an unhappier man in his life.

They had to stay awake all night to watch the herd. Sister was allowed to stay in camp, rolled in her blanket, with Ned hovering over her, dozing and jerking awake, scared to death that she'd do something crazy and bring down Stretch's wrath on him.

Stretch was as twitchy as the horses, walking up and down all night, never sitting down and resting like the others. A couple of times she threatened to kill someone she caught dozing. She got mad when Cat Shawnessy, usually quiet, said she was so tired she didn't care what happened to her. Stretch jerked her to her feet and slapped her awake. Some of the horses whinnied at the sound.

Morgan was glad to see first light. It had been a bad, edgy night, the dark hours crawling by like a long funeral procession. Only Morgan and Stretch and Pretty Woman were fully awake, and even Molly was dull-eyed like the others, hungry but not showing much interest in her food. Sometime toward morning, worn out by nervousness, Ned had fallen asleep sitting up and was still in that position. Stretch picked a small rock and hit him in the back. His startled yell woke Sister who began to cry.

"You may have to shut her up," Stretch said to Pretty Woman. "She's getting on my nerves."

Pretty Woman just nodded. After four cups of black coffee, Stretch told Morgan it was time they moved on. Morgan said they better scout for the water before they started up the herd. "It could be dried up," he said. "At least we'd know for sure if it is."

Sister was still crying, and Stretch yelled at Ned to keep her quiet. "Where's the next water?" she said to Morgan, angry and wanting to blame him for something.

"Down from here. Getting down will be dodgy if the herd isn't watered first."

Stretch didn't want to buy that. "How'd they manage it, the drives before this?"

Morgan said, "They had water and enough wranglers, men who knew what they were doing. The people you have around these horses are making them nervous."

"You're a horse's ass if you believe that. How can a horse tell the difference? All right, maybe they can. You're still a horse's ass, Big Boy. Let's go find water before Christmas."

Molly didn't even bother to look when Morgan rode out with Stretch and her shadow. Stretch rode alongside, Pretty Woman behind. Can't go anyplace without these two ladies, Morgan thought with grim humor. Can't kill one without killing the other. Maybe today he'd get lucky. A wish without much hope in it.

For once, Stretch was ready to listen. They rode for miles and were getting close to the end of the plateau, when they came on a wide split in the earth that went down into shadows. It was as wide as a street at the entrance; then it widened out further before it got to the bottom. Trickling water formed a pool at the bottom.

"Well, I'll be damned!" Stretch said. "That goddamned map had it wrong. What was that signboard shit supposed to mean? Why didn't they mark this place? Enough for ten herds."

"Looks like they came a different way than we did. A few miles on the flat don't mean much."

"Who gives a shit!" Stretch was back in what passed for a good mood. They rode down to the pool to water their horses, then started back to the herd. Stretch was delighted with what she thought of as her discovery. "Imagine us frettin' over a fuckin' mudhole. They ought to name that pool after me, Big Boy."

Morgan didn't tell her that the pool at the bottom of the split was probably known to dozens of people. The Indians that hunted over this country, gone now, would have known about it. A good guess was that the oldtime Spanish did, too, as well as other odd travelers since then.

They were climbing up from shadow to sunlight when Stretch looked back. "Even if I wasn't a wanted woman they'd never name it after me. You notice they never name anything after a woman. Move it, Big Boy! We ain't got all day."

There was enough light left to drive the horses down to the pool though they had to take it slow. Getting the wagons down was the hardest part. Lester took over the reins from Molly, but even then the big freight wagon lurched and swayed, threatening to overturn, before it got to the bottom.

For a while, there was no need to watch the horses. The pool was wide and deep, and the horses, frantic at first, grew calm as they drank the clear, cool water. While the horses were drinking, they built a rope corral around the open end of the pool and strung it to both sides of the chasm. That way the horses were free to drink during the night.

This was the first night they didn't have to guard the herd too closely. The camp was sheltered from the wind, there was plenty of good-tasting water, and it would have been a pleasant place to spend the night if the circumstances had been different. It could be worse, Morgan thought.

He changed his mind when Pretty Woman handcuffed him and Molly so Stretch could sleep, though that wasn't actually explained. Pretty Woman never said anything. All she did was gesture with her gun, pointing them toward the wagon. Stretch trusted Pretty Woman to do anything, but didn't want to leave her without support.

Jimmy and Lester watched the herd for the first watch. Soon everyone in camp was asleep except Morgan and Pretty Woman. Lying flat with his eyes closed, Morgan pretended to sleep. Everything was quiet except for the snoring of Stretch and the cook. Carlos made the most noise, but Stretch gave him plenty of competition.

Morgan was dozing when he heard voices at the fire—Sister and Ned. He couldn't turn around all the way because of the goddamn handcuffs, but he was close enough to hear most of what they were saying. Ned's polite voice was clearer than Sister's. Ned was saying he hoped she was feeling better.

Sister said, "Much better, thank you, Ned."

"It won't be so bad. You'll see," Ned said. "It's been a very bad time for all of us."

"Yes, it has, Ned."

Ned said, "Stretch told me I must look after you. I hope you don't mind."

"If it's not too much trouble," Sister said.

Morgan smiled in spite of all. Kindly doctor with nervous patient, or concerned minister with troubled member of his flock. Looked like the two misfits were getting on like a house afire. Maybe there was something there he could work on. Stretch had taken Sister's rifle and pistol away from her, but Ned still had his. It wasn't that he didn't know a thing about guns, he simply was afraid of guns. That much was obvious from the way he carried the rifle, holding it far forward on the stock so the muzzle always pointed skyward. His pistol was also a menace to him. Afraid of losing or dropping the pistol, he kept jamming it down into the holster. Maybe something there, Morgan thought again, but what?

Now Ned and Sister were talking about the things they liked to do in their other lives. Sister liked to read uplifting books, and so did Ned. But not always serious books, Sister said. Once in a while, she enjoyed a light romance. She stopped short when she said that, and Morgan could picture her blushing. "I'll never again read a romance story," she said firmly. Ned said there were plenty of things to do besides reading books. Appreciating the wonders of nature was just one of them.

Poor bastards, Morgan thought.

Molly woke up and whispered, "Are you awake, Morgan?"

"I'm awake. The Indian is watching us."

"She can't hear what I'm saying. Have you thought of anything yet?"

Morgan said, "I've been thinking till my head hurts. Nothing."

"I picked the wrong man when I picked you," Molly said. "I was sure you'd be able to handle any kind of trouble. I was wrong."

"I guess so."

Molly's handcuffs rattled as she tried to get comfortable. "Why don't you try fucking the Indian and see where that gets you?"

Oh, Lord, this was like being forced to sleep in the same bed with a wife you couldn't stand. "Pretty Woman doesn't like me."

"I don't like you either, you spineless coward. A real man would have done something by now."

"I guess so." It was bad enough to be chained up, but he had to listen to this shit, too. "Good night, Molly."

Molly's handcuffs rattled so hard, Morgan thought she was going to bring Stretch or at least the Indian down on them. "Don't you good night me," Molly raged. "I'm beginning to think I'd do better being nice to Stretch."

Morgan felt his stomach turn. "You don't want to do that."

Molly said, "Anything is better than being dead."

Chapter Ten

Morgan wondered if Molly knew what a dangerous game she was playing. She didn't start off
wiggling her ass or shoving her crotch at the
big dyke. Nothing as obvious as that, but she
didn't give her usual defiant stare when Stretch
said good morning. The handcuffs were off, and
they were eating breakfast by the fire. After a
moment's hesitation, Molly said good morning,
then busied herself with her food.

That's how it started, and it was all a mistake.
No point telling her again, even if he got the
chance. Telling Molly something she didn't want
to hear would make her even more stubborn than
she was. One of Molly's main troubles—and she
had more than a few—was the high opinion she
had of herself. Too clever by far, she just knew she
was smarter than anyone else. This was true in
some ways. Morgan knew she was pretty smart,
had gone to a private school and thought she

had people figured, but how did that compare with an animal like Stretch, a savage creature that belonged in a zoo? Yuma was a zoo, but she'd broken out of it, and now she was going to take what she wanted, no matter what pain and misery she inflicted on others. With nothing to lose, knowing her days were numbered in spite of all her bragging, she was going to do anything she pleased.

The herd moved out, well-watered and well-behaved, and they fell into the daily routine. They were coming to a bad patch of country, not as hard to get through as the desert but bad enough. The landscape was strewn with big rocks and dotted with mesquite and thornbush. There were gullies where horses could get lost. To get them out would mean backbreaking work and hours lost. Morgan knew what it would be like. One stretch of bad country was much like another.

They hadn't hit the bad stretch yet, and the herd was giving no trouble. Once in the morning and once before noon, Stretch left the herd and rode back to Molly's wagon. Both times she was back there longer than usual, and when she returned there was a faint, puzzled smile on her face. Goddamn Molly! Did she really believe she could string along somebody like Stretch? This was no dirt-scuffling yokel or middle-aged businessman she could bat her eyelashes at and have him turn into a puddle of butter. Teasing or promising more than you meant to deliver could only succeed for so long, and even the yokels and the others got tired of it in the end.

If Stretch got tired of it and realized she was being played for a fool, she'd do more than turn sulky. Morgan didn't want to think about that. It would have to be bad. Stretch wouldn't just tear her clothes off and attack her. There would have to be physical punishment and humiliation to go with it, and if Stretch did it once, it would be worse when she did it again and again. People like Stretch always got worse.

Stretch would get tired of Molly after a while. No matter how much she wanted Molly now, there would come a time when she'd want to get rid of her. With Stretch that would mean a bullet. Molly's good looks would be no good to her then. The world was full of beautiful women, and in Stretch's crazy mind she could have any of them she wanted.

The trouble he feared might not come right away. It would surely come before they got to the end of this godawful drive. Stretch was impatient and would want a payoff long before then.

Unless—and Morgan was sickened by the thought—Molly meant to go through with it.

Right now, eating the noon meal and looking at her, it was hard to tell. She made some reply when Stretch spoke to her, but no more than that. Stretch's barnyard joshing brought a wan smile that didn't last. He knew what she was up to, but did Stretch know? Ignorant as a hillbilly, the big crazy killer was no fool. Molly was buying a whole mess of trouble, and there was nothing he could do about it.

None of the others noticed. There wasn't much to notice. Ned was too busy with Sister. Jimmy and Lester had no interest. Cat Shawnessy brushed hard at her cropped black hair. Pretty Woman, sitting with half-closed eyes, didn't do anything at all. She knows, Morgan decided.

That could mean trouble for Molly if the Indian killer got jealous enough. Stretch had complete control over her, or so it seemed, but what if she

had a mind of her own? People didn't always
do what you expected. If Stretch saw the Indian
as just a brainless but useful redskin, Morgan
did not. There was intelligence behind those dark
blank eyes that seemed to see nothing. Morgan
knew they saw everything.

Early afternoon brought the start of the badlands, rugged, rocky country crossed by low hills
with sliding shale on the slopes and deep sand
in other places. Here and there, mesquite thickets blocked the way and had to be circled. It
was much hotter here than in the high country, and everybody was drinking more water. In
the heat, the fresh water in their canteens was
already warm and had a brackish taste. More and
more, as they moved on, the horses floundered
in deep, powdery sand or balked at climbing the
slopes.

In a way, Morgan was glad they had to work so
hard and were kept busy all the time. Molly had to
handle the wagon alone since Jimmy and Lester
had to stay with the herd. Stretch rode back to see
Molly only once in the long afternoon. The rest of
the time she had to keep her mind on the job. To
judge by the look on her face, the quick visit had
not been unrewarding. It was a hell of a way to
run a drive, Morgan thought.

But for all the hardship, there was only one
moment of real danger, and that came when a
diamondback struck at Lester, who was leading
his horse through a patch of rocky ground. The
snake's fangs struck Lester's boot without getting
through to the skin. Lester cried out, drew his
gun and would have fired at the snake if Morgan
hadn't yelled at him. The snake slithered away
into the rocks and there was no stampede, though
the horses closest to where this happened showed

signs of panic at the yelling and the sudden movements.

Snakes could do it. Anything could do it. Morgan sometimes thought horses liked to spook. It was a game with them, like kids pretending to be scared of ghosts. Luckily, they weren't doing it now, which didn't mean it wouldn't happen in the next five minutes. So far they'd been fortunate with the horses since they hadn't come up dry on the water. That could change.

He looked at his watch—nearly five o'clock. At least three hours to the next water. Whatever they found—if a rockfall hadn't buried it or the sun dried it up—wouldn't be anything like the water they had left behind at the pool. This wasn't a country for water; it wasn't fit for anything but snakes. Getting through here had slowed them down, and the day after wouldn't be any better.

Ned and Sister rode in Molly's wagon. Fat Luz had been put back on a horse and didn't like it. Morgan could picture Molly gritting her teeth, trying not to hear the peculiar couple's conversation. Molly was getting better at handling the wagon, but this was rocky country and he hoped she wouldn't turn it over. A broken wheel could be replaced, but if the wagon overturned and spilled its load, the dynamite was sure to be discovered. He kept trying to make some plan that would figure in the dynamite, but nothing came together. In the meantime, the box of dynamite, plainly marked, just sat there under the spare wheels and harness. No one thought to look under there, not even Stretch. The rope and stakes were carried in the back of the long wagon so they could be loaded and unloaded without wasting time. And the dynamite just sat there, protected by sandbags but likely to be discovered at any time.

Stretch remained in an even mood, yipping at the horses but yelling at no one. She even joshed Cat Shawnessy about the way she sat on a horse, saying, "Stick to it, gal. You're getting better every day." The lover wanting to share her feeling of well-being, Morgan thought. Too bad the rattler didn't sink its fangs into her instead of Lester's boot.

They found the waterhole, wide but shallow, and it didn't fill up too fast after the first bunch of horses drank from it. That's how they had to do it, letting a small bunch of horses drink while the others remained penned in a lopsided circle of rocks with too many places where they could get out. Poor though it was, it was the best place they could find anywhere close to the waterhole. The horses that had to wait were restless, kicking up and wanting to get to the water.

Jimmy and Lester cut thornbush to block the holes in the rocky circle. Morgan, Molly, Stretch and the others saw to the horses, getting them to the waterhole, waiting while they drank, then driving them out again. It wasn't easy to get them away from the waterhole before they had drunk their fill, but there was no other way to do it, no matter how balky they got.

Morgan tasted the water in the hole. It had a slight alkaline taste, but it would do as long as they didn't have to drink it for more than one night. Longer than that they would start coming down with different ailments. Strong as a horse wasn't a true saying when it came to sickness. Horses were laid low by any number of ailments, from intestinal bleeding to pneumonia.

The food and coffee tasted good after a long day with so much hard work at the end of it.

Finally, with hardly any water seeping into the hole, they had to take the water barrels from the chuck wagon and empty them into the hole. A drop in the bucket, Morgan thought. It helped, and that was the best that could be said for it.

With only one full barrel of water left, they would have to go easy on their consumption. A fair-sized barrel seemed a lot of water, but not with ten people sharing it, and then there was the coffee and the cooking. Water in canteens evaporated even with the stopper in. No shortage yet, just something to think about. It was funny to be figuring water, Morgan thought, when every day brought him and Molly closer to the final bullet.

Molly seemed to think she'd found a way to avoid that, and it might work for a while if Stretch didn't blow up in one of her demented rages. At best, Molly was just putting it off, but for her the end would be the same. Leaving Sister out of it, Stretch had absolutely no pity, and if she'd ever had any, it had long since been beaten out of her. Sister might arouse some sort of twisted pity in the lanky killer, but Molly would not. Sister was a weepy misfit and far from good-looking. Molly was arrogant and beautiful, with a rich girl's upbringing.

Stretch said she had feelings for Molly, but Morgan thought there must be a store of buried hate. Love and hate, as the wise old billygoat said, weren't so far apart. Not yet 30, Stretch wasn't that much older than Molly, but the mark of the hard life was stamped on her face.

Sitting by the fire, Molly was still going through her act of unbending, loosening up and accepting the inevitable. One way or another, Stretch was the inevitable, a fact to be faced. Molly's behavior—the quick nods, the little smiles—seemed to hint that having Stretch as her protector wasn't so bad. She played it well, Morgan had to admit. Her nods of agreement weren't too vigorous, and her smiles weren't too wide. All well and good, but how long would Stretch be satified with that? Stretch claimed to have lived the outlaw life for a lot of years, and even if it hadn't been as hard and desperate as she said, still it was the kind of life where things happened fast and decisions had to be made in a split second. Mad with hunger, Stretch would want to get to the main meal.

Molly could never understand a life like that or people like that, and that's where she was making her mistake. Morgan could picture her face when Stretch, tired of waiting, suddenly said, "Let's get to it, gal." However she said it, it would be like a mad bull charging through the bedroom door. Saying she had a headache wasn't going to put off this female bull. Submitting too late wouldn't work, not if Stretch thought Molly was trying to trick her out of the crotch rights she wanted so badly.

Right now, though, Stretch had a grip on her feelings. Her voice was a mixture of country and jailhouse. Molly spoke girls' school English, clear and polite. A funny pair, the two of them. They were pairing off here, Morgan thought—Stretch and Molly, Ned and Sister. He preferred the pairing of Ned and Sister. There was no viciousness there, no trickery, and what they said to each other was harmless. They sat away from the fire with the shadows on them, talking quietly.

Molly and Stretch were fencing; there was no other word for it. Lovestruck though she was, Stretch must have been aware of the lunge and parry in their somewhat one-sided conversation, but for now their fencing was careful. They were fencing with the covers on. So far, neither had even been nicked.

Morgan didn't mind being ignored. Anyway, how could he feel ignored when Pretty Woman was giving him all her attention? Eyes half-closed, still as a statue, cross-legged, she watched him but listened to Molly and Stretch. Not so much as a twitch betrayed her inner feelings.

Stretch was saying, "You prob'ly know I come from East Texas. Ever been there?"

Molly said no. She had been to Texas but never that far east.

"Nice country there, some of it. A lot of woods still standin'. Good huntin' in there. Wild boars and such."

Molly said she'd like to see East Texas.

"Nice country if you got money," Stretch went on. "We had kind of a ranch there. Not much land to it, more like a farm some ways. Call it what you like, it didn't amount to much. Good times we had a fair amount of livestock, horses and cattle, and a few good cotton crops. Bad times come and we was poor again."

"No, I've never been to Galveston," Molly said.

"Used to be a great town to hide out in," Stretch said. "If you had money there was nothin' too good for you. Law looked the other way and even tipped you the wink if there was outside law in town lookin' for you. Then the reformers got in an' all that changed. All of a sudden, the local law got religion an' started runnin' people out of town, the crooked bastards."

That side of life in Galveston left Molly with nothing to say, so she made polite noises.

Stretch didn't mind.

A dark shape under the chuck wagon, the cook snored like a sawmill. Odd thing, Stretch for all her quick temper never yelled at Carlos for snoring. Cooks drank and snored, no changing that. Morgan wondered how his whiskey supply was holding out and where he was hiding it. A few times, fearful but thirsty, Jimmy and Lester had poked around when the cook was asleep and Stretch was standing her watch. Nothing. Not a bottle in sight. Not a mouthful.

It was late, and Cat Shawnessy was already asleep. Ned and Sister were fussing with their blankets. Ned, a queer and a gentleman, didn't set his roll too close to Sister. Stretch and Molly continued to talk, still not quite at ease with each other but friendler than they had been, and even when Stretch moved a little closer to Molly, she remained the well-mannered gentleman caller.

Stretch had been yawning. Now she stood up and told Molly it was time to get some sleep. "I hate to cuff you, gal, but it's more to keep you out of trouble. Big Boy keeps lookin' for a way to start trouble. Can't do it, but just the same he keeps thinkin' on it. If he starts talkin' trouble and you don't want to hear it, sing out and I'll deal with him. You hear what I'm sayin', Big Boy?"

"I hear it," Morgan said.

"Hear it good," Stretch said. "This good gal ain't interested in nothin' you got to say. Just leave her be."

"Sleep good, gal," Stretch said to Molly: "Won't be long we'll be havin' this arrangement."

"Here we are again," Morgan said after Pretty Woman handcuffed them and left. Later they would have to stand guard with Stretch and

Pretty Woman. Molly didn't answer at first, and Morgan didn't much care. If she wanted to be a bitch, let her.

"Didn't you hear what Stretch said?" she asked after yawning several times. "She doesn't want you talking to me. I don't either."

"Then why are you?" Morgan said wearily.

"Because you spoke to me. Nothing you say means anything."

Molly was determined to pick a fight with him. After dodging around Stretch for hours, maybe it loosened up the tension, lighting into somebody she had no reason to fear. He didn't especially mind that, except the tension would be there the next time she saw Stretch. It vibrated between them like a telegraph wire.

Morgan didn't say anything. Molly said angrily, "I saw you tonight. You were listening like a snoop at a keyhole. Why didn't you go and talk to your friend Dallas?"

"Dallas was asleep. You should get some sleep if you're going to stand watch."

"Don't tell me what I should do. You've forfeited the right to even suggest."

Pretty high-toned talk, Morgan thought. He listened to the scratching sounds made by some small night animal. Stretch and Carlos were snoring their nightly serenade.

"Listen to me," Morgan said. "You're getting in over your head and there's nothing I can do to help you. You go on with this and you're going to get yourself killed. Me, too, I'm sorry to say."

"Hah! Still thinking of no one but yourself. What am I doing, if I may ask? Come on, Big Boy, tell me."

"You're trying to outfox that demented woman. It can't be done. She'll turn on you."

Molly didn't stop to think about it. "Would any-thing I do make any difference?"

She had him there. "I don't know," he said slowly. "You don't have to encourage her."

"That's no answer. If she wanted to . . . to take me, is there anything to stop her?"

Another one he couldn't answer. "I guess not."

"I guess not," she mimicked him. "Can't you give a simple yes or no? I'll give you the answer. She can do anything she likes. Your friend Dallas isn't going to help us. No one's going to help us. What I'm doing is all I can think of. I'm taking a chance, but it's better than no chance at all. Look, Morgan, we don't have many days left. What is it? About a week?"

"More or less. Crossing the desert will be the hardest part."

"Whatever it is, there isn't much time. I'm hoping to play her along until we're close to the fort; then I'm going to make a break for it. The soldiers will wipe them out if they don't give up."

"You'll never make it," Morgan said. "She'll send the Indian after you. You can't outride the Indian."

"It's my life." Molly said it so softly that he could barely hear.

"And if you can't play her along that far?" Morgan didn't think she could.

"Then I'll submit. I've seen enough of that in Yuma. It won't shock me so much. Anything to stay alive. You're on your own in this."

Morgan had no more questions. Nobody could blame her for wanting to go on living, no matter what the price. In a way, she had no choice. There were two ways she could go, easy or hard, and she still wouldn't have a choice. The third choice—the one she wouldn't even think about—was killing herself.

Molly said in a whisper, "Even if I stay on her good side, I can't plead for you, Morgan. It would spoil any chance I have. She intends to kill you and all the others. If she lets me live, if she decides to take me along after she gets the money, I'll accept that, too."

"She won't kill the Indian," Morgan said. "You'll always have the Indian watching you. No chance to escape."

"Perhaps I can persuade her to get rid of the Indian."

"Only one way she can do that. Pretty Woman won't just walk away.

"I know that. Stretch will have to kill her. Then there will be just the two of us."

"What then?"

"I'll find a way to kill her," Molly whispered. "If there's any of the money left by then, I'll go back home and try to save something. I won't let anything destroy my life. . . ."

Molly's voice trailed off, and he knew she was asleep. There was a hardness in her he admired even as he was put off by it. If anybody deserved to die, surely it was Stretch, but the way Molly talked of killing her was so casual. He got the feeling that Molly would kill Stretch even if she got a chance to turn her in. And he wasn't sure she wouldn't claim the reward money.

Morgan woke when he heard Jimmy and Lester coming in from their watch, so he must have been asleep for hours. Molly didn't stir. Stretch turned out when she heard the rattle of the coffeepot. With Pretty Woman trailing behind, she came over to the wagon, poked Molly awake, unlocked the handcuffs and handed her a damp kerchief. "Get some of the dirt off, gal, and you'll feel better."

Molly rubbed her face. "Let me do it, gal," Stretch said, taking the kerchief. "Alongside the crease of your nose there's a big smudge." Molly allowed her face to be cleaned.

Stretch saw Morgan looking up at her and gave him a playful kick in the leg. It hurt just the same. "Well, looka here, Big Boy is back from the land of dreams. Bet I can tell what you was dreamin' about. What you was goin' to do to me should you get the chance. Am I right?"

She turned to Molly without waiting for an answer. "Get a move on, gal. We got horses to look after."

"What about me?" Morgan asked.

Stretch said, "You get to sleep in tonight, Big Boy. Herd is quiet, so I don't need you. Us gals goin' to lazy around out there an' have ourself a nice talk. Come on, Pretty. You, too. Big Boy ain't goin' to break no wagon spoke or fiddle no Yuma handcuffs."

Morgan looked after the three women.

Chapter Eleven

Morgan wrapped his hand around the chain of the handcuffs and pulled. The spoke didn't budge, wouldn't turn in its socket. He tried again and pulled on the chain until the veins stood out on his forehead and he was gasping for breath. No good. Wheel hoop and spoke were fashioned from seasoned wood, nearly as hard as rock. Hours of working with a good knife would have pried the spoke loose, but there was no knife and no time.

The handcuffs were the new kind that clicked shut and had to be opened with a key. A veteran criminal would know how to pick the lock in a minute flat if he had a sliver of steel, but Morgan had nothing. Stretch wasn't fooling when she said he wouldn't break loose. With nobody guarding him, this was his first real chance, and he might as well be in a padlocked steel box and buried six feet under.

If Stretch had decided to attack Molly, while Pretty Woman watched, no sound of it came from the darkness. Nothing at all. They could have gagged her before they threw her down. Maybe nothing was going on but that "nice talk."

Sleeping soundly, the ones by the fire had guns, if he could only get to them. A short kick to the temple with a pointed boot would put anybody into a deeper sleep. That would be risky, but he couldn't even do that.

At first, he was angry at himself for not being able to think of something, but forcing himself to think with a calm mind didn't help either. All that was going to turn him loose from the goddamned wagon was the key in Stretch's pocket.

His heart beat faster when Dallas rolled out of her blankets and stood up. Jesus Christ, maybe there was a way to get loose after all. He didn't call out to her. She either was coming to him or she wasn't. But before she did anything at all, she stood still and seemed to be checking if the others were asleep. Then, after waiting for another few moments, she started toward him. Nobody had built up the fire for a long time and there were deep shadows, so he couldn't be sure if Sister had raised her head for an instant. It looked like she had, but it was too dark to be sure.

Morgan held back the blanket with his free hand, and she crawled in with him. This wasn't like the first night when his hands were free and Dallas had Stretch's permission to get fucked. Right then, fucking her was the last thing on his mind. That first night she'd seemed on the edge of doing it when he urged her to kill Stretch or give him her gun. She had been scared then, and who could blame her? Maybe she was still just as scared but had changed her mind.

"What's going on?" he asked, holding her close because she seemed to want him to. "Stretch and the Indian could come back any minute."

"Don't forget your friend Molly. She's edging over to their side. You know that. They won't be back anytime soon. I know Molly, and I know Stretch."

"They won't be out there all night," Morgan whispered, wanting a straight answer. "Are you going to do it? Get me a gun and we'll do it together. Shoot Pretty Woman in the back and I'll shoot Stretch from here."

Her answer nearly drove him crazy. If only she'd make up her mind. "But you're handcuffed," she said. "If you miss . . ."

"I won't miss. Give me your gun. You can use your rifle. They'll come walking in not expecting anything. It's a sure way of getting clear of all this."

"Clear for you and that bitch," she whispered back. "When we're clear you'll help me to get to Canada or South America—where was it?"

Morgan managed to control his impatience. It wasn't helping and it might make her balkier than she was. "There's no time to go over all that again. You have my word."

Dallas said, "I won't do it for Molly. Why should I risk my life for a selfish bitch like that? I won't do anything unless she's left out of it. Last time you said you wouldn't leave her behind."

"I've changed my mind." Morgan hoped he hadn't said it too quickly.

"Then you're not to be trusted." Dallas pressed closer to him. "If it's true, you're not. You're lying."

Oh, Lord almighty! Crazily he wondered what it would be like to live in a world without women.

"I'm not lying. I've had time to think it over. I'll go with you and leave her behind."

"Would you leave her behind dead? If I can kill the Indian, it will be no trouble to kill Molly; then you'd have to leave her behind. Say yes and I'll get ready to do it. Molly has no gun and won't be quick enough to get her hands on one."

"I don't know," Morgan said. He hadn't expected this turn of events.

"I'm not asking you to do it. I'll do it. You'll be where you are. I'll get behind the Indian and Molly, shoot the Indian and then Molly. You'll shoot Stretch at the same moment. Then I'll take the key from her pocket. Once Stretch is dead, the others will run away. That's what they'd do if she let them."

Morgan couldn't figure her. She could be dead serious. He couldn't risk trying to shoot her between the time she killed Pretty Woman and then put the gun on Molly. He could probably do it standing up, but he was lying on his back and handcuffed to a wagon. Killing her that way was out. He didn't want to kill her at all. It was just too risky.

"I don't like it," he said. Molly was as shifty as a tinhorn gambler, but he didn't want her dead.

"I knew you would never agree to that." She had his pants unbuttoned and was rubbing his cock. "You have a chance to escape and you won't take it. I wish I could inspire that sort of loyalty in a man." She unbuttoned her pants and put his hand inside. Stretch might be on her way back to camp, but his cock didn't know that. He might be edgy, but his cock wasn't. It didn't just get hard. It bulged.

"I don't see what's so special about Molly?" Morgan wondered how she could be so calm. If

Stretch caught her now, it would mean at least a bad beating. Dallas had left her gun by her blankets. She was a young, strong woman, but no match for Stretch. Even if she downed Stretch—something unlikely to happen—she'd still have the Indian to face. The Indian wouldn't use the shotgun. She'd use the knife.

"I'm just as good looking as she is," Dallas said. The way she spoke was so deliberate, as if she had all the time in the world. Morgan wanted to shake some sense of urgency into her, but she was not to be hurried even with Stretch just beyond the edge of camp. He hoped Molly and Stretch were having a nice long talk.

"I'm better looking than she is." Her hand on his cock was moving faster. He was starting to rub her clit, knowing that would shut her up for a while. How good-looking she was didn't interest him too much. He knew he was going to fuck her, handcuffs or no handcuffs, and if it got him killed, all this useless planning would be out of the way.

It wasn't so easy to fuck her in handcuffs. She would have to get in under him, closer to the wheel, and he would have only one hand for ass-squeezing and breast-squeezing. There were people who liked to fuck and be fucked in chains. Now he was going to find out what it was like. Whatever it was like, it seemed to excite her, because all of a sudden there was a bossiness about her movements that hadn't been there on that first night when she had walked directly to him, honestly and without bravado, a proud woman who wanted cock but wasn't too proud to express her need.

He had to rise up as best he could so she could wriggle under him, and he kept forgetting his left

hand was useless because it couldn't move more
than a few inches. Finally she was under him and
her pants were open and pulled down below her
knees, and so were his. She opened her legs as
wide as she could, and he got his cock into her.
If Stretch had been near there was no way she
could miss the groan Dallas let out. Morgan felt
like a man having a last fuck on a sinking ship.
One moment to the next could mean disaster.
Stretch had joked with Dallas that first night,
but there would be no joking if she caught them
fucking behind her back. But as he quickened his
thrusts and Dallas responded, Stretch wasn't as
much in his mind as she had been at first. She
was still there but not altogether so threatening,
and the smell of danger wasn't so strong. What he
smelled a lot stronger than danger was the heat
and wetness of Dallas's cunt. It was a lovely smell,
and Stretch and her meanness were no part of it.
This was the here and now, and nothing else mattered but the moment. The danger gave it spice,
heightened every feeling, made every movement
feel more important because it might be the last.
A bullet in the back could end an orgasm or pro-
long it. But nothing like that ended Dallas's first
string of orgasms, and she didn't hold back as
she did that first night. As the spasms of intense
pleasure hit her, took hold of her and lifted her,
she bucked under him as if trying to control him
as he was controlling her, keeping her pinned in
place with the driving motion of his cock. He
thought he heard something and shot his load
into her before Stretch—if that's what the sound
was—crashed down on them with her guns and
her cursing.

But it was nothing, and after he came he
wanted to come again. This time he would do it

to please himself and not be rushed. The thought of Stretch did have something to do with how he felt. He knew Dallas must be feeling the same way because she clung to him, as if using his body for protection. He listened but heard nothing except the small sounds of the night, the wind stirring the brush and small animals prowling in search of prey. Dallas kept grinding her crotch into his, and before long he was hard again. Now for some reason he was as calm as she was, thinking you can only die once and there's no use thinking about it too much. He was sure that Sister was awake, and that could mean some of the others were awake and listening as she was. But that didn't stop him, no more than the thought of Stretch had. Let them run to Stretch like kids running to Mommy. Lester was the real sneak of this sorry outfit, and he would do it quicker than anyone else. But even when nothing like that happened, he couldn't shake the feeling that Sister was listening.

They came again, and still Stretch hadn't come back. Morgan resigned himself to things as they were. He knew Dallas was going to get back to the whys and why nots of escaping, and he knew she was going to lay out some argument he didn't want to hear. If the key to the handcuffs had been in her pocket, he would have knocked her out to get it. He might have done it to get hold of her gun, but she had left the gun where he couldn't get it. Too bad she didn't trust him. Too bad she was so smart.

Knowing he was spent for the moment, she got back to the subject of Molly, the last thing he wanted to talk about. "Your plan could work if you'd just agree to kill her," she whispered.

"Why does she have to be killed?" A dumb question. The answer was because she wanted to do it.

That didn't seem like a good enough reason, and maybe she was more of a killer than she knew. Or having killed more than once, killing again wasn't such a big deal.

"She could spoil it by trying to pick up a gun. That's what she'd try to do when we started to shoot. She'd think we were trying to kill her, too. Naturally she'd want to defend herself."

Morgan said wearily, "If I know Molly, she'd throw herself flat and hug the ground and hope she didn't get hit."

"It's too big a risk," Dallas said. "I don't want to kill the Indian and then be killed by that bitch."

Morgan couldn't see what bitchiness had to do with it. "It wouldn't come to that. I know her."

"You only think you do. Even in Yuma where you have to scheme and cheat to survive she was known for her lying and scheming. Your Molly darlin' has a heart like a bullet. All this talk and you're forgetting one thing. If I don't kill her and she kills me instead you'll still be chained to this wagon. That's what you should be thinking about, not that bitch."

Morgan couldn't think of anything to say. Talking to her was like being on a merry-go-round that wouldn't stop. It wasn't going any faster; it just wouldn't stop.

"You wouldn't regret going with me," she went on. "I know you like me. You don't have to say it. We're good together, and you know it. Come with me and I promise to drive you crazy in bed for the rest of your life."

The rest of my life, Morgan thought. I'll be lucky if I see my next birthday. He got a quick crazy picture of himself and Dallas in bed at the age of 80. All he wanted to do was drink his barley water and get some sleep—and she was driving him crazy.

Dallas went on some more. "Stretch is always talking about all her big bank robberies. We're much smarter than Stretch. We could pull off a bank robbery that would set us up for the rest of our lives. My uncle is the president of a bank in Fort Worth, Texas. If we . . ."

It was getting worse. First she was going to deprive him of his sleep in his old age. Now she was trying to lead him into a life of crime. It was way past time to get rid of her.

"Before you give me a definite yes or no," she whispered, calm as before, "I am going to show you what you'll be missing if you don't come with me on my terms."

Morgan wondered what it could be that warranted such a statement. He never made light of any woman's efforts to please him, and there was nothing smart aleck in his thoughts. But all she did was suck his cock. "All" surely wasn't the right word. She sucked his cock with such loving tenderness that it might have been the first time for her. It wasn't, of course, but she made it seem so. The way she took the head of his cock into her mouth was like somebody discovering something entirely new, and even when she began to suck it with great expertise, that same feeling remained. Tense yet relaxed, enjoying every moment, he wished there was something he could do to help her. In spite of her unexplainable hatred for Molly and the people she had killed, there was something decent about her. People often used the word integrity to describe somebody, usually without much thought, but she had it in spades. Her proposal that he go away with her and rob her uncle's bank had more in it than was said.

She wanted to bind herself to someone who would see her for what she was, loving and loyal, strong but tender. Her husband, the rich man with the wandering dick, had been a fool.

At first Morgan lay still; then he began to move in time with the sucking of her mouth. She held the hilt of his cock with her forefinger and thumb while she sucked it. He could use only one hand to stroke her hair. He wanted to grip her head with both hands and move it up and down on his cock. Sensing what he wanted she began to move her head up and down until his bulging, swollen cock seemed to fill her whole mouth. Her breath was coming as hard as his, and his ass rose up to push his cock deeper into her mouth. Then with a sudden convulsion that gripped her whole body she came, though no finger or cock stimulated her clit. Morgan's jism volleyed into her mouth when he felt her coming. Unbearable tension had built up in him and he had to let go. She had come by sucking his cock, and he could tell she was happy to be able to do that. He felt good for her and for himself. He didn't know what she was going to do, and he didn't ask. They had talked themselves out and fucked themselves out, and there wouldn't be any more of either. They were, in spite of everything, some sort of friends.

All she said before she left was, "Goodbye, Morgan."

He lay on his side and watched her after she went back to her blankets and few belongings. It was too dark to see what she was doing. Some evenings he'd seen her writing in a schoolkid's copybook with the stub of a pencil. A diary of her life in Yuma? Stretch used to josh her about it. She seemed to be writing in it now. That's

what she was doing all right. He heard the sound
of a page being ripped out. And then, after a
last look around, she walked off into the darkness.

He waited. A half hour passed and nothing happened. She had been gone for most of an hour
when he heard Stretch and Molly coming back
into camp. They were talking, but Pretty Woman
was as silent as ever.

He waited for Stretch to discover that Dallas
had run out, but she was too busy talking to
Molly to even look over to where Dallas's blankets
were. Stretch had no special reason to look in that
direction, and it was likely that Dallas had fixed
the blankets so they'd look as if somebody was
under them. Come sunrise, there would be hell
to pay—that is, if Sister didn't blow the whistle
before then.

But Sister did nothing, didn't even move in her
blankets. Good for her, Morgan thought. Lester,
the sneak-faced son of a bitch, would run yowling
like a cat if he knew. So the only one who knew
was Sister. The longer start Dallas had, the better
chance she had of getting away. It was possible
that Stretch might just let her go. Dallas was a fair
hand with horses, but going after her would slow
them down. He didn't think Stretch would see it
that way. In her crazy mind, she would take it as
a personal insult. Stretch was the boss. Stretch
had gotten them out of Yuma. Nobody ran out
on her. Seen that way, it didn't look good for
Dallas.

Stretch and Molly sat by the fire, drinking coffee. Pretty Woman just sat, watching. It was too
late to bother building up the fire. Pretty soon
even Stretch would need to get some sleep.
She was in what passed with her for good

humor. Morgan wished to hell she would call it a day before she discovered Dallas had gone. All it would take was some question that only Dallas could answer, maybe something about Yuma, the details of the escape, some woman convict's name—anything. She never hesitated before waking somebody, no matter how tired they were.

But for now Molly kept her close to the fire, and there was a liveliness in her voice as she talked. As usual, Stretch did most of the talking. Right now, she was telling Molly about the first bank she robbed and how green she was at the time. "Was just a kid," she was saying. "Truth is, I never been in a bank before that. Back home we didn't have hardly enough money for sugar an' coffee, the things you got to have cash money to buy. Makes me laugh when I look back on it. Here I was without a pot to piss in, walkin' into the biggest bank in that town . . ."

Morgan couldn't hear what Molly had to say to that. When Stretch was starting in the bank business, Molly was starting her lady's education in some private school. Poor old Molly. She had let herself in for this kind of bullshit, and now she was getting it by the bucketful. Bad though it was, she might get a lot worse before this was over. Stretch talked on for a while, then stood up and told Molly, almost apologetically, that it was time to be handcuffed for the night. After Molly was in place, Stretch and Pretty Woman went into the tent, leaving Lester on guard for the short time until dawn.

Molly was silent. Morgan watched as Lester, yawning and scratching, got up and walked around with his shotgun. If he got too close to where Dallas was supposed to be sleeping he might see that she wasn't there, but all he did was sit down again. Dallas had been gone for two hours.

"Why aren't you asleep?" Molly asked, sounding peeved.

"How could I sleep with all that woman talk going on?" First light would start to glimmer in about an hour. If Dallas's absence wasn't discovered before then, she would have a three hour start. "You have a nice chat out there?"

Molly's handcuffs rattled. "No, we did not have a nice chat out there. I swear I'll go crazy if I have to listen to one more of those stories."

"Count yourself lucky. Better to be talked to death. It's slower and less painful than the other way. You bought this raffle ticket, remember?"

"I know what I'm doing."

"I hope so. She's not one to cross." Morgan wondered where Dallas thought she was headed. New Mexico was a long way east of where they were. She might make it there if Stretch didn't catch up to her or if she didn't get lost. "You making any headway with the lady?"

Molly didn't like that. "That's a dirty thing to say. I am trying to escape. It's more than you're doing, isn't it?"

True enough, he thought, and she'd said it more than once.

"I have to believe I'm going to succeed," she said.

Morgan didn't know what she hoped to succeed at. He had listened to her spin out one plan for going with Stretch after the army money was paid, then somehow getting Stretch to kill the Indian, then killing Stretch herself, then taking what money was left and making a fresh start. It was a bloody stew with too many ingredients in it, but even planning a meal like that showed her determination.

"I'm going to live through this," Molly said. "No matter what happens I am going home to rebuild my ranch. I couldn't go on if I didn't think that." Her tone of voice suggested that he wasn't taking her seriously.

"It's a good way to look at it." He had to say something or she'd get mad. "What did you talk about with Stretch?" You'd think they were a couple chatting in bed early in the morning.

"Bank robbing stories, stories about ambushing posses that were getting too close, a story about the prize bull she kidnapped and held for ransom. I doubt if she's done half the things she says she has."

"She's done enough," Morgan said.

"Whatever she's done she insists on talking about it. She's a bore."

Morgan could think of a lot of other words to describe Stretch. Only someone with Molly's background would call her a bore, especially under the present circumstances. It was something like complaining that the hangman wasn't wearing a clean shirt on that final morning.

"I'm going to sleep for a while," Molly said, trying to get comfortable.

Morgan continued to watch Lester, who couldn't seem to settle down. Maybe it was the late hour or the thought of all the ass-breaking hours in the saddle that lay ahead. Lester hated work as much as he loved to play cards with Jimmy. He fidgeted and rubbed the growth of beard on his face. He got up, looked around, then sat down again. No difference what he did, Morgan thought. They'd all know when the sun came up.

They knew a little earlier than that. A sheet of paper blew past the fire, just missing it, and snagged on one of Lester's spurs. He picked it up and stared at it in the first gray light. Then he read it again, and when he jumped up he was yelling. Stretch was out of the tent before he got to it. She snatched the sheet of paper and looked at it. Lester kept yelling, "Dallas ran out. It wasn't my fault!"

Stretch shut him up with a slap, then looked at the paper again. "Don't trust Molly," she read in a loud voice.

Chapter Twelve

"Gone! How can she be gone?" Stretch stomped up and down in a rage. "The rotten bitch! The dirty cunt! I got her out of Yuma and she does *this!* We got money cookin', money that'd take us far outta this fleabite territory. Fuck her! She won't get away with it."

She waved her arms and drew her gun. Pretty Woman tried to give her a mug of coffee, but she knocked it out of her hand.

"I'm sorry, Pretty," she said. An instant later she started up again. Everybody stayed out of her way. Nobody was guarding the herd. This was big trouble. Anything that got Stretch this mad was big trouble.

"You have anything to do with it, you sneaky bastard?" Her finger was pointing in Morgan's face. "You show her the way with your big cock?"

"I was asleep," Morgan told her. "You told me to sleep. I was cuffed to the wagon."

"I'd like to chain your balls to the wagon." She crumpled up the paper with Dallas's warning on it and threw it in his face. "You tell her to write that? Don't Trust Molly."

"Why would I tell her to write that? I didn't even talk to her last night."

Sister looked at Morgan but said nothing. He had a friend there, at least not an enemy.

"I'm not talkin' about last night, shitface. The night of your big fuck with her. You tell her then?"

Morgan said, "I didn't tell her anytime."

"I think you put her up to it," Stretch said furiously. "Maybe it's time to punch your ticket, Big Boy. I'm sick of your lookin' and schemin'. I'm goin' to think real hard about you."

Luz and Cat got it next. Ned and Sister were left out of Stretch's tirade. "What good are you, lettin' her sneak off like that? Didn't you hear nothin'? How can you sleep so fuckin' sound?"

"There was nothing to hear," Cat said.

Cat was as sly as her name, Morgan thought. She even looked a little like a cat. She tried to stay out of trouble.

Stretch gave her a terrifying look. "You sleep like you was home in bed. Don't you know you're on the run and will hang if they catch you? You got to keep one eye open, dimwit. How could you not hear that cunt sneakin' off? Me, I can hear the fuckin' snow fall."

Luz got the least abuse. Most of Stretch's rage was spent by then. " 'Course you didn't see or hear nothin', you sack of guts. I don't know why I waste my breath on lamebrains like you."

Pretty Woman had slipped away and was back. Stretch had to bend down so the Indian could whisper in her ear. "You sure?" Stretch asked.

Pretty Woman nodded. Suddenly Stretch was smiling. "Well, will you listen to this? The cunt don't have a horse. She lit out without a horse. She's afoot. How far does she think she'll get? Depends what time she took off, the kind of start she's got. I would think she wouldn't leave too late. Three or four hours, maybe. That's just down the road."

Pretty Woman stood waiting.

"Go after her, Pretty," Stretch said, "and don't be bringin' her back. Would never trust her again. Don't hurry with the doin' of it. You can catch up with us easy. Let her repent a bit before she goes."

The Indian's cow pony was already saddled. She ran to it and raced away.

They broke camp and moved out. Too bad about Dallas, Morgan thought. She was gambling that Stretch wouldn't come after her, a bad bet any way you looked at it. She should have known that Stretch just wouldn't let her go. She should have figured that Stretch would send the Indian after her. The gamble was that Stretch wouldn't want to be without the only person she trusted. She might have won if not for Pretty Woman. Stretch thought she could spare her for as long as it took to catch up to Dallas and torture her to death.

Morgan wondered what drove Dallas to leave the message for Stretch. Dallas didn't like Molly, and neither did some of the others. Even as a captive, Molly looked down her nose at people and got their backs up without even trying.

Up ahead, a horse had broken a leg and Morgan had to kill it with his big Bowie. Stretch gave the knife to Jimmy and he gave it to Morgan. Both of them held their guns on Morgan while he was

killing the horse. Taking no chances, Stretch got
the knife back through Jimmy, but Morgan knew
she wasn't feeling as safe as if Pretty Woman had
been there. There must have been a time when
she depended on nobody, and if Yuma hadn't broken her, it might have damaged her in ways she
didn't realize. If she did know that her nerve had
cracked a little, she would strive to bury any such
thoughts. Despite all her boasting and bragging,
she did depend on the Indian.

Right now, Morgan saw no way to get at her.
She was good with a gun, and she didn't take her
eyes off him for long.

Ned and Sister had been put back on horses,
and now Luz rode in the wagon, not beside Molly
but behind her. Morgan hadn't heard Stretch tell
Luz to kill Molly if she made a false move, but
he knew the order had been given. Luz, the pious
whore, had killed a customer for pissing on a
statue. Killing Molly wouldn't be as important
as that.

Pretty Woman had left not long after first light.
Now they were eating the noon meal. Morgan
knew everyone was thinking about Dallas. Nobody
said anything, but it was in their faces. Stretch
looked at Molly, then looked away. Things weren't
working out so well for Molly, after all. If she
hadn't started playing up to Stretch, the warning
from Dallas wouldn't have meant so much. Dallas
wanted to do Molly dirt and rile up Stretch at the
same time, and that's just what was happening.

The next patch of bad country they were
laboring through was hard on the horses. Morgan
thought maybe Dallas was smart not to take a
horse. Anyway, it wouldn't have been easy. Just
the same, she was going to need a horse if
she made it out of this country. Ten to one

she wouldn't. Yuma had toughened her some,
but Pretty Woman was tougher. A mountain or
desert Apache would be tougher than any white
woman. An Apache woman didn't need Yuma to
make her hard. Life in the sunbaked, half-starved
Indian camps would do that.

Dallas was as good as dead. She had taken
three canteens, her own and two stolen from Sister and Ned. Morgan wondered if they'd heard
her. If they had, they didn't tell Stretch. Morgan
had seen Ned sneaking two spare canteens from
the wagon before they started out.

Stretch stayed angry and restless as the afternoon wore on. Pretty Woman had been gone for
close to 11 hours, and there was no sign of her
yet. Even when you figured in the bad terrain she
had to cross and Dallas's three or four hour start,
she should have been back by now. It was good
not to have to look at her, Morgan thought.

Stretch didn't share the sentiment. She kept
looking, shading her eyes with her hat, and she
cursed the dust for making it hard to see. But
even as she did that, she never let Morgan get
too far away.

The two trips she made to the freight wagon were short, and when she came back, her
face had a stiff look to it. Molly wasn't in the
doghouse yet, but she was getting there. At the
moment, Stretch was more concerned about why
Pretty Woman was taking so long to return. Once
she got back, Morgan knew, Stretch would start
thinking more about Molly.

They found the water where it was marked on
the map. A few evergreens grew nearby, always a
sign of water. The water here was a spring that
formed a pool and ran off to nowhere. No circle
of rocks here, they had to sweat building rope

corrals. It was well after dark when the horses were corralled and they settled down to eat.

Everybody but Stretch had a hearty appetite; she just picked at her food. The cook was drunk, but he regarded her with some anxiety. Ned talked quietly to Sister while Jimmy and Lester played cards on a blanket. Cat and Luz did nothing but doze in the heat of the fire. Morgan noticed that Molly was sitting closer to him than she usually did. What good she thought that would do her he didn't know.

But Stretch paid Molly no heed. She kept walking out past the firelight so she could see better. Morgan didn't know what she expected to see in the dark. Pretty Woman had been gone going on 16 hours. It stayed dark, but Stretch kept on looking.

Later, the moon broke through, and Stretch finally could look with some expectation of seeing something. The way she walked in and out of camp, muttering to herself, scared the others into silence. Ned and Sister stopped talking. Lester and Jimmy put away the cards. No one dared sleep because Stretch might take offense. So they fidgeted and yawned, not knowing what she'd call on them to do. Form a search party? Build the fire into a beacon? But they all knew the Indian would find her way back—if she could, if she wasn't dead or injured, if she hadn't gone over the hill like Dallas.

Morgan liked the picture he had of Pretty Woman lying dead with the buzzards picking at her. Far more likely she was heading home, back to the southern deserts and mountains where her people lived, some on reservations, others as hunted animals on both sides of the border. But if she wanted to head

home, why hadn't she done it after she broke
out of Yuma, which was in the far south,
a good distance from Apache country but a
lot closer than where she was now? Or if
she'd been swept along with Stretch and the
others in the first desperate dash for freedom, why hadn't she slipped away on the way
north?

Just the same, it looked like she'd run out
on Stretch. Morgan wondered if Stretch was
thinking the same thing. Not yet, it looked
like. There was more concern than anger in
her face. Morgan knew the anger would surge
out eventually but not until she was sure she'd
been left holding the dirty end. Then there
would be hell to pay, and who knows who
was going to get jumped on? First Dallas, then
Pretty Woman. Stretch would want to take it
out on somebody. Morgan thought he was a
likely candidate, with Molly a close runner-up,
but she might take it into her head to shoot
poor old Sister because she was no good for
anything. She might shoot the cook because he
snored.

Coming back into camp—she'd been standing
in the dark for a long time—she told everybody
not with the herd to get some sleep. Lester,
watched by Stretch, handcuffed Morgan and
Molly to the wagon and was left to guard them.
Stretch went into the tent. It remained as quiet
as it had been.

Molly spoke first. "Do you think Pretty Woman
has deserted?"

"I hope so," Morgan said. "It might give us a
chance with Stretch. It might give us less of a
chance. She's working herself up to do something."

Molly thought for a minute. "Dallas is to blame for this. I hope the Indian kills her."

"I'd rather have the Indian gone. If Stretch doesn't go wild over it, maybe she'll settle down."

"I don't like the way she looks at me," Molly said.

"The way she looks at me isn't any better," Morgan said.

"What if she takes Dallas's warning seriously?"

As well she might, Morgan thought but didn't say. Molly wasn't one to be trusted. She was in trouble and he was her friend again.

"She may decide it's just spite. Then you're back in business."

Molly doubted that. "I don't think she'll ever trust me."

"It was dumb to think you could make her."

Sitting with his rifle across his knees, Lester was craning his neck, trying to hear what they were saying. But he was too far away and their voices were too low. Stretch was snoring, as was the cook.

Molly didn't like to be called dumb, but she let it pass. "I was trying to do *something*."

Morgan had a thought. "What were Stretch and Pretty Woman like in Yuma? I've seen Pretty Woman going into the tent and sometimes staying for hours. You think it's to guard Stretch or the other thing? You know."

"Stretch had a lot of girls in prison. Pretty Woman was one of them, maybe more so than the others. So was Cat. Even then Pretty Woman did things for Stretch. I know she killed a big rough woman who stole food from Stretch. The guards smuggle in food and sell it. Stretch had the money to buy some, but the woman stole it. Pretty Woman killed her, stabbed her in the dark.

No one got too excited about it. The woman was a real menace."

"Why didn't Stretch kill her herself?"

"She intended to. Pretty Woman did it first as a favor. I mean, Stretch didn't tell her or ask her to do it. They weren't so close then."

"And later?" Morgan was getting a picture of the loudmouth Stretch and the silent Indian. Pretty Woman did what she was told to do, not because she was afraid but because she wanted to. She was the stronger of the two but would follow Stretch anywhere. No wonder Stretch was fretting.

"Tell me about Cat," Morgan said. "You can forget Luz."

"Cat was sentenced to life imprisonment for poisoning her mother—not her stepmother, her real mother. Her father was dead and the mother was the only one who stood between Cat and some money. It can't have been much. The mother and father had a music academy in Phoenix. Father, the violin. Mother, the piano."

"What's she like?" It was time to cut in on this family history.

Molly snorted, not a ladylike sound. "What do you mean? You're not thinking of . . . ? Wasn't Dallas enough for you?"

Morgan said, "Nothing like that. I was thinking if Pretty Woman is gone for good, Stretch will have to get herself another woman as a steady bedmate. Cat has to be it. I can't see her choosing Sister or Luz."

"She won't choose me. She's suspicious of me."

"She wouldn't want you as a steady," Morgan said, then stopped, not wanting to say any more.

Molly said it for him. "You mean she can take me as many times as she wants, then throw me aside like soiled lavatory paper. Her steady would be more like a regular wife. Yes, I can see where Cat would suit her very well. Don't you think so, Morgan? Of course you do. You suggested it. Cat for wife, Molly for slut!"

"Calm down. Nothing's happened to you yet." Molly's voice was starting to rise. Lester, busy rolling a cigarette, looked over at them. Stretch came out of the tent, saying, "Who's that talking out there?"

Lester pointed with his cigarette. "Them over there. Molly and Big Boy."

"I thought maybe Pretty was back," Stretch said quietly. Then she let out a yell loud enough to spook the horses. "You hear me over there. Shut your fuckin' mouths and go to sleep. I'm tryin' to listen."

A few minutes later she was snoring again.

Morgan whispered, "Best we do like she says. We'll get out of this. Good night, Molly."

"Good night, Morgan," Molly whispered back. "I'm glad you're so optimistic. I'm not."

Morgan wasn't optimistic. He just wanted Molly to get some sleep. Next time they roused Stretch from her slumbers might get them kicked until the big dyke was too tired to go on. So let the vicious bitch sleep. The time she slept was the only bearable part of the day.

But she was up and out again before first light. Lying still, Morgan heard her building up the fire and slamming down the coffeepot. She poured coffee and walked out of camp. The sun was coming up.

She came back, and the yelling started. "Everybody up! Up! Up! Up! Roll out, you sons of bitches! You got five minutes to eat and then we're on our way! Lester, you lousehead, get Big Boy and Lady Molly on their feet."

Morgan got up stiff from lying too long in the same position, but he managed to dodge a kick Stretch aimed at him. He knew this was going to be a real bitch of a day. "You lost a good horse yesterday," she yelled at him. "Lose another, you careless fuck, and you'll be destroyed along with the horse."

Morgan drank coffee and chewed on a biscuit. No point heaping a plate and then having it slapped out of his hand.

Molly got some hard looks, but that's all she got. Nightfall might see her naked and beaten, but for now Stretch let her take her place on the wagon box with fat Luz behind her. Luz smelled. They all smelled, but Luz smelled worse. They started out after the horses drank.

Stretch was all business today, as if she felt herself slipping and wanted to regain absolute control. There wasn't a person who wasn't called down for something. Lester and Jimmy weren't showing enough energy. Cat was daydreaming instead of watching the horses. Ned and Sister were just fuckin' hopeless.

Morgan got most of the shit. It was like she was blaming him for Pretty Woman's disappearance. This wasn't said, but he thought he knew the way her mind worked. Fucking Dallas had got her all dissatisfied, and that's why she ran. Pretty Woman had to be sent after her and hadn't come back. So whatever had happened to Pretty Woman was all Morgan's fault.

Stretch didn't want to mention Pretty Woman, so she lit into Morgan for anything she could think of. A lot of what she said made no sense, and Morgan tried not to listen. She caught on to that and yelled all the harder. Morgan knew how a recruit must feel when a mean sergeant got down on him. "Grin and bear it" didn't apply here. Morgan didn't feel like grinning. Besides, it wasn't allowed.

Stretch kept at it even when she should have shut up. They had to find a way across a deep gully that slashed through from north to south. There was no way to get across where they were. The gully was too deep, the crumbling sides too high. Stretch yelled at Morgan to look at the fuckin' map. Morgan said she had the map. Nothing about the gully was marked on the map, and that brought a fresh torrent of abuse. Only a shitfaced, so-called boss of the drive would start out without a proper map.

It was worse than being married to a nagging wife. Morgan could joke with himself in the grimmest situations, but now his humor was wearing thin.

They had to leave the herd where it was while they looked for a place to cross. Stretch rode with Morgan, the first time they'd gone anyplace without Pretty Woman. They rode south along the lip of the gully for about 200 yards. Morgan kept looking for a chance to jump Stretch. If he could knock her cold or kill her, he figured he could run and crawl through the brush until he got behind Molly's wagon. Luz was perched high on the wagon load and the only way to down her was to kill her. If the shot started the herd running, fuck it!

But he didn't get to do any of that. Stretch stayed away from him, the gun in her hand. Farther down, the gully broke apart and widened out. They rode back to the herd with Stretch staying behind him all the way.

Getting the herd across in the wide place wasn't so hard. Morgan braced himself for trouble as the horses clattered over scattered rocks on the floor

of the gully, but the horses made it up the other
side without breaking any legs. Morgan didn't
know if Stretch would carry out her threat to
shoot him if another horse had to be destroyed.
It was one of those questions he couldn't answer.
Sure as sunrise, she was capable of it.

That night she made them build not one fire
but three, real signal fires that lit up a whole
patch of country. As soon as a fire started to
burn down, she yelled at them to pile on more
brush. They kept chopping and tearing up brush
until their hands were sore and swollen, and still
that wasn't enough for her. Another fire had to
be built.

The herd was penned in a wide gully with a
rockfall at the north end. Ned and Sister and
Luz, too fat to work, watched the open end where
a rope fence had been built. None of the three
misfits could have done a thing if the horses came
charging out.

Stretch must have known the herd was being
neglected, but she didn't care. Molly was more
worried about the horses than she was. Morgan
knew she still hoped somehow to get the 10,000
dollars from the army. Why not? Better to hope
than to give up. He had to give her that much.
She wasn't just a schemer, she was a fighter.

Evening turned into night with still no sign of
the missing woman. Stretch let them eat long past
suppertime but didn't eat herself, just drank one
cup of coffee after another. Once she roused the
cook from his nightly stupor and told him to
bring some food to the three shitfaces standing
watch. Carlos ran as fast as his rheumatic legs
would carry him.

Finally, getting herself under some sort of control, she told them they could get some sleep

after they topped up the fires one last time. After that was done to her satisfaction, she walked off into the darkness, but before she left she made sure Morgan and Molly were securely handcuffed to the wagon. Tonight it was Jimmy's turn to guard them, and he settled down with a pack of cards that he kept shuffling, teaching himself some crooked deals.

Molly slept, but Morgan waited for Stretch to come back.

Chapter Thirteen

First light was glimmering when Stretch walked into camp with Pretty Woman slung over her shoulder. The Indian's eyes were closed, and her cropped black hair was clotted with blood. Her hands, arms, shirt and pants were caked with dried blood, and hanging from the back of her belt was a blood-soaked hairy thing that, even at a distance, Morgan recognized as a human scalp.

Dallas's scalp—what else could it be?

Lester, Jimmy and Cat were by the fire. Ned, Sister and Luz were still standing guard. No one had relieved them. During the night, after Stretch had been gone for hours, there had been fear and confusion. This got worse as time passed and Stretch hadn't returned. Unable to move, Morgan heard Lester and Jimmy talking by the fire, ignoring Cat completely. Morgan couldn't make out what they were saying, but he didn't have to.

171

Half-convinced that they were the new bosses of this outfit, they were badgering the cook for a bottle when Stretch walked out of the dark like an avenging angel with a dead soul on her shoulder. Lester and Jimmy stood like bad boys caught in a naughty act. The cook got behind the chuck wagon, and Cat didn't move.

Ignoring everyone, Stretch walked to the tent and pushed her way inside. When she came out a few minutes later, her face was drawn with fatigue, her eyes bright with anger. She hated nobody and everybody. She hated the world. "You there." She snapped her fingers and Cat jumped. "Get them three fools in here. Never mind the herd, just get them in here!"

Nothing else was said until Cat shooed Sister, Ned and Luz into camp. Morgan and Molly had been freed and were waiting with the others. No sound came from the tent. The cook was rousted out of his hiding place when Stretch caught him peeping around the end of the chuck wagon.

"I found Pretty and brought her in," Stretch said. "I don't know how she is. Comes to, can talk sensible as anybody, then blacks out agin. Dallas was afoot and Pretty tracked her easy. Caught up to Dallas in a flat place with no cover. Should have waited, but she didn't. I don't know why. They traded shots. Dallas got killed. Pretty got creased. Came to. Getting dark. Pretty crawled over to Dallas and . . ."

Stretch reached behind, took Dallas's scalp from her belt and shook it in their faces.

Cat vomited. The others looked sick but stood their ground. Ned put his arm around Sister, and the cook crossed himself. Stretch threw the scalp into the fire, where it flamed and sputtered. She watched it until it dissolved into ash.

"Now listen to me," Stretch said. "You're all goin' to help get Pretty well. Took me half the night to find that gal. Horse got killed in the shootout. That Dallas sure could shoot. Pretty was crawlin' back here. Come to when I found her, put water on her face, could talk. Blacked out again. We ain't goin' to move no herd today and maybe not tomorrow. Then, if Pretty looks better, we'll make a bed in the back of the wagon and she can travel comfortable."

Morgan thought of the dynamite.

"You know anythin' about doctorin'?" Stretch asked Ned. "You been to schools back East."

"I studied bookkeeping," Ned said.

Cat said without being asked, "I just know music."

Stretch spat out her disgust. "Bookkeepin' an' music! That's what we need to doctor a sick woman." She gave Molly a flat stare but didn't ask her anything. "What about you, Big Boy? You know anythin' about head injuries?"

"Not a lot," Morgan said. "She could have a concussion. I'd have to look at her."

"What's this concussion?"

"An injury to the brain. Happens when the brain is jarred by a hard blow. A bullet crease could do it. I'd have to look at her."

"Look at what?"

"Her eyes. If they're blood-streaked, it could mean concussion."

"How bad is this concussion?"

"It can be serious," Morgan said. "It depends. I'm telling you I don't know that much about it. What you described sounds like concussion."

Stretch stared at him. "You ever have it? That why you know about it?"

"A friend took a fall and hit his head on a rock.

The doctor explained it to me. Can be serious or mild. My friend's case was mild. Best thing for it is rest. Not a lot else you can do for it."

Stretch asked the big question. "Can you die from it?"

"I don't know about dying. Doc did say there can be lasting damage to the brain if the patient doesn't rest long enough and gets up too soon. My guess is you could die from it."

Stretch's gun came out fast. "Pretty better not die from it, Big Boy. Take a look and tell me what you think. Better be straight talk."

Sister spoke up. "I'll help, Mr. Morgan. My mother used to be a nurse. I've watched her."

"Come along then," Stretch told her. "The rest of you see to the herd. Don't make me have to find you, cookie. Warm up water to wash the blood off."

Pretty Woman lay on her back on the folding cot. The tent had the sickly smell of old blood. Morgan told Sister to hold the flap open so he could see better; then he peeled back the unconscious woman's eyelids and bent down to look at them. Tiny blood vessels were broken at the top curve of the eyeballs.

"Looks like concussion," he told Stretch. "You want me to look at the wound?"

"Do it," Stretch said. "It's a deep crease."

So it was. "The doctor put ice wrapped in towels on my friend's head," Morgan told Stretch. "Cool cloths will have to do here. After Sister washes her off, she should be kept quiet. Somebody should stay with her so she won't roll off the bed."

"Don't worry about that, Big Boy. That'll be taken care of."

Sister had gone to fetch the basin of warm

water. Morgan thought it was funny, Stretch telling him not to worry about the Indian. He recalled his thought about the buzzards.

When Sister came back with the basin, it was too crowded in the tent. Morgan went outside, followed by Stretch, who had holstered her gun but kept her hand on it.

"This friend. For how long did he have to stay in bed?" Stretch's hand didn't move from the butt of her gun.

"A week to be on the safe side, the doctor said. It worked."

"You're telling me Pretty should stay in bed for a week?" Stretch regarded Morgan with deep suspicion.

"I'm telling you what the doctor said about my friend. I don't know how long she should stay in bed. A week may not be long enough. You're the one has to decide. She's your friend."

Stretch said, "You think we should hang around here a week so the Rangers can catch up? Don't play the fox, Big Boy. I can see right through you."

Without waiting for an answer, Stretch gestured Morgan toward the fire. Then she called the cook over. "Coffee for him, coffee for me," she told Carlos. "Don't get between me and him."

Still taking no chances of being jumped. Morgan picked up the mug of coffee. "The Rangers are your business. You have to decide."

Stretch held her mug with her left hand. "The first Rangers show, you're dead. They won't bargain, so you're dead." The coffee was bitter, boiled and reboiled, but she drank it anyway. "All right. We'll stay two or three days and see what happens with Pretty. What about the horses? Think they's enough water to hold them?"

"I'll have to look. This was a one-night camp. If the water comes in too slow, what then? The herd'll die if you don't move on."

Another time she might have given him a sly smile, letting him know she was on to his tricks. She always liked to prove how smart she was, but there was no smile now, just a hard stare. "Let me decide about the herd. It gets past three days, then I'll decide. A bed of blankets would soften the joltin' of the wagon."

Morgan said nothing. Stretch was trying to decide between her Indian and the 10,000 dollars. That's how she was, moods swinging back and forth. Not 30 minutes before, she was ready to let the herd rot. Now she was back to thinking of the money.

"Go and look at the water," Stretch said. "But you'll do it with handcuffs on."

Morgan said, "I can't do it right with handcuffs."

"Sure you can," Stretch said. "I figure you won't try to run long as Molly has a gun in her back, but I don't want to tempt you. Even a man of honor such as you are gets tempted. You could've run a lot of times. I don't know if you could've outrode Pretty. Maybe you could."

Morgan drank the rest of his coffee.

"Surprised you let yourself be took in by Molly. Poor ol' dead Dallas, may she rot in hell, was right. Don't trust Molly is a good rule for anybody has to deal with her. Day or two back she changed her tune and started givin' me sweet little shy smiles, like butter wouldn't melt in her cunt. You think I didn't twig what she was up to?"

Stretch twigged all right, Morgan thought, but she liked it at the time. With just a little more coaxing she thought Molly would drop her drawers and not have them ripped off. Hard-bitten Stretch wanted hearts and flowers, a real romance, and now she'd decided it wasn't going to be that way. Poor Stretch. One hell of a shame.

"Anybody'd be a fool to trust Molly," she went on, giving him her newfound wisdom. "You're a fool, Big Boy. You think she wouldn't be a stranger to you if she got on the right side of me?"

"You're just going by what Dallas said."

"Not one bit, fool. You're just tryin' to make it easier for her. You haven't gone soft on her, have you? Don't think so. You like fuckin' too much to settle for one woman. You gave her your word when you hired on with her. Not in words, no sir, Big Boy, but you gave it just the same. Now you're stuck with it. You think you're a great big hard man that knows what's what, but you won't let Molly down, long as they's breath in your body, which may not be all that long. Say it ain't so."

Morgan said, "The hell with Molly!"

"You're a bad liar, Big Boy. Maybe I can do without the handcuffs. Go on, fool. Check the water."

Sister came out of the tent saying, "I washed the wound. I'll need something to cut her clothes off before I wash her all over."

Stretch handed her Morgan's Bowie knife. "See that knife don't slip. I'll be watching you good."

Morgan checked the water source and thought it would hold up. It might run low in the full heat of summer, but that hadn't come yet. If Stretch let the Indian rest up long enough, there might be no need for a bed in the wagon. If they started fooling with the wagon, goodbye dynamite. What he planned to do with the dynamite he still didn't know. For now, the guns were out of his reach, but the dynamite was there waiting to be used, if only to blow them all to hell.

Grazing here was poor. This was a time when baled hay, a whole wagonful, would have solved that problem. The idea had occurred to him before they started out, but they were shorthanded and it looked like this was going to be a fairly easy drive. Going a few days without grass wouldn't kill the horses. At the same time, it wouldn't make them any easier to handle. A horse couldn't understand why it had to go without fodder. It just knew it wasn't being fed, and when an animal was hungry it became troublesome.

He heard a sound and turned to find Stretch behind him. She trod easily for such a big woman. Not just big, she had the muscles to go with her size. Back when they were spilling water into the drying-up water hole, he'd seen her lift a full barrel by herself. It took Jimmy and Lester, heaving together, to lift a barrel of the same size and weight. True, Jimmy and Lester were not so young and not in good shape from drinking and laziness. Even so, Stretch had lifted that barrel right off the chuck wagon.

"The water's all right," he told her. "No grass though."

"I can see there's no grass, Big Boy. Much as I hate to disappoint you, Pretty's all washed and clean and startin' to look better. Woke up a few minutes, smiled at me, then closed her eyes again. It's not like she blacked out. More like she went to sleep."

Morgan saw she had gotten the knife back from Sister. The big bitch wasn't careless. "Then maybe we can move on sooner." Saying the opposite would make her suspicious.

"That's the spirit, Big Boy. Keep up the good work and maybe, just maybe, I'll let you live.

You figure I mean to kill you, am I right? Answer up."

"Where's the profit in killing us?" Morgan answered with a question. "You'll have the money and a clear road to New Mexico. The army's not going to chase you. Not their business. And what harm can we do you?"

Stretch said, "I could answer that by sayin' I hate your guts. What's one more killin'? The other hand, where's the profit, like you say? So keep on doin' as you're told and I'll think about your case. Like a judge, you understan'."

Morgan and some of the others were back in camp. Stretch was in the tent talking to Sister. Morgan and Molly sat under the eye of the cook's double-barrel, held by Lester. So much for the new freedom Stretch had been allowing him, with Molly as the guarantee that he wouldn't do wrong. Nothing odd about that. Another change in mood.

There was an air of restlessness in camp. Other days they got out of their blankets, ate and moved on. Monotonous though it was, it was part of the daily routine. Now there was nothing to do. Watches had to be stood, but they were hours apart with nothing in between. This wasn't a time for catching up on sleep, even if Stretch had allowed it. Stretch was twitchy, barely controlling her anger, and everyone was nervous. Lester and Jimmy couldn't even play cards anymore. Stretch had thrown the pack in the fire. Ought to organize games for them, Morgan thought, like they did in hotels when it was raining and the guests were fretful.

It dragged on like that the first day. Bulletins from the tent were issued every time Stretch had something to tell them. It was like the best-loved woman in the country was sick and crowds were gathered outside telegraph offices, waiting for news of how she was. Morgan could only guess what the others were thinking. Come to think of it, he didn't have to guess—he knew. They wanted the Indian to die, and at the same time they were afraid what would happen if she did. Even Luz, who couldn't do much besides eat and sleep, was nervous.

Morgan wouldn't have minded some sleep. That last night with Dallas had been a corker, and there hadn't been much sleep since then, what with all the dramatic doings being played out around him. The hell of it was not being able to do anything. In all his experience, this was the worst pickle he'd ever been in. He'd been in some good ones, but this beat all.

It really was having to deal with women. In the world of men he'd know what to do, figure something out. You could hardly count Ned and Lester and Jimmy as men. The women were the movers here, and even Sister had some kind of importance. The wronged woman, the little mouse, was finally doing something that mattered.

Molly was silent. When the cook fixed the noon meal, she ate it. It could have been chopped cardboard, the way she ate it. Nothing Morgan could do would cheer her up. Cheer her up? She'd be lucky if she got to the end of the day without a beating. For now, Morgan was pretty sure that she was safe from having her drawers ripped off and her legs spread. Stretch was too busy ministering to her sick friend, but that was still no guarantee that it wouldn't happen. If the Indian started to get on the mend, Stretch might want to celebrate—or punish.

Nothing happened. The afternoon was as slow as the morning with Lester still watching with the shotgun.

Late in the day Stretch called Morgan to take a look at the Indian. Sister had bandaged her head and washed her, and she lay naked under three blankets. Her face was in repose, and she looked different than her usual stony self. She muttered something in her own language when Morgan looked at her eyeballs. If she wasn't unconscious, she was in a deep sleep.

"I don't see she's any different," Morgan told Stretch. "She's sleeping, so let her sleep."

"You don't think her forehead is hot?"

Morgan felt the Indian's forehead. It wasn't all that hot, considering the wound she'd suffered. Probably no more than a slight fever, he told Stretch. "She doesn't need all those blankets," he said. "Two is enough."

Sister hovered nearby. "I keep trying to give her water, Mr. Morgan. That isn't wrong, is it? It isn't a stomach wound."

Sister was earning her canned beans. "Keep trying," Morgan said. "She needs water."

Stretch followed him outside. "You think she's going to be all right?"

"There's a fair chance of it."

"Then we'll move on day after tomorrow. Pretty ought to be sittin' pretty by then." Stretch had gotten off a good one and was pleased with herself.

Morgan thought it unseemly to smile. What he said was solemn. "If she's strong enough to stand a jolting wagon."

Stretch dismissed his remark with a wave of her left hand. Her right remained on the butt of her gun. "She'll be strong enough, you bet your life. That's a joke, Big Boy. I'm right cheerful about the way Pretty's comin' along."

Stretch and Pretty were two gals trying to get by in the murder and cattle stealing business. It was hard to say which of them was worse. Six of one, he decided. The Indian was a merciless killer, but Stretch was the one who sent her out to kill.

"But I ain't goin' to do nothin that'll hurt that gal worse'n she's hurt now. That would be flyin' in the face of Providence."

Providence? Next she'd be calling on the Lord to deliver her from her enemies. "You don't want to do that." The moment he said it he knew he shouldn't have.

Stretch's short bark of a laugh jeered at him. "You are such a hypocrite, Big Boy. Want to kneel down and join me in a prayer for Pretty? You care as much about religion as I do. If you're prayin', it's for Pretty to kick the bucket."

She was wrong there, much as he would like to see Pretty Woman gone to the happy hunting grounds. The way things were, the Indian was less of a threat alive than she was dead. He wanted to see her up and around and able to sit a horse, but not riding on a bed in the wagon. That dynamite had to be good for something.

It was well past dark and the horses were hungry. They were moving about restlessly instead of settling down for the night. Horses were among the most excitable creatures on earth, and these horses were showing signs of it now. By morning, they wouldn't be just restless, they'd be milling around. The sound of their discontent was already there.

Later, Molly was handcuffed to the wagon, but Morgan was told to sit by the fire. Stretch said, "I want you ready in case Pretty takes a bad turn."

Morgan sat there in handcuffs, guarded by Jimmy and the shotgun.

Finally, without calling for his professional services, Stretch had him chained up for the night. Only one good side to that. Molly was asleep, so he didn't have to talk to her.

Chapter Fourteen

They were still handcuffed to the wagon when Stretch came out of the tent and went to look at the herd, not even stopping for a mug of coffee. It was morning, and those not standing guard were at the fire eating breakfast. Stretch didn't look at them. She glanced at Morgan and Molly but said nothing. Easy to see she was in a worse mood than usual. Had to be or she would have stopped for coffee.

Molly said, "I wonder how the Indian is."

"She can't be dead or we'd have heard about it. Stretch is more worried about the horses."

"Do you think she'll put the Indian in the wagon and move on?"

"She might do that," Morgan said. "Another day without fodder and the herd will be set to break loose."

"Would the wagon be so bad? I mean, for someone with a concussion?"

184

Morgan said, "I don't know. Depends how bad the concussion is. In flat country it wouldn't make much difference. In these badlands with nothing but rocks and gullies, a wagon would rattle the teeth out of her head."

"I wish I could get some of that coffee," Molly said. "Why is she leaving us handcuffed like this?"

"Why don't you ask her? Here she comes."

Stretch strode into camp and didn't stop until she was standing over Morgan. She fished in her pocket for the handcuffs' key and threw it beside him. "Throw it back before you stand up."

Stretch pocketed the key, and Morgan got up. "You're goin' to look at Pretty an' I don't want to hear none of your bullshit. Tell me how she is. No beatin' about the bush, no maybes. Get on now."

Morgan moved too slowly, and Stretch gave him a shove that sent him staggering. If she did that again, he'd be ready for her. Spin and grab her and let her kill him if she could. But she didn't.

Sister was in the tent, changing the cold cloths, and Stretch told her to get out. "There's your patient, doctor."

The Indian looked much the same, perhaps a little better. The tiny hemorrhages in her eyeballs seemed to be fading and her forehead was cool. He shook her gently by the shoulder. She opened her eyes, looked at him and closed them again.

"See! She opened her eyes," Stretch said. "Ain't that a good sign? Can she be moved or not? We can make a nice soft bed in the wagon."

"The wagon will jolt the hell out of her. She's better off here."

Stretch started to yell at him, then remembered the Indian and ordered him outside. She cursed Sister for standing around doing nothing, and Sister scurried into the tent.

"Say that again," Stretch told him. "Think before you talk."

"I wouldn't move her till she's up and walking," Morgan said.

"That's your final word, is it?"

Morgan hoped it wasn't. "That's right."

Stretch stared at him as if she couldn't believe what she was hearing. "The herd'll break out and die of hunger if we don't move on. You're askin' me to give up ten thousand dollars."

Morgan didn't answer.

"Answer me."

"How can I ask you to do anything?"

Stretch called him every dirty name she could think of.

Suddenly he was tired of this whole go-round. "Go to hell, you demented loony."

Stretch's gun swept out of her holster. "What did you say?"

"You heard it."

"Take it back." The hammer went back with an easy movement of her thumb. A squeeze of the trigger and it would be all over.

Morgan shook his head. "Like hell I will."

"I ought to shoot you," Stretch said, but she eased down the hammer and put the gun away. "Finally showin' some spunk, are you? I thought all you showed was your cock. Demented loony, am I? Guess I must be. By rights you should be layin' there dead an' the herd movin' on to the money. Stead of that I'm debatin' with you. Ten thousand fuckin' dollars! I never saw that much money in my whole life. Frank gambled the bank money away, then ran out on me when I got shot."

She wasn't talking to him. She was talking to herself. Morgan stood there, waiting. Her eyes moved back to him. "I got to think more on this. Back to the wagon, Big Boy. You can talk it over with your sweetheart."

Before Morgan got down beside the wagon, he said, "How about some coffee?"

Stretch walked away without answering. She went into the tent, and Sister came scurrying out followed by Stretch's rasping voice. "Don't wander off, peabrain!" Then the tin basin came sailing out. "Clean water, cheeseface! Fetch it now!"

"I'm afraid," Molly said in a low voice.

"You ought to be," Morgan said. He was as tired of Molly as he was of Stretch.

"You came close to being shot."

"I'm always close to getting shot. So are you." What the hell, it wasn't her fault. "I shouldn't have said that."

"It doesn't matter," Molly said, trying to move to a less cramped position. "I don't understand you, Morgan. Why did you tell her the Indian shouldn't be moved?"

"She could die if she's moved. Then it would be worse for us."

Molly was exasperated. "How much worse could it be? You saw her face just now. You're lying, Morgan. You're up to something, but you won't tell me what it is. Tell me. I have a right to know."

"I don't know what you're talking about." He couldn't tell her about the dynamite. It was in the wagon, but she'd forgotten it. No way he could trust her not to tell Stretch.

The sun beat down on them, and they sweated in the heat. Once a camp was more than a day old, with food scraps and people shitting in the bushes, it drew flies. Morgan forgot the coffee and thought about water. It would be hell if they had to go without water. They weren't that bad off yet. That wouldn't happen till the sun was at its peak.

Calling for water was a waste of breath. The miserable bastards by the fire were too scared to help out. There was no need of the fire except to cook, and yet they sat around it as if they'd been ordered to stay there. From where he was, he could see the cook tilting a bottle at the chuck wagon. The others couldn't see him. Good for him, Morgan thought. Drinking was one way to get through a day that looked like it was going to be very bad.

He had no doubt of that. It was in the air. It was like waiting for a twister to hit and knowing there was no place to hide. Stretch was still in the tent. No sounds came from it. The only sounds were the hot wind and the restless whinnying of the herd.

He was surprised when Molly asked him what time it was. "Not long before noon. Why do you want to know?"

"Because it's too late to move the herd today. It would be night before the herd got to water, if it got there at all."

Morgan knew that. So did Stretch. The best part of the day was gone, and she still hadn't made any decision. Well, letting the hours drag by was some kind of decision, if only a left-handed one.

It got to be noon. Lying with his hat over his face, Morgan listened to the cook working at the chuck wagon. Nobody brought food or anything to drink. Food didn't matter. You could go a long time without food. He knew he could go without water longer than Molly could. He'd done it, but she hadn't. No good telling her not to think about it. That kind of talk was dumb and didn't work. If you needed water, you thought about it. Once, when he was very far gone with thirst, he thought about nothing but beer—great, foaming schooners of ice cold beer. It took days before you reached that stage.

Nothing like that would happen here. Something would break long before then. Unless he was wrong, the blow-up, so long in coming, would happen today. What form it would take could only be guessed at, and he was tired of guessing.

With the noon meal over, the cook washed the pots and dishes and put them away. There was no wind now, and the flies buzzed in the hot sun. Molly was asleep, her hat covering her face. The herd sounded more restless than before. It was a long day all right and far from over.

About an hour later, Stretch came barging out of the tent with her eyes snapping and her fists clenched. The twister had struck. "All right, listen good!" she yelled. "We'll not be movin' the herd today. Sure as hell, it'll move tomorrow. We're losin' a day and riskin' the horses, but I'm doing it for Pretty. Now get out there, every goddamned one of you, and keep them horses together if you got to lie down in front of them. Watch them till your eyes are sore. Comes night there'll be no sleepin', no changes in the watch. I catch a one of you sleepin' or noddin' off, I'll nail your hide to the fuckin' cross. Get goin'. Run, you worthless lumps of shit!"

Sister came out of the tent untying the makeshift apron from around her waist. "Not you, dimwit! Get back in that tent and see to Pretty. Use

your goddamned brain and try to think!" Next
she flushed out the cook from behind the chuck
wagon. "Get your bony ass out of there and help
with the horses."

Carlos shook his head when she asked him
where the whiskey was. "Ain't got no whiskey,
missus. All drank up, ever'ting. No lee-core."

Morgan knew Carlos was the kind of hardrock
drunk who'd been drinking for 40 years, a soak
since the first day he tasted the stuff. He was
more terrified at being cut off from his booze
than he was of Stretch.

Stretch broke his nose with the barrel of her
gun. Carlos screamed as spraying blood hit
Stretch's shirt, and she hit him again, this
time across the ear. He tried to get away from
her, but she pushed him against the side of the
chuck wagon and held him there with her free
hand.

"Where's the goddamn liquor?" she shouted.

The old cook's eyes pleaded with her as he
mumbled. The next blow tore his mouth. With
no teeth to break, it split his lower lip. Stretch
held him up and battered his face to a pulp. Then
she raised up on her toes and brought the gun
barrel down on the top of his skull. When she let
him go, he dropped. He was dead.

Stretch turned away with blood all over her.
Even her boots were wet. She stuck the bloody
gun in her holster and started to take the chuck
wagon apart. The work table got in her way, and
she ripped it off the hinges and tossed it away. She
threw pots and pans after the table. She dumped
out cannisters of flour and sugar. She lifted the
water barrels and upended them. "Where's the
fuckin' liquor?" she kept shouting. "Where's the
fuckin' whiskey?"

One barrel lay on its side with dough still oozing out of it. Stretch kicked the barrel and two bottles rolled out. With a whoop, she picked up the bottles. One was full, while the other was half-full with the cork pushed in hard. She stuck the full bottle inside her belt, uncorked the other with her teeth and drank from it. Standing there like she was planted, she took two long swallows of whiskey, then wiped her mouth with her blood-soaked sleeve.

We're going to get it, Morgan thought. If not now, then not much later. There was no one in camp but the three of them—Stretch, Molly and himself. Sister and the Indian didn't count. But even if the others had been there, it wouldn't have made any difference. Stretch didn't care who saw her doing what.

Morgan expected her to start in on Molly or himself. They were handcuffed and helpless. Instead, she went to the tent, and it was quiet in there until she started yelling at Sister. Then she came out and stood drinking from the bottle, as if trying to make up her mind what to do next.

The bottle had been half-full when she started. Now it was empty and she threw it against a rock. It bounced off without breaking, and she picked it up and hurled it against the rock with all her might. It shattered like a glass bomb, some of the splinters nicking her in the face. She looked at the broken glass, then at the tent, then put her finger to her lips and made a loud shushing sound. A giggle turned into a string of curses as she looked over at the freight wagon.

Here it comes, Morgan thought.

Stretch stood over them with the second bottle in her hand. It was corked, and she needed a corkscrew to get the cork out. She knocked off the neck of the bottle by hitting it against the iron wheel rim. Then, holding the bottle so the jagged edges wouldn't cut her, she poured whiskey into her mouth. She caught Molly staring at her and screamed, "How would you like to get your sweet little face all cut up? How would you like your little doll face slashed so bad no man in his right mind would look at you? Many a time I seen you lookin' at me with your doll face an' your cold little eyes like you was sneerin' at me on the sly. Fuck you, doll face. I'm better'n you are any day. You was thinkin' to lead me on, huh? With the little doll smiles an' the little lady voice. Fuck you, you cunt!"

Holding the jagged bottle, Stretch started to walk up and down, like a prosecutor presenting a damning case to a jury. Her anger wouldn't let her stay still. The more she walked, the angrier she became. Now and then, she stopped and gestured with the bottle. For the moment, Morgan was ignored.

"You didn't want to lie down for me in the place," she shouted at Molly. "What was wrong with me? Did I have a hump on my back? Did I have one leg? I stank, sure. So did you. So did everybody."

Stretch paused to pour whiskey into her mouth. Spattered by the dead cook's blood, her face cut by broken glass, she was like something out of a horror story to frighten children. She started pacing again, talking all the time.

"You was fuckin' and gettin' fucked by others. You'd deny that now. I know it for a fact. So why couldn't I get my tongue into you? Wasn't like I was tryin' to get inside of a virgin, for Christ's sake. Day you was a virgin was long since and it didn't happen in the place. You'd been lyin' down for men and women since you first knew what you got that thing for."

Stretch paused to drink, then went on. "Good thing for you you was payin' protection to them two guards. You wasn't no less a killer than the worst killer in the place. No matter. Your daddy was gettin' you money through the back door, so his little doll of a daughter wouldn't have no poor people's heads stuck twixt her legs. Fuck it! It ain't fair. You only got fifteen for a planned murder and you got a pardon in a year. Money under the table. Everythin' about you is under the table. That man you shot. Wasn't for doing your ol' man, I betcha. You was fuckin' him and somethin' went sour and you killed him."

Stretch was good and drunk by now, and every time she tilted the bottle, she got drunker. It showed in her movements more than her voice. Normally, she was a large ungainly woman with big feet and big hands. Her face had been roughened by work and sun in her early years and made vicious by her later life. Now it was twisted by hate.

"Pretty gal, I'm going to take you down a peg or two," she said, dropping her voice from a shout to a quiet, deadly threat. She reached into her pocket, took something out and waved it. Shaped like a man's cock, it had rubber straps hanging from it. "My rubber cucumber, my dildo. I fucked more gals with that than I had hot meals. Don't say you ain't never seen one, sweet gal. You're goin' to feel it in a minute."

Morgan knew Stretch wasn't going to throw Molly the handcuffs' key, not like she did with him. When Stretch stooped down to unlock the handcuffs, Molly went at her like a big cat. She came right up off the ground, tangling arms and legs with Stretch and knocking her backward. It wouldn't have happened if Stretch hadn't been drunk. Stretch hit the ground with Molly on top of her. They rolled over and over, Molly getting hit in the face with the rubber cock. Both women were screaming. Molly got the gun, but Stretch twisted her wrist and the gun flew out of her hand. Molly fought like a tiger, but Stretch had the weight and the strength. Her big fist came up and took Molly on the chin, and her body went limp. Morgan yelled at Stretch, calling her every bad name that came into his head, names that she would have killed him for any other time. But she wanted to get at Molly so bad, that all she did was twist her head to one side and spit at him. Molly started to come to, but Stretch didn't hit her again. She wanted her awake. She pinned Molly to the ground and strapped the dildo on. It was crazy looking, strapped on over her pants. Morgan's yelling had no effect. Yelling herself, she tore open Molly's pants and pulled them down over her knees, pulling and fumbling until she got them down over her boots. When she got them off, she whirled the pants in the air and threw them away. Molly had no drawers on under the pants and that made Stretch howl with crazy excitement. Molly screamed as Stretch spread her legs, threw herself on top of her and shoved the dildo in. Now Stretch was gasping instead of howling and her breath gusted into Molly's face.

A wild shout, not from Stretch, jerked Morgan's head around. Sister was out of the tent with the Indian beside her, standing without support. Pretty Woman was naked, her skin bright copper in the sunlight. Sister shouted again, and this time Stretch stopped what she was doing and turned

her head. Then she got up on her knees, still
looking, her face blank with surprise. She heaved
herself to her feet with the dildo dangling down
in front of her. Sister and the Indian didn't move.
They stood and stared at her. Stretch unstrapped
the dildo without looking at it. Still with a vacant
look on her face, she stuffed the rubber thing
in her pocket. Then she began to walk toward
Pretty Woman. Sister walked to where the gun
was, picked it up and put it in her pocket under the
apron. Then she found Molly's pants and helped
her to pull them on. Molly looked dazed. Morgan
looked over at Stretch and the Indian. Stretch had
her arm around the other woman. Morgan said to
Sister, "You have the gun. Kill her now. She'll kill
you if you don't kill her. It's your only chance. Our
only chance."

It didn't work. For an instant it looked like it
would, but Stretch's hold on Sister was too great.
Sister helped Molly to stretch out beside the wagon and walked away. Stretch and the Indian were
in the tent. Sister was standing outside, looking
fearful. Molly was awake, but Morgan didn't say
anything. What could he say that would mean
anything?

After a while, Molly crawled under the wagon to get out of the sun. Morgan could see her
lying there with her eyes open. It was a hell of
a thing, what Stretch had done to her. They had
come so close—the gun and the look of indecision
on Sister's face—and now they were back in the
same fix. Molly was free of the handcuffs, but
what could she do? Morgan felt bad about her
and forgot all the bullshit she'd been giving him.
She'd been beaten and raped and maybe it would
happen again. He looked up and saw Sister coming with a canteen.

"I won't listen to you," she said to Morgan
before she crawled in under the wagon and held
the canteen to Molly's mouth. She poured some
of the water over Molly's face and wiped it with
a rag. Then she let Molly drink again before she
crawled out.

Morgan drank from the canteen. "I won't listen to you," Sister repeated. "I don't have the
gun. Don't try to get it. I can't leave the canteen.
Stretch would be angry when she wakes up."

Morgan took another long drink. "You mean
she's passed out?"

"She's on the cot and Pretty is looking after her.
Don't ask me any more questions. I don't want to
talk to you. You're not my friend. Hurry up. Drink
as much as you can. I don't want Stretch to see
me doing this."

After Morgan had another drink, Sister took
the canteen and went back to the tent. She looked
inside and what she saw made her turn away.
She stood there with the canteen hanging by the
strap. There was fear in her face, but she wasn't
shaking anymore. Unless she still had the gun
and had lied about it, the Indian had it by now.
No other guns in camp, Morgan thought. Nothing
Molly could do, even if she came out of the shock
she was in. She could run, but she couldn't get to
the horses and she couldn't get far on foot.

He had to face it. The Indian was up and walking. That would mean they'd be moving on. If the
Indian was strong enough to look after Stretch,
lying there drunk, then maybe she could ride.
Stretch would have something to say about that.
Anyway, they wouldn't be going anywhere today.
It was well into the afternoon, and Stretch might
be passed out for hours, depending on the kind of
drinker she was. He wondered why she hadn't hit

the bottle before. Maybe she knew she couldn't handle it and stayed sober. Anger and disappointment and the thought of losing the money had driven her to get drunk. Killing the harmless old drunken cook showed how much she wanted to blot out what she didn't want to think about. Molly had been there so she had taken it out on her, but the hatred and the lust had been there anyway. Drunk or sober, it would have been just a matter of time before she went at Molly the way she did, and it would have been a lot worse if Sister hadn't distracted her.

Molly's voice came in a whisper. "Are you there, Morgan?"

"I'm here," Morgan said. He didn't know what else to say. Then he said, "How do you feel?" Dumb question. How did he expect her to feel?

"I hurt, but I'll be all right." She wasn't making the pain sound worse than it was.

"Just lie still."

"Where is she? What happened?"

Morgan said, "The Indian's recovered enough to walk around. Stretch is dead drunk in the tent. You remember Sister giving you water?"

"I remember," Molly said. "She took a risk."

"The hell with her!" Morgan said. "She could have helped us more than that."

"Oh, my God!" Molly cried out.

Stretch was awake.

Chapter Fifteen

First they heard a whoop, then nothing. A minute or two later, Pretty Woman came out of the tent and said something to Sister and waited while Sister hurried off to get coffee from the pot that always bubbled by the fire. Sister handed her the mug, and she took it inside.

The dead cook lay where he'd fallen, with flies crawling on his bloodied face. No one had come in from the herd to see what all the screaming was about. They knew Stretch, and that was all they needed to know. Somebody might venture in when they got hungry enough. Suppertime wasn't far off, and the cook was dead. But there wasn't much to opening bean cans and making coffee.

Buzzards were circling overhead, a few bold ones lighting down but keeping their distance. As long as there was movement in camp, the buzzards wouldn't come any closer to the body. Coming out of the fog she was in, Sister threw stones at the buzzards. The ones on the ground squawked, flapped their heavy wings, rose a few feet into the air, then settled down again.

The Indian came out again and handed Sister the mug without saying a word. She gave the Indian what was left in the pot, then went to the chuck wagon to get water and fresh coffee. To do that she had to walk past the dead cook. It must have bothered her, but she didn't hesitate or turn her head the other way. Sister was finally showing some backbone, Morgan thought. Too bad she didn't have enough courage to kill Stretch when she had the chance. But she had given them the water, and that was something.

Molly hadn't said anything for a few minutes. "It's not so bad now," she said when Morgan asked her how the pain was. "She did worse to other women. My guards, the two I paid, had to beat her to keep her away from me. She could have fought them and won, but they hit her from behind with a blackjack."

Molly had some nice memories.

"How does the Indian look?" she asked.

"Pretty good. I was surprised. Made a quick recovery unless she keels over again, but I doubt it."

"Good," Molly said. "They can get back together and Stretch can leave me alone. Did the Indian see what was going on?"

"She saw some of it, maybe all of it. The screaming must have woke her. All she did was stand there, watching. With the face she has, there's no way to know what she's thinking."

Molly turned on her side so she could see him through the spokes of the wheel. "She must have hated what she saw. She's been loyal to Stretch. It may be different after this."

"You mean they won't . . ." Morgan found it hard to find the right words. "They won't be going to bed together?" he finished.

"I don't know. It's possible. Stretch has been always after me, but this is the first time she did anything about it. The Indian saw her doing it. I don't know how she'll take it. She's an Indian, after all. Who can tell what a savage will do?"

Morgan didn't know much about queer Indians, men or women. He knew the men flounced around in the camps without getting the shit beaten out of them, something that could happen to a white queer anywhere. Fact was, he'd never heard of a queer Indian woman. It was hardly saloon talk, after all. Looking at it the other way, there was a good chance Pretty Woman had been turned into a dyke in Yuma. A good looking gal by any standard, she would have had no shortage of admirers. She looked to be no more than 19 or 20, so she'd started early.

Molly's voice was stronger. Like Pretty Woman, she seemed to be making a rapid recovery. "Morgan," she said, "all those horrible things Stretch said to me about doing things with women in the prison. She was lying. They're absolutely not true. I swear it."

"I believe you," Morgan lied. When people took a solemn oath so readily, usually they were lying. If they swore on their mother's grave or the lives of their children, nothing they said could be believed.

"She's just trying to drag me down to her own level." Molly was indignant. "She's a barefaced liar and a pervert."

Morgan thought the last part sounded a bit prim. Stretch could lie like a salesman and love all the women she wanted for all he cared. First and last, she was a killer, and everything else took a back seat to that. He didn't think Stretch was lying about Molly and the women. Not that he minded a whole lot, though it seemed a waste of good pussy when women should have been panting for a big cock.

"You can't believe anything she says," Molly went on, pressing the point too hard. "God, how I hate her! And what she said about Crockett Mapes was also a lie. Why would I shoot him if not for crippling my father? The idea that I would have anything to do with a hooligan like that! It's beyond belief."

"She was just trying to tear you down," Morgan said.

"I just hope she stays with her Indian and lets me alone. I don't want her filthy hands on me."

Morgan was still thinking about Pretty Woman. "What's the story on the Indian? I mean, how did an Apache girl get sent to Yuma? Usually the army deals with Indians."

"It's a bit mixed-up, her story. She stabbed a married Indian agent who had taken her into his house as a servant. It didn't happen on the reservation. The agent owned a small ranch somewhere else. That's where she killed him. Somehow she was tried in a territorial court and sentenced to life imprisonment in Yuma. It was an awkward case."

Awkward for Pretty Woman, Morgan thought. He could picture it, the married agent fucking the pretty Indian girl and then trying to turn her out for one reason or another. Like the old slave owners and overseers, some Indian agents saw their charges as a ready source of poon. The uncommon part of the story was that this horny agent got killed.

You'd think the cook wasn't lying there dead, the way Molly talked on, and he found himself wondering if Stretch's rape had been painful enough to bring on all that screaming. It certainly must have hurt, the way it was done, without flowers and mandolin music as a lead-in. The question was, had Molly been dildoed before? And had she done it to other women? You've got your mind in the latrine, partner, Morgan told himself.

What Molly said next surprised him more than anything else he'd heard that day. It was as out of place as trying to pick up women at a funeral. Her life was in danger and a dead cook was starting to rot a few yards away, but she said, "You don't think I have a doll's face, do you, Morgan? Stretch kept going on about it, and I'd hate to think I looked like that."

Morgan said, "You sure don't look like any doll I ever saw. Pretty as a picture surely—beautiful, I should say—but no doll."

He was almost glad when Stretch came out of the tent. It was time to get back to the real world. He heard her before he saw her. Sister got out of her way. After looking around, Stretch walked over to the wagon with Pretty Woman behind her. Her hangover made deep creases between her eyes. Sister had given her the gun back and it was in her holster. Pretty Woman was carrying Morgan's Colt. Stretch's eyes were bloodshot, and she rubbed at them. The dead cook didn't get more than a glance.

"What's she doing under there?" Stretch asked Morgan, meaning Molly. "Why ain't she cuffed like you?"

Morgan looked up at her. "You took the cuffs off." He didn't say any more. Either she'd forgotten everything or was pretending to.

"Guess I killed the cook, too. Come out of there, you," she said to Molly.

When Molly crawled out Pretty Woman stared at her in a way she'd never done before. It wasn't threatening, but it was different.

"I'm not putting you back in cuffs," Stretch said to Molly. "Go sit by the fire where Pretty can watch you. You, Big Boy, get that body out of here."

Morgan tossed the key back after he unlocked the handcuffs. "You want me to bury him? There's a shovel in the chuck wagon."

"Do what you like with him. We'll be movin' on in the mornin'. Pretty's well enough to ride, she says. No wagon, won't hear of it. Guess we won't be hangin' around till the Rangers show up. Get busy, undertaker."

Morgan buried the cook with his own shovel, then went back to see what new misery Stretch had in store of them. But she was surprisingly quiet and didn't even call him down for fixing a mug of coffee without permission. Molly asked if she could have coffee and Stretch told her no. Then she changed her mind and said she could have it. Pretty Woman watched Molly pouring the coffee. Her eyes moved as Molly moved. That wasn't her way. Her way was to sit stock-still, stone-faced, seeming not to blink.

It would be dark before long. No buzzards now, but the feeling of menace that hung over the camp was worse than any buzzards. It never went away. Not so bad in the daytime, it hung heavy at night.

Stretch was trying to be all business and not making much of a job of it. There was no shake in her hands, but one eyelid twitched. "Tell Luz to get in here and start cookin'," she told Morgan.

"Then look at the herd and tell me what you think. Shake a leg, Big Boy."

Luz looked sullen when he told her what she had to do. "How come the cookie don' do it? What's goin' on in there, Big Boy?" Morgan said the cook was dead and Stretch wanted her to cook, pronto. The rest of them were just as sullen as Luz. Downcast was more like it. Morgan thought he'd never seen a sadder looking bunch in his life. They all wanted to know what was going on. He told them Pretty Woman was all right again, but the cook was dead. He said nothing about Molly.

Stretch just nodded when he told her the herd would probably hold until morning. It was more or less the truth. Hunger could make horses rebellious or listless. Horses were horses, and you could never be sure what they were going to do. He hoped these horses would stay put until morning. There had been enough excitement for one day.

Luz was opening cans of beans and dumping them into pots. Then she sliced salt bacon and put it in with the beans. She worked at the hinged board Stretch had tossed away during her search for liquor. Stretch's bloody handprints were on the board, but Luz didn't try to wipe them off. If she knew what they were, it didn't interfere with her work. By the time she finished, there were beans and scraps of bacon all over the board. She scraped them together and put them in her mouth.

Ordinarily, Stretch would have yelled at her for being such a pig, but she didn't. Morgan knew she was troubled by something. It wasn't the herd or she would have said something. So it had to be the way Pretty Woman was watching Molly. Nobody talked except Luz, who muttered at the bacon and beans.

Something was going on, but Morgan was the odd man out. Molly was too nervous to look at him, Stretch didn't want to, and Pretty Woman had no interest at all. Morgan felt like an invited guest who comes to dinner on the wrong day.

When the bacon and beans were ready, Stretch told Luz to take everything—pot, plates, forks— and let the others eat where they were. "You stay there, too," Stretch warned. "I don't want to see your fat face in here tonight."

Morgan and Molly got to eat, but Stretch was too sick. Pretty Woman shook her head. Fuck it, Morgan thought, I'm going to eat.

Pretty Woman watched Molly eat. It didn't take long for that to get on her nerves. Molly didn't know what to do with the beans she didn't want to eat, but Stretch decided for her. "Scrape them back in the pot. You ain't back at the big house now."

Morgan expected her to go on like that, but she let it drop. That wasn't like her. When she started with the badmouthing, it didn't let up till her cesspool of a mind was empty. Only once did she yell, and that was when she spotted Sister, still standing by the tent. "What do you think you're doin', lamebrain? Get out there an' help guard the horses."

Stretch drank coffee until the pot was empty; then she told Molly to make a fresh pot. While Molly was getting water, Stretch said to Pretty Woman, "Ain't you tired, gal? Ought to be. How's about you gettin' some sleep?"

The Indian shook her head.

"Ain't right, you not gettin' some sleep. I guess you know what you want to do. How's about a laydown on the cot? Suit yourself. Should you get tired later, go right in and lay yourself down. No

need for you to guard old Molly. She ain't goin'
nowhere. Me and Big Boy got to go guard the
herd."

Morgan didn't want to leave Molly with the
Indian. Stretch laughed at the look on his face.
"What're you so worried about, Big Boy? Nothin'
goin' to happen to your lady friend. Who'd want
to put a finger in her?"

She remembers, Morgan thought. Maybe it
wasn't clear in her screwed-up brain, but she
knows something about what she's done, and
Pretty Woman knows because she saw it. That
would explain the tension between the two wom-
en. Pretty Woman, so obedient and so loyal, had
caught Stretch raping another woman. It was
enough to cause problems in any family. It was
no joke though if Molly got caught between the
two dykes.

Stretch took the pot of coffee out to the herd
and drank it all by herself. Luz was ordered to
keep the black coffee coming. "I'll run some of
the lard off you," she threatened. "Coffee and
then more coffee. These lazy good-for-nothin's
got to stay awake."

Stretch stayed with Morgan as he checked the
herd, so there was no chance to jump her in the
dark. No matter what he did, she stayed about
four feet behind him. Four feet was close enough
for a killing shot but too far away for him to get
at her. Molly was like a ball and chain, hampering
his every movement. If it had been just him and
Stretch, one of them would be dead by now. He
wasn't sure he could take her, but at least he
could give it a try.

Nerves all jangled by coffee and whiskey,
Stretch was the only one fully awake. All the
others wanted to sleep, and it wasn't so much

ordinary tiredness as nervous fatigue. Day after day, Stretch's craziness had worn them down. They knew she had killed the poor old cook for nothing, so where did that leave them?

Jimmy deserted before morning. The tramp cowhand with the cockeye just vanished into the darkness. He slipped away like Dallas, on foot. Lester, who was supposed to be his friend, ran to tell Stretch when he found him missing. If he hoped to get a pat on the head, he'd come to the wrong schoolmarm. Stretch's anger at the news came and went like a gust of wind.

"Fuck him!" she said. "He wasn't much good no how."

Lester was disappointed. "Ain't you goin' after him?"

"He ain't worth goin' after," was all Stretch said to that.

Two down, Morgan thought. Dallas and Jimmy were no big threats, but they were gone, and every little bit helped.

He kept listening for sounds from the camp. Molly could scream pretty good when she wanted to. She wasn't screaming now, but that didn't mean she was all right. Pretty Woman, stealthy and silent, didn't need to make noise. For all he knew, Molly could be dead and buried by now.

In spite of everything, it got to be morning, and the herd was still there. So was Molly, awake but bleary-eyed. Watching the Indian while the Indian watched her had taken a toll on her nerves. It had been a longer night for her than the rest of them.

Stretch was all over the place, pushing them to get ready. What food Luz was able to throw together was eaten standing up. Nobody talked. The coffee was bad even by trail standards, but it was hot and strong and they gulped it down.

After a lot of confusion, they moved on. Stretch caused most of the confusion, stalking around and getting in the way. She asked Pretty Woman for the third time if she'd rather ride in the wagon. Pretty Woman was already mounted up, waiting for the rest of them. Morgan's Colt rode on her hip, and she looked all right except for the bandaged head. Sister had done a good job and no blood had seeped through. Morgan couldn't figure her. She had crawled over miles of rough country, gone without sleep, and none of it showed.

According to the map, there was water and grass 20 miles away. They would have to push hard to get there in one day. Morgan didn't have to look at the map. It was in his head. How much water and what kind of grass was the question. If Stretch was thinking about it, she said nothing to him. Ordinarily, she didn't talk to him at all, except to yell at him or blame him for something, yet there were odd moments when she'd speak to him in a normal tone of voice—or what passed for normal with her. He had heard or read somewhere that kidnappers and their victims often got to talking about everyday things if they were cooped up long enough in the same place. At times, it was that way with Stretch, or something close to it, but there was none of that today. The strain was beginning to tell on her, and she showed it, not by slumping in the saddle but by keeping busy with things that didn't have to be done.

One thing she didn't do was bother Molly. She bothered Luz about the way she drove the chuck wagon, but stayed away from Molly. Cat Shawnessy, who was no hand with a horse or with a herd, sat behind Molly with a gun in her hand. Ned and Sister were back on horses, not much good as riders but not as bad as Cat. Morgan saw that Stretch hadn't given Sister back her gun which meant she knew about Sister's good samaritan work.

They went without a noon break. The terrain got rougher with more gullies, mesquite thickets and rock falls. A hot sun made them sweat, and a hot wind did nothing to dry it. But in spite of it all, they kept moving. With a halfway decent crew of wranglers, it would have been nothing, but with this bunch of misfits and loonies, it was one for Barnum's Hall of Wonders.

There were delays. The chuck wagon got a wheel jammed between two rocks and had to be levered out. When Stretch did some of the lifting, once again Morgan saw how strong she was. A horse developed a sprung tendon, couldn't keep up and had to be destroyed. Ned was thrown when his horse spooked at something and it took ten minutes to revive him and get him back in the saddle. All this took time.

Well after dark, the horses ran for the water when they smelled it. There was no use trying to control them. It couldn't be done. One minute they were moving along at a plodding pace, the next they were off and running. The water would stop them running, but not all would get that far. Already, horses were down screaming in the rocks, trampled, maimed, killed by those behind. The running horses raised so much dust that it was hard to see anything. The other riders were just shapes in the dust. The horses had run ahead of them, and there was nothing to do but let them run. Through the dust, Morgan heard the wagons coming up behind. Then he could make out Molly's floppy white hat but not her face. He couldn't see Cat, but he knew she was wedged in behind the seat, holding the gun.

Morgan turned his horse and rode ahead to where Stretch was yelling. Morgan caught up to her, but not before the Indian came out of the dust cloud like a spook in the mist in a ghost story. "What you hangin' back for, Big Boy? Go ahead now so's we can see you."

They took it easy getting to the pool where the horses were drinking. Some of the lead horses had been driven into the pool by the wild push of those behind. These horses stood chest-high in water, drinking. The water had quieted the horses for now, and they took advantage of that to start building rope corrals. Everybody had to work at it. The ground was rocky, and it took a long time to drive the stakes in so they would hold. When they were done, the corrals enclosed what grass there was.

Penning the horses took some doing after they had run wild, but water was plentiful and that made even the wildest animals easier to handle. The grass they had wasn't much, but it would keep them occupied. There would be fights over the grass when they got through drinking, and even the fiercest biters wouldn't get their bellies full. However it went, they would all get something.

That night Pretty Woman didn't sleep in the tent with Stretch, who declared she had to sleep no matter what. The cracks in the iron lady were beginning to show. She had come in from the first watch and now sat by the fire, yawning so hard her jawbone cracked.

Morgan was handcuffed to the wagon. So was Molly. Molly didn't have to stand the late watch because Stretch didn't trust her out of her sight. Morgan and Molly had eaten at suppertime, something they couldn't always be sure of.

Now Stretch stood up, stretching her arms and yawning loudly. "You comin', Pretty?" she asked the Indian. That got a no and a shake of the head. "Suit yourself, gal." Stretch tried to sound casual, but Morgan could tell she didn't like it. If the tent had a door, she would have banged it hard when she went in.

Pretty Woman rolled herself in a blanket by the fire. An hour or so passed and no snoring came from the tent. Morgan knew Stretch was lying awake for all her yawning. The Indian lay still. She could be asleep, or she could be planning death and destruction. New developments every goddamned day, Morgan thought.

He heard Molly moving. "I'm too tired to talk," she told him. "I'm going to sleep. If I sleep I don't have to think. I don't care anymore."

"We both need sleep," Morgan said, hoping that was the end of it, but it wasn't. Molly moved again, raising up a little. "Stretch isn't asleep. She'd be snoring."

"Maybe she's sleeping on her side."

"People who snore do it in any position. She can't sleep. She's thinking about the Indian, wondering why she's been so distant since she recovered. Only a brute like Stretch wouldn't understand the reason. Oh, she knows there's a coldness there, but she thinks an invitation to bed will solve everything. No wonder she can't sleep."

"It could be all that coffee," Morgan said. "You sure you're not making too much out of this?"

"Do you think I'm wrong?"

"No. What is it? Jealousy? Anger?"

"Mostly anger," Molly said. "The Indian doesn't know where she stands with Stretch, and it's making her angry. They have slow minds, these people, so she's keeping away from Stretch while she mulls over it in her savage brain."

Molly had it right, Morgan thought. Maybe it wasn't as neat as that, but she was close. Pretty Woman would have a savage's way of looking at things. She had killed many times, and there was no reason to think she wouldn't do it again. But he didn't say that to Molly, because she knew it as well as he did.

He was relieved when at last he heard loud snores coming from the tent. Sleep had won out over anger, jealousy and indecision. By the fire, the Indian lay still.

Chapter Sixteen

Next morning's breakfast was as festive as a condemned man's last meal. Morgan had been through so much, was thinking so sourly of the day ahead, that he didn't much care as long as the coffee was hot. But it wasn't just hot, it was good. Cat had made it instead of Luz, not that he expected that to be much of an improvement but it was.

Cat got no argument from Luz, who was too lazy to scratch, and it was understandable why she'd want to make coffee you didn't have to hold your nose over before you gulped it down. Just the same, there had to be some other reason, because Cat tried to keep out of the way as much as possible, saying little and never venturing an opinion. According to Molly, she had been one of Stretch's women in Yuma. There was no way to be sure of that since Molly didn't always speak the gospel.

But he thought he knew what Cat was up to when she poured a mug of coffee and offered it to Stretch.

"What's this about?" Stretch asked suspiciously.

"Luz doesn't make good coffee," Cat answered. "Not her fault. My coffee is better."

"Anything is better than Luz's coffee," Stretch said after taking a sip. "You're the new cook, gal."

They moved out. Cat rode in the wagon behind Molly, cocked her gun and held it behind Molly's head after she climbed aboard. She wanted Stretch to see she was taking her job seriously. Stretch saw her all right, and that got her yelled at. "What in hell you think you're playin' at? Ease down the hammer on that fuckin' thing! You want it to go off?"

Cat didn't look as put out as she usually did when Stretch yelled at her. In Morgan's opinion, she even looked pleased with herself. The schoolmarm had yelled at her, but there had been no follow-up, no torrent of abuse about how dumb she was. Cat had been yelled at, she seemed to think, for her own good.

They were coming out of the badlands, heading down on a slope into dry country. It wasn't desert country yet, though there were desert flowers and yuccas. The desert was still days ahead, but they could feel it in the air. It got hotter every mile they traveled. The herd moved on without any trouble. They had lost 11 horses in the stampede. It could have been worse, Morgan thought, considering the broken ground the horses had run over. Stretch was mad about it, as he expected her to be, but for once she didn't burn his ass with scorching obscenities. At the moment, the standoff, or whatever you could call it, with Pretty Woman was getting most of her attention.

After the last plentiful pool, water was no immediate problem. The barrels had been refilled as well as their canteens. It was hot, and they drank more and sweated more. They stopped at noon where the cactus grew thick and gave shade. Cat seemed to have taken upon herself the responsibility of guarding Molly on and off the wagon. Molly made some sort of quick movement—a thorn or a biting fly—and Cat drew her gun. They all looked at her. "Put that thing away," Stretch said. "What'd you think she was goin' to do? Grab a gun and shoot it out?"

"Who knows what she'd do?"

"Not a chance. This rich brat uses her brains stead of guns or thinks she does. Don't mind you watchin' her good, gal. Just don't get the jitters doin' it."

Trailing the herd and eating dust like Molly, Cat didn't get any chance to show off for the rest of the day. Morgan wondered what she'd try to fix for supper. That had to be her next time to show off for Stretch. There was no fresh meat, but there was plenty of salt bacon and canned stuff. Only so much you could do with stuff like that. Even so, she would try something that would make Stretch salivate fit to beat the band. Morgan got the feeling that Cat, crafty-looking though she was, wasn't all that bright. What she was trying to do, whether she knew it or not, would get her on the sore side of Pretty Woman.

But that was the least important thing that happened that evening. They got to the next water hole with the sun still high, and an hour later Morgan was checking the stakes on a stretch of rope corral. Stretch was behind him as he straightened up and saw something flash miles back. Gone in a wink, but he knew he'd seen it. He turned to put the hammer where Stretch could get it, hoping she hadn't seen the flash. He found her grinning at him.

"Wasn't goin' to tell me, was you, Big Boy?" she said. "But I seen it quick as you did. Bet your heart is jumpin' with hope it's the Rangers. You think it's the Rangers?"

"Could be, less you can think of something else."

Stretch squinted, but there was nothing more to see. "I can think of a lot of things. A wandering drunk tossin' away a dead soldier like that ol' prospector Pretty killed way back. Don't have to be the Rangers."

"The flash came from high ground," Morgan said. If the Rangers were out there, this was a whole new barn dance. According to Stretch, there were only four Rangers hunting them, more than enough if they were good men and had at least one long range rifle with a scope sight. "The only high ground we passed today was a bunch of tall rocks sticking up from the flat. You'd have to climb hard to get up there."

Stretch pulled at her chin with her left hand. "I remember it, six or seven miles back. You're sayin' nobody'd climb up there less they wanted to use glasses. You got a point there, Big Boy."

"You could ride out soon as it's dark," Morgan told her. "Close to it now. Build up the fire and let them think you're staying the night. With a good start, you'd be long gone."

Stretch eyed him. "You want me to pass up ten thousand dollars. In a pig's prick I will! Let them come, whoever they are. We'll be ready for them."

Smoke drifted out from camp, and there was the smell of cooking. The sun would be gone in less than 90 minutes.

"You're ready to tackle the Rangers?" Morgan said.

"These ain't the Texas boys," Stretch said. "They ain't so great neither. Arizona Rangers ain't no reg'lar force. They got a few reg'lar lawmen. The rest just sign on temporary, get paid for their time, then go back to beggin' on street corners or swampin' out saloons. They ain't shit."

"They got this far, whatever they are."

"You give them too much credit, Big Boy." Watching him, Stretch picked up the hammer and stuck it in her belt. "Guess they're thinkin' to hit us tonight, come slow and quiet, creep in close, the bastards. Like I said, we'll be ready for them."

"Like how?" Morgan said.

"Like an ambush, that's how," Stretch said. "Step lively, fella. Time to tell the folks."

Morgan knew she was enjoying this. There was a jauntiness about her that hadn't been there before. After days of dragging along with the herd, she wanted to see some action. The thought that she could get killed didn't seem to occur to her. Or if it did, she didn't care. Once again, in her own words, she was "the toughest, baddest woman that ever lived." Morgan could see what had taken her from an East Texas farm to Yuma Penitentiary.

She got them all together before she broke the news. "We won't be guardin' no herd tonight," she started off, "cause we got more important things to do."

Morgan thought it sounded like the beginning of a speech, but she got right down to cases, told them what was probably out there and what they were going to do about it. One by one, they took the bad news in different ways. Nobody there wasn't scared except Molly and Pretty Woman. Molly tried to hide how she felt, and Pretty Woman didn't have to. The others were startled.

"Cheer up, folks. We ain't dead yet." Stretch clapped her hands and let out a little whoop. She even gave Lester a playful punch in the shoulder. "Cheer up, boy. You'll live to steal a whole herd of cows. Now get out there and keep your eye and ear peeled. My guess is they won't be comin' anytime soon, but you never know."

Morgan had never seen Stretch so full of herself. Now that she had to face real danger, she was bursting with life. Cat gave her a mug of coffee which she drank in a few gulps. "We got the edge," she said. "They don't know we know they're out there. Less I'm dead stupid wrong, they'll wait till late before they try to hit us. That's how I'd do it, with most everybody sleepin'. They may start early, but they'll hang back till the right time. Whatever they do, they got a good piece of country to cover. Six or seven miles, maybe a little more, is what I make it. You saw the glasses' flash, Big Boy. You think my figurin' is about right?"

"Close enough," Morgan said. "They've got powerful glasses."

"Won't do them no good," Stretch said. "Bastards can't see in the dark, and it'll be full dark soon. Pretty here will get out there and take a look-see. Get out there fast and get back fast, right, Pretty?"

The Indian nodded, and Stretch went on. "We got to ambush the bastards a good piece back from the horses, and by that I mean a right good piece. Seems to me there's not a bad place about three miles back where there's rocks both sides of the trail, kind of in a hollow. You recall it, Big Boy?"

Morgan said he didn't.

Stretch laughed. "Big Boy's lying. Sure he remembers it, only he don't want to kill his Ranger friends. It's there like I said, not the best place for an ambush but pretty good. It'll have to do. But we got the edge, see. They'll be slowed down by then, coming in on us like they planned. Comin' in slow they'll be easier to shoot at. Now that don't mean they won't wake up real quick, so we got to fire every damn thing we got at them. Some of you ain't no hand with a gun, but you're better than nothin'. Point your gun at a man and let fly and don't stop till your gun is empty. There won't be no time for reloadin' less they manage to get into cover and start shootin' back. They'll be shootin' back anyhow. Bone stupid they may be, but they know that much. We got to keep them from ridin' through, turnin' back and gettin' to cover. We got to slaughter them the first thirty seconds. More than that, I don't know how it'll go. If we do it right, they's nothin' to stop us between here and New Mexico."

Stretch paused to drink more coffee. Morgan glanced at the others, thinking Stretch's ambush plan didn't look as good to them as it did to her. Sister had shot a man up close, but that didn't count. He doubted if Ned, Cat and Luz had even handled a gun before they got into this. They could have used Dallas and Jimmy now, but Dallas was dead and Jimmy was gone.

Stretch said, "We got two shotguns and that's how we're goin' to get them. Ain't nobody lives in the face of a shotgun blast. Two double-barrels can do an awful lot of damage. We're countin'

on that. We got to. I'll have one shotgun, Lester
the other. Split second the shotguns let loose, you
start firin' and don't let up till there's no more
bullets to fire. If you got any questions, now's the
time to ask 'em."

Nobody had a question but Morgan. "Where'll
we be when all this is going on?"

"I don't know," Stretch said. "Would puttin'
a gun to your sweetheart's head make you kill
Rangers? You don't have to answer that. Fine,
upstandin' citizen like you never'd murder Rangers, even if the price of not doin' it was your little
honey-gal's life."

Morgan started to say something, but Stretch
cut him off. "Don't be givin' me no shit, Big Boy.
Too late to be joinin' this little army. You just
want to get your hands on a gun."

Pretty Woman whispered in Stretch's ear.
"You're right, gal." Stretch looked at the dark-
ening sky. "Time you was off. You know where
we'll be?" Pretty Woman nodded. "Get back quick
as you can," Stretch said.

Morgan found Stretch staring at him. "Was
goin' to leave you an' the rich gal chained to
the wagon with Luz holdin' a gun on you. Then
I got to thinkin' suppose—just suppose—one of
them Rangers comes on ahead of the others, gets
off the trail, makes a wide swing round with the
fire to guide him in. He finds nobody there but
Luz, and if he ain't got a cowbell on him she
ain't goin' to hear him sneak up on her. Maybe
he's even got time to ride back and warn the
others, you an' the rich gal with him. Not a good
idea leavin' you, Big Boy. You folks're comin'
with us."

They rode out after the fire was built up.
Watched by Stretch, Lester put the handcuffs

on them after they mounted up. Still fired up, Stretch went around checking guns and ammunition, trying to get their nerve up. "Think the herd'll stampede with all that killin' noise out there?" she asked Morgan.

"Three miles, maybe not," Morgan answered. Stretch might win the battle but lose the herd. In a few hours, they could all be dead.

Clouds drifted across the moon, and Morgan wondered how Pretty Woman was doing with the Rangers. A light, swift rider, she ought to be there by now, maybe even on her way back. What she'd seen would make all the difference. Stretch said there were four Rangers, but there could be more. Even a handful of possemen they picked up along the way would make a difference. So there could be as many as 12 or 15 men on the move, not such an easy number to ambush with what Stretch had. But you'd think she had a force of crack guerrilla fighters, the way she carried on. If spirit had any influence on the coming fight, then she ought to win it all by herself.

They got to the place Stretch had picked, and from there they could see the glow of the campfire three miles away. "Like the good Lord's light leadin' them on," Stretch said, giving that little whoop of hers. The others looked at her, wanting to be anywhere but where they were. Still and all, Morgan thought, they just might pull it off. In the Civil War, it was said, aged militiamen had turned back some veteran Yankee cavalry raiders before they could burn their town. Anything was possible.

Before Stretch showed them their positions, the horses had to be tethered a good way off.

Lester drove in the stakes and secured the reins. Back in the rocks, Stretch climbed around, looking for the best places to put her downhearted little force. Only when they all knew their positions did she get them together to wait for Pretty Woman. The only new thought Stretch had was to handcuff Morgan and Molly together.

"I now pronounce you cock and cunt," she said when it was done. That was supposed to be a joke, but suddenly she turned vicious. "You'd do better marryin' a weasel, Big Boy. Least you can trust a weasel if it gets to know you."

Stretch turned away like a woman with more important things on her mind. It took an effort for her to stay in one place, but she managed to do it. Even so, she kept cupping her hand to her ear, listening for sounds, and when somebody gave a muffled cough she told them to shut the fuck up. Morgan knew she was listening for Pretty Woman, but so were they all. The difference was, Stretch had her own special reason for feeling uneasy. If Pretty Woman could disappear once, she could do it again, this time of her own free will, and her running away would have nothing to do with fear of the Rangers. A very good guess, Morgan thought, would be that the Indian was afraid of nothing.

Stretch was getting fidgety again, like a commander who plans an engagement and can't wait for the fighting to begin. She jumped to her feet when a three-note whistle came from the dark, and when she called out, "Come ahead, Pretty," there was the sound of a horse being walked in.

Stretch took Pretty Woman aside so she could tell what she'd seen. Morgan could hear nothing. A shy killer and silent by nature, she liked to talk to no one but Stretch.

Stretch put her arm around Pretty Woman and drew her toward the others. "Ain't Rangers out there," Stretch told them. "An older man, fifty or so, and four younger men that look to be his sons. They all got the same reddish hair and eyes."

"That's Alamo Mapes and his sons," Molly said. She tried to move her hand, forgetting she was handcuffed to Morgan. "Mapes—"

Stretch cut her off. "Who is this Alamo Mapes?"

"I killed his son," Molly said. "That's why I was in Yuma."

Stretch was angry. "You brung trouble down on us, that's what you done. Pretty got close enough to hear this ol' Mapes sayin' they was goin' to kill you an' the rest of us an' take the horses. Ol' man was goin' over how they was goin' to come in quiet an' slow, just like I said. One of the sons was prodding the ol' man, sayin' was they goin' to rape us before or after they killed us? Ol' man didn't like that kind of talk, said all he wanted was you dead and the horses his. Couldn't leave no witnesses though."

Morgan spoke up. "Time you gave us a gun." He lifted his right arm, pulling Molly's arm along with him. "Take these things off and give us a gun."

Stretch's eyes moved to him. "What you so panicky about? Them Mapeses ain't goin' to rape you. All right. You'll get a gun but not till they get close."

Morgan said, "They may get too close. They won't be coming with a brass band."

"Do tell. I thought maybe they was. Don't play the dumbshit, Big Boy! You know well as I do Pretty'll be out there watchin'. They'll still be a mile off when we're in position an' ready to drop

them outta their saddles. That's when you'll get
your gun."

"I want Lester's shotgun," Morgan said. "All
the cartridges he's got. I can do more good than
he can."

Stretch was getting mad again. "Better than
me, you think?"

Morgan didn't answer that. "There's more to a
shotgun than just pulling the triggers. You don't
have to loose both barrels the same time. If one
barrel does the job, you get to save a load for
something else."

Stretch shook her head at Morgan's shotgun
talk. "Custer should've had you at the Little Big-
horn. I just hope you're as good as you think you
are. Ain't seen no evidence of it yet."

Morgan's fingers were itching for the feel of a
gun, a shotgun most of all. Get Stretch and the
Indian together for a second and there would
be an end to this. Just raise it on the hip and
blow them to bits—after he got through helping
to kill the Mapes family, he thought sourly. That
was the knot in this tree. He had nothing against
the Mapeses other than they meant to kill him,
but that wasn't personal, so he couldn't work up
much hate. Stretch he wanted to kill so bad he
was almost beyond hate. You didn't hate a mad
dog. You killed it.

The kick in the ass was that whatever chance
he had with Stretch he would have none with the
Mapeses. They wanted Molly dead, the witnesses
to her killing dead, and they wanted the horses.
It was hard to understand a man supposedly as
rich as Mapes going to all this trouble to kill one
woman, but there it was. Mapes probably didn't
want the horses as much as he wanted Molly, but
if the horses were to be had, why not? He couldn't

sell them to the army, which was not to say he couldn't get rid of them somewhere else. But right this minute he wouldn't be dwelling on that.

Stretch came back down out of the rocks and told them to gather round. "This place starts wide, then narrows down. Me an' Big Boy will be on both sides of the narrow part with the shotguns. The rest of you will be above an' below us, like I explained before. Above us, Ned and Cat on one side. Sister and Luz on the other. Below Big Boy and me, Molly on one side, Lester on the other. Big Boy and me will start blasting before they get to us. They'll be trapped. We'll all be shooting down at them. You get that? You fire the fuckin' guns *down!* Don't want you killin' our own people."

That was a good one, Morgan thought. Now he was one of Stretch's people. So was Molly, so arrogant and well-brought up. It had to be galling her ass if she wasn't too busy thinking about Alamo Mapes and his killer sons. But to give this tricky beauty her due, she wasn't stiff-faced with fear like the others, and he knew she would fight like a wildcat when the time came. If Mapes and his sons took her alive, she would be beaten and raped, over and over, before they finally put a bullet in her head. It was the best reason to die fighting.

Everybody was wound up tight, waiting for Pretty Woman's three-note whistle. Morgan knew she wouldn't come in except to tell them the Mapeses were on their way. The light came and went as black clouds ran across the face of the moon. Not a good night for an ambush. There would be hell to pay if the light failed just as the Mapeses rode in.

They had to be coming soon, if they hadn't avoided the trail and were approaching from some other direction. That was the unspoken fear among them, and it was well-founded. Mapes and his sons didn't have to keep to the trail. With no herd to drive, they had a free range of movement. They could split up and send one man to scout ahead.

The three-note whistle came from the darkness, and there was no longer any doubt.

Chapter Seventeen

"You stay with Big Boy," was all Stretch said to Pretty Woman after she came back. No shooting position had been fixed for her before. Now Morgan knew why. Even here, Stretch wanted him watched. Pretty Woman looked at Molly and then at Stretch and nodded. Lester was already taking the handcuffs off. He balked when Morgan reached out to take the shotgun. "Give him the fuckin' thing!" Stretch grabbed the shotgun out of his hands and slammed it at Morgan.

Molly got back her .38 revolver and short-barreled .44-40 Winchester carbine. Morgan didn't ask for his Colt .44 because Pretty Woman was wearing it. He got a Remington Army Model .45 and a Winchester rifle. All three weapons he had were loaded, and Pretty Woman had the spare ammunition in the big pockets of her canvas coat. Her own long gun was a .44-40 carbine like Molly's.

"Get set," Stretch said quietly. "You know your places. For Christ's sake an' your own, do this right."

Stretch was the last to get into position. Morgan watched as she ran across and climbed up into the rocks. The moon clouded over before she got all the way up. Crouched close to Pretty Woman, Morgan smelled her sweat and his own and the gun oil of the shotgun. From where they were, after the moon cleared again, he had a clear view of the trail as it came through the rocks. The wind gusted, blowing dust, and dropped as suddenly as it came. It had been doing that for hours. Along with the balky moon it wouldn't make things any easier.

Below him, about 40 feet away, he could make out Molly's blond head in the rocks. You wouldn't see it if you weren't looking for it. She had left the big white hat in camp. Her blond hair, dirtied by travel, didn't show near as much as the big white hat would have. Across from Molly, staying low, Lester was in position, though he couldn't see him. He hoped Lester would show his face when the shooting started.

The moon was still playing tricks, shining down strong, then blacking out the light like a curtain had been dropped. Every time that happened the eyes had to adjust. A few seconds lost in an ambush could get you killed. If they had to open fire in half-darkness, they'd only have vague shapes to shoot at. Best thing then was to shoot at the widest part of the shape and hope you hit something. If they had to do that, the shotguns would be a godsend.

They had to get there soon. Even if Pretty Woman had heard them more than a mile off, enough time had passed to bring them close. He still hadn't heard them when Pretty Woman rested her carbine on a rock and sighted down the barrel. He hefted the shotgun, an old 10-gauge with twin triggers, and then he heard them—faint sounds at first, not voices, just the quiet movement of horses, their hooves thudding the sandy dirt. They were coming slow and quiet, wanting to get there late. Moving like that they'd make good targets. The twin hammers of the shotgun were already eared back.

Now there was enough light to see them, not bunched up but riding two by two, with one rider out in front. They separated and rode in a line when the trail began to narrow. They started in, and none of the forward shooters fired too soon, always a danger with amateurs. They got closer. Morgan took a quick look and saw Stretch rise up with the shotgun. She was aiming the shotgun when the moon clouded over. The light just quit, and Stretch must have hesitated before she fired. She fired both barrels at the same time, and the blast lit up the trail and the rocks like a lightning flash. Morgan fired one barrel, then the other. A horse was screaming. No way to tell if it was hit or just scared. Men were yelling, and the horse was still screaming. Scattered fire came from the rocks behind them. All Morgan could see was movement down below. Now they were firing back, shooting at gun flashes. Morgan broke open the shotgun, thumbed in two cartridges, snapped it shut and fired without taking aim. There was nothing to aim at. Down below one man was yelling louder than the rest. Stretch let go another double blast. Morgan could hear her yelling. Beside him, Pretty Woman was firing steadily, firing and levering like a machine.

Powder smoke drifted, was snatched by a sudden gust of wind and carried away. There was better light as the clouds blocking the moon began to clear. It might be gone in a minute. One horse and one man were down. It looked like the horse had fallen on the rider. The horse kicked, but the man didn't move. The four other riders were turning their horses this way and that, firing back at flashes. The man with the big voice was shouting. "They got Travis! Sons of bitches, they killed Travis! Pull back! Pull back!" He kept on shouting as he fired back. A woman screamed, and Morgan thought it sounded like Luz. The light died again. Morgan fired again, and a horse screamed. Maybe it wasn't a horse. Maybe it was another woman. Screams could sound the same. Ned and Cat, Luz and Sister were back of the Mapeses and under heavy fire. It looked like Luz was dead. Scattered shots came from where Ned and the others were, but Morgan didn't think they were doing any good. The Mapeses were already heading back the way they'd come with nothing much to stop them. Stretch fired and yelled at Morgan to get down from the rocks. She fired again and started to climb down. Morgan and Pretty Woman were there before her. Reloading as she ran, stumbling and cursing, she started after the Mapeses. She stopped and fired both barrels, but neither horse nor man went down. The last rider to break out turned in the saddle, fired back at her and then was gone.

Reloading and still cursing, Stretch started to walk back. There was a dead horse jammed up against the rocks but no dead or wounded rider. Morgan was looking at the man who'd been thrown off or shot off his horse. The horse was dead, and the man lay pinned by its forelegs. The full weight of the horse would have crushed him like a baked potato. Instead, he was breathing. Stretch cursed and pointed the shotgun at his head. Morgan grabbed the barrel and turned it upward as the gun went off. Then something hit him in the back of the head, and he dropped.

Molly was pouring water over his face when he came to. He held his hand out for the canteen, and she held it while he drank. He saw Stretch and Pretty Woman standing behind Molly. His head hurt like hell. He tried to get up.

"Stay where you are," Molly said, pushing him back down.

"Let him get up," Stretch said. "We don't have much time. Fuckers could be fixin' to come back in. On your feet, Big Boy!"

Molly helped him to stand. His gun was gone from his holster. When he touched the back of his head his hand came away wet with blood. A headache was banging away inside his skull.

"It was Pretty put you to sleep," Stretch said. "Thought you was fixin' to murder me. Grabbin' that gun was pretty dumb, Big Boy. Could have made me blow that fella's head off. You thought I was about to kill the lad, that's how dumb you are. Never would do that. Don't you know we got Mapes's son here, alive and well."

"He's alive for now. I don't know how well he is."

"Then see to him, Doc. You done good with Pretty. I'll give you a hand there."

Stretch gave her gun to Pretty Woman before she lifted the horse's legs and Morgan dragged out the unconscious man. His breathing got better after the weight was off him. He looked young.

"Water here, Nurse Bitch," Stretch said to Molly.

Molly poured water on young Mapes's face, and he opened his eyes when she slapped him hard. He tried to grab at Molly but fell back with a groan. Stretch pushed Molly aside and leaned over him. He stared up at her. His right arm was twisted at an awkward angle. A dislocated shoulder or a bad wrench, Morgan thought.

"Don't go grabbin' at me, son," Stretch said, "or they'll hear you screamin' in the next county. What do they call you?"

"Fuck yourself, jailbird!" Young Mapes's eyes were scared but defiant. Morgan could tell his arm was hurting bad.

Stretch reached down, grabbed his wrist and gave the bad arm a twist. Mapes screamed before he passed out. "Well, I do declare," Stretch said, letting the arm drop. "This boy is a baby. Wake him up, Nurse Cunt."

This time it took him longer to come back to life. Molly got out of the way before Stretch could push her.

"We better get out of here," Morgan said. "They'll be coming back to look for him."

"Can't go nowheres without horses, Big Boy. The others've gone to fetch them. Luz and Lester are dead. Pretty checked while you was dozin'. Mapes attacks now he'll have one dead son."

She leaned over Mapes and started again. "What's your name, crybaby?"

"Travis."

Stretch nodded. "The truth now, Travis. Your ol' man got any remounts out there? One of your brothers got his horse killed and is presently ridin' double. Answer up, crybaby. Think of your poor little arm."

"He's got remounts," Mapes said.

"Where, for Christ's sakes? Out by the tall rocks where you was spyin' on us? Don't make me beat it out of you?"

"That's right. Where you said."

Stretch straightened up. "That's right good news. Daddy Mapes got to go back six, seven miles to get a fresh horse. Can't see two boys ridin' double and chasin' us the same time. Get him on his feet, Big Boy. Treat him gentle, you hear. This boy is worth somethin'."

Ned, Sister and Cat came in leading the horses. Morgan and Molly were handcuffed after they mounted up. There were no handcuffs for Travis Mapes. Stretch tied his wrists to the saddlehorn after he was heaved into the saddle. Morgan thought he looked about 18. They rode out, leaving Luz and Lester for next morning's buzzards. There was a bright moon all the way back to camp.

Stretch shook her fist at the moon. "You two-timin' son of a bitch!" she yelled. "But we did good in spite of you!" But that was just fooling. She was in the best humor Morgan had seen her in since that first night. It wouldn't last, but it was there now.

The herd hadn't run, which was more cause for good humor. "I tell you the Lord's been good to us tonight. Fuck the Lord! We done it by ourself. Lost Luz an' Lester, no big loss. And we got ourself a hostage."

Morgan was by the fire, handcuffed to Molly. "Mapes doesn't have to go back all that way. One of the sons can do it. Mapes and the other two are probably looking for this one."

Morgan nodded at Travis Mapes, who was sitting in the full light of the fire with Pretty Woman directly behind him with a shotgun trained on his back.

"This is where he'll find him," Stretch said, "sittin' pretty with Pretty. Don't be throwin' a wet blanket on the party, Big Boy. We're holdin' all the cards, I tell you. Mapes can't see in the dark with them glasses. Only way he can get a look at his boy is to come in real close. Knowin' what we're like, would you do that if you was a father?"

She looked at Travis Mapes. "Your father know about us?"

"Yes, he knows, ma'am. News got to Niles City before we started out. That had nothing to do with Molly, so he wasn't interested. Then we caught up to the herd and saw you with the binoculars. The paper had your descriptions."

"How did they describe me? A tall ravin' beauty, am I right?"

Travis Mapes tried not to look at her. "I didn't read it, ma'am, just heard about it."

"A little bird told me you was fixin' to rape us." Stretch looked at the women. "That true?"

Travis Mapes shook his head.

"You was just goin' to murder us in cold blood?"

"We were goin' to hold you for the law." Travis Mapes was a bad liar and it showed.

Stretch was getting mad. "Every citizen's duty, am I right? That why you was sneakin' around out there? You and the rest of your kin was goin' to drag us back to Yuma to be hung."

"We was goin' to leave it to the law, ma'am," Travis Mapes said, trying to keep his head down.

Stretch pointed at him. "Don't you ma'am me, you hypocrite little bastard, and look at me when you talk. Leave it to the law, my East Texas ass!

You and your tribe was goin' to murder a bunch of people never harmed you in your fuckin' life." Her anger began to ebb. "Tell me, Travis, was your father thinkin' to collect the reward money?"

Travis Mapes had to look at her. "He wasn't doing it for the money."

"Course not, a rich man like that. If he did collect it, he'd prob'ly give it to the poor an' needy, God bless him. While we're talkin' about money, how rich would you say your father is?"

Young Mapes blinked at the question. "Pretty rich, I guess."

"That's no answer, son. Is he rich enough to pay a fifty thousand dollar ransom for you?"

"Christ, lady, I don't know. You want to hold me for ransom?"

Listening to this, Morgan thought Stretch was really going crazy. They'd be lucky if they got away from Mapes with their lives. Even now, holding the son, there was no guarantee that they'd live till sunrise.

"Well, you got to admit it's a pretty enticin' idea," Stretch said. "We got you and your ol' man's got the money. What's wrong with a trade? What you think, Big Boy?"

Morgan said, "Mapes could hate his son's guts."

"There you go again with the wet blanket," Stretch said. "Course the ol' man don't hate Travis's guts, but we'll let the ransom idea go for now. So what you want to talk about, Travis? Religion an' politics is out. Before the money we was talkin' about rape. You want to talk about rape?"

"I'd just as soon not, lady." Mapes's face twitched with pain.

"You're just bashful, is all. You ever rape a woman, Travis?"

He hung his head. "I never did."

Stretch was smiling, but her eyes glittered with meanness. Morgan had run into a few people like her in his time. Their pleasure was to torment people who couldn't fight back.

"But you get your reg'lar ration of pussy," Stretch went on, digging in the needle. "A good lookin' boy like you, 'course you do. I'll bet your cock don't cool off a single night of the week. What you mumbling for, boy?"

Travis Mapes said he wasn't mumbling.

" 'Course you was mumblin'. Was you tryin' to tell me you don't get no real woman pussy? What you do then when it gets hot? Stick it in a cow? The other hand, maybe a cow'd be too much woman for you. To me you look more like a chicken man. I'd be willin' to swear it. Ever fuck a chicken, Travis?"

No answer. Young Mapes looked around as if looking for someone to rescue him from this ordeal. Let him stew, Morgan thought. The little bastard had come here to rape and murder and steal. No matter that his old man might have pushed him into it. You don't have to do everything your father tells you.

"I would say you've fucked your share of chickens," Stretch said. "What growin' boy ain't fucked a chicken or a duck? Still an' all, that ain't why the Lord give you that thing twixt your legs. The Almighty don't hold with chicken fuckin'. But listen to me, son, you must think about real women even when you romancin' the poultry. You ever think of fuckin' Miss Molly Niles here?"

Travis Mapes shook his head.

"You do know her, don't you, seein' as you're neighbors?"

"I know her."

"And you mean you never wanted to fuck her? They tell me she's one fuckable gal."

Travis Mapes's chin came up. "I wouldn't touch her with a ten-foot pole."

"Good for you." Stretch clapped her hands, an oddly childish thing to do. "Did your brother—the one she murdered—ever fuck her?"

"Crockett had her plenty of times," Travis Mapes said.

Molly started to her feet, but the other loop of the handcuffs pulled her back. "You're a dirty rotten little liar," she yelled at Travis Mapes. "Your brother was trash, and so are you. You're a family of trash."

"Quiet her down, Big Boy," Stretch warned Morgan. "She talks again I'll put her face in the fire. You got to excuse Miss Molly's manners, Travis. Now about your brother, may God rest his soul, why do you think she murdered him? Was it because he took his coconuts to another stand?"

Young Mapes gaped at her. "Coconuts?"

"Was he fuckin' somebody else?"

"I don't know. Me and Crockett wasn't close. I guess she killed him on account of her father, not that he didn't have it comin', the lyin' old windbag. Listen, lady, my arm hurts real bad."

That didn't get much sympathy. "Doctor Big Boy says it's just a bad wrench. It's not—what was that big word, Big Boy?"

"Dislocated," Morgan said.

"Ain't education a wonderful thing," Stretch said, back in good humor. "What can you do for a bad wrench, Big Boy? Wouldn't want Daddy Mapes to think we wasn't treatin' his boy right."

"Make a sling for the arm. Tell him not to move it."

Stretch made a sling by tearing an old shirt she found in the dead cook's box. "You got the head lady lookin' after you, Travis. Tell me somethin', boy, how well do you get on with your daddy?"

"We get on good."

"You're the what—the youngest son?"

"That's right," Mapes said.

"Then you're the apple of your daddy's eye," Stretch said. "You'd better be. Your life depends on it. Was foolin' with you a while back. Ain't foolin' now. Tell him I ain't foolin', Big Boy."

Morgan said, "She ain't foolin'."

"See how nice me and Big Boy get along," Stretch said. "That's cause Big Boy does what I tell him. Don't rile me. Don't try to run off. Try to run, boy, and I'll tie you tighter than a Christmas turkey. That understood?"

Young Mapes nodded. "All right if I lay down? My arm hurts."

"It's not all right. You got to sit up straight like you're doin' case your daddy takes a notion to jump us. I'm bettin' he'll do no such thing. Come morning though, he'll be wavin' a white flag and wantin' to know can we do business. The pain? You brought the pain on yourself. If you can sleep sittin' up, go to it."

Another long night, Morgan thought. Stretch was probably right about Mapes waiting till morning. She was wrong in thinking all the Mapeses would go for the remounts. One man could do it. Mapes would have used the time in-between searching for his son. He might figure the boy had been able to crawl away under cover of darkness, so he would look all over. Not finding him, he would have to conclude the ambushers had him. Mapes knew where they were camped—their fire could be seen for miles—so the next move was up to him. To come in the dark would put the boy's life at risk. Mapes and his three sons might be able to kill everybody in camp, but his youngest son would die, too.

Travis Mapes had his eyes closed, and his head was nodding forward. His sweat-matted hair was the color of a carrot. He had a big nose, a slack mouth and a short chin. If all the Mapeses looked like that, Morgan thought, they were not a good-looking family. What spirit the kid had, and it wasn't much, must come from his father, who had to be the man with the big voice.

"Is he sleepin'?" Stretch asked Pretty Woman.

Pretty Woman nodded.

"She can tell if they're fakin'," Stretch said to Morgan. "You ever see such a mis'rable little shit? Odd thing how kids with money in the family turn out to be such shits."

That was a dig at Molly. "Some of them do," Morgan said. Best to let her talk. Better than having her go on a rampage.

"Most of them do," Stretch said. "They all do. They think they got it all tied up with ribbons till they get in a tight place like this. Then they wonder how come Daddy don't do somethin' about this. Only Daddy ain't around."

"Mapes is around."

"Sure he's around, but he ain't workin' wonders like this snotnose thinks he can. A big man he may be, but when it comes down to the wire he'll have to come hat in hand. He'll have to deal with me, me that didn't have a pot to piss in till one day the burnin' bush up and told me, listen gal, the only way to get money is to take it. Too bad we can't soak Ol' Man Mapes for a big piece of his hoard. Ten thousand for the horses don't seem enough, this stage of the game. Would be nice to waltz away with, like say, fifty thousand. Forget the fuckin' horses an' do a nice neat trade for snotnose here."

"You could tell Mapes you'd wait a certain place for the money, then ride off with the kid. Without the herd you'd be able to move around any way you liked." Even as he tried to sell it, Morgan didn't think she'd buy it.

She didn't. "There you go again, Big Boy, tryin' to outfox me. Can't be done. I'm the one that taught the fox his tricks. I'm not sayin' what you said ain't a good idea. Would be a blessin' to get out from under these fuckin' horses. Trouble is your idea is only half good. The ol' man's readiness to pay would sort of depend on how much love he has for this kid."

Morgan tried again. "A man like Mapes couldn't refuse to pay. It would make him look bad if the kid got killed."

Stretch looked at Travis Mapes, his slack mouth open, his head hanging down. "Lord, I wouldn't pay a plug nickel for that. I'd pay to get rid of him. Not the point though. We're talkin' of family ties. It could go like this. Even if Mapes hates the kid he'd pay somethin'. Family honor and so forth. If he loves him a little bit he'd pay more but still small. So we get to fifty thousand and Mapes has to make the big decision. He thinks this fuckin' kid is the moon and the stars, but is he worth fifty thousand? Now fifty thousand ain't nothin' to a millionaire, which Mapes ain't. He got that fifty thousand by workin' his balls off one way or another. Cheatin' is just as hard work as work. My last thought is Mapes won't pay any big ransom."

"Then there's no change in the plan?"

"Not a one. We talk to Mapes, he keeps his distance, the horses get to the fort, and we ride off with the money. The deal with Mapes will be the kid gets turned loose after the deal is done. But he's got to wait a day so's we're long gone by the time he collects his kid. A few wrinkles got to be ironed out."

"What about us?" Handcuffed or not, Molly was asleep. "I asked you before. Why kill us?"

"Nobody's goin' to kill you, Big Boy. Hate to let the rich girl go, but I'll do it. Kick myself later, but I'll do it. I told you I'd think on it, so I did. You got nothin' to worry about, less it's Mapes. And we'll be talking to him come mornin'."

Morgan slept like Molly with his chin on his chest. You got your sleep any way you could. His last waking thought was, if Alamo Mapes wasn't any better than Stretch, at least he'd be a change.

Chapter Eighteen

"No sign of them," Stretch said, handing Morgan the binoculars. It was well after sunrise, a windy morning, not hot yet, without a cloud in the sky. Morgan scanned the country all the way back to the tall rocks where he'd first sighted the Mapeses. Nothing showed. He moved the binoculars the other way, to where the ambush took place. Nothing moved there either, but he thought he saw something. It was a lighter gray than the rocks, maybe a man's hat. When he looked again, it was gone.

With the glasses he had a clear view of the rocks, three miles away. Except for a few low, bare hills in-between, there was nowhere else they could be.

"Let them make the first move," Stretch said. "We don't want them to think they got us scared." She half-turned. "Get the kid out here, Pretty."

Stretch put Travis Mapes between Morgan and herself. "Watch the birdie," she told him. "Look

serious so your ol' man won't think you're havin'
a good time with these fallen women."

A flash of light came from three miles away.
Stretch put the binoculars to her eyes. "There
goes the white flag."

Morgan used the binoculars and saw a white
rag waving back and forth. It was tied to the
end of a rifle barrel. The man waving it was
some years older than Travis but looked much
the same. There was no sign of the father.

"What's it going to be?" he asked Stretch. "You
going out there or you want them to come here?"

Stretch took another look. "I ain't goin' no place.
They'd grab me, knowin' I'm the boss of this outfit.
I'm not goin' out there, and I don't want them
comin' here. You go, Big Boy. You got no hostage
value. You go palaver."

"I thought you wanted to do it."

"In a pig's prick I do! We already went over the
terms, so you'll be talkin' for me. Don't say more
than we agreed. Understand?"

This was one time he could talk any way he
pleased and there was nothing she could do about
it. "All right," he said.

Stretch said, "Mapes ain't goin' to kill you long
as we got the kid. Wave your good arm, Travis,
so your ol' man won't think we got your body tied
to a board. Keep wavin'. Listen to me, Big Boy.
Don't get any ideas out there. We got Molly, but
you could decide your own life is worth more.
Out of sight, out of mind. Should you be tempted,
just remember Mapes'll kill you soon as you're
no more use to him. So come on home when it's
done. We'll keep a light in the window for you."

Morgan rode out without a flag of truce. Alamo
Mapes had called the palaver under his own flag.
That wouldn't stop them from killing him anytime

they liked. As soon as he got close enough, they
would have their rifles on him all the way in. They
could have a big rifle with a scope that could knock
him out of the saddle at 1000 yards. What would
be the point of that? He hoped there was none.

Midway between the two camps there was a
point where he was out of range of the best rifles
they had, even a big one with a scope. There were
long range rifles that could kill at a mile and a
half, but the shooter had to be the best there was.
The target had to be in the same place, and the
scoped rifle had to have a solid rest. If he made a
break now, they would never hit him. They would
have to decide whether to split their force and go
after him or let him go. He figured they would let
him go.

But even as he thought about it, he knew he
wasn't going to run. Stretch and others like her
would call him a fool, but there it was. If he ran,
he could tell himself that an untrustworthy bitch
like Molly wasn't worth his life. The hell with it.
He wasn't going to run.

Soon he was past the point where he could have
run. They had their rifles on him now, and none
of the rifles had a white flag tied to it. Two were
up in the rocks, and two were standing where
the trail came out in the open. They didn't do
anything, so he kept coming. He didn't get down
till Alamo Mapes told him to.

Mapes looked like his sons but was taller. It
was one of those families where the mother's side
hardly shows. The father and sons had the same
carroty hair and reddish brown eyes, the same big
nose, slack mouth and short chin. Pretty Woman had described Mapes as an old man, but at
her age anybody over 40 looked old. Mapes was
around 50 but far from old in his movements.

There was more weight on him than the sons, and the bulk gave him a sort of force the others didn't have.

One of the sons stayed high up with the binoculars. Before Mapes spoke to Morgan, he called up, "Don't be lookin' down here. Watch what they're doin'." He turned to Morgan. "What do you call yourself?"

Morgan told him.

"You're the one Niles's daughter hired after the set-to in town?"

"That's right."

"She didn't send for you? You're not related? You're not a friend of the family?"

"She just hired me that day," Morgan said. Not a word had been said about the hostage son. Maybe that wasn't so strange. Mapes had a slow, deliberate air about him.

"What I mean is," Mapes said, "you work for the wages she pays you—or did. No reason for any special loyalty. Course she's one good-looking woman—for a killer. You been gettin' more than wages from her?"

"Suppose you tell me what you're driving at. They'll be getting edgy if I don't get back."

Mapes's expression or tone of voice didn't change. "You'll go back if I let you go back. Forget that. You could join with us and help get back my son. You'd find me not ungrateful."

"Your son wrenched his shoulder, but he's all right," Morgan said.

"I saw the sling," Mapes said. "That big woman wants to dicker but won't come herself. Her description was in the paper. Did you know she was sent to prison for five murders? Two bank managers, two lawmen, one man that got in the way. Five was all they could prove. She killed the bankers in cold blood with their hands in the air."

"What about your son?"

"We'll get to that. If I hadn't seen him myself, standin' up an' wavin', you wouldn't be talkin' to me. What does the big woman want?"

"Safe passage out of here."

"I'll agree to that."

Sure you will, Morgan thought. "Stretch, the big woman, thinks you mean to kill all of us. You want to kill Molly Niles so you have to kill us, too."

"What does my son say?"

"He says you want to hand them over to the law. Stretch doesn't believe him."

"What do you believe?" Mapes asked.

"Stretch is the one you have to convince," Morgan said. "If you kill Molly Niles, you have to kill the witnesses. That's what she thinks."

"I could have killed Niles's daughter anytime since she got out of Yuma. Why would I wait till now?"

"Because it's a long way from Niles City. We're out here in the middle of nowhere. By rights there shouldn't be any witnesses, just me and the Mexicans we started with."

"That's better. Now you're talkin' for yourself. How do I get my son back?"

"By staying well back till the big woman sells Molly's herd to the army at Fort Buell. After she gets the money your son will be turned loose where you can find him. But you've got to give them a day's start. That's the only deal she'll make. I'd say take it."

Mapes pulled the end of his big nose. "How do you and Niles's daughter fit into her plans? First sight of you two she was holding a gun on you."

Morgan said, "She says we'll go free if we don't make trouble. Why should she kill us?"

"Because she's a killer, that's why. We found two Mexicans picked clean back there. Tell by the clothes. What happened to the cook?"

"She killed him, too," Morgan said.

"And she'll let you live out of the goodness of her heart?" Mapes spat in the dust. "You and Niles's daughter are dead meat. A killer is a killer."

One of the sons cut in. "This is draggin' on too long, Pa. Do we get Travis back or not?"

Mapes didn't move his eyes from Morgan. "You keep quiet, Houston. We'll get him back, damn right we will! Why would this murderin' woman keep her word to me? Suppose I do take her deal—what's to stop her from killin' my son?"

"She'd be a fool to do that," Morgan said. "Molly has told her a lot about you. Molly told her you'd chase her to hell and back if she harmed your boy."

Mapes spat. "Comin' from the likes of her, that's a compliment. But she's right. I wouldn't just chase the big woman. I'd nail her to the cross when I caught her—and catch her I would. You tell her that."

"I'll tell her. The deal is for you to hang back and not stampede the herd. No night crawling, no riding ahead to poison the water. You've got powerful glasses. You can see your son is alive and well."

Mapes's smile was just a twitching of the lips. "I got more than powerful glasses." He called to the son on lookout. "Show him the rifle, Bowie."

Bowie Mapes stood up holding a .50 caliber Sharps rifle with a telescopic sight. Grinning, he slammed it to his shoulder and pointed it down at Morgan.

"Quit your foolin'," his father said.

Morgan waited while Mapes thought about something. He talked as slow as Sunday, but he wasn't stupid. Sometimes crafty people liked to give the appearance of being slow in the head.

"Bowie can knock a fly off your nose with that thing," Mapes said, giving another thin smile. "Any distance you like he can do it. What I mean is we can kill you any time we want. By you I mean the big woman. That's what'll happen if somethin' don't look right in there. I don't want my boy knocked about, you hear. I'd as soon have Bowie shoot him than have him shamed an' abused by that jailhouse scum."

"He won't be." Morgan knew he couldn't guarantee that.

So did Mapes. "You're walkin' a thin line, mister. There's no tellin' how this'll go. If you were bossin' the show—never mind that. That big woman don't even belong in Yuma. Too soft for her. She ought to be hung down with chains in a madhouse."

Not a bad idea, Morgan thought. "Then is it a deal?"

"This place where my boy is to be left at. You can't say where cause you don't know. That right? The big woman don't know either. Don't know this country. I do. There's a trading post about sixty miles east of the fort. Suppose she leaves him there?"

Morgan said, "I don't know if she'll agree to that. What kind of people run this place?"

"Just one old man and his son. No threat to the big woman, if that's what you're thinkin'."

"Not me. It's what she'll be thinking. She's suspicious of everything and everybody." Morgan knew Mapes would try to get at them before they got to the fort. The trading post was too far away for a man worried about his son. Anyway, if they got to the fort it might bring the army into this. Mapes wouldn't want to tangle with the army.

"Ask her," Mapes said.

"You mean there's no deal if she doesn't agree to the trading post?" Morgan knew Mapes would agree to most any deal. Why not, if he didn't intend to keep his word? Keeping his word to somebody like Stretch would depend on what he got out of it. Above all, Morgan thought, Alamo Mapes was a practical man.

"I didn't say that, but the big woman's got to fix a definite place and I got to agree to it. We'll leave that open. For now it's the tradin' post less she's got a strong argument against it. But you got to let us know."

"How will I do that?"

"Don't act simple, mister. It don't suit you. We'll be hangin' back far like she wants, but we'll be watchin' every minute. Wave a shirt, somethin', any color, and we'll know you want to talk."

Morgan nodded. "I should be getting back."

"Somethin' else," Mapes said. "Should have talked of it before. Would make things a lot more simple and get to the lean meat, so to speak. Ask the big woman if she'd consider a straight trade, my son for Niles's daughter. Give me the woman that murdered my son and she can go about her business. I ain't interested in catchin' or killin' escaped jailbirds an' she ain't about to run to the law to tell what happened out here. I will say this straight. Me an' my sons are out here to get justice for my dead son. I swear on my dear wife's grave, give us Niles's daughter an' the rest of you can go. You're thinkin' the rest of you could be witnesses. What kind of witnesses? A drifter, no offense, an' a gang of murderers. Not so good. In fact, downright bad. You advised me before. Now I'm advisin' you. Convince the big woman this is the best way out."

It wasn't a bad try, the way he spoke his piece. "Stretch can't get the money for the horses without Molly. Plan is that Molly's to be left under guard while Stretch takes the herd and a letter from Molly to the fort. Letter explains Molly is sick and can't leave the ranch. Stretch is acting for her, is authorized to deliver the herd and collect the money."

"What'll you be doin'? Seems to me if the Indian is left to guard Niles's daughter an' my son an' maybe you, she'll be hard-pressed to get that herd anyplace. The man don't look like he can ride a tame donkey, which leaves the big woman an' the small woman."

"She means to do it," Morgan said.

"How much was Niles's daughter gettin' for the horses?"

"Ten thousand."

"Less than that," Mapes said. "You lost a few along the way. All right, make it ten thousand. I can't match ten thousand, not here, but I got about five hundred on me. See for yourself."

Mapes dug into his pants pocket, took out a roll of bills and pretended to count them. A man like Mapes would know to the dollar how much he had, but he counted anyway. "Five hundred and four dollars," he said finally. "Tell the big woman she can have all of it when we trade Niles's daughter for my son. It ain't ten thousand, but it's free an' clear with no risk in it. Suppose that major smells a rat, then where is she? Headin' back to Yuma to be hung. It's that or take on every soldier in the fort. Tell her."

"I'll tell her. All right to mount up?"

"Not yet." Mapes clenched his fist and moved it up and down like a man aiming a hammer at a nail. His thumb stuck out as if it had been broken years before and badly set and the knuckles were scarred by work or fights long past. Clenching his fist was the first emotion he had shown.

"I will tell you what will happen if anything happens to my boy. The big woman may be the meanest thing ever walked, or thinks she is, but not like I can be. If my son dies or is hurt bad, I'll put all business aside and hunt her till she drops. I'll follow her up and down the country, anyplace she goes. I'll put every detective agency in the country on her. I'll pay the police to look harder. I'll buy crooks that'll help me nail her. I have the money to do all that, and I'll spend every cent of it and borrow more if I need it. You get the picture?"

"I'll tell her everything you said."

Mapes narrowed his small reddish eyes. "What I said includes you, too. Right or wrong, you're in it. Now you can leave."

As he rode away, Morgan had the feeling that the Sharps rifle was aimed at his back. Bowie Mapes looked like the kind to do something like that. One look at Bowie and you knew the Sharps was more to him than a top quality rifle. The Sharps was his darling, his sweetheart, his own true love. If his father could be believed, Bowie was a better shot than most men, and in his own mind that made him king of the hill. That didn't make him a worse man than his father, but it made him more dangerous in a situation like this. He might obey his father, but he wouldn't want to. He'd want to prove how well he could kill.

Taking his time, Morgan passed out of range of the big rifle, but he kept on riding easy. Stretch would be cursing as she watched him. Let her. It was good to be on his own for even a little while, with nobody talking tough or making threats. It gave him time to think.

It galled him to have a rifle and pistol and still be riding back to be put in handcuffs. Yet the only other way was to come in like a storm and hope to kill Stretch and the Indian before they killed him. Stretch would have a rifle on him by now. So might the Indian. He kept coming, still thinking of the guns he had and wasn't going to use, ready to halt when Stretch yelled her warning. It came, loud and threatening, but not from camp. Then he saw Stretch come up from behind a clump of brush. The rifle was rock steady at her shoulder and aimed at his chest.

"Let the guns slide," she yelled. "Don't even think what you're thinkin', Big Boy. Watch him, Pretty." Morgan didn't turn his head, but he knew Indian was rising up from somewhere with the shotgun.

He rode in slowly with the two women behind him. He climbed down when he was told. Ned and Sister held guns on him until Stretch told them to get the hell out of the way. Molly and Travis Mapes were handcuffed to the wagon. Mapes looked frightened, but Molly looked as if she didn't care. The shotgun in Cat's hands was pointed at Molly's head. I'm home, Morgan thought, but there's no light in the window.

"I wanted to shoot you," Stretch raged at him. "There's news I'm waitin' to hear and you come back here with lead in your ass. You were defyin' me, you evil bastard son of a bitch! All right, let's hear it."

"Mapes will take the deal," Morgan said.

Chapter Nineteen

"Well, now, ain't he the one?" Stretch said when Morgan got through talking. "You tell him everythin' I said? You tell him I'd kill his son if he farted too loud?"

"I didn't tell him that," Morgan said.

"Least you're honest. I wouldn't have believed you if you said you did. But you laid down the law like I wrote it? Everything?"

"All but the farting part," Morgan said.

They were at the fire, and Morgan wasn't handcuffed yet. Molly and Travis Mapes were still under Cat's shotgun. He had gone over it twice, and Stretch still kept asking questions, especially about what Mapes said about her. It seemed like that was as important to her as the deal itself. She couldn't hear enough of it.

"He knows you mean what you say," Morgan said. "He keeps calling you the big woman."

Stretch looked doubtful. "I don't know as I like that. Makes me sound like a horse. The hell with him an' his tradin' post! He ain't lookin' that far ahead, no sir. How dumb does he think I am? He's got money, but I got brains. Course we can tell him anythin' we like."

"It would be a mistake to sell him short. He talks like a shit-kicker, but he's thinking all the time." Morgan wanted to give Mapes's brains a boost. Stretch thought everyone but herself lacked brains. "He's got a high-powered rifle with a scope sight. Anytime he decides to turn mean he can pick us off one at a time."

Stretch drank some of her coffee. "Why would he do that?"

"I don't know," Morgan said. "If his patience wears out."

"All the threats he made, followin' me to the North Pole, the detectives, so forth. You don't believe that?"

"No. Mapes wouldn't go bust tracking you down, but I'd say he'd follow you far if he didn't have to tap the till too hard. He's too stingy for that."

"How can you tell? Not that I don't think he is. All these rich bastards are stingy."

"You can tell by the way he counts his money, like he's afraid somebody's about to snatch it."

Stretch nodded. "It figures. Tryin' to buy me off with five hundred and four fuckin' dollars! Who does he think he's dealin' with? Some shitass hayseed?" She gave Morgan a foxy smile. "But I wouldn't mind takin' that five an' change off his wrinkled ol' corpse."

Oh, Christ, Morgan thought, another double-crosser heard from. "You don't want to rock the boat when you're sailing smooth."

"I'd like to rock it before he does. You can't believe he'll stick to the deal. Nobody's that dumb."

"I believe he'll kill us if he gets the smallest chance. He could get it if we don't do this straight, or look like we are. For instance, I wouldn't keep the kid cuffed to the wagon. Mapes went on a lot about him being shamed and abused."

"What shamed an' abused?" Stretch was indignant. "He's layin' there comfortable with a saddle under his head, his hat shieldin' his face from the sun. Cat fixed him as good a breakfast as the rest of us. You think Cat should suck his cock so his ol' man can watch and know he's bein' treated right?"

"Nothing like that," Morgan said, not sure she wasn't serious. "Even with binoculars Mapes will find it hard to see him where he is. Keep him handcuffed, but let him sit by the fire when it's light."

Stretch didn't like the idea. "He can eat his food by the fire. The rest of the time he'll stay cuffed to the wagon. We'll show him to his father every mornin' and every night when there's still light in the sky. That'll have to do." She looked up at the sun to fix the time. "Too late to move the herd on, I guess."

"We'd be still moving after dark, like before."

"I'd surely like to put some distance tween us and the Mapeses. They got to hang back an' stay back. I won't have them crowdin' us."

"I warned Mapes about that," Morgan said.

"Lord, I got to get some sleep," Stretch said. "Go fetch a spare wheel from the wagon, Big Boy." She yawned mightily.

"What for?"

"So's you can be cuffed to a spoke. Can't go far with a wheel draggin' after you. You're goin' to stand a day watch. Sing out if you spot the Mapeses headin' this way. They'll be comin' to kill you same as the rest of us."

Stretch stood behind him while he unfastened the tarpaulin that covered the front part of the wagon. Under it were the spare wheels, harness, boards, carpenter tools—and the dynamite. If Stretch looked over the side of the wagon she would see the box covered with sandbags and want to know why, but she was too busy yawning and telling him to get a move on. He removed the wheel and retied the tarpaulin; then she made him carry the wheel to where there was a gap in the brush that screened the camp.

"Lay yourself down," she said. "Don't nod off, Big Boy. You could wake up dead." She put the binoculars within reach before she headed for the tent.

Morgan used the binoculars and saw another of the Mapes sons, the one called Houston, was on lookout. He didn't have the sharp, twitchy look of Bowie. He drank from a canteen while Morgan watched, then went back to scouting the country. He moved the binoculars more than Morgan did, fiddling with the screw from time to time. There was no sign of the Sharps. It would be propped against a rock, ready to be picked up and slid out if something looked wrong. Houston Mapes yawned and drank more water.

There was no wind, and Morgan could hear Stretch snoring in the tent. Pretty Woman wasn't in the tent but asleep under the chuck wagon. It was the first time he'd seen her asleep. He'd never seen her any other way than awake and alert. She lay perfectly still, but he knew it wouldn't take much to wake her.

He didn't think there was much chance of loosening the spoke that held him where he was. It didn't budge or turn in its socket. He looked over at the Indian as he picked up the binoculars. She had turned on her side and was looking at him. That left him with nothing he could do but go back to watching for the Mapeses.

By early afternoon, Bowie Mapes was back in position. This time Morgan saw the Sharps because Bowie slid it out and looked through the scope. There was nothing to shoot at, but that didn't keep him from playing with the big rifle. He went through the motions of firing and reloading, squinting and scowling as he did. He was like a kid with a wooden gun killing imaginary badmen or hostile Indians, except that Bowie Mapes was no kid. Morgan put him between 25 and 30, old enough to stop behaving like a stupid asshole.

Looking at him, Morgan wondered what Mapes thought of this particular son. If a father could love this son, then he could love anybody. All the Mapeses were dangerous, but Bowie was probably the most dangerous of the lot. It was a pain in the ass to keep tabs on him, but that's what Morgan did. Now and then he checked the string of low, bare hills that lay between the camp and where the Mapeses were holed up. To get to the hills they would have to crawl. No way to get there on a horse without being seen. They could do it after dark if they wanted to move in closer. There didn't seem to be much advantage to that unless they were planning something.

The hours crawled by, and now there was the heavy, dull heat of late afternoon. Ned, Cat and Sister were still watching the herd. The water supply was holding, and there was grass enough for another night. Molly and Travis Mapes were asleep, their shirts stained by sweat. Pretty Woman crawled out from under the chuck wagon, went out of camp and came back with her hair wet from washing. She sat on a rock, a rifle across her knees, drying her hair with a rag. Stretch had used Molly's towels when she washed. The Indian wouldn't touch them.

An hour before sunset, Stretch came out of the tent, clapping her hands and yelling. "Time for junior to stand inspection," she yelled. "Let's show Mapes his kid ain't bein' shamed nor abused." Standing over Travis Mapes, she yelled down at him. "Rise an' shine, chicken plucker!" She unlocked his handcuffs but left Molly as she was. Travis stumbled, still groggy from sleep. Stretch caught him by the collar of his shirt and marched him over to the gap in the brush. "Smile like you're gettin' your picture took. Wave to Daddy an' the rest of your poxy kin."

She held him there while he smiled and waved until she told him he could quit. "You had your visit with Daddy," she told him. "Now go sit by the fire where Pretty can watch you. Cat'll be comin' in to cook supper. No shamin', abusin' or starvin'. All we can offer you tonight is bacon an' beans, but it'll be a change from all the porterhouse you been eatin' back home. Yes sir, Travis, we're goin' to fatten you up for the kill. Just funnin', son. You'll be goin' home fat and sassy an' full of stories you can tell your grandkids about."

Out of handcuffs and rubbing his wrist, Morgan thought Stretch was back in her usual nasty high spirits. A good thing she didn't have whiskey or

she'd be singing young Mapes a different tune.
For someone who had to deal with Stretch he
was getting off easy, but that could change in the
blink of an eye. It was dark now and the Mapeses
could no longer use the binoculars. Anything that
Stretch might do to him would be under cover of
darkness.

Molly got to eat with the rest of them. Stretch
unlocked her handcuffs almost like an afterthought and took little heed of her after that.
Pretty Woman had stopped watching Molly and
watched Cat instead. Cat was very frightened by
the turn things had taken with the Mapeses. The
death of Luz must have rammed home the fact
that she also could be killed. And now, more
than ever, Morgan thought, she seemed almost
desperate in her efforts to please Stretch. She
kept Stretch's mug filled with coffee. She gave
her more lean bacon than the others. She smiled
nervously. Stretch was busy talking, but she
took time out to call Cat a good gal and
pat her absentmindedly on the ass. As she
did she darted a quick look at Pretty Woman, who sat on the other side of the fire.
The look seemed to say—if you don't want
my hands on you I can find somebody who
isn't so standoffish. Morgan saw all this and
marveled at it. Women? Who could understand
them? These three women were walking a tight-
rope, with Mapes sawing at one end of it and
the hangman at the other, and still they were
playing games that could come to no good end.
Women, it was said, were a mystery. Morgan
agreed with that, but they were also a pain in
the ass.

The proof of that was right in front of him.
Stretch was telling Travis about her exploits as

a bank robber. The husband, the one who left her wounded in the street, was never mentioned. Anything that was done was done by her alone. Naturally she had a gang to back her up, but they were nothing without her. Travis was doing his best to goggle at her lies. Some of her stories had to be lies, Morgan thought, but some had to be true or close to true. He wondered if Stretch herself could separate truth from lies. What she wanted to believe was true. What she didn't was lies. In the end, he thought, it was the thing that was going to get her killed. He might not get to do it, but somebody else would. Stretch would talk herself to death.

At the moment, though, she was telling Travis about the famous town marshal she'd killed in Texas. "Was in the middle of the state with a lot of Germans livin' there. These Germans was pretty good with their guns when there was Injun trouble and bushwhackers an' such. Now all that's over an' they can go back to their old ways of not carryin' guns. Like it's a part of their church rules or somethin' like that. We was lookin' around for a fat bank to rob an' we heard about this place. It was like a dream you have. Here was a bank in a town with nothin' but fat Germans. Better than that, nobody in town carried a gun 'ceptin' the marshal who was famous for cleanin' up a lot of wild towns before he took the job there. The citizens figured we won't be carryin' guns no more so we got to hire a top lawman to protect us. So they hired this fella and he's there for years and the town is quiet as a graveyard, the most law-abiding place in all of Texas."

"So how did you kill him?" Travis asked, as if he really wanted to know. Careful, boy, Morgan thought, don't overdo it and get her mad at you.

"Simple as potato pie is how we done it." Stretch was all caught up in her story. "See, this famous marshal was as famous for his chili eatin' as he was for lawin'. Had to make it for him special, this bein' a squarehead town, with pork and dumplin's and such. Fact is they called him Chili Beeder, so fond was he of it. We done our homework on this famous lawman. Anyway, it's known he always has his mornin' chili at a little three-stool place run by some woman, who otherwise cooks nothin' but German chuck. He's there as usual, reg'lar as clockwork, ready to start spoonin' in his first chili of the day. I come in dressed like a widow lady, all in black, and there's another gal with me, like maybe my sister. It's a three-stool place so I sit next to Marshal Chili Beeder. Me and this gal order somethin' that takes time, but the marshal's chili is dished up right then. Marshal's about to start spoonin', and the cook is bangin' around in the kitchen. "Look out there, sir," I says to the marshal. "Don't that look like . . ." Well, sir, he looks out the window, goin' "Where? Where?" and quick as lightning I tips my little bottle of Mickey Finn into his bowl."

"By God," young Mapes said, "that was some nerve!" This boy belonged on the boards, Morgan thought.

Stretch acknowledged the compliment with a nod. "Nerve is what it takes. Anyhow, the marshal turns back to me an' wanted to know what he should be lookin' at. That don't stop him from startin' to down the big bowl of chili. It's goin' down real fast an' I'm talkin' real slow. 'I could of sworn, sir, I just seen Gen'ral Phil Sheridan out there wearin' store clothes.' I prob'ly shouldn't

have said that 'cause he jumped up all excited
and makes for the door only he dint get there.
He came crashin' down like a log and starts to
snore. I tell you robbin' the bank was real easy
after that."

"But how did you shoot him?" Travis asked. Not
such a smart question, Morgan thought. Shooting the marshal before the robbery would have
aroused this quiet town, that is, if such a place
ever existed.

"I shot him after we robbed the bank," Stretch
said.

"That's some story," Travis said admiringly.
"How much did you get?"

Here Stretch was on safe ground. "Twenty thousand, give or take a few thousand. Took our time
and cleaned them right out. Maybe more than
twenty thousand. Prob'ly more. Hard to recall all
the banks we took."

Talking about money put Stretch in a jubilant
mood, and she was still that way at first light. It
was still too early to show Travis Mapes to his
father, but she bustled about, washing her face
in the dead cook's wash basin and tugging at
her cropped hair with a broken comb. She was
like an actress preparing to go onstage, Morgan
thought. Morgan and Molly and Travis were out
of their handcuffs and sitting by the fire drinking
coffee. Stretch had put them close together so
Pretty Woman had them within the spread of a
double shotgun blast. The sun was inching up.
Stretch's spirits were lifting faster than that. She
gave a final tug at her hair, let out one of her little
whoops and did a few steps of a jig. The others,
not so cheerful, just looked at her.

"From here on in we're goin' to call all the
shots," she said to nobody in particular. Drinking

coffee, she went to the edge of camp and looked off to where the Mapeses were. No way she could see three miles in that light, but she looked long and hard before coming back to the fire. "Soon as we display Travis here we'll be movin' along. I want to feel a horse under me and know I'm ridin' to the money. Ain't nothin' to make the time pass like somethin' good at the end of a hard journey."

Travis said, "I'm going to tell my father you treated me right. That's what I'll tell him."

"An' never a truer word spoken," Stretch said. "You folks do right by us an' we'll do right by you. Tit for tat, as the sayin' goes."

"You said it, lady." Young Mapes looked like a sly kid who thought he was putting one over on his stern aunt. Watch it, sonny, Morgan thought again. This auntie will do more than take you to the woodshed if she turns sour.

"You're all dirty," Stretch told young Mapes. "Put some water in that basin and wash some of it off. Then wet your hair an' run a comb through it." She took the gap-toothed comb from her back pocket and tossed it to him. "Wash good now. Don't want your Daddy to think you're bein' shamed and abused." She laughed. "I like the sound of that, I don't know why. Did you make that up, Big Boy, or did Daddy Mapes say it?"

"Mapes said it." The twists and turns her mind took. Anything that came into her head was going to be said.

Now she was thinking of something else. "Tell me somethin', Travis, what would your ol' man do if the Rangers happened along? Would he be on their side or ours? We got you, remember."

"We didn't see no Rangers, lady. It was in the paper they were lookin' for you, but that's all."

"Got to set you straight," Stretch told him. "I'm a woman, not a lady. We got one lady with us and more'n that I can't stomach. So don't call me lady. Now about the Rangers, what would your father do?"

"I guess he'd try to talk them out of attackin' you." Young Mapes seemed to think that was a good answer.

It didn't please Stretch. "He'd talk, but if they wanted to go ahead he'd let them. Attack us and get you killed. Got to tell you you'd be dead the first shot they fired."

Travis swallowed hard, and his reddish eyes got watery. "You'd kill me for somethin' wasn't my fault?"

Stretch said wisely, "When the shootin' starts there ain't no time to be fixin' blame. All you Mapeses would be a lot better off at home tendin' to your own business. Now you're thinkin' the rich lady here is your business, and maybe she is. Only the whole thing got turned around so we're all your business. 'Course it's all your ol' man's doin'. Got money an' land an' he thinks his shit don't smell. He thinks your dead brother, his son, dint get justice, so he's goin' to make his own kind of law. I don't like the law. I don't even like the word."

"We got to have some kind of law," Travis said bravely, thinking an honest opinion might do him some good. Dumb kid, Morgan thought.

Stretch was grinning. "Sure we got to have laws. You know why? 'Cause if we don't have 'em, I can't break 'em." The grin turned into a loud laugh. "That's a good one, huh?"

"That's a real good one," Travis said.

Stretch was smiling at some new thoughts. Morgan had seldom seen anybody so cheerful so early in the morning. That's how she was, smiling one minute, ready to kill you the next.

"If you live through this," she said to young Mapes when she had her thoughts together, "you can tell people you knew Stretch Harrelson back when. I done a lot of things in my time, and I'm goin' to do a lot more. It's been said you can't break out of Yuma, which I must tell you is the toughest prison in the country, maybe the world. Have to be honest though. A few—a very few— have broke out from that place, but did they get away? No, sir, none of them did. They was caught or killed in no time a-tall. You know why?"

Travis tugged his big nose the way his father did. "They didn't have a plan?"

"Zackly right," Stretch said. "Not havin' a plan done them in. It's a great thing to break out, but what do you do then? Less you have a change of clothes, guns an' money, you're just runnin' through the desert with your thumb up your ass. No wonder the poor fuckers get caught. Well, sir, that dint happen to us, an' it ain't goin' to. I planned the whole thing, if I do say so myself. Wouldn't surprise me if they wrote up my life story in one of them dime novels."

The sun was coming up strong. Stretch finished her coffee and got to her feet. "Come on, boy. Time for daddy to take a look at you. Too bad your daddy don't have a camera that'll make a picture at three miles. What a keepsake for the family album that'd be. You and me an' Big Boy. Not Pretty though. Pretty'll be right in back of you with the two-barrel."

Stretch could never make a joke without adding a little meanness to it. The meanness always won out, Morgan thought. Travis Mapes was bound to feel her boot or her fist before she was through with him. For now, she was posing him for a make-believe photograph. But there was malice even in that.

"Chin up," she was saying. "Smile. You got to show them teeth. I'll just put my arm around your shoulders. Hold still now."

A bullet blew her left earlobe away.

Chapter Twenty

Stretch yelled. Travis Mapes's mouth gaped open with surprise; then he was off and running before the sound of the shot died away. Stretch and the Indian were down in cover, and Morgan was running after the kid. The rifle boomed again and burned a crease along Morgan's side. Ahead of him the kid was running toward the sound of the shots. The kid was light and fast and was yelling. Another shot came at Morgan and missed, and he ran harder. They were well out of camp by now. Morgan could run, but the kid had the speed of youth. He was starting to outdistance Morgan when he caught his foot on something and went down flat on his face. A third bullet missed Morgan as he dived onto the kid and knocked the breath out of him. The shooting stopped.

He lay on top of the kid, waiting for it to start again, but it didn't. Underneath him the kid was struggling, and when he rabbit-punched Travis on the side of the neck, he went limp. Stretch was yelling from camp, but he couldn't hear what she was saying. He raised the kid's head when he raised his own, and no shots came. Then he saw a white flag waving wildly from the top of one of the low hills about 500 yards away. Without binoculars, all he could see was the rapid movement of the white flag against the brown of the hill. He slung the kid over his shoulder and started to walk back to camp.

It was the longest walk of his life. The kid's head and shoulders covered some of his back, but the rest was exposed. A .50 caliber bullet would drive his spine out through his belly. It had to be Bowie, the son of a bitch! Trying to walk faster wouldn't make any difference. The telescopic sight would follow right along. Stretch was still yelling, but he couldn't see her in the brush. He didn't know if they were still waving the white flag. When he had only a few more yards to go, the big rifle remained silent.

He walked through the gap in the brush, Stretch rose up to grab at the kid, and they went down in a tangle of arms and legs. Blood from the torn ear was all over Stretch, and she kept kicking at the kid. When Morgan tried to stop her, she kicked him, too. Morgan yelled at her, and she yelled back at him. She scrambled to her feet, drew her gun and chopped at Morgan's wrist when he tried to grab it. "Fuck you! Damn you! Get out of the fuckin' way! I'm goin' to kill that fuckin' kid!" She stuck the gun in Morgan's belly and kept on screaming. "I'm mad! I'm fuckin' crazy mad!"

Morgan took hold of the gun but didn't try to take it away from her. Even here the Indian would shoot him. She was down in cover, her six-gun moving as he moved, and she wouldn't miss.

Morgan's and Stretch's faces were close together, and her spit wet his face as she screamed at him. "Stop! Stop it!" he roared in her face. "We can't kill him! Stop it!" She started to pull away from him, and he let her go. She jammed the gun in its holster and stared at him. "There's been a mistake," he said, no longer having to shout. "Something went wrong. We have to find out."

Travis Mapes was coming to, and Stretch told Pretty Woman to put handcuffs on him. "Fix him to the wagon and watch him," she said. Her voice was under control, but Morgan knew she was boiling inside. She looked at Morgan. "They made a mistake all right, and somebody's goin' to pay for it. I say we kill the kid." Her temper was starting to break loose again. "The rotten bastards tried to kill me. Can you credit that? I'm showin' the kid to his ol' man, keepin' my part of the bargain, and they try to kill me."

Morgan decided she was more insulted than scared. So must a noblewoman feel when she's been spattered by a rotten egg thrown at her by a beggar. "Bowie Mapes did this. The father didn't order it. We have to take a look. They were waving a white flag."

Stretch didn't want to be convinced. "Sure they were. They missed killin' me so now they're wavin' a white flag. You're a fool, Big Boy."

"It's worth a look," Morgan said. "At least they've stopped shooting."

"Why wouldn't they? They'd be firin' blind if they didn't." But she unslung the binoculars and gave them to him. "Keep your goddamned head down." She touched her ruined ear with her forefinger. "That was a good ear. Goddamn you, look if you're goin' to look!"

The same white flag was still waving from the

top of the hill. Morgan brought in the face with the binoculars and it belonged to Alamo Mapes. He waved the flag with one hand and gestured with the other. The hand he gestured with held a pair of binoculars. Now and then he raised them to his eyes. Morgan felt Stretch beside him, and he handed her the binoculars and pulled his shirt off over his head. The crease in his side burned, but there wasn't much blood. "He's wavin' all right," Stretch said. "I wish I had a gun long enough to blow his head off."

Morgan had to stand up straight to wave the shirt. They could buy him a bullet, but all Mapes did was keep on waving. Mapes's face was a mixture of panic and rage. He gave one more wave and disappeared. "Where the hell is he?" Stretch said when he gave her the glasses. "What trick is he tryin' to pull now?"

Morgan put his shirt on. The crease in his side was nothing. "I don't think there's any trick. Bowie did the shooting on his own, and now Mapes is trying to save his kid's life. He wants to talk."

Stretch took another look. "Nobody there. How does he know the kid ain't dead already? By every right the little bugger should be dead."

Morgan got the shirt buttoned. "Mapes is hoping he's not. It's no good arguing about this. I have to talk to Mapes. I won't go up there, but I'll meet him halfway."

Stretch used the binoculars again. "That would put him in range of our rifles."

"And me theirs." He held out his hand, and she gave him her gun. "You want to get me killed? Bowie would nail me with the Sharps."

Stretch said quickly, "You could throw yourself flat, and we could cover you. Killin' Mapes would end this whole thing."

"Like hell it would. Mapes is the only thing keepin' Bowie from running wild. If he goes wild, the other two will. You don't start shooting unless they do. Blaze away and don't stop. I need a rifle. I'm going to ride out there and hope you keep your goddamned head. Maybe we can save this deal."

Stretch glared at him. "Don't you be goddamning me, Big Boy. I'm still the boss here. You tell Mapes nothin's been decided for sure. His kid's alive but standin' right in death's door."

Morgan rode out easy and saw two riders coming toward him. One of them carried the truce flag. As they got closer he made out Alamo Mapes and Bowie. They were closer to midpoint than he was and reined in and waited for him. Walking his horse toward them he saw Mapes was wearing a gun, but Bowie wasn't. Mapes's face was stony with held-back anger. Bowie was angry, too, but for a different reason. He looked hangdog, and Morgan knew he had been forced to come out here.

Morgan stayed on his horse. "Your son's alive," he said to Mapes, "no thanks to you. What the hell is going on? You had a deal."

Mapes spat to one side of him. "This dumb idjit did the shootin'. I rapped him to make him stop." The left side of Bowie's forehead was beginning to swell. "It was none of my doin', I swear it." More solemn oaths, Morgan thought. "I'd like for the deal to stand," Mapes said. He got down and told his son to get down.

Morgan dismounted. "I don't know about the deal. The big woman's ear, part of it, got shot away. This dimwit isn't as good with a Sharps as he thinks he is." Bowie told Morgan to go fuck himself. His father jerked around and slapped

him in the face. He put his hand to his face and
rubbed it. His eyes told Morgan how much he
wanted to kill him.

"Go on," Mapes said.

"The big woman is mad," Morgan said. "I had
to fight to keep her from killing the boy. It could
still happen. Depends on what I bring back to her.
Is this dumb sniping going to go on, or is this the
end of it? You won't get another chance like this.
One more shot fired by you and the boy is dead.
That's not even a threat—just a fact."

"Then we still have a deal. We hang back, make
no trouble, and the boy isn't harmed."

Morgan looked at the hill the shots had been
fired from. "You didn't stay back like we agreed.
You snuck up there in the night. What were you
figuring? Crawl in close for a night attack?"

"I thought we ought to get closer," Mapes said.
"It was a mistake, but this one"—he jerked his
thumb toward Bowie—"kept arguin' for it. I didn't
know he was plannin' to do what he did."

Morgan looked at Bowie Mapes. "What did you
figure to do? Kill the big woman and everything
would fall apart? We'd all turn and run or stand
there with our hands up waiting to be killed."

Bowie stared back, trying to look defiant. The
slap in the face, in front of a stranger, was a blow
to his shitkicker pride. "That's right. That's what
I figured. Something like that. I didn't think you
would put up much of a fight with the big woman
dead. Goddamn! I oughter've blown her head off.
You say the ear?"

His father said, "Shut your damn mouth. Ain't
you done enough harm?"

If this was an act, Morgan thought, it was a
pretty good one. He didn't think it was, but you
never knew. Alamo Mapes had messed with the

deal by getting up behind that hill. They had come in leading the horses. What they meant to do wasn't clear, probably not even to themselves. They wanted to be there, closer to camp, waiting for some chance they could use.

"I ask you again," Mapes said. "Can we let the deal stand?"

Morgan gave him a short sermon. "Not every man gets a second chance to save his son's life. There won't be a third—count on that—so make the most of it. Stick to the deal and your son will ride home with you."

What he said might have some truth in it. Young Mapes might go home as bones in a bag. "Stick to the deal," he repeated, "and the boy will go home alive."

Mapes pulled his nose, off in thought. "I wish I could believe that. That boy means a lot to me."

Bowie Mapes had been keeping quiet. Now he flared up in defiance of his father. "That's shit, Pa. You can't trust this scum to do nothin' more than what they did all their life. They'll kill Travis sure."

Mapes didn't turn his head. "Why is that? They didn't kill him just now."

"Because they will, that's why." Bowie was searching for a reason. "We're too close, and they're scared shitless. But they'll do it. I know that and so should you. I tried to give Travis a chance an' he nearly got away."

"You nearly got him killed," Mapes said.

Bowie started again, and Morgan told him why didn't he shut his fucking mouth. Mapes had to get between them. Bowie was smaller than Morgan, but he was quick and wiry, bursting with mad energy. His nose was bent, and his face was marked by old blows. Morgan thought he had the look of a saloon brawler. His father had to use his bulk to push him away from Morgan. Even then he danced around, shifting his weight from one foot to the other. Light on his feet, he would be quick with his pointy boots.

Morgan was sick of this whole thing—sick of Stretch and sick of the Mapeses. "Fuck you, pigface!" he roared at Bowie. "You couldn't shoot yourself in the foot, you drooling little loudmouth." Bowie dodged his father and rushed at Morgan with his head down. When Morgan sidestepped Bowie went past him, but he was already turning. Morgan pulled his gun and threw it toward the father. The father picked it up and got out of the way. Bowie was coming again, small but ferocious. Morgan thought of a wolverine snapping at itself. A kick at Morgan's knee got him in the leg, and he grunted with pain. He swung at Bowie, but the little bastard wasn't there. He swung again and the same thing happened. Every time he missed he got hit himself. The kicks to the legs hurt more than the punches. Morgan was used to fighting bigger men, and Bowie was shorter and lighter than the men he'd tangled with. Bowie was just below average height, and he fought like a killer fighting cock. He didn't curse. He hissed through snapping teeth. He got Morgan with an onrushing butt in the belly, but he didn't manage to hang on after Morgan went down. Morgan jumped to his feet. Bowie was already up and dancing around. Morgan was quick on his feet but no dancer. He tried boxing with the little bastard, feinting with one hand so he could land a punch with the other. He knocked Bowie flying with a right to the jaw that sent him staggering back. Morgan went in after him, still trying to use what boxing he knew. He quit and went

back to slugging when he saw it wasn't doing
him any good. They circled, Morgan edging in and
Bowie backing off when he got too close. Bowie
backed off some more, then came at Morgan in
a rush and tried to kick him in the balls. Morgan
blocked the kick by moving his thigh, and the
leg nearly collapsed under him. He was wobbling
when Bowie dived straight at him and knocked
him on his back. In a flash Bowie was on top of
him, trying to get at his face with his teeth. His
hands jerked up from Morgan's shoulders and tore
at his eyes. One of his thumbnails scraped across
Morgan's eyelid, and his teeth snapped at the end
of Morgan's nose. Morgan didn't feel panic. He
didn't know what he felt. He knew he had to end
this or be disfigured or killed. He broke Bowie's
grip on his head and jerked his head up hard
into Bowie's face. The butt was meant to break
his nose but smashed him in the chin instead.
Morgan's hands grabbed at Bowie's throat, but it
was slick with sweat and Bowie twisted free and
fell backward. He was scrambling up again when
Morgan kicked him in the face and he crashed
down on his back a second time. His body jerked
and his eyes fluttered and his breath came hard.
Morgan stood over him, ready to kick him again
if he tried to get up.

"Enough," Alamo Mapes said, placing his hand
on Morgan's arm. "You beat him. That's enough.
Go back and tell the big woman what was said.
Tell her she'll have the safe passage she wants."

Morgan just nodded and got on his horse. He
knew Mapes could have shot him during the fight,
but it wasn't going to happen now. No doubt about
it, it was the damnedest fight he'd ever been in.
His legs hurt like hell and the crease in his side
was leaking blood. The crease burned and blood

soaked his shirt. All things considered, it had been a bitch of a day. Hell, the morning wasn't even over yet and he'd been shot at, kicked till his legs ached, nearly lost the end of his nose, and came close to being blinded.

What he wasn't in the mood for was any more of the bullshit he had to face in a few minutes. Every waking moment he'd been trying to figure a way out of this and was no further along. Win, lose or draw, it was time to take a stand.

The Indian held a shotgun on him as he rode in. This was the big woman's way of saying welcome back, Big Boy. You done good, Big Boy. What she actually said as he got down was, "Drop the gun and do it quick."

"No," he told her. "I won't give up the gun, not this time. You want it you'll have to kill me."

Stretch laughed, but her hand dangled close to her gun. He knew she was fast because he'd seen it when she pulled it in a rage. No matter— he couldn't win against the Indian's shotgun. He didn't want to. For now, the Mapeses were the enemy.

"Pretty will kill you if I say so," Stretch said.

"Then say so. Say or do what you like. I'm keeping the gun, and I'm not going back in any handcuffs."

"Such balls all of a sudden." The others were listening, and Stretch didn't like this challenge to her authority. "You think because you beat up that runt out there you can take me on?"

Morgan said, "Nobody's taking you on, but I can't do any good chained to that wagon. I want to have a gun when I need it. They come at us unexpected I don't want to be rattling my handcuffs and begging for a gun. May be too late then."

Stretch stared at him. "You want a gun so you

can shoot me in the back. Don't tell me you ain't wanted to kill me a hundred times. You're still thinkin' it. Why should I let you keep a gun?"

"You're letting me keep nothing. I already have the gun."

"Another ten seconds you have it." She began to count and the others moved out of the way. "Five . . . six," Stretch called out.

"The Mapeses hear a shot they'll think the kid is dead." Morgan got ready to draw against the shotgun. Small chance of that. If he could just kill Stretch.

"You're right," she said. "I have to kill you quiet. Keep the fuckin' gun. Think on this while you're keepin' it. You got to sleep. You got to take a shit. So watch out for me, Big Boy."

The danger had passed but it hadn't gone far. He had bested Stretch, and it left a sour taste in her mouth. Stretch followed him to the fire when he went to get coffee. The gun felt good on his hip, but he kept his hand well away from it. All this stalking around with your hand dangling was bullshit. The coffee tasted better because he poured it himself.

Stretch got coffee for herself. "All right, Big Boy, you want to move the herd or sit there thinkin' how brave you are?"

"Why are you asking me? You're still the boss."

"Don't try to soft-soap me. We'll move the herd right away, and you'll be takin' orders like you been doin'. Don't push me too far."

Morgan set down his tin mug. "There's no need to keep Molly in handcuffs all the time. What's the good of it? What can she do?"

"Run off when it's dark."

"Run where? To the Mapeses? They'd like nothin' better than to see her running. Turn her loose and I'll watch her, but she won't run. She has more reason to fear the Mapeses than any of us."

Stretch touched her ear and winced. "I'll think about it tonight. What about the shitass kid? You think he should be walkin' around, too? Let me know. Explain. Set me straight on that. I'm dumb, get it?"

"Day or night he should have the cuffs on," Morgan said. "Why don't you see to that ear before we start? It could get infected."

"Why don't you see to the crease in your side? Why are you worryin' about my ear? Whatever I do to it, it's always goin' to look lousy."

"Grow your hair long," Morgan told her. "Nobody would ever know the difference."

"I'd know," Stretch said.

The shooting hadn't spooked the horses into a stampede. Maybe the horses were worn down by the poor grazing lately. As long as they had enough water they behaved until real hunger began to gnaw on them. That could happen by the time they reached the next watering spot.

Travis Mapes rode in handcuffs but wasn't too hampered because there was a chain between the loops that circled his wrists and he could hold the reins. Morgan put him to work and Stretch didn't object, and it turned out he was better than Jimmy and Lester together. He was nervous about Stretch, and Morgan warned him to stay away from her best he could. Morgan didn't like it when the kid started calling him "sir" and told him to cut it out. Stretch was touchy enough without having her think the kid was looking up to him.

They abandoned the chuck wagon and put the water barrels and cooking gear in the back of the

freight wagon. Molly was put on a horse in handcuffs, and Sister drove the wagon. Stretch said
nothing to Morgan before she made the switch.
Molly was no great shakes with horses, in spite of
her father's ranch, but at least she knew something
about them. Cat and Ned were as useless as before,
but riders moving alongside the herd helped to
keep it in line. All in all, Morgan thought, they
were making better time.

There was one more camp to be made in semi-
desert country before they reached the real desert.
Morgan didn't look forward to it. Bad enough to
move horses through the desert in the best of times
with a good bunch of men working together. This
was like a bad dream at the tail end of a five-day
drunk.

They skipped the noon break because of the
late start. Everybody but Stretch made do with
biscuits and water. Stretch drank black coffee
from a canteen and ate nothing. Morgan wondered why she didn't smoke. A long thin black
cigar stuck in her mouth and maybe an eyepatch
would have completed the desperado picture she
had of herself.

After scouting their back trail, she handed the
binoculars to Morgan. Nothing to be seen but
rocks and cactus and brush. Stretch said, "They's
crawlin' on their bellies like the snakes they are."

"That'll really slow them down," Morgan said.
It was hard to know what to say to Stretch. If you
didn't talk you got yelled at, and if you did talk
she took it the wrong way. She didn't like jokes
unless she made them herself. There wasn't much
to joke about here.

"You're kind of a snake yourself," she said,
giving him one of her long stares. "No, that's
wrong. You're more of a weasel, the sneakiest

animal there is. In one day you weaseled your
gun back and your sweetheart back onto a horse.
What else you thinkin' to weasel?"

"I'd like to weasel myself a cold bottle of beer."

That got no comment. She was off in thought.
She kept touching her bullet torn ear, and sometimes she cursed and got a strange look in her eyes.
The deliberate attempt on her life had unsettled
her more than she let on. Morgan didn't doubt that
she'd been shot at plenty of times, but somehow
this wasn't the same. The Mapeses should have
been catering to her every whim, but instead of
that they tried to kill her.

The deal with Mapes would get the hard test
once it got dark. That was when they could ride
in close if they had a mind to, their movements
covered by the sounds of the herd. Dark and dust
would give them all the cover they'd need if they
came to get the kid. Deal or no deal, they might
decide to do it. Mapes didn't look like the kind
of man who could be talked into anything he
opposed, but what if the sons, egged on by Bowie,
cut loose and took things into their own hands?
Fool or not, Bowie had a deep distrust of Stretch
that was well-founded. Morgan knew he would
never trust Stretch to keep her word about anything. The difference was that he knew her a lot
better than they did, and their uncertainty might
keep them in line for the time being.

As well as he could, working to keep the horses
together, Morgan kept a watch on the kid. So did
Stretch. But there was no trouble there. The events
of the morning had given him a good shaking-up,
and now all he wanted was to stay alive.

Chapter Twenty-one

Cat Shawnessy was a fool, a bigger fool than he'd thought before. They were in camp, and she was offering him a mug of coffee right in front of Stretch. Earlier in the day, she'd smiled at him a number of times, but Stretch hadn't seen it. There was not much playing-up she could do on the trail. They were all too busy.

Now was different. The herd was penned in a small, deep basin with water in the middle. Grass was dry and yellow but plentiful, a last oasis before the desert. The herd would stay put unless the Mapeses sneaked in and started a panic. In camp, with the herd quiet, they could let up a little for the first time that day.

It was a dark night, about an hour before midnight, and everybody was tired. Morgan would have said no to Cat if she hadn't shoved the mug in his face. Saying no would be more noticed than accepting, so he took it. All he wanted from Cat was for her to leave him be.

That late, Molly should have been handcuffed to the wagon. Instead, she was sitting by the fire, silent and yawning. Nobody could say she hadn't worked hard that day, and she'd worked just as hard to get the horses settled before they came in to eat.

Cat did the cooking but didn't fawn over Stretch the way she'd been doing. Stretch took no notice of her. The peculiar mood of the afternoon was still with her. She ate little and drank a lot of coffee. The Indian watched everything.

Sister and Ned were watching the herd, and the late watch would be decided when they came in later. By the look of her, the horses weren't much in Stretch's mind, and she stared into the fire, saying nothing. Travis Mapes was handcuffed to the spare wagon wheel in the full light of the fire. Trouble was unlikely, with the kid like that and Pretty Woman watching him with a shotgun. Morgan still hurt from the fight and would have been content just to sit if Cat stopped fussing like a spinster with a gentleman caller.

"No thanks," he said as quietly as he could when she offered him more coffee. Stretch looked up at the sound of his voice, then drifted back into private thought. Morgan knew that wasn't the end of it. Not much later, Cat would be urging him to try some of her delicious dried apples. It was a dumb play and sure to cause trouble if she didn't quit. To get away from her, he got up and said to Stretch, "I'm going to take a look around."

Stretch raised her eyes and grunted. Then she said, "Don't let the Mapeses get you, Big Boy."

Morgan picked up his rifle and walked out of camp. It was dark and still with no wind blowing, but Ned and Sister didn't hear him until he was right on top of them. If the Mapeses came they'd be dead.

"Take it easy," he told them. "Looks like nothing's going to happen tonight."

Sister reached out to touch him, then drew her hand back. "Mr. Morgan, do you think we're going to get out of this?"

"I don't know," he said. "It looks better than it did. Thanks for giving us the water that day. Didn't have a chance to tell you before."

Her face was vague in the dark. "I . . . I should have done more."

Morgan left them, walked away from the herd and sat on a rock with deep sand underfoot and brush growing in close. It was darker here than out in the open. He knew he couldn't stay long, but for the moment it was quiet where he was and he didn't have to talk to people. He thought it was Stretch coming to look for him when he heard someone moving through the brush. It couldn't be the Mapeses. They wouldn't make that much noise.

It was Cat, the town girl not doing so good in the wilds, and she swore mildly at the spiny braches that snagged on her clothes. "Mr. Morgan!" she kept calling in a low voice. "Where are you, Mr. Morgan?" Morgan didn't rise up because she would have screamed. "Over here," he called back, and for some reason he felt like a fool. Then she was close and saying, "I've been looking all over. I'm so glad I found you."

"What do you want? You shouldn't be out here," he said. She was so close he could smell the lemon soap she used. Cat was a fool but she was a very clean young woman, and what the hell did she think she was doing?

"I must talk to you," she said. "I've never had a chance to talk to you."

"Go ahead and talk, but make it quick." She sat down beside him on the rock. "I don't want Stretch to find you here," he said.

"Stretch has gone to sleep. I doubt if she'll miss me with the mood she's in." Cat put her hand on his thigh and squeezed it. "I'm sure she won't."

Morgan wasn't as sure as she was, but what the hell! Still squeezing, her hand was moving up his thigh, and his cock stood up like a soldier. If the Mapeses were lurking in the bushes, they were going to get an eyeful.

"What do you want to talk about?" he asked, not too interested in anything she had to say. If she said the cavalry was on its way—fine! Otherwise, she could talk about the price of turnips for all he cared.

"I admired the way you stood up to Stretch," she said, unbuttoning his pants. "It's time somebody stood up to her. She's going to get us into terrible trouble if she keeps on as she is." Cat took his cock out and gave it a gentle squeeze.

Morgan didn't see how much more trouble they could be in. "I had to do it," he said. "For all our sakes."

Somehow, in a minute or two, they were straddling the rock, facing each other. He was unbuttoning her shirt and she was working on his with her free hand. Her other hand was stroking his cock. He got her shirt open and leaned down to suck her breasts. "Oh, my God!" she cried out when his tongue touched her nipples.

"Shush now," he said. "We don't want anybody to hear."

"I don't want Stretch to hear. I'm afraid of her

and that Indian. I caught the Indian looking at me tonight."

You finally noticed, Morgan thought. He had her pants open and was working his hand through her drawers. Her drawers smelled of lemon soap like the rest of her. He'd seen her hanging wet drawers on bushes in the evening. She was clean as a pin, given the circumstances, and she sure knew how to stroke a man's cock.

"I'm asking for your protection, Mr. Morgan. Oh, my God!" she said when his finger began to tickle her clit. She was a very genteel music teacher and mother-poisoner, and she was very wet down there. Morgan eased her off the rock and down onto the cushion of sand. He didn't know how much protection he could give her. It was enough to have Molly to think about without taking on an extra lady, but he would protect her if he could.

He pulled her pants off and got his own out of the way. She was trying to tell him something but wasn't finding it so easy. She spread her legs and he got between them and she guided him in. His cock went deep inside her in one powerful thrust, and she gasped though not with pain. He didn't want to hurt her, but it wouldn't have mattered if he did. After Yuma, she was a lot more desperate than he was, and there must have been long bleak nights when she used her finger or let herself be used by other women. He hadn't shafted in and out of her more than four or five times when she creamed all over her crotch. It gushed out of her and wet her thighs and dripped in the sand. Morgan drove in hard and came while she was still squirming and gasping under him.

She was still trying to talk. Morgan said it could wait. He would listen to her later. With his cock still in her, trying to stop gasping, she said, "Oh, please, will you listen to me now?"

Talking never got in the way of fucking, but it was better when nobody talked. "I'll do my best to see you're all right," he told her.

"I hope you will, Mr. Morgan, but they're very dangerous people. You don't know how dangerous." Morgan thought he had a pretty good idea. "I'm as afraid for you as I am for myself."

Everybody laid it on too thick, he thought. Cat had no reason to hate him, but his welfare was the last thing on her mind. Nothing wrong with that. After all, she was just a little genteel music teacher thrown in with a pair of merciless killers. That she was a mother-poisoner didn't seem so terrible compared to the trail of corpses Stretch and Pretty Woman had left behind them. Maybe her mother was the only person she ever wanted to kill. Maybe the old bat deserved it. Morgan found it hard to pass judgment on a willing woman with his cock inside her.

"You have a gun now and could kill both of them." She gave his ass a squeeze of encouragement. "They'll kill you if you don't kill them. Stretch said it. You heard it yourself. 'I have to kill you quiet. You have to sleep. You have to take a . . . '" Cat didn't want to say shit. "That's what she said, and I believe her. You believe her, don't you?"

Morgan said, "I believe she's capable of it, but I don't think she'll try it with the Mapeses dogging us. I'm good with a gun, and she knows it. Why kill somebody you may need later?"

"Yes. But you're talking as if she were a normal person. The things she's done, the brutal way she killed that poor old cook. I can't forget how she murdered those soldiers. The Indian tortured a

storekeeper after the escape. Stretch watched it
and laughed. It was horrible."

"I don't doubt it." What could he say? For now
they were on the same side and he wasn't going
to kill her till the time was right.

"You must think about it," she told him with
a touch of sternness in her voice. Probably that
was the voice she used on some poor kid who
hit the wrong note. "Promise me you will think
about it."

"I promise." Promising came easy because he
thought about little else than killing Stretch as
well as the Indian. You could hardly kill one without killing the other.

"I'm so glad," she said, and the way she began
to move her ass showed she meant it. There was
nothing she wouldn't do and nothing he didn't
want her to do. With the talking out of the way,
everything got better. Morgan couldn't imagine
how or where she'd learned all the things she
knew about pleasing a man. After he'd come for
the third time, she took his cock and sucked it
until he came again. That took some doing, but
she kept sucking until he wanted to jump out of
his skin. Sure he was conscious of time passing
and of Stretch, but there were worse ways to
die than with your cock in a willing woman's
mouth.

But after it was all over, when they were lying
together, quiet and drained, he reminded her that
she should be getting back to camp. She kissed
him and started to get dressed. Then she pushed
her way through the brush and disappeared into
the dark. He gave it half an hour before he went
back himself. When he got there, Stretch was
coughing in her tent. Molly was rolled in blankets
by the fire. The kid was handcuffed to the wagon,

his head slumped in sleep. There was no sign of the Indian or Cat.

Morgan was fixing his blankets by the fire when Pretty Woman came back and settled down to watch Travis Mapes. Even killer Indians had to piss. That's where she'd gone. He wondered where Cat was. He lay in his blankets and waited for her to return to camp. If she'd gone to piss, she was taking too long to do it. He raised up when he heard what sounded like voices coming from the tent. It could be Cat was in there, or it could be Stretch talking in her sleep, something she did all the time. If Cat was in the tent, talking to Stretch, she was doing it of her own free will. There was no yelling. So much for Cat, he thought. He couldn't think of anything she could tell Stretch that she didn't already know. Telling her that he'd like to kill her would be no news at all, unless Cat told lies and spun a yarn that Stretch would want to believe. Morgan couldn't worry about what hadn't happened yet. He went to sleep.

Movement and Stretch's hoarse whisper woke him when the darkness was thinning to first light. Stretch was outside the tent, and Pretty Woman was pointing. "What the fuck am I whisperin' for?" Stretch yelled. "How could she sneak off and you not know it?"

Morgan got up. He knew Stretch was yelling about Cat. It was just like the night Dallas disappeared. Stretch ignored him and strode over to Cat's blankets. Pretty Woman and Morgan went after her. Stretch kicked the blankets in a blind rage before she got hold of herself and turned back to Pretty Woman. "Bitch rolled them so it looked like she was sleepin'. Sneaky fuckin' cat's tricks. The hell with her. Let her go. Was no rider, wasn't nothin'. One less mouth to feed."

"It doesn't make sense," Morgan said. "It isn't like with Dallas. The Mapeses hadn't showed up then. Cat would never wander off in the dark. She was scared to death."

Stretch eyed him suspiciously. "Then where is she? If she ain't here that means she's gone, get it? You have anythin' to do with it? I seen her feedin' you coffee last night. A few days back she was feedin' *me* coffee."

"She gave me coffee and I drank it." Something wasn't right here. Sneaking off was the last thing Cat would do. "I'm telling you she hasn't run off."

Pretty Woman whispered to Stretch. "Pretty says she followed you out of camp after you got through lappin' up the coffee. What about that, Big Boy? You get her in a dark place and kill her? After rapin' her first?"

Before Morgan could answer, Stretch turned to the Indian. "You see her come back into camp?" Pretty Woman shook her head. "I think you raped and killed her," Stretch said to Morgan.

"Ask her why she didn't get suspicious when Cat didn't come back."

More whispering. "Pretty says she thought she was out there fuckin' you. You come back while Pretty was takin' a piss. When she saw you she thought Cat was back, too. Wasn't till just now she took a look at Cat's blankets an' found her gone."

"Why didn't she look last night? Why now?" This could turn dangerous.

More whispering. "She felt somethin' was wrong. Injuns feel things. Looks like we're back where we started. You against me an' Pretty. We should've had it out then. Move away from me, Pretty."

"I didn't kill her. Why in hell would I kill somebody like Cat?"

Stretch's hand was brushing the side of her holster. "Because you got the chance, that's why. Poor gal was harmless, loved music. What the hell!"

Buzzards were wheeling down some distance from camp. Others, higher up and gliding on the wind, were on their way. "Aw, Christ!" Stretch said. "I kinder liked that gal."

Cat's body lay in the brush about 200 yards out. She lay on her back with her throat cut. Flies buzzed on and around the gaping wound. Her nose and ears had been cut off and her eyes gouged out. Morgan knelt beside the body and looked at the bloody eye sockets that had been cut with a razor sharp knife. Her pants had been ripped open and her crotch slashed. There was not much blood; she had been mutilated after she was dead.

Standing with Molly, Travis swayed on his feet. Molly moved away from him. She was pale but holding up.

"I never did this," Morgan said.

Stretch's eyes didn't move from the body. "No, I guess you didn't. Have to be a real fiend to do somethin' like that. You think the Mapeses?"

"It wasn't my folks. They wouldn't . . ." Travis was shaking.

Stretch told him to shut up. "Hard to believe they'd go this far. Had to be them, no other explanation. Guess they thought to do the worst thing there is, then did it. Meant to scare the shit out of us. Seen some bad things. This is pretty bad."

Morgan took another look at the body. "The

Mapeses didn't do this. An Apache did this." Pretty
Woman's face stayed deadpan. "Pretty Woman
did it."

Stretch blew up in a mad rage. "You're fuckin'
crazy, that's what you are." Her voice got louder,
and her face twitched. "You think Pretty . . . little
Pretty here . . . you're out of your fuckin' mind!
Aw, Christ, what is happenin' here?" Her voice had
some strange anguish in it. Maybe she sees herself
lying there, Morgan thought. "You didn't do this?
You couldn't," Stretch said to Pretty Woman.

The Indian shook her head.

That was all the testimony Stretch needed.
"There! See!" She gestured toward Pretty Woman
as if that settled it. "It was Alamo Mapes and his
rat bastard kids. My Lord, is there goin' to be a
reckonin'."

It sounded good and biblical, but Morgan knew
she didn't believe the Mapeses had caught Cat
running and murdered her. She looked at Travis
with mean eyes, yet made no move to kill him.
When she had to be, Stretch was as practical
as Alamo Mapes. The practical side of her was
buried under a load of bullshit—the threats, the
wild statements—but it came to the surface when
it was needed. If the Mapeses caught Cat they
would kill her or hold her hostage. Throat slit-
ting would be the sensible way to keep a killing
quiet, but they wouldn't do the rest of it. Stretch
knew that as well as he did and had chosen not
to believe it—or believed it and wouldn't face it.

Morgan figured Mapes was watching all this
with binoculars, and no doubt he was wondering
what to make of it. There was some high ground
about a mile back. It wasn't all that high, more
like a bump in the ground, but he was more likely
to be there than anywhere else. The hell with all

that! It was time to bury Cat deep so the coyotes couldn't get at her.

"What d'you mean you'll bury her?" Stretch raged at him. "By rights the snotnose ought to bury her. His kin done it. All right, you bury her. I don't want this little bastard touchin' her. Me an' Cat had some times together. You know that?"

After Morgan buried Cat they moved on, another late start. They sure were dwindling down, with four dead and one gone. Now if there was only a way to get Stretch and the Indian to face off and kill each other, but it wasn't going to happen. They were sisters now as they had never been before—or were they? Stretch had defended the Indian against his charge of murder, yet there was uneasiness in the way she looked at her. It wasn't fear so much as uncertainty that seemed to be digging at Stretch. Not knowing was getting her down though she would be the last to admit it. Things were out of control. Things were falling apart.

"What are you thinking about? Your mind was off somewhere? Were you thinking about Cat?" Molly put the three questions together without looking at him. They had stopped at noon in the shade of a barrel organ cactus, and the desert was no more than 15 miles away. The sun beat down, and the horses were sluggish in the heat. Stretch and Pretty Woman were under the spiky arms of another cactus about 30 feet away. Ned and Sister were standing together, wiping the sweat from their faces. It was like a picnic where people separate along certain lines.

"I was thinking about cold beer," Morgan said.

"You're a liar," Molly said calmly. "Was she good? Was she as good as me?"

Morgan was tired. "Nobody's as good as you. By that I mean—"

"I'd like to slap your face." Molly drank warm water and didn't like the taste. "I thought you were fond of me. You got Stretch to take the handcuffs off, so I thought you cared for me."

Our first quarrel, Morgan thought. That wasn't true. This was just one of many. He wished she'd stop talking and let him rest. He looked over to where Travis sat alone by the side of the wagon. He was lucky. Nobody was talking to him. Stretch had put him there because it looked like she wanted to have a private get-together with Pretty Woman. As usual, Stretch was doing all the talking while the Indian just nodded or shook her head.

At one point, Stretch turned her head and looked over at them. There was no way to tell which of them she had in mind. Maybe both. She turned back to the Indian and said something that took a while. The Indian nodded at the end of it.

"Did you see that?" Molly said.

"Yes, she looked over here. She's always looking. It doesn't have to mean anything."

Molly didn't want to be put off. "I'm sure they're talking about me. Stretch is trying to decide if she should hand me over to the Mapeses or go on as we are. We're not so very far from the fort, and she's trying to decide if the Mapeses will settle for me and let her go. It would be an easy way out, except she can't make up her mind what Mapes will do."

Molly was reading a lot into a look, but there was something in what she said. The same thought had come to him. There was a good argument for trading Molly with the fort right there on the other side of the desert. The major might be short of

horses, but unless he had no horses at all, there
had to be some patrols going out. That was the
argument for trading Molly now. On the other
hand why would the major be sending a patrol
into the desert?

"I think she'll risk it," Molly went on. "I don't
think she can take the strain of having the Mapeses
so close behind her."

"She's used to being hunted." Stretch was still
gabbing away to the Indian. It was getting to be
a long lunch.

"Not like this." Molly tipped her canteen again.
"At first I was sure she was enjoying it, crazy as it
sounds, but that's when she thought the Mapeses
would jump when she snapped her fingers. Then
they shot her ear off, and she knew nothing was
for sure."

"It's not the whole ear," Morgan said.

Molly was ready to hit him. "You're missing the
point, you blockhead! Losing the ear has rattled
her. She doesn't know what to expect. If trading
me will ease her crazy mind, she'll do it. She's
thinking the Mapeses will be too busy with me
to ever catch up, if they bother to chase her at
all." Molly drank more water. "I don't know what
she'll decide for you. You still have the gun."

A lot of good it's doing me, Morgan thought.
Without actually putting it into words—she was
such a proud bitch—Molly was asking him what
he'd do if Stretch decided to make the trade. She
didn't have to ask. Stretch would make the decision for him. It might not happen.

"I won't let her trade you," he said.

As he spoke, Stretch turned again and looked
over at them. The look didn't last more than a
few seconds. He didn't know why she bothered
to look at all, but that's how she was. She did

anything that came into her head. Talking to the Indian, she kept on touching her ruined ear. It wouldn't look that bad after it healed up, yet it seemed to bother her more than a wound like that should have. The life she led, she had to expect to be wounded, and in fact she had been wounded before she was captured and sent to Yuma. So maybe Molly was right. Where she was wrong was in thinking he'd missed the point altogether. He hadn't. He'd been thinking about it. It just wasn't as clear to him as it was to her.

Stretch was on her feet, brushing sand from her pants. One last thing she said got a nod from Pretty Woman. A long hot afternoon lay ahead with who knows what at the end of it, Morgan thought.

Molly stood up. "If it comes to shooting, I hope you'll save a bullet for me."

Morgan watched her swing into the saddle—a fine figure of a woman, a foxy female and a terrible nag. Trading her to the Mapeses would be like selling a princess into slavery, only the Mapeses would do worse than put her in chains.

A trade? He had the glimmering of an idea.

Chapter Twenty-two

"Keep your hands where they are," Stretch said. "Don't touch the gun. Sister will take it from you. Go round behind him, Sister. Don't snatch it. Just reach down and take it. Then walk over here and put it beside me." It happened just like that.

The Indian had moved the shotgun from Travis to Molly. It was night, and they were in camp. The hammers of the old 10-gauge were pulled back. Pretty Woman always sat with the shotgun like that, and even with her finger resting outside the trigger guard, it was as dangerous as hell but a lot more dangerous now. Her finger was on the trigger.

Sister took his gun. "What's going on?" Morgan said.

"What's happenin' is I just took the gun back. You defied me to keep it. How come you ain't defyin' me now? You ain't so brave now, is that it? You ain't been beatin' on no runt to give you

a head of steam. When you beat the runt you
thought you could defy me. You was wrong, Big
Boy."

She put a heavy stress on the word, and she was
right in a way. The shotgun hadn't been pointing at Molly then. It was pointing at him. The
difference now was in the way the Indian held
the shotgun. They were always threatening to kill
Molly if he didn't do what Stretch said. He had
given up the gun because this time they really
meant to do it.

"You got the gun. What now?" he said.

"Nothin'," Stretch told him after she picked up
his gun. "Simple fact is, I dint like you with that
gun. Made me kind of uneasy in my mind. Now I
got it back and things go on same as before. Only
they ain't zackly same as before. You don't give
me no more arguments, not a one."

Nothing had been said about trading Molly.
That didn't mean the idea wasn't on a slow boil.
Stretch looked pleased with herself, as if taking
the gun back was the right decision to make.

"Suppose the Mapeses come?" he asked.

"Then you get the gun back, and I expect you
to do your duty like a man. A thing to remember,
Big Boy. Don't be tryin' to scare me with the
Mapeses. I ain't the kind you can scare with a
bogeyman. That ol' man's learned his lesson, I
would say. He'll follow right along, hangin' back
like he's doin' now."

Morgan reached for his mug of coffee, and
Stretch drew her gun. "Big Boy, you ain't asked
can you have that coffee. Sure you can have the
coffee, but you got to ask."

"Thanks," Morgan said.

"None of that sour talk," Stretch said, putting
the gun away. "Look at it this way. You don't

have the gun you won't be thinkin' about killin' me. I have to tell you that would get you in the last trouble of your life. Hate to say it an' hurt your feelin's, but I don't think you're much good with a gun."

Morgan drank the coffee and said nothing.

"Quit sulkin'," Stretch said. "Try to look at it from my point of view. Fort's the other side of that blamed desert. You got a gun and horses close at hand. Not a minute you ain't been thinkin' you could make a break if not for your little sweetheart here."

Molly looked at Morgan.

Stretch laughed. "You can't get your balls out of the wringers less you take your sweetheart along, but you ain't sure you can do that. You don't know if she'll fail you when it comes to makin' a try for it. Still an' all, the closeness of that fort is a real temptation to you. Least it was before I took your gun back." Stretch barked out another laugh. "Temptation is all round us, Big Boy, but like the preacher said, you got to fight it tooth an' nail."

Morgan didn't think she was going to kill them. The practical side would keep her from doing that, but she kept going on about the gun, like it meant more than just taking it away from him. It was dangerous to taunt her, but maybe it was worth the risk.

"You'll get no more advice from me," he said. "You and General Mapes can fight this out by yourselves."

Stretch's temper stirred. "I don't need your god-damned advice. Never asked for it, never needed it. If I'm a gen'ral then you're the lowest soldier in my army. You ain't even a soldier. You're a prisoner. If you don't obey orders you can be shot."

"Fuck you, General!" Morgan said.

The Indian's shotgun didn't move from Travis, but her eyes did. Then she looked back at the kid, who was gaping at this new twist in events.

Stretch held herself in check. "We're back to that, are we? I ought to put the boots to you which don't mean I won't do it if you keep this up. Like Miss Molly could tell you, you're forgettin' your place, shitkicker. When I talk to you, you got to sort of shuffle your feet an' mumble polite like a field hand."

"That'll be the day," Morgan said.

"Why do men think they're hard cases an' always say that?" Stretch pretended to look puzzled and put on a deep voice. She didn't have to. Her voice was rough enough. "Tha'll be the day! Like it was suppose to mean somethin'. Like you're suppose to think this ain't no hombre to tangle with. Ain't you pitiful though. I could tangle with you any day of the week an' beat your two brothers on Sunday."

Morgan said, "Why don't you? You brag enough about it. What do you do with all these hard men you put down? Sit on them? You're horse enough to do it."

That got the biggest laugh he'd ever heard from Stretch. "Ain't you the one! Don't you know I know what you're up to? Get this woman mad enough to lay aside her gun an' I'll lay her out like a corpse. That'll be the day, my weasel friend. But keep it up an' maybe I'll kick your balls off with one hand tied behind my back. If you tangle with me, Big Boy, it'll take Nurse Molly a year to get you walkin' again. Hush up now and be a good big boy."

"Fuck you." Morgan didn't know what he was buying at this store. He might not like it when he got it unwrapped. "Fuck you for an East Texas sharecropping loudmouth."

Stretch just looked at him. "Sticks an' stones will break your bones—an' in the end they will. You're gettin' away with this cause you're disappointed. You're kickin' yourself for not doin' something with that gun. Poor Big Boy! But the barn door's open an' you're the horse's ass, as the stablekeeper said." She pointed at him. "You may badmouth your way into somethin' you can't back out of."

"Fuck you double," Morgan said. He wasn't good at badmouthing.

"You are a man of few words," Stretch said with a malicious grin. She was enjoying herself. The peculiar look she had earlier was gone, and her knife was sharper than ever. "You think you're a hard man an' all the time you got a soft middle like choc'late candy. Why, you mis'rable excuse for a man, you couldn't beat up on Sister. That Mapes runt had you till you got in that sneak kick."

"I'd like to kick you in the cunt."

Stretch doubled over with laughter. She laughed so hard she had to wipe her eyes. Then she cupped her hands and shouted, "You listenin' out there, Gen'ral Mapes? Big Boy's puttin' on a show, dirty words an' everythin'. Come on in! Get yourself a front row seat!"

But the joking stopped, and she was dead serious. "You was shittin' on East Texas just now. You want to know how I come to leave there? Listen an' learn. You see I had these four brothers I mostly raised cause my mother was dead. They dint like me and I dint like them, an' that's how it went for a long time. Then one fine day, with some full growed, some not, they decide I got to be more'n a sister to them. These farm stories

ain't all true, an' I never in my life fucked a one
of them. This day they decided they was all goin'
to fuck me, with the ol' man in town an' nobody
around. They tried coaxin' first. It got mean, an' I
got mean. Come an' get it if you can. The biggest
one, James, said he was goin' to make me suck his
cock. Four against one, nice odds! House near fell
down, the fight there was."

Stretch paused to drink coffee. "Bet Miss Molly
is gettin' all wet an' excited. Anyhow, they come
at me in a rush. James, the oldest, was fixin'
to crack my head with a piece of stove wood.
Another was tryin' to kick the legs out from under
me. Two more were comin' at me from behind. I
killed James with his own chunk of wood. Didn't
know he was dead, but he was down. Rest of
them backed me up by the fire where a kettle
of lye soap was boilin'. I let fly with the kettle
an' blinded an' scalded two of the bastards. The
youngest one ran, and I let him run. Ain't been
heard or seen since then, least not by me. Now
ain't that a nice family story, Big Boy?"

Morgan decided it was probably true. It sounded true, not like some of Stretch's other yarns. He
didn't think he wanted to push her on this. Family
was family, even one like hers. There was more
to be gained, if it didn't get him shot dead, in
poking at her pride in being what she called "the
toughest, baddest woman that ever lived."

"An' you think you could beat up on me," she
said to Morgan. "It's pitiful, the notions men get.
'Cause they're bigger and stronger than most wom-
en, they think all women are the same. Well, I
ain't most women. I have taken the worst shit
they could throw at me an' tossed it right back.
Big Boy, listen to me for your own good. Are you
listenin'?"

"I'm listening but I don't hear you," Morgan said.

"You hear me all right. Big Boy, my shitkicker chum, I have beaten up on big men an' bigger women. In Yuma I near killed a bear of a woman used to be a wrestler in a dirty show in New Orleans. In Yuma the toughest guards walked shy of me—mean men I'm talkin' about. Only time they got me was with a blackjack. You seen that, Miss Molly?"

Molly didn't answer.

"She seen it all right. An' you will feel my fists an' boots. Keep on an' you will—but not yet. Every boy got to get a chance to mend his ways. Grin an' bear it is my good advice. Face it. You're swimmin' in shit an' I got the only rope."

Before she went to look at the herd, Stretch attached a can of kerosene to Travis Mapes's handcuffs. The dead cook had been using the kerosene to start fires in the rainy foothills. Stretch sloshed the can about to make sure there was plenty of kerosene still in it.

"The bullets start to fly, you'll be one roast piglet," she told the terrified kid. She left him by the fire with the spare wheel to hold him in place. He was too far away to be blown up by the fire, but he twitched every time it crackled. When he wasn't doing that, he stared out into the dark. There were no rocks here, just cactus and sagebrush, no cover at all. They were in flat country, and the horses were in rope corrals. The water was poor, and so was the grass.

Morgan and Molly were back by the wagon, handcuffed to wheels. It was a starry night with a chill wind blowing from the desert. There were scorpions and other vicious creatures here, but nothing as dangerous as Stretch. They had no blankets to keep out the cold, and it would get colder as the night wore on.

Molly stirred. "You took a terrible chance tonight. For God's sake, what did you think you were doing? What did you hope to accomplish?"

"Get her riled up."

"You did that all right. My God, for a while I thought it was the end of us. Anyway, the end of you. You must be as crazy as she is. You were challenging her to a fight. A fight! I mean . . . it's ridiculous. A man challenging a woman to a fight."

"She's not your Aunt Matilda," Morgan said.

"Such rubbish you spout. Do you think she'll actually fight you?"

"I hope so. You heard her bragging about all the big men she's whipped."

"That's just bragging. Beating up women isn't the same as men. I never saw her beating up any guards. If you have this stupid fight, you'll win and she'll have to kill you—or the Indian will."

Morgan looked up at the starry sky. Peaceful up there. "How do you know I'm going to win? Don't be taking bets on it."

"The way you talk!" Molly said. "It's insane. You may find yourself fighting her in handcuffs. I've never known her to do anything that wasn't to her advantage. God knows what she'll do to you."

Molly didn't need to tell him the hard facts. "I'm gambling what you said won't happen. She's crazy with pride. If she hobbled me before the fight, she'd never know if she could beat me square."

"Are you saying she's not a cheat?" There was astonishment in Molly's voice. That would change to peevishness in a minute. It did. "In spite of everything, she isn't a cheat? No sane person would think so, but you do."

"In some ways she's not. Keep your temper. I'm trying to explain."

That got him nowhere. "How can you say anything good about her? She's a . . . I don't know what she is. You can't have some queer liking for her?"

"For Christ's sake!"

Molly pretended to look at it sensibly. "That's not so impossible. Both of you are pretty queer customers, if you ask me. She lets you get away with an awful lot."

"I hadn't noticed."

"Like tonight. She'd kill me if I said half the things you said. She even laughed when you called her a horse. And she laughed harder when you said you'd like to kick her in the . . ."

"She laughed, but she's going over it in her mind," he said.

"That's what I'm afraid of," Molly said. "I'll be beaten with the same stick if she gets mad enough. And I thought you cared for me."

"I guess I do care," Morgan said reluctantly. "In my way I do."

"What a way to say something nice! I guess. In my way. You're a roughneck, so what can I expect? Is it true what she said? That you haven't tried to escape because of me?"

Morgan didn't like that kind of talk. You showed what you felt by doing something, not talking about it. "I wouldn't want to leave you behind."

Molly pretended she couldn't hear him. "What was that again?"

"You heard me," Morgan said with clenched teeth.

Molly said, "That's the sweetest thing anyone

ever said to me. Are you sure that's the only reason?"

She was asking for it. "I still have a mind to collect that five hundred dollars."

"You're a liar." She thought for a while. "If someone gave you five hundred dollars, would you try to escape?"

"Right now I can't even get out of these handcuffs, but if it'll set your mind at rest I wouldn't leave you behind for any dollars. That good enough for you? Will that hold you for a while?"

Molly doubted everything you told her. For some reason she had no trust in anybody.

"You intend to kill her, don't you?" Molly started again. "Get her to fight you and then kill her if you can."

"That's right," Morgan lied.

"Why don't you just challenge her to a gunfight?"

"That's not the way to do it."

"Do what? If I knew what you were talking about, perhaps I could make some sense of it. Do you think she's afraid of a gunfight? That you're better with a gun than she is?"

"A gunfight doesn't scare her. In a gunfight even a tiny woman is the equal of a big man. All that counts is the gun and how good the shooters are. If the tiny woman is better with the gun, she wins. If Stretch fights me, she'll be wanting to prove to herself that a woman can have the brute strength of a man. You heard the story about her brothers, how proud she was of killing one and half-killing the others. I doubt if she's fought many men. Men don't get into fights with women, at least not like that. Could even be she's never really fought any man."

"You mean she's always wanted to?"

"I think so. But she doesn' want to fight a man she doesn't think is a match for her. Where would be the satisfaction in that? She wants to fight somebody like me."

Molly chewed on that for a while. "It's crazy, but you could be right. The way she calls you Big Boy all the time. She's always showing off how strong she is. Have you noticed that?"

"Oh, yes," Morgan said. "She lifts wagons and dead horses and throws water barrels around. She's quick on her feet for such a horse of a woman. She boasts she's the toughest, baddest woman that ever lived, and maybe she is. I've never met tougher."

"You sound as if you almost admire her." The peevishness was back in Molly's voice. The slightest hint that you appreciated something about another woman was poison to her. For a woman who had bedded other women—and surely she had—she seemed to regard all other women as enemies. It was hard to figure.

"Well, do you?" she wanted to know. "Do you admire her?"

"Like the grizzly bear," Morgan told her. "The grizzly is a vicious killer, but you can't help admiring the son of a bitch."

"Both of you should be locked up, you and your grizzly bear. Now listen to me. You're forgetting the Indian. If you do kill Stretch in this insane fight, what about the Indian? She'll kill you, Morgan. Give it up. It won't work, unless you have some plan you aren't telling me about."

"I'll tell you as soon as I work one out," Morgan said. He expected her to accuse him of holding back, but she didn't. It would come after she chewed on it for a while; then she'd spit it out like a shot from a gun. Sometimes she was right on target. All you could do was try to dodge the question which wasn't an easy thing to do, the way she kept harping at it. It was even harder when you were chained to the same wagon.

"I'll never forgive you if you don't tell me," she said. "If you can't tell me, who can you tell?"

Nobody, he thought. "I need more time to think," was what he said. They were in the same boat, and while it wasn't likely she'd push him overboard, he couldn't take the chance. There was no need to tell her anything; she'd know when it happened.

It was true, more or less, about needing more time to think. He had been going over a number of plans, none of them very good. He had to make a better plan, one that would get Stretch and Pretty Woman and the Mapeses together when the dynamite exploded. One big bang would end this misery.

Chapter Twenty-three

It started with the coffee. Or maybe it started when Stretch left them in handcuffs until the coffeepot was empty and the food gone. She turned the pot upside down to show there was nothing in it.

"Not a drop," she said to Morgan. "Just as good. You been drinkin' too much of the stuff. It's gettin' your nerves frazzled an' your temper on edge and makin' you say things you'll be sorry for. Best you lay off for a while. Drink water like the horses do. What's good for a horse is good for a horse's ass. Relay the message to your rich lady friend."

Morgan didn't answer. He surely missed his morning coffee, and she knew it. But if it hadn't been the coffee, it would have been something else. There was a meanness in her voice that was different from her usual malicious joking. Usually when she told him he couldn't do something, she changed her mind a few minutes later. This time she didn't.

They hadn't moved out yet. First the kid had to be put where his father's binoculars could pick him up. The light wasn't strong and clear enough for that. They had to wait for the sun. Without the kerosene can tied to him, the kid didn't look so nervous. Stretch told him to wash his face and comb his hair.

Stretch banged her mug on the empty pot and told Morgan to make more coffee. That was all right. He had been trying to get her more riled than she usually was. It would get worse as it went along. That was what he wanted, what he was going to get. The business with the coffee was just a light tap to get his attention.

When the coffee was ready, she tasted it and spat. "Lord God, are you stoopin' so low as to poison me? You want to be a poisoner, you should've took lessons from Cat, God rest her little soul. Got to do better, Big Boy. You're the new cook."

Morgan didn't sit down. If she threw the coffeepot at him, he could dodge it better standing. Stretch drank the rest of the coffee, then poured another mugful. The sun was creeping up.

"You get to cook, but you don't get to eat," Stretch told Morgan. "You're gettin' too fat, I am sorry to say. Should you get into a fight with somebody, you would not be at your best. You got to be like these prizefighters that take off the weight by runnin' an' fastin'. You may not want to do either, but I'll make you do both. What do you say to that?"

She had the coffeepot in her hand. Morgan said, "I say kiss my ass!" He waited for scalding coffee to come at him, but it stayed where it was.

Stretch set the coffeepot down. "How dare you say a thing like that? We ain't even engaged yet."

Stretch never could pass up a joke, even an old one like that. Morgan waited.

The joke over, Stretch got down to cases. "Tonight when you cook an' serve dinner I'll expect you to wear an apron. Now what do you say to that?"

"That's the mean way to do it," Morgan said. "The cowardly way to try and tear somebody down. You're like a mean old woman."

"You're right about the mean, but I'm a mean young woman, and I'm goin' to show you how young an' strong an' mean I am." There was a calmness about her he hadn't seen before, as if she meant everything she said. A lot of the time she blustered and bragged, letting her temper run wild, and some of the threats she made weren't always carried out.

Sister and Ned were in the camp, their breakfast over with, standing away from the fire. Most of the watch on the herd had been left to them, and they looked worn out. Sister had the look of trying not to listen to Stretch. Ned was afraid to look away, as Sister was doing. Stretch ignored them in her eagerness to get at Morgan. The sun was up, but she made no move to show the kid to his father.

Pointing, she said, "You've had it soft till now, Big Boy. That's all changed. Startin' tonight we're goin' to have a reg'lar latrine back of camp. Not just a hole to shit in, a reg'lar trench like they have in the army. One for the ladies and one for the men, though Ned may object to you usin' his. If he does you'll just have to drop your pants in the brush like you been doin'. Now what do you think of that?"

"What I said before," Morgan said. "You're a vicious old woman. You've got the mind of one." Morgan repeated what Alamo Mapes said. "You should be hung down with chains in a madhouse."

That struck a spark, but nothing caught fire. Morgan wondered if she'd ever been in one. She'd left home as a kid and was now close to 30. She could have done time behind other bars than Yuma. The spark in her eyes was long gone by now.

"The one that's mad is you. If you ain't ravin' mad now, you will be before I get through with you. I'll make you so droolin', babblin' mad you'll eat shit an' think it's punkin pie. I will break you, Big Boy."

"What if I don't? I've met tougher women than you." Morgan couldn't think of any. "What'll you do? Shoot me? That's what you have in mind for me anyway."

"Sure I'll shoot you," Stretch said. "But it'll be like how you shoot a wounded animal, an act of mercy. That's what you'll be—a poor crawlin' whinin' critter that has to be shot. I'm goin' to kick an' beat you so bad you'll beg for a bullet. What is it, Pretty?"

The Indian whispered in Stretch's ear.

"Ol' Mapes is flashing his binoculars." Stretch got up and pointed at Morgan. "I'll be talkin' to you later. Think on what I said. You got to learn to crawl."

They got young Mapes squared away and moved out. Stretch had sense enough not to make Morgan try to work in handcuffs, as she did the kid. There was no badmouthing because there was too much to do. Molly stayed on a horse, and Sister drove the wagon. Deep sand was still ahead, but the wagon hadn't bogged down yet. Foremost in Morgan's mind was the thought that it would overturn. Without the dynamite there would be no plan.

In open country it was harder to keep the herd together. It kept spreading out at the edges and required constant effort to keep it in any kind of shape. They could have used Jimmy and Lester now. The herd moved ahead, but it was slow going, trying to keep the mass of horses together and cover distance at the same time.

They started into the first real desert they'd seen. It didn't happen all at once. For a long time, they'd been moving through terrain thick with patches of chaparral, sage and greasewood. While there were no sand dunes yet, it could kill you if you weren't wary. To run out of water here was to die a lingering death. A man dying of thirst could crawl to a clean, clear pool only to die of the arsenic that had seeped into it.

They drank more water here. Desert sand didn't absorb heat; it threw it back. Heat waves shimmered in the distance as the sun beat down. Raised in high country, the horses were dazed by the heat, and locowood was an ever present danger. There were snakes and lizards and kangaroo rats here, none to be seen in the heat of the day.

They stopped at noon in the shade of a saguaro cactus, drinking warm water and chewing jerked beef. There was canned food, but it was too hot to eat. Nobody talked. The herd was spreading out but going nowhere because the horses were too hot. It would take hard work and a lot of patience to give the herd a movable shape.

There was no sign of the Mapeses and no cover even remotely close to their noon camp. Stretch checked their back trail before she lighted down. Nothing she saw caused her to say or do anything. She didn't pass the binoculars on to Morgan,

something she usually did even when she was
mad at him. It was getting dark by the time they
reached the water hole marked on the map, and
she hadn't said a single word to him since they
started out that morning.

The water was protected by a scattering of rocks,
but there was no other cover. Rope corrals had to
be built before they could rest. Heat from the day
was still heavy, but the temperature would drop
as the hours passed. Night on the desert could get
biting cold, and the fire was welcome.

Though the water hole was large, it was not to
Stretch's liking, and before the horses crowded in
to drink, there was greenish scum on the surface
of the water and blobs of tadpoles. The water
looked poisonous enough to kill the entire herd,
but there were no bleached animal bones anywhere around it, a sure sign that the water was
drinkable. To drink the water as it was, without
first boiling it, might give you the shits, but it
wouldn't kill you. Morgan didn't tell Stretch any
of this because she didn't ask.

He didn't start looking for an apron or start
opening cans. It was up to Stretch to start bull-
shitting him again, if she wanted to. Ned got the
fire going, and Sister filled the coffeepot and set
it on to boil. Then she went back and filled two
more pots, drinking water for the night and the
following day. A lot more than two pots of boiled
water would be needed. Stretch watched Sister
dragging the heavy pots from the water hole but
didn't say anything.

Stretch still didn't say anything when Sister
began to heat up cans of beans. She continued
to watch while Sister dug out dried potatoes and
canned tomatoes. Stretch looked as if she'd never seen anyone cooking before. There would be

no biscuits because Stretch had spilled out the sourdough barrel the day she killed the cook. The boiling coffee smelled good as the night wind got colder.

Everybody was drinking coffee but Morgan and Molly. What the hell! Time to start the party. He picked up two mugs and reached for the coffee-pot.

"I told you no coffee!" Stretch's voice cracked like a whip. "No coffee an' no food. Touch that pot an' I'll shoot a finger off! Now stand back from the fire."

Morgan stood back. He could see her better without the flames shooting up in front of him. Through the flames and smoke she looked like the she-devil she thought she was. Sister and Ned sat close together like people expecting a storm to break. Molly did nothing but sit with her hands together. Travis Mapes gaped, nervous but fascinated, his slack mouth hanging open. Pretty Woman held the shotgun midway between Morgan and the kid.

Stretch snapped her fingers at Sister, and the food was dished up. Ned took his plate and nodded thanks without taking his eyes away from Stretch. Sister put plates beside Stretch and the Indian but didn't fill a plate for herself. Morgan and Molly got nothing.

Stretch put the plate between her legs, forked up a mouthful of food with her left hand and made a great show of chewing and swallowing. "Well now, don't that taste good. You're goin' to make ol' Ned one hell of a wife, little Sister." She was looking at Morgan but couldn't pass up the urge to downgrade somebody else. "Don't feel too bad, Big Boy. Think on all the lardy pounds you're goin' to be sheddin'. Bring you down to fightin' weight. Won't do Miss Molly a bit of harm either. She's got an ass on her like the backside of a horse."

Morgan watched her forking in the food. "You're fixing to starve us, is that it?" Might as well push on with this, wherever it led. "You can do that—the coward's way. You missed your true calling. You should've been a prison guard, beating up on the sick and helpless."

Anger flickered and then went dead in Stretch's eyes. She was trying to remain calm, hard for her. "Don't be lookin for pity. You ain't sick or helpless. You may be useless, but you're not helpless. How about gettin' started on them latrines? Dig the ladies' right. I want to be your first customer. Get your little shovel, Big Boy."

Morgan didn't answer.

"How come you don't say that'll be the day?" Stretch's laugh was as sour as her face. "Bet that's what you told your ma when she told you to get up an' go to school. Only I ain't your ma an' don't have her sweet nature. Seems I recall an old whore name of Morgan was abandoned by her son an' was sellin' her ol' ass when she wasn't scrubbin' floors. Couldn't be your ma, could it?"

"Fuck you, gutless woman-licker!"

Stretch put her plate aside and stayed calm. "Come on, Big Boy. You never said that to your ma, or am I gettin' this mixed up? If you did, shame on you! I will tell you somethin' I ain't mixed up about. I surely am a woman-licker, but I surely ain't gutless."

"Surely you are," Morgan said. "Denyin' people food is the only way you can get at them and beat them down."

"I can beat you with this." Stretch held up her fist. It was as big as Morgan's fist and just as hard. Yuma toughened women as well as men. Stretch's fist looked like a club. Beating her, if it came to that, would be no taffy pull. "I can beat you down into the ground with this. I can beat on your kidneys so bad you'll be pissin' blood for a month. When I get you down I can stomp you flat with these." Stretch dug her bootheels into the dirt. "I can boot your face till no woman that don't like freaks would look at you."

"You're all mouth," Morgan said. "You got a mouth like a sow and a brain like a rat. The rat bites babies and sick people and runs. You turn my stomach."

"Lawsy me! If you can't stand to be around me, why don't you leave? Walk out. Pick up your big feet an' mosey along. Head on out, cowpoke. I'm tellin' you to leave, Big Boy. Take your sweetheart with you."

"You'd shoot me in the back first step I took." Morgan wasn't sure of that. "Back-shooting is the safe way."

"Ask your sweetheart about back-shooting." Stretch didn't look at Molly. "I can shoot you any way I like—back, front, standin' up, layin' down, takin' a shit. Tough men, so-called, think they want to die with their boots on. How about you dyin' with your pants down?"

She was a lot better at abusing people than he was. A lifetime of hard knocks had given her a mouth like a shark. "You're still just a windbag," he said. "All you do is fart from the wrong end."

Stretch gave Morgan an evil grin. "Can't get your mind out of the shithole, can you? That reminds me. Time you started diggin' latrines. Forgot you don't want to do that. Then how about gettin' into Sister's dress an' doin' a little waltz with Ned?"

Ned looked startled.

" 'Course you'd have to let it out a wee bit," Stretch said. "Would look good in a dress, maybe even a poke bonnet. You got a poke bonnet, Sister?"

Sister's plain face was a mask of misery. "No, Stretch, I don't have a poke bonnet."

"That's a shame. It'd suit you and suit Big Boy even better." Stretch made hand motions like she was fitting Morgan for a dress. "I could make you wear it. I could make you run around in Sister's drawers pretendin' Ned is tryin' to rape you."

This time Sister looked over at Stretch, her face more of a mask than before. Stretch wasn't earning any loyalty there.

She held up her hand to cut off anything Morgan might have to say. Then she walked out of camp, took a look around, then came back in. "What I have in mind for you's got to be private. Don't want the Mapeses to see it even from a distance. Might get the idea to move in fast, you an' me too busy to notice. Pretty's good, but she can't deal with four men comin' in from four sides. Get it?"

"What's wrong with now?"

"I just said you won't want the Mapeses buttin' in less you think they'd kill everybody but you. We don't know where the fuckers are. Could be anywhere. Things here look normal, an' they got to stay that way till they can't see so easy. That means better cover from pryin' eyes."

"Sure you won't change your mind by tomorrow?" He knew she was right about the Mapeses. The binoculars he'd seen the Mapeses using were too old to be night glasses like the new ones the army was starting to use. But even ordinary binoculars could pick up movement by firelight. If they were close enough, they wouldn't need binoculars.

"I'll change my mind anytime I like," Stretch told him. "You know what women are like." That made her laugh, but it was short and ugly. "You think you got women figured, like every man does. Go on thinkin' of me as a woman all you like. Only this time this woman is goin' to grind your face in the dirt." She tried to pout. She was being coy. "Has to be private, like men and women do."

Morgan let himself be handcuffed to the wagon. There wasn't much choice with the Indian's shotgun pointing at him. Stretch thought she was joking about the way women changed their minds from one minute to the next, but she was a woman herself and she just might do it. A nod would make the Indian trip the two triggers of the 10-gauge, which was not to say it wouldn't happen. But so far his half-figured plan seemed to be working. The next camp would decide it, he felt pretty sure. By then they'd be mostly out of the desert with the fort 30 to 40 miles away. Stretch knew, as well as he, that it couldn't go on the way it was going. The army was in front, the Mapeses behind, and this thing between them had to be settled—or at least she seemed to think so. Most anybody else would settle it by killing him, and that would be that. Unless he was really digging his own grave, really and truly this time, Stretch had to settle this to her own satisfaction, to prove once and for all that she was different from all other women. He could see Molly at the other end of the wagon. She might be asleep. More than once he had accused her of reading too much into things. Maybe he was reading too much into what he thought was Stretch's state of mind. Who could read the mind of a madwoman?

Molly wasn't asleep, more's the pity. All this rehashing was getting to be a nuisance. He didn't need to be told for the umpteenth time what he was getting into. If he'd read Stretch wrong, then he'd read no more.

"This fight . . ." Molly started to say, then changed to, "If I'm not handcuffed I'll try to get at the Indian—knock her down, kill her. Sister and Ned won't help, but they won't try to stop me. They're too afraid to do anything. If I could just . . ."

"Wait and see," Morgan told her. "It might not happen." If it didn't happen—if Stretch changed her mind—they would never see another sunrise. Of that he felt sure. The idea of Molly tackling Pretty Woman didn't offer much hope, but he knew she wasn't just talking. She'd do it, knowing that if he died, so would she.

"I think she means it," Molly said, "by the look in her eyes and the way she sounded. I felt the way she sounded when I set out to kill Alamo Mapes." A pause to reflect on the past. "It's a pity I didn't. There would have been none of this. Have you ever fought a woman?"

"Not with my fists."

"Don't be stupid. It's stupid to joke at a time like this."

"No, I've never fought a woman, any woman," Morgan said. "Does it matter?"

"Of course it matters," Molly said irritably. Then she went on to tell him the best places to hurt a woman. Morgan wasn't squeamish, but he found it hard to listen. "Go after her face. Keep hitting her in the face, break her face, break her nose so it can't be fixed, break her teeth. All women are afraid of their faces being marked, even a brute like Stretch. But it's the breasts you must concentrate on. Hit there and kick her there if you get the chance. A woman's breasts are the most vulnerable part. You have to forget she's a woman and remember she can be hurt as a woman. She'll kill you if you hold back or show pity."

Oh Christ, Morgan thought, women were so merciless. The weaker sex, my ass! Nothing she'd told him he didn't know, but hearing it from another woman made his stomach turn. But what she'd said was what he'd have to do. It was that or be crippled for life or killed. The truth crowded in on him like it never had before. He was going into a no-rules fight with a woman!

"You can't be having second thoughts," Molly said. "She said she won't let you back out, and I believe her. Whatever she says now, I believe her."

Morgan felt like a battered old pug being forced to fight the champion. "I don't want to back out. Just ease up, will you?"

Molly said, "You've got to show more fighting spirit. I've attended prizefights. I know something about it. You've got to hate your opponent. You've got to want to kill your opponent. Think of all the times Stretch has insulted and belittled you. Think of all the terrible things she's done."

Morgan was thinking of all the terrible things she'd be trying to do to him, but it was no good trying to work up what Molly called the fighting spirit. It usually came to you the first punch you took in the face. Then you got it right away or you were in for a licking. Now there's a word Stretch would like. He was getting punch-drunk and the bell hadn't sounded yet.

"Got to get some sleep," he said and meant it. A day of hard work and no food had left him tired. Maybe he could prod Stretch into giving him some food come morning. He sure as hell wasn't going to eat a heavy meal, if she offered it, before the fight.

He was dreaming about food when he awoke in the gray light before sunrise. Travis Mapes, with the can of kerosene attached to him, nodded beside the still-smoking embers of the fire. Pretty Woman, sitting opposite him with the shotgun, had her eyes closed. She opened them when Morgan moved and the handcuffs rattled. Then Sister and Ned got out of their blankets, Ned to build up the fire, and Sister to start the first meal of the day. A little later, smelling coffee, Stretch came out of her tent.

She didn't even glance at Morgan as she ate a few mouthfuls of dried apples washed down with coffee.

Morgan wasn't all that hungry yet, but he could have used some food. He decided not to prod her about food or coffee. This wasn't the place to do it. He knew Molly was as hungry as he was, but she said nothing about it. If she expected him to promote some food, she was in for a disappointment. By the morning of the following day they would have food in their bellies or have no need of it.

Sister unlocked their handcuffs and gave the key to Stretch. After young Mapes was put on display for a few minutes, they moved out.

Chapter Twenty-four

This was the longest and hottest stretch they had to cross to get to water. One of the horses fell down and wouldn't or couldn't get up. It lay in a patch of sand and flaking rock, with twitching muscles and bulging eyes. Stretch dismounted, kicked the animal and jabbed its hindquarters with Morgan's knife until blood flowed freely, but it refused to budge. Morgan, who stayed on his horse, couldn't see what was wrong. The animal could have swallowed a poisonous spider in a mouthful of grass. It could be the start of one of the many diseases horses came down with. Whatever it was, the horse, a good one, was done for.

Stretch killed it with Morgan's big Bowie. She didn't ask him to do it. Her eyes met his as she put the knife away, and they moved on. Like the day before, she hadn't said a word to him since they broke camp. He didn't expect her to, but you never knew.

They didn't stop at noon this last day. Stretch didn't say anything to the others. Noon came and went, and nothing was said. Ordinarily she would have said something but not this time, and the lines of impatience in her face got deeper as time after time they had to go after stragglers. Every bothersome move the horses made made her angrier and more impatient, but the only way she showed it was in the grim set of her mouth. She yipped at the horses but didn't curse them. Everything she did was like an afterthought, as if she had to make an effort to remember where she was and what she was doing. More than once, horses she should have been keeping in line broke loose and were getting away before she realized what was happening and galloped after them. Twice she failed to bring them back—five horses were lost—but she said nothing about it. She didn't rage, didn't shrug it off, didn't do anything. If it hadn't been for Morgan, Pretty Woman and the kid, they would have lost more horses than they did.

In the late afternoon, dragging along in the heat, they saw a line of hills in the distance. Morgan knew from the map that this long stretch of narrow hills was all that separated them from rocky scrub country that ran another ten miles to the fort. From where they were they could see only the high line of the hills, but they would begin to move up out of the desert before they got that far. On the map, the next water and grass could be found at Paint Rock, with an arrow pointing at something called Scoop Basin. Morgan saw Stretch looking at the map, then using the binoculars. If she spotted the painted or naturally colored rock, she gave no sign of it. But she must have seen it because she told Ned to tell Morgan the herd had to move

about a mile southeast and then head in straight.
Easier said than done, Morgan thought, and it
took a lot of slow, hard work to get it done. About
five miles from where they got the herd moving in
the right direction, he could see the rock, tall and
white in the red glow thrown over everything by
the setting sun.

Stretch turned in the saddle and used the binoculars while there was still light enough to see,
using her hat to shade the lenses. There was a
long stretch of featureless desert behind, miles of
it, and if the Mapeses had been there she would
have seen them. Morgan knew they were there—
they had to be—but too far back to be spotted in
the thickening light. Up till now, they were keeping their part of the deal. If they were planning a
move they were cutting it fine, with the fort not
too far off. Could be they had circled out wide and
were waiting in the hills. The way the herd was
moving and all the time lost, they could have been
there long since. But the Mapeses could wait,
Morgan thought. The coming night, if he lived
through it, would bring this thing to an end.

It was close to dark, and they were moving to
higher ground. They had left Paint Rock about
half a mile behind. In the half-dark its natural
gray color could hardly be seen. By day, in bright
sunlight, it would look white and be seen from
miles away. What was marked as Scoop Basin
was dead ahead, a winding passage between two
low hills that ended in a long, wide place with
slightly elevated sides. Right down its middle it
was scattered with rocks, some rising to a good
height, but a good part of it was flat and grassy.
There was a spring forming a pool about halfway
to the other end of it. Tall rocks crowded the pool
and would give some protection from the sun a

good part of the day. Alders grew to one side of the pool, and the ground was spongy there. Getting the horses to the pool, they had to drive them through gaps in the crooked stand of rocks. No need to pen the horses here. It was a good place to defend as well as to make camp in. Sister, driving the wagon, came through last.

Morgan waited. That's what he'd been doing lately, waiting for Stretch to do something or say something, but for the moment she seemed to be at ease, and that was as ominous as if she'd been making threats. Maybe more so. She watched Ned and Sister doing their chores, starting the fire and putting the coffeepot on to boil.

She ate none of the food that Sister prepared. Instead, she took the shotgun from Pretty Woman and sent her out to scout for the Mapeses. She looked from the cookpots to Morgan and Molly, but she didn't tell them to eat. Morgan wouldn't have eaten if food had been offered. A tight feeling in his gut told him this wasn't the time to be packing away a load of beans. Stretch drank very little coffee, which was unusual for her. With no food and a few mouthfuls of coffee, maybe she was thinking of a belly blow that would make her puke.

Pretty Woman was gone for more than an hour, and when she came back all she did was shake her head, which meant the Mapeses weren't anywhere close. That brought Stretch to life with an abruptness that surprised even Morgan. Suddenly she was her old self again. It showed immediately in the way she stood up, flexing her long legs, socking one fist into the other, giving a little whoop. "You're goin' to see somethin' this night, ladies an' gents," she said, not shouting but loud. She had the air of somebody addressing a large

crowd of spectators. All she needed was a top hat
and a megaphone.

"You are about to see a fight to the finish tween
me, the champeen, and the contender, Big Boy
over there." She pointed at Morgan and waggled
her fingers. Nobody applauded so she did it herself. It's crazy, Morgan thought. "This fight's been
a long time coming," Stretch said, shouting now.
"And here it is, ladies an' gents! Can't be put off
one more minute."

She took off her hat and sailed it away. Nobody
picked it up. "The rules are there are no rules.
We're going to fight the dirtiest way we know
how, am I right, Big Boy?"

Morgan nodded and raised one hand. "You're
right."

He would always remember how it was—Sister and Ned standing together back from the far
side of the fire, Molly and Travis handcuffed to
the wagon to keep them out of the way, Pretty
Woman standing apart from everyone, holding
the shotgun, the coffeepot still steaming in a bed
of coals, darkness outside the circle of light.

"You're right I'm right," Stretch shouted. She
took the dildo from the pocket of her canvas coat
before she peeled it off and threw it aside. She
shook the rubber dildo and the leather straps
flapped. Morgan sure as hell hadn't expected this.
"You're goin' to get fucked in the ass, Big Boy!"
The shout was closer to a scream. "You been
tellin' me to go fuck myself. It's you is goin' to
get fucked! You been wantin' to fuck me. It's in
your face every time you look at me. Here's your
chance to try. You want to try?"

"Sure," Morgan said.

"You heard him!" Stretch shouted. "Says it so
casual like it's nothin'. The big man is goin' to

fuck me, he thinks. Then do it, you prideful bastard. With your hard man's face and big ugly cock, try it. But there's a kicker in there, Mr. Contender. You down me you got to fuck me. That'll be the day, but you got to try. You got to get that big ugly cock in me or Pretty'll kill you quick. You hear that, Pretty?"

The Indian nodded.

It was quiet enough for Morgan to say, "What do I get out of it if I win?"

Stretch roared with laughter. "You get to fuck me. Ain't that prize enough for you? Ain't a man don't want to fuck me nowhere. You want to go free, is that it?"

Morgan got time to answer. "That's it."

Stretch gave him a pitying look. "God love you for a mis'rable fool. If the likes of you can fuck me you deserve to go free. You have my word on it. Pretty won't shoot you. Nod your head, Pretty."

The Indian nodded.

Morgan said, "How do I know you'll keep your word? Pretty'll do anything you tell her."

"You should've done the same stead of talkin' back all the time. Now look where you find yourself. If I wanted Pretty to kill you I'd tell her to do it right now. You ain't goin' to get killed that quick." She brandished the dildo, still clutched in her left hand. "You're goin' to get punished with this. Who can say? Maybe you'll like it. I got to think on what to do with you after you're lyin' there with a sore asshole. Maybe I'll let you live so's you can remember how you was fucked by a woman."

"You're no woman." Morgan wanted to get on with this. He was as ready as he'd ever be. Unreality crowded in. He drove unreality out of his head. This was real. She was unbuckling her gunbelt.

Stretch waved the hand with the dildo in it. "That don't make me mad. Because I am a woman, the kind of woman I want to be. None of your badmouthing can change that. And think on this." She stuffed the dildo in her pants pocket. "Think on it good."

She came at him in a rush. Ready or not, it took him by surprise. Stretch's big body stuck him and drove him back. The way she moved she was trying to get the feel of him, find out how he fought. She waded in after him and landed a punch to his jaw, rocking his head with her hard fist. She tried to follow it up by a hook with the other hand. That one he dodged, but the right hand hit him again, this time in the side of the neck. She spat at his face as the blow landed. They circled, but it wasn't like fighting Bowie Mapes. Morgan and Stretch were sluggers, and they wanted to get down to giving blows and taking them. Her reach was as long as his. That was because of her height. She knew he was going for her jaw, trying for a knockout punch. He swung and got her with a side of the head punch that would have knocked anyone else off her feet. It jolted her head but didn't knock her down. She pretended to be dazed for an instant; then she came at him swinging both fists and kicking at the same time. A swing clipped him in the jaw. A kick below the knee sent him wobbling. Then he drove her back with wild swings that didn't do much damage. Her fists came up to block his swings, and while he was still trying to bust her face, she kicked him in the same leg. Kicking out at her with that leg made the pain worse and threatened to collapse him. He switched to the other leg and kicked at her crotch, but she blocked it with her thigh. A grunt of pain came from her mouth. Her jaw was

set, her eyes narrow, as she bored in again. He
got her with a blow to the breast that made her
cry out. That was where to hit her. He knew he'd
been holding back. He cursed himself for doing
it. He tried to hit her in the same breast, but
she knocked his arm up and aimed a kick at his
balls. His legs were wide apart, and he had to
jump to avoid it. The kick got him in the thigh of
the damaged leg and nearly brought him down.
Stomping his foot, moving from one foot to the
other, he tried to get the bad leg working right.
The pain got worse, but he was moving better.

They were still on their feet and hadn't yet gone
down in a welter of arms and legs. That might
give him an advantage, maybe not. He had some
pounds on her, if that made any difference. What
she had going for her was ferocity. She wanted to
cripple him or kill him. She hadn't worked herself
up to that yet. The fight had just started, and
she showed no signs of tiredness. Her wind was
good, and her movements were controlled. The
bad part was coming. It came with a whoop and
a rush like a mad bull at his middle. Her long legs
carried her forward, and she was quicker than
he was. Her head knocked the wind out of him
and crashed him down on his back. Flying back
with her diving on top of him, he grabbed her
wrists, raised his legs and threw her into the air
and over his head. She landed on her feet before
the force of the throw made her stagger and fall.
But she was back on her feet as fast as he was.
The throw and the fall had rattled her, and she
was a little more wary as she moved in again.
She aimed a kick and missed and then kicked
with the other leg. One leg was as quick as the
other. Same with her fists. She didn't look to be
right-handed or left-handed, the way she jabbed

and threw punches. He hadn't noticed it before, but he noticed it now. A right to the jaw was followed by a left to the ribs; then she switched and left-handed him in the jaw and right-handed him in the gut. He dropped his hands to protect his gut, and she landed a right and left to the jaw. White sparks were in his head and a sudden weakness in his arms. He backed away from her, shaking his head, trying to clear it. She came after him, swinging and kicking at the same time. The kick that got him in the balls wasn't the strongest, but it made him yell. It cleared his head and drove him at her in a killing rage. The ferocious swings he aimed at her drove her back.

The Indian moved as they fought back and forth. She had a holstered pistol but still held the shotgun. Stretch backed off a few feet, then charged at him again. They met in a savage exchange of blows that decided nothing. A stiff-armed right to her breast made her grimace with pain. He thought he saw doubt in her eyes. Maybe he wanted to see it. He tasted blood when she punched him in the mouth and tried for an uppercut with the other hand. The upward swing went wild and threw her off balance, and he landed a solid blow to her gut. It was like hitting a board, but it told on her. He hit her again in the same place, and she backed away puking coffee. He bored in after her, and they clinched. Blood dripped from his chin, and she smelled of puke. So did he after she tried to spit the last of the puke in his face. Some of it spattered in his eyes and he had to back off, sleeving at his eyes, half-blind, trying to see. His eyes burned, and he saw her through a mist of pain. She jabbed at him, trying to goad him into another swing that would leave him open for another kick. Another jab that took her too far forward got her a kick in the crotch that made her dance with pain.

She shook it off, but there was doubt in her eyes for the first time. He wasn't imagining it. It went as quickly as the pain, but he knew he'd seen it for real. He didn't know how tired she was, if at all. They circled flat-footed, looking for an opening. Morgan knew he wasn't a graceful fighter. Neither was she, but she could hit. They moved in fast and met head-on like before, and when they clinched she tried to knee him in the balls. His balls still hurt from the kick. A knee in the balls would put him down. He blocked it with his thigh and punched her in the face. It should have smashed her nose. It opened a cut in her cheekbone. She pushed him back with both hands, and he let himself go. His arms felt heavy, and suddenly he felt tired. No food, a lot of punishment, punches, kicks—he was tired. Her next swing carried her past him, and he kicked her in the back of the knee before she could turn. Her knee buckled and she hit the ground with her face. Turning fast, she nearly got up before he threw his full weight on her. It knocked her on her back, and she started kicking wildly at his legs. She grabbed his head and tried to bite him in the face. He grabbed a breast and twisted it until she screamed. Her hands slipped down to his throat, the hard fingers digging it, trying to cut off his air. He reached up and bent her thumb back until it snapped, and still she tried to hit him in the face with the damaged hand. All her strength was behind the effort to throw him off. Instead, they grappled and rolled over and over. Rolling, he got flashes of Ned and Sister, the Indian; then the same faces flashed again. They rolled into the edge of the fire and rolled out with ashes all over them. Their bodies were smeared with blood and puke and ashes and sweat. A fierce jerk of her body put her on top of him, and one hand was trying to tear his ear off. He tore her hand away from his ear, but she was still on top of him.

She had grunted or screamed when pain hit her. Now she was screaming words. All the hate spilled out of her in a wild, crazy torrent of words. Her hand was trying to reach down to claw at his crotch. "I'm goin' to fuck you!" she screamed over and over. Then she started daring him to fuck her. "Fuck me! Fuck me! I'll kill you! Fuck me! Kill him, Pretty! Fuck me!" She shuddered and screamed as they rolled again, and this time they ended up with Morgan on top. The shotgun was close by. He was going to fuck her. He was as crazy as she was. His fist swung in a short arc and hit her squarely on the chin. Her head snapped back, but she wasn't knocked out. Her hands still clawed at his crotch. He ripped her pants open, then opened his own pants and took out his cock. It was hard as rock. Saliva dribbled from her mouth, and her eyes were crazy. He forced her legs apart and shoved his cock into her. It went in all the way, and she screamed as her whole body shuddered with a fierce orgasm. Morgan shot his load on that first thrust. "Kill him, Pretty!" Stretch screamed. "Kill him! Kill him for me!" Morgan hit her again, and she went limp. He was getting up off her when there was another scream, and he saw Pretty Woman clawing at her face. Sister, screaming just as loud, smashed her over the head with the empty coffeepot. She was sinking to the ground and covered with blood, when Ned hit her on the head with the iron bean pot. She fell hard, and Sister snatched the pistol from her hand and kicked her in the face. Ned kept beating her with the heavy pot until her skull caved in. Her legs kicked once; then she lay still.

Stretch was still unconscious, and while Morgan was taking the handcuffs key from her pocket, Sister came over and handed him the Indian's pistol and shotgun. "We had to do what we did," she said simply. "It couldn't go on any longer. What are you going to do with her? Try to turn her over to the law? That means us, too."

Morgan gave her back the shotgun. "You'll need this later for guarding her. Nobody's going to turn you over to anybody. You and Ned are going to disappear. Nobody will ever hunt you. I'll explain later. I'd be dead if not for you and Ned." For some reason, Ned was standing over the dead Indian. Morgan waved to him, and he waved back.

He unlocked Molly's handcuffs and tried to help her up. Instead of being relieved, she tried to slap his face, but he grabbed her wrist before she could do it. Enough of being beaten on by women. "Have you gone stark raving mad?" she said. "In all my life I've never seen anything so disgusting. I couldn't believe my eyes. I mean, did you have to . . . ?"

"I don't know," Morgan said. He took the handcuffs away from her and told her to strip off. She was going to switch clothes with Stretch. "Soon as you're stripped, take her clothes off. Don't argue—do it."

Molly wanted to argue. "Why must I put on her filthy clothes? What is this all about?"

"Damn you, there isn't time to explain." Morgan pulled the clothes off Stretch and threw them at Molly. "Put them on, then the hat. For Christ's sake, get your clothes off. Nobody's going to look at you. Hurry up." Travis Mapes was trying to be heard, but Morgan ignored him.

Stretch came to in Molly's clothes but didn't notice it at first. Like a drunk coming out of a whiskey fog, she looked as if she couldn't quite remember what had happened. Morgan knew he couldn't have hit her that hard. She had a jaw like oak. His hand still hurt. Stretch looked down at Molly's shirt, then over at Molly herself. "What's going on?" she said to Morgan. The handcuffs on her rattled.

"Fight's over. You lost," he said.

"You didn't win. The Mapeses will kill you yet. How're you goin' to trade me for her?"

She was quick. Groggy or not, she'd caught on to some of it. They would have to watch her as closely as she'd watched them. He got her on her feet and handcuffed her to the wagon after handing the pistol to Molly. The kid was terrified. Morgan called Sister over and told her to watch Stretch good. "Don't listen to her. Don't kill her. We need her to get out of this."

"I'd like to kill her," Sister said. "She can't be allowed to do any more harm."

"You have my promise on that," Morgan said.

Molly followed him to where Ned was standing guard over the dead Indian. "Bury her right outside camp," Morgan told him. "Dig deep as you can, and cover her good. We don't want any buzzards flapping in the morning. You and Sister did good."

Ned took the body by the heels and dragged it away.

Morgan picked up the blood-spattered coffeepot. "Wash it off and fix good strong coffee," he told Molly. "Then I'll explain."

This time she didn't argue. He eased himself down by the fire, favoring the leg that had taken the worst kicks. His face was lumpy and would look worse by morning. If Alamo Mapes asked about it he would blame it on Stretch, which would certainly be true. Might even be a good reason for agreeing to trade Molly. He was sick of getting knocked around.

Molly put the coffee on to boil; then she settled down to listen.

"When we show the kid to his father you're going to be Stretch." Morgan massaged his aching knee. "I'm going to wave like I want to talk some more. If he waves, which he will, we'll meet way out like we did before. Deal will be Stretch is tired of being dogged and wants a straight trade for you. The fort is close, and she wants to be rid of you. We'll leave Stretch dressed as you chained to the wagon with the kid. But I'll tell Mapes to give us time to move on before he comes for the kid."

Molly fretted with impatience. "For God's sake, what happens then?"

"Stretch and all the Mapeses get blown up." Quickly, Morgan told her about the dynamite and how he'd explode it with a long range rifle shot.

"But that will stampede the horses." Molly suddenly was back in the horse business.

Morgan was tired and hurt and could have used a long soak in a hot tub. He said wearily, "You and Sister and Ned will have to move the herd as far ahead as you can. Forget the goddamned horses. Mapes may smell a trap. The whole thing could fall apart, but it's the best chance we have. If we don't kill the Mapeses they'll keep coming. Even if you get to the fort and sell the horses, they'll kill you sometime. They won't let up on you."

Molly touched the front of Stretch's dirty red shirt. "If this doesn't fool them they'll shoot me.

I'll be standing there like a target. They have that rifle. I'll never pass for Stretch. She's taller than I am, has a different build."

"Look tall. Pull the hatbrim down over your eyes like she does. Do it now so I can see. Walk away a bit."

It would have to do, he decided after he looked at her. The high crowned hat with the forward crease and the red shirt was close enough. What other option did they have? But she was right. It could get her killed. It's not likely that Bowie Mapes would miss a steady shot a second time.

"You'll pass," Morgan said. "Wet a rag with hot coffee and wipe off the front of that shirt. It's got puke on it."

Molly glared at him. "I wish Mapes would shoot *you*."

That was altogether possible, Morgan thought.

Chapter Twenty-five

"Better warn your pa, kid. They're up to something sneaky." Morgan was unlocking Travis Mapes's handcuffs, and Stretch was trying to scare him. She didn't have to try. The kid was scared and confused and couldn't figure out what was happening. It was just before first light, and Morgan wanted to be sure they'd do it right.

During the night he had explained the plan to Ned and Sister. Ned was astonished, but Sister wasn't. "If I get to the fort my story will be that you were blown to bits with the others. It's a whole box of dynamite. If anybody wants to look, all they'll see is a hole in the ground. A blast like that will turn them into confetti."

Ned shuddered; Sister did not. "That's how we'll disappear," she said.

"Off the face of the earth," Morgan said. He wanted them to believe him. He needed their help. "Once the story gets out they'll stop looking for you. After it's done you can take what money Stretch had and start for New Mexico. I owe you my life."

"I think we saved our own lives," Sister said.

Now it was morning and he was set to pull it off. Molly had cleaned the shirt and was wearing Stretch's hat. She didn't look much like Stretch, but he hoped Mapes would be giving most of his attention to the kid. Sitting by the fire and drinking coffee, the kid didn't know he had only a short time to live. Neither did Stretch, but she was brighter than he was, knew some sort of trade was in the works and was yelling about it. Let her yell, Morgan thought. They can't hear her with binoculars. Molly wanted to gag her, but Morgan said no, keep away from her.

"Now listen to me," he said to the kid. "I'm going to try to make a deal with your father. We're going to pass off Stretch as Molly so he'll let us go. You'll be left with her, handcuffed to the wagon. The deal will be he has to hold off nine hours before he comes to get you."

Morgan didn't know why he said nine hours. He might as well have said 24. Mapes would start in as soon as he saw his kid chained to the wagon. "If he keeps his word we'll be through the hills and right on top of the fort. It won't be too bad. We'll leave you plenty of water."

"My father always keeps his word," the kid said. A real choirboy, Morgan thought. "I hate to be a part of deceiving him."

"You'll be doing it for a good reason. Once he admits to himself the whole thing was a mistake, he'll turn about and go home and take you with him." Morgan added a bonus. "He can hand Stretch over to the law. You understand all

I've been saying? That's good. One last thing—
act natural or I'll kill you."

Morgan thought this must be something like an
actor feels before he goes on stage, except actors
usually don't get shot no matter how much the
audience hates them. The sun was up and he
had the binoculars to see how Mapes responded
when he waved the shirt. Molly was nervous, and
he didn't blame her. There was some warmth in
the sun when he looked again and saw Alamo
Mapes looking their way from the top of Paint
Rock. That was the highest point from which
Mapes could use his binoculars and still keep
his distance. It was closer than he liked. No help
for that. He told the kid to wave.

He waved the shirt when the kid got through;
then he held the binoculars steady to see what
Mapes did. The glasses brought Mapes's face in
close, but he saw no change in it. That didn't
mean much. Mapes had a face with as much
expression as a potato. He waved again and Mapes
waved back. He waved and pointed and his mouth
moved.

Morgan mounted up and rode out to meet
Alamo Mapes for what he hoped was the last
time. He was tired and hurt and wanted this
to end. Molly said she would have the horses
harnessed to the wagon when he got back. It
just might work. He started into the long rocky
passage that led back to the desert. Mapes would
be coming in from the other end. He was closer
to midpoint than Mapes, so he took his time, not
wanting to get there first and make a target. But
Mapes was in a bigger hurry than he was and
came riding in hard. Mapes reined in and walked
his horse forward. He looked the same, maybe a
little dirty and sort of tired.

They stayed on their horses. "You wanted to talk," Mapes said.

"Stretch wants to give you Molly," Morgan said. No good leading up to it. That wouldn't go with what he had to say. "You offered her the same deal before, but she didn't like it. Now she does. You can have Molly if you let Stretch ride out and don't come after her. The fort isn't far off, and she thinks you won't want to get too close to the army. She wants a full day's start so the herd will clear the hills and get to the fort. Is it a deal?"

Mapes pulled his nose. "What happened to your face?"

"Stretch got drunk and beat on me, no special reason. I had to take it, with guns pointing at me. She killed one of the women a while back. Same thing. Bad blood to start with."

"Is that so?" Mapes's reddish eyes searched Morgan's face. "I been wonderin' about that. She hasn't hurt my boy?"

"You saw him just now," Morgan said. "She's too smart for that."

"She's a vicious woman," Mapes said. So far it looked like Mapes was buying it. "I don't know that I'd trust a woman like that."

"You don't have to. You heard the deal. What is there to trust? The boy and Molly are left behind, we move on, you come and get the boy."

Mapes did some more nose pulling and gave his lost-in-thought stare. "Why are you pushing this deal? You were against it before."

"Stretch was. I just want to get out of this whole thing. I hired out to drive horses, nothing else. I look after myself."

Mapes studied his lumpy face. "Looks like you ain't been doin' too good a job of it. All right, it's a deal, but I want the boy an' Niles's daughter where I can see them. Can't see nothin' now. The wagon's got to be out front of them rocks. Tell the big woman this time business don't matter. We won't be comin' after her."

Morgan nodded. "I'll be getting back then."

"Hold on, mister. How soon do we see the boy?"

"Soon as I get back and we're ready to move."

Mapes was ready to turn his horse and head back. "No tricks now. The Lord help you if there's tricks."

Morgan rode in through the rocks and got down. The wagon was harnessed and waiting. Stretch and the kid lay on the ground on their backs, kept there by three guns. "Mapes agreed to it," he said. He took one last look at the wagon before he climbed up on the box and drove it out through the rocks. During the night, he had set the box of dynamite up high in the wagon bed, put the tarp back in place and marked where the box was with a dab of wet ashes. The ashes had dried out to a grayish color. He had already picked the place he was to shoot from.

He halted the wagon, unharnessed the horses and drove them back through the gap in the rocks. Then he went to get Stretch and the kid. "Start moving the horses," he told Molly. "Go easy, but keep them moving. I'll catch up to you."

Even in Stretch's clothes, too big for her, Molly looked like her old arrogant self. Once again the horses were her horses and she was wearing her belted-high .38.

"How long will that be?" she said. "You don't have a horse. Can't you leave a horse here?"

"Too close. The blast would kill it. Rocks big as barrels will be raining down. I'll catch up soon as I can. Depends on how long I have to wait. Go on now."

The herd started to move after some prodding. The animals didn't want to leave good water and good grass. He pointed Stretch and the kid to their feet with his gun. "Walk on ahead of me. Try to run and I'll shoot you in the back. I said turn around and walk ahead of me."

Stretch knew she was going to die. How she knew he didn't know. "Kill me now," she said over her shoulder. "I could've killed you many a time. A favor. I'm askin' you—kill me now."

"I'll kill you if you run," Morgan said.

She was still talking when they got to the wagon and he told the kid to chain her up. Not all the fight had gone out of her, and she cursed him for pinching her wrist with the handcuffs. Morgan told the kid to jam Molly's big floppy white hat down on her head.

The kid laughed at her, and Morgan told him to cut it out or get belted. "You better not hurt me," the kid said. Morgan handcuffed him to the wagon and straightened up. Sitting on the ground, Stretch raised her head to look at him. "I should have killed you, too, Big Boy."

"So long, Stretch," Morgan said and turned away.

"I nearly did fuck you in the ass," Stretch called after him.

Back in cover, he picked up the Winchester rifle and started up to the rim of the basin. Down toward the end of it the herd was moving into the opening that went to the hills. The horses weren't moving as fast as he would have liked, but with only three riders, none of them experienced, that was too much to expect. Like everything else, what happened next was chance.

He climbed, keeping low. There was no way the Mapeses could see him unless some of them had moved up in the night. All he could do was keep climbing and figure it was going to work. Once he was up on the rim he would have to move forward until he could sight down on the wagon. It would be a long shot, but he couldn't get any closer. The wagon was in place and he'd have to shoot the way he planned. Nothing happened by the time he got up to the rim and went over it. A few minutes later he was in position.

From where he was now he could see the wagon and the two people who were about to die. He had no feelings about killing them, no more than he felt anything about the rest of the Mapeses. They had put themselves in the way of sudden death, and it was waiting for them in a wooden box. He had used dynamite but never a whole box, all the sticks at the same time. The force of the explosion would be so great they would just disappear. Funny to think of Stretch going out that way, the big mouth and the big bang. Where the hell were the Mapeses?

Patience, boy! They'd want to scout around before they rode in since Mapes had been wary of this final deal. He'd be safe enough if some of them didn't start up to the rim. They might do that. More likely they'd come in real slow, stretched out in a line. He hoped that big white hat of Molly's would draw them in toward the wagon. They'd seen her wearing it any number of times. No reason why her head shouldn't be under it now. But even if they had their suspicions, they'd still ride in to get the kid.

It was still early, and since the sun was behind him, there was no risk in using the binoculars. Stretch's hands were handcuffed behind her, the chain looped around the spoke. No easy way she could get Molly's hat off no matter how hard she shook her head. That's what she was doing, shaking her head and banging the back of it against the wagon. He should have tied it when he had the chance. Too late now. If he risked going down to fix the hat, the Mapeses might ride in and that would be the end of it.

Stretch was still shaking her head like a madwoman. Goddamn, he should have tied it. Even if she knocked the hat off, the Mapeses would still come in for the kid, but it wouldn't be like he'd planned it. If they saw Molly wasn't there and someone else was in her place, most likely they'd send one man ahead. Not good—he had to get all of them. He raised the binoculars away from the wagon and saw them coming.

It was just like he figured—single file, riding slow, with Mapes out in front. While he watched, Mapes reined in his horse, raised his binoculars to his eyes, then waved the others to come ahead. Morgan's rifle was already pushed out, ready to fire. They were still coming in slow, and it took time before Mapes stopped using the binoculars. As soon as he did he spurred his horse to a gallop and they came in at a fast clip. Morgan sighted down the barrel, his finger resting on the trigger. They got to the wagon, and he blew them to bits.

High on the rim, Morgan felt the hot blast of the explosion. If he'd been standing it would have knocked him over. Brush was burning, and what looked like chimney soot was raining down. Sunlight was blotted out by smoke, and the brush fires were spreading all the way up the slope to the rim. Because of the smoke, he couldn't see the crater the explosion had left, but he knew it was there. He got away from there fast.

That didn't last long. As soon as the tension drained out of him his bad knee began to hurt so badly he had to stop and rest. It hurt worse now than earlier in the day, and if it went on like this he'd never catch up to the herd. The only thing he could think of was to bind the swollen knee with a strip of torn shirt and hope that would hold it long enough to get back on a horse. It took him a good while to get to the end of the basin. There he used the big Bowie knife to cut a crutch from a branch, and the going was easier after that.

It took him two hours to catch up to Molly. That's all there was—just Molly. Her horse was tied to a bush, but the herd was gone as well as Ned and Sister. She was sitting on a rock, looking like she was carrying the weight of the world. She turned when she heard him coming. Morgan limped up to her and said, "Move over."

She made room for him, and he sat down on the rock. God, it was good to take the weight off the bad leg. "My horses are gone," Molly said. "Your explosion caused a stampede. My horses are out there in those hills." She waved her hand. There were hills in all directions.

Morgan took a drink from her canteen. "You were long gone by the time the dynamite blew. I wouldn't have thought . . ."

"The explosion made them run. It made a sound like thunder, and they ran away from it."

Morgan felt as beaten down as she was, and it wasn't just the pain in his knee. Knowing it was the letdown after too much strain didn't help.

"Did Sister and Ned stay long enough to see the stampede?"

"Oh, yes. They were with me when it happened. After it was over they decided to move on. I didn't try to stop them."

Morgan looked at her. "Why should you try to stop them?"

"They were part of Stretch's gang. They're criminals."

"They saved our lives, goddamn it." Morgan wondered why he had limped so far just to get into an argument. "Did you give them the money I took from Stretch?"

"I gave them half of it. I should have kept all of it. If not for them I'd still have my herd. Now what the hell am I going to do?"

Morgan looked around. There was grass in these hills and a good chance of water. "You're going to the fort and ask the major's help rounding up your horses. If there's water that's where you'll find them. You won't get back the herd you had but maybe a big part of it."

Molly brightened at the thought. "That's exactly what I'll do. Frederick is so nice. He needs the horses, and I really do need the money. You know what I'll do as well? I'll try to persuade Frederick to pay me for the entire herd, as if none were missing. He's such a lovely person, I'm sure he'll agree. I'll give him my word of honor—a note, perhaps—guaranteeing to provide the missing horses as soon as my ranch is back on its feet. There's really no risk."

No risk to you, Morgan thought. He got a picture of Frederick being drummed out of the army, his insignia and brass buttons ripped off, his sword broken. But maybe they didn't do that for misuse of government funds. Frederick didn't know it yet, but he could be heading for Leavenworth.

"You'll help me, of course," Molly said.

Morgan thought he'd been around Molly long enough. "I don't know about that."

"It's the only way you're going to get your five hundred dollars." With Molly, when all was said and done, it always came down to money. When she saw a good horse she saw 50 dollars. When she saw a better one she saw 100.

"Five hundred doesn't seem so important," Morgan said. "I'm thinking more of peace and quiet, a thick steak and a cold beer. You can send me the five hundred. I'll let you know where I'll be."

Molly was indignant. "But you didn't earn it."

Now it was his turn to be indignant. "What do you mean I didn't earn it? I could have run out on you a lot of times. Instead, I stayed around and have been kicked and starved and I don't know what. I had to fight a madwoman. I just got through blowing up all the Mapeses. You don't think all that's not worth five hundred."

"You didn't earn what I hired you to do," Molly said firmly, "which was to get my horses to Fort Buell."

"You can't blame me for Stretch."

"You can't argue that Stretch was an act of God." Molly Niles, Attorney-at-Law, Morgan thought. "The only way you'll be paid that five hundred dollars is to help me round up my horses."

They had only one horse between them. Morgan wondered if he should steal it and leave her sitting on the rock. "The hell with the five hundred! It's not worth it. I'll catch one of your horses and ride it bareback. I'll get away from you somehow."

"You'll help me find my horses or I'll tell Frederick you helped Ned and Sister to get away. Frederick will inform the authorities and that will be the end of them."

Morgan turned to stare at her, trying to make some sense of the woman. "You'd do that?"

She put on her good citizen face. "I wouldn't want to, but I would."

Morgan didn't say anything for a while. The woman was beyond understanding. "You shouldn't run a horse ranch; you should open a school for blackmailers and schemers. You'd be good at it. Nothing you couldn't teach them. Stretch was a terrible woman, but at least there's the excuse she was crazy. You aren't crazy, by any chance?"

Morgan shut up. No good talking to Molly unless you liked the sound of your own voice. She was one of those people who always knew they were doing the right thing.

"Of course I'm not crazy," she said. "How dare you compare me to a creature like Stretch? By the way, did you enjoy yourself last night? You might say your fight with her had a happy ending, if that's the right term for it. I realize you had to fight her, but my God, did you really have to go that far?"

"I don't know if I did or not," Morgan said. It was a question he'd been asking himself. A ready answer didn't come to mind.

"Do you mean you don't remember?"

"I remember all right. You heard what she said before the fight. I'd be killed if I didn't . . ."

"If you didn't fuck her." Molly seldom talked dirty, but she seemed to taste the word. "You were forced into it, poor man."

It was a dumb conversation to be having with a bum knee, an empty stomach, the horses gone.

"Sure I was forced into it," he said. "It was do it or die."

"Yours not to reason why," Molly said. "But you can scarcely have enjoyed it."

"I'd just as soon not talk about it." Morgan squeezed his damaged knee, trying to ease the pain. It was good to be off his feet, but they'd have to move on sometime. The way Molly was carrying on, the sooner the better.

"I think you've always been secretly attracted by Stretch's muscular charms. Last night was just the culmination."

"The what?"

"You got to fuck her at long last. Not in an ideal setting to be sure. Or perhaps it was. You were well-matched, you two. But the way it ended was disgusting."

"It's always disgusting if you do it right." Morgan used the crutch to get to his feet. "I'm going to get on your horse and leave you if you don't stop talking. I'm hungry and I hurt. I need to see a cook and a doctor."

Morgan climbed into the saddle, and she got up behind him. "I'm only riding like this because you're hurt," Molly said. "You won't run out on me, will you, Morgan? We've been through some terrible times together."

Morgan started the horse walking. Molly was light so carrying double wouldn't be such a chore for the animal. It was getting on for noon, and they'd probably reach the fort by nightfall or shortly thereafter. Food was first in Morgan's mind, then a bed to stretch out on. A bath could wait. Now if only Molly would shut up for the last few miles ahead, but even as he wished for it, he knew it wasn't going to happen.

"I won't let you leave me," she told him. "I'm going to blind you with so much fucking, you'll never find your way home. Night after night I'll fuck you until the sun comes up. You'll get out of bed weak and shaking in every limb."

"That's no way to round up horses," Morgan said.

"Does that mean you'll help me?"

"I'll help you, but there has to be time for sleep." What the hell! Idaho or wherever he was going could wait. Fact was he'd gotten used to her. If he lived to be 90, which wasn't likely, he'd never meet another like her.

"You'll get your sleep. We'll go to bed early."

Morgan wished he could go to bed right now. He didn't have a hard-on, he had a pain in his knee. The hills they were passing through were long but not wide. Pretty soon they'd be looking down on the last stretch of country before the fort.

"We have to get our story straight," he said. "The way it is now, nobody would believe it. It has to be set to rights with a lot left out."

Molly had her arms around his waist. "Are you asking me to perjure myself?"

"You won't be under oath. All the Territory will want to know—are these people dead? Yes, they're all dead. But we'll keep the rest of it simple. Stretch killed all the Mexicans, including Trinidad. I didn't kill him, all right?"

Molly was rubbing her chin on his back. "Nobody cares about Mexicans. But whatever you say."

"Stretch didn't attack you, and I didn't fight with her."

"Aha!" Molly said. "So that's what this is about. You don't want to become notorious as the man who fought and fucked Stretch Harrelson, the famous bank robber."

Morgan had a comeback. "You don't want to get your name in the *Police Gazette* as the refined young lady Stretch fucked with that thingamajig. You've been riding me about her and if I enjoyed it. Did you enjoy it?"

Molly's hand had moved down to his crotch. "You have a filthy mind," she said.

"About the explosion," Morgan said, trying to get his thoughts together in spite of his hard-on, "the Mapeses were out to kill you, so they were chasing Stretch and her people because they had you. Stretch tried to deal with them, shooting started and the box of dynamite was hit. Up went Stretch and the Mapeses, Sister, Ned and Pretty Woman."

"Where were we?" Molly had her hand inside his pants. "We've got to get this story as straight as your cock."

She sure was starting to talk dirty. "We were rounding up runaways," he said.

"Perhaps we were fucking. They thought we were rounding up runaways, but we were fucking."

"You don't want to put that in an official statement." Molly was in a mood he'd never seen before, as if she'd gone a little cracked. Too much strain for too long. He felt a little cracked himself. She was right—they had been through terrible things together.

"Let's talk about the statement later," she said in her practical voice. "We'll reach the fort before too long, and after that it will be nothing but talk. Frederick will want to know everything, and so will the ladies. A fort is such a small place that everybody knows everybody's business. I think we should have a quiet time together before we get there."

"I'm game if you are," Morgan said.

Chapter Twenty-six

They watered the horse, using Morgan's hat as a bucket, before tying the animal securely to a bush. The horse looked at them as they lay down under another bush where the grass was soft and hadn't been bleached yellow by the sun. The sun was hot, but not as hot as it had been in the desert. Morgan felt at peace with the world in spite of his bad leg. No birds were singing, but it was nice to lie down with a good-looking woman on soft grass in the shade.

Morgan got all her clothes off, then all of his. He was sick of fucking in handcuffs and under wagons, with people close by. This was more like it, with no threat of Stretch or the Mapeses. Up above the sky was blue and the clouds were white. He was getting to be a poet.

"Oh, my God, your poor knee!" Molly said when he took his pants off.

"It's not that bad," he said, taking her hand away from his knee and closing it around his cock. It was good to see her naked with her legs spread. For all their bickering they were a great pair as long as they stuck to what they were doing now. Nothing to bring people together like a good fuck.

There was no hurry. The fort would be there tomorrow. Morgan was in no hurry to get there. Not now. Even the steak and the beer could wait. Molly was food and drink all by herself.

He got between her legs and fucked her until they both came. It was like this was their first fuck under normal circumstances. At the ranch she'd been drunk, and the same for that other time on the trail. Nothing wrong with fucking a drunk woman as long as she was over 16 and didn't think you were somebody else.

His knee throbbed, as did his cock. The pain hadn't gone away, but somehow it made everything more enjoyable. Lying on top of her, with his hands stroking her hair, he felt his cock getting hard again. If they could ignore the hunger, they could stay here all day, even all night if they liked. Right now they were hungry for each other, for man did not live by bread alone, and sex made a better meal than corn dodgers.

As the afternoon passed peacefully, she sucked his cock and he licked her clit. There was nothing hurried or desperate in the way they did all that, and for the first time since they met in Niles City they seemed to have all the time in the world. Morgan took her from behind, and she said she wished she could do it to him. In the afternoon, when the sun was very hot, he got up once to give the horse most of the water, keeping a little for Molly and himself. She said there was jerked beef in the pocket of her coat, so they chewed strips of leathery meat and sipped water.

Her mouth was salty, and the head of his cock burned when she sucked it again. She said she loved sucking his cock even though it had been in so many women. He said not so many as all that, and she said sure it had, but she forgave him. What she was forgiving him for he didn't quite know, so he guessed it must be for fucking women he met before he met her. This was a bit of a puzzle but he didn't dwell on it. It was hard to think with his head between her legs and her thigh muscles squeezing hard.

They took a rest and lay together looking up at the sky through the branches of the leafy bush. All that unpleasantness with Stretch was so far behind it might never have happened. Morgan knew he wasn't going to lie awake in nights to come, thinking about it, and he felt pretty sure Molly wasn't like that either. What surprised him, if there were any surprises left, was how well she had come out of it. Living so long under threat of sudden death should have left some marks on her, but as far as he could see, she was the same Molly he'd started out with. The only difference was the way she talked about fucking, always putting a stress on the word. In her other life, that is before Stretch, she probably would have called it lovemaking, if she talked about it at all. Back then it had taken whiskey to get her pants off. Now she took them off herself and was impatient if it took too long, so who said people couldn't change? The greedy, shifty part of her would never change, but the sex part had.

"I suppose you've been wondering about me," she said quietly. "All those things that came out, the things Stretch and even the Mapes boy said."

"Makes no difference to me." Morgan didn't want to go into all that. Truth was, he didn't give a damn.

Molly turned toward him. "No, please, don't try to put me off. They're all true. I had men and women before I went to prison. I had women in prison and they had me. That Mexican, Ana, at the ranch—we did things together before prison and after I got out. That's the way I' am. I can enjoy women as much as men—perhaps not quite as much—but I don't feel there's anything unnatural about it. You're a man, you probably do."

Morgan knew she wasn't just talking. This seemed to be important to her, so she deserved an honest answer. "It's not something I've given much thought to," he said, trying to find the right words. "Thinking about it now I can't see anything wrong with it. If you want it, take it. Not hurting the other person is what's important, I guess."

That was a lame finish, but it was the best he could do. Talking about horses would have been more in his line.

"I did fuck Crockett Mapes," Molly said. "I despised him but I fucked him. Can you understand that? No need to answer. We met in all sorts of places—shacks, under trees, several times at the ranch, once in the freight company office on Sunday. We had to sneak around because of my father and his. I think he hated me. Somehow he learned about Ana—these things are hard to keep secret—and he taunted me about it. Then he started fucking some young Mormon girl from the colony, and he began to jeer at me as worn-out and too old for him, the swaggering son of a bitch!"

She was getting worked up, so much so that Morgan said, "You don't have to go on."

"Damn you, Morgan, keep quiet. I want to go on. It got worse and worse. He was threatening to tell people about Ana, and I knew I couldn't put up with that—so I killed him." She started to cry. "I used my father as an excuse, my poor father. I wasn't thinking about prison. I just knew I had to kill Crockett Mapes, and I did."

Morgan wiped her face with his dirty neckerchief. "Enough," he said. "We've all done things we're ashamed of. You think we should move on?"

She took that the wrong way. "You're saying that because you're disgusted with me, the things I just said. You don't want to fuck me because you think I'm dirty."

Morgan grabbed her hand before she could hit him. "For the love of Christ, you've got it all wrong. I just asked a question. You're out of your crackpot mind."

That got a wan smile. "Thank you, Morgan. Perhaps I am out of my mind. I thought you didn't want to fuck me anymore."

Morgan was exasperated. "Enough of this fucking talk. It's getting on my nerves. You don't have to say it to do it. Make it a habit and Frederick and the ladies will have nothing to do with you."

Another smile, this time with a little more cheer in it. "Frederick is a horse's ass. Pardon my French. Before we go, would you like to make love to me again?"

"You bet," Morgan said, and that's what they did. It went on for so long that it was close to dark before they started for the fort. They saw some of Molly's horses in the hills, and it looked good for a roundup if they got started the next day. Fort Buell was a cavalry post that was sure to have experienced wranglers they could use. If nothing went wrong Molly would get most of her herd together inside of a week. She would have fared a lot worse if the stampede had happened in the badlands or the desert.

"I don't know where we'll be sleeping tonight," Molly said when the lights of the fort were in sight. "I'll probably be staying with Captain and Mrs. Todd. There won't be many opportunities for, well, lovemaking while we're at the fort. But we had a wonderful day, didn't we?"

"Best I ever had," Morgan said truthfully.

Major Van Horn greeted Molly with a brief hug and a kiss on the cheek. Morgan got a nod but not even a handshake. They were in the major's quarters. They had arrived so late that they found him asleep, and he asked that he be excused while he changed into something more suitable than a nightshirt. His manner was so stiff, Morgan wondered why he didn't wear his uniform to bed, and when he came back from his bedroom he was dressed for parade inspection.

Molly told her terrible story, and the major listened without interruption, except for an occasional "By Gad!" He also muttered "Shocking!" "Disgraceful!" and "Damned awful!" But he listened right to the end, his frown deepening, his look of concern growing with every word. The story, as Molly told it, was more or less what they had agreed on.

"You have been through hell, my dear," he started off. But that was all he managed to get out before Molly asked if she might have another brandy and water. The major went to get it, but he didn't ask Morgan if he wanted

another. The first drink had been offered only
when Molly suggested it. Officers didn't drink
with hired hands, but for Molly the major
made an exception and gave Morgan a drink.
Naturally he didn't say he was making an exception. It was in his face and especially in his
voice, which had some kind of Eastern accent
to it. "I'm afraid we have no beer," he'd said
to Morgan.

Major Van Horn picked up his own brandy and
water and toasted Molly. "Here's to a very brave
young lady," the asshole said. Molly had called
him a horse's ass. Morgan thought asshole suited
him better. "You must be exhausted, my dear.
You'll be staying with Mrs. Todd, of course."

Molly was careful not to belt back her drink
in front of the major. She had to walk and talk
and drink like a lady or this stiffneck would put
a padlock on his purse or at least hide it under
the mattress. Morgan thought asking for a second
drink so soon after the first was a mistake, but
the brave little lady had been through so much
and had suffered so terribly that the major understood, even if he frowned ever so slightly.

"I promise you my fullest cooperation, my dear,"
he said when Molly mentioned the roundup. "It's
to my advantage, you see, and if I may say so, it
gives me great pleasure to be of assistance to one
so brave."

By Gad, Morgan thought, there's a mouthful
for you. He felt pretty sure the major could recite
the Lord's Prayer backward. Hard to believe a
woman like Molly would even consider marrying
such a donkey. If she did, he wouldn't get out of
bed bleary-eyed and shaking in every limb. He
wouldn't leave his bed until the undertaker took
him away.

"We have two good wranglers here," the major went on. "Doolin and Danzig, fine fellows. The two Ds the other troopers call them. No need to worry anymore, my dear. We'll start looking for your horses as soon as you feel up to it. Say no more. You're in good hands."

Morgan thought that was kind of a daring thing to say, for the major, that is. And he really did intend to get a little second meaning into the everyday expression. He even blushed a little as he said it. He hadn't said a word to Morgan after making the remark about the beer. Morgan thought he could use a kick in the ass to bring him down from the high plateau he lived on.

"We'll be having dinner at Captain and Mrs. Todd's tomorrow evening." The major took a bird's sip of brandy and water. "I've had Mrs. Todd on the alert, you see. Priscilla will be so glad to see you, and of course the captain himself. Priscilla will entertain us with some airs on the piano, and we'll have Corporal O'Hare and his fiddle in for a bit of a laugh. It will be a jolly evening, I can assure you. It's not every day we have such a heroine in our midst. No need for modesty, my dear. You've earned all our respect and admiration."

"Mr. Morgan was brave, too," Molly said.

"Yes, I'm sure he was," the major said without looking at Morgan. The stuffed shirt was trying to sound like an Englishman and doing a good job of it. A lot of young officers, especially cavalry officers, were like that. Most of them gave it up as they got older. Frederick was the exception—50 if he was a day and still playing Major Muck of the royal something or other.

He wondered how long this bullshit would go on. The drink was weak, and no food had been mentioned, at least not to him. It was assumed that Molly would have a bite before she retired for the night at Mrs. Todd's. Still and all, he'd come this far and might as well bear with it. If only they'd get on with it, he could retire to wherever they put hired hands. Being treated like a hired hand didn't bother him a bit. It might even be good for a laugh if he felt like laughing. And he didn't even mind the major all that much, come to think of it. The prissy son of a bitch might turn out to be a tiger if there were any more wars to fight in.

Molly had downed two drinks on an empty stomach. Maybe that was why she brought up business when she should have waited for a better time, that is, when she and Frederick were by themselves. "I'm afraid we'll never recapture all the horses I promised you," she said. "I know our financial arrangement . . ."

The major gave Morgan a sideways look. "I'm sure we can come to some agreement satisfactory to both of us. Yes, I'm quite sure we can."

That was the end of it, and the major said he would escort Molly to the Todds' quarters. A sergeant was summoned, and Morgan was handed over to him. "This way, mate," he said to Morgan. "A nice bit of crumpet, your lady boss. Wouldn't mind a bit of a go at her myself, I can tell you."

"Watch your language, you blackguard," Morgan said, but not so the sergeant would take it the wrong way.

The sergeant laughed. "Mapes is my name," he said, "an Englishman and proud of it."

"I knew some people called Mapes," Morgan said.

"Never met another body called Mapes in my life. Morgan's your name. Welsh, are you?"

"I don't know what I am. What I am right now is hungry and thirsty. Can you do anything at this late hour?"

"Not a bit of trouble," Sergeant Mapes said. "The food is gratis, but you'll have to pay for the whiskey. Sorry, mate, no beer. There's no money in beer. Bulks too large, if you know what I mean. Whiskey you can smuggle in."

They were heading for the stables, and the smell of old horse piss nearly stung his eyes. Except for five or six horses, the stables were empty. "You'll be snug as a bug in that hayloft," the sergeant said.

"I'll have to owe you for the whiskey," Morgan said. A lot of sergeants were moneylenders and sellers of secondhand goods.

"I'm sure your lady boss is good for it." Five minutes later the sergeant came back with a quart bottle of whiskey. There was no label on the bottle. Morgan pulled the cork out with his teeth and tasted it. No use going blind. It was bad, but not as bad as he expected. In some forts, sergeants sold whiskey so awful you had to hold your nose before you drank it.

"That ought to hold you till I get back with the grub. Don't set fire to the hayloft, mate. Be back in a jiffy."

And so he was. Morgan hadn't even taken a second drink before the limey sergeant was back with a plate of bacon and beans. Morgan looked at the mess on the plate. Where had he seen bacon and beans before? Where was his thick, juicy steak?

"Just what I wanted," he told the sergeant.

"You must be daft, mate," the sergeant said. "Good night, sleep tight, don't let the bedbugs bite."

Morgan was alone with the smell of old horse piss. Climbing up to the hayloft while trying to maneuver the plate and the bottle, he wondered how Molly was doing at Mrs. Todd's. Cold chicken probably. Certainly a soft bed.

He ate the bacon and beans before he settled down with the bottle. It wasn't so bad in the hay, and his knee hardly hurt at all after the third drink. Down below the few horses left in the fort made the usual noises. Peaceful night sounds, hay to sleep on, a bottle of Gilligan's Breathless—what more could a man ask?

A lot, he decided. Molly had a lot of nerve eating cold chicken and sleeping in a soft bed while he was stabled with the horses, and he'd tell her so first thing in the morning. Morgan knew he was a little drunk and took another drink to celebrate that. He yawned and fell asleep, but not before he put the cork in the bottle.

He didn't know how long he slept, but when he woke up he was cold sober. Somebody was climbing up the ladder. He drew his gun from habit and waited for a head to appear. The light was bad, just enough to see, and what he saw was Molly's blond head. A smell of soap came to him in the half-darkness.

"Morgan, are you there?" she said.

"Right here," Morgan said.

She snuggled up close to him in the hay. "Is that a bottle you have?"

Morgan gave her the bottle, and she drank from it. "Oh, my God," she said, "what a taste! I couldn't get to sleep at the Todds' so I decided to come and find you. But I really shouldn't stay all night."

"Frederick won't like this if he hears about it."

"Frederick is a horse's ass," Molly said. "Have you missed me, my dear?"

"Missed you something awful, by Gad," Morgan said.

It takes a man with quick wits and an even quicker trigger finger to survive in a vicious world of fast guns and faster women—it takes a man like the Kansan. Get a double blast of beauties and bullets for one low price!

Showdown at Hells Canyon/Across the High Sierra.
__3342-9 $4.50

Red Apache Sun/Judge Colt.
__3373-9 $4.50

Warm Flesh and Hot Lead/Long, Hard Ride.
__3395-X $4.99

Trail of Desire/Shootout at the Golden Slipper.
__3421-2 $4.99

The Cheyenne's Woman/The Kansan's Lady.
__3450-6 $4.99

LEISURE BOOKS
ATTN: Order Department
276 5th Avenue, New York, NY 10001

Please add $1.50 for shipping and handling for the first book and $.35 for each book thereafter. PA., N.Y.S. and N.Y.C. residents, please add appropriate sales tax. No cash, stamps, or C.O.D.s. All orders shipped within 6 weeks via postal service book rate. Canadian orders require $2.00 extra postage and must be paid in U.S. dollars through a U.S. banking facility.

Name_____

Address_____

City _____ State _____ Zip _____

I have enclosed $_____in payment for the checked book(s).

Payment <u>must</u> accompany all orders.□ Please send a free catalog.

by Gene Curry

**The hardest-riding, hardest-loving cowboy
who ever blazed a trail or set a heart on fire.**

#5: ACE IN THE HOLE. Working as a gunslinger for the notorious Butch Cassidy, Saddler found the action was real hot real fast. For when there wasn't a bank or a train to rob, or a woman who was eager for his attention, there was always a shootist itching to outdraw Cassidy or any of his hired guns.
__3127-2 $2.95 US/$3.95 CAN

#6: YUKON RIDE. Three things Saddler thrived on were gold lust, loose women, and hot lead, and he found them aplenty in the icy Yukon. But life was cheap in the frozen north, and if Saddler wasn't careful he'd end up an unlucky stiff in a pine box.
__3167-1 $2.99 US/$3.99 CAN